FALL OF DAMNOS

Spreading out, the necrons had enveloped them. Bolters tracked and fired to compensate, relying on advanced targeting sensors – the mist was so bad that the enemy were literally appearing as if from nowhere, and in numbers.

'Brother, my flank has been compromised.' It was Atavian through the comm-feed in Iulus's helmet.

'Close up battle-formation, there are more necrons than we first believed.'

An affirmation rune flashed on Iulus's retinal display. The tac-icons representing the Devastator squad started to move closer to the Immortals. Iulus noticed there were several red markers that remained static.

Squad Fennion and the two Devastators – they were the rearguard. Glory belonged to others.

'Take and hold the ground.' Those had been his orders during the mission briefing. Thirty Ultramarines to keep a simple esplanade from the enemy. It had seemed like overkill; now, Iulus Fennion wasn't so sure.

FALL OF DAMNOS

NICK KYME

BLACK LIBRARY

*For brothers. For Richard and Anthony, and for Paul, Mike and Kev –
brothers in spirit, if not by blood.*

A Black Library Publication

First published in Great Britain in 2011 by
The Black Library,
Games Workshop Ltd.,
The Black Library,
Nottingham, NG7 2WS, UK.

10 9 8 7 6 5 4 3 2 1

Cover illustration by Jon Sullivan.
Internal illustrations by Neil Hodgson and Carl Dafforn.

A CIP record for this book is available from the British Library.

UK ISBN 13: 978 1 84970 040 5
US ISBN 13: 978 1 84970 041 2

See the Black Library on the Internet at
www.blacklibrary.com

Find out more about Games Workshop
and the world of Warhammer 40,000 at
www.games-workshop.com

Printed and bound in the UK.

IT IS THE 41st Millennium. For more than a hundred centuries the Emperor has sat immobile on the Golden Throne of Earth. He is the master of mankind by the will of the gods, and master of a million worlds by the might of his inexhaustible armies. He is a rotting carcass writhing invisibly with power from the Dark Age of Technology. He is the Carrion Lord of the Imperium for whom a thousand souls are sacrificed every day, so that he may never truly die.

YET EVEN IN his deathless state, the Emperor continues his eternal vigilance. Mighty battlefleets cross the daemon-infested miasma of the warp, the only route between distant stars, their way lit by the Astronomican, the psychic manifestation of the Emperor's will. Vast armies give battle in his name on uncounted worlds. Greatest amongst His soldiers are the Adeptus Astartes, the Space Marines, bio-engineered super-warriors. Their comrades in arms are legion: the Imperial Guard and countless planetary defence forces, the ever-vigilant Inquisition and the tech-priests of the Adeptus Mechanicus to name only a few. But for all their multitudes, they are barely enough to hold off the ever-present threat from aliens, heretics, mutants - and worse.

TO BE A man in such times is to be one amongst untold billions. It is to live in the cruellest and most bloody regime imaginable. These are the tales of those times. Forget the power of technology and science, for so much has been forgotten, never to be re-learned. Forget the promise of progress and understanding, for in the grim dark future there is only war. There is no peace amongst the stars, only an eternity of carnage and slaughter, and the laughter of thirsting gods.

PROLOGUE
274.973.M41

THE PRIMARY GENERATORS were dead. No litanies to the Machine-God, no entreaties to the Omnissiah were about to revive them. The last tremor had been the largest – the Mandos Prime fusion stations were down.

It was the job of Gorgardis and his crew to repair them.

'Critical failure across all facilities,' the exofabricator muttered. His breath fogged the air with the cold from the permafrost.

'My lord,' a voice crackled through the vox-implant in Gorgardis's ear. The heavy ice and some kind of latent, as of yet unspecified, radiation marred his reply with static.

'Present,' said the exofabricator, distracted with his scanner read-outs. The seismographic returns were incredible, more than merely tectonic plate shifts. Perhaps the planet was destabilising.

The voice's next words made Gorgardis stop what he was doing.

'We've found something.'

He licked his lips, tasting the blandness of ice crystals, and put away the scanner. Artak's position in the facility came up on the retinal display of his optic implant. It was flashing, and a small binaric code indicated the other exofabricator was a further eighty-six point two metres down.

Gorgardis paused to think, the logic engines supplementing his organic brain functions making swift correlations. 'I'll be right down,' he said, and made for the nearest rail-lifter.

MUCH OF THE hard ice around the structure had melted, but it was buried so deep and seemingly without end that it was impossible to tell just how big the thing was.

There were icons upon the smooth outer wall. It looked like metal but very dark, shimmering, almost vital. Despite a wealth of experience in runic symbolism and semiotics, Gorgardis didn't recognise any of the iconography.

'Unknown provenance,' he muttered, tracing his hand over the symbols but being careful not to touch them. He turned to Artak, who was waiting anxiously behind him. Gorgardis waved him on. 'Bring up the servitors – drills and hammers, heavy-bore.'

MAGOS KARNAK OBSERVED the pristine surface of the half-buried ruins with cold detachment.

'Incredible…' he breathed. It had been many years since he'd experienced awe, let alone expressed it through his organic vocal cords. Karnak was mostly machine, but he still retained the gamut of human feeling. Presently, it was being stimulated to a greater extent than he'd thought possible since his apotheosis from the flesh.

Mechadendrite scanners performed a full spectral, auditory and metallurgic analysis of the structure, feeding the results to the tech-priest's machine-cortex for later study. An initial review made little sense.

'And you went to every length to open it?' he asked.

Gorgardis gestured to the half-dozen wasted servitors slumped in a pile nearby. 'We exhausted our every resource,' he said.

Upon witnessing the slab-sided ruins, he'd summoned the tech-priest of the facility at once. Karnak had been swift to respond, bringing in his adepts: a horde of enginseers, transmechanics and genetors. The tech-priests were baffled.

Gorgardis went on, 'Returns from our sonar-staves reveal that this is but one structure amongst a series of many. Most are buried deep beneath the ice bed.'

'And this?' Karnak referred to a floating grav-bench on which several items of alien origin were arrayed.

Gorgardis singled out a six-legged creature with silver chitin across its back and mandibles not so dissimilar from mechadendrite tools.

'My best estimate is a repair drone of some sort. It's dead.'

'Or dormant,' Karnak countered, his gaze absorbing and cataloguing the other mechanical finds on the bench. Some were perhaps weapons; others were harder to classify. Partial degradation from exposure to ice moisture made the task difficult but not impossible. 'I'm taking all of them,' he decided, before showing Gorgardis his back and driving away on the tracked impellers he had in lieu of his legs.

'M– my lord?'

'All finds are to go to Goethe Majoris where they can be better studied.'

Gorgardis made the sign of the Cog and went about his orders.

'Seal this site,' Karnak added by way of afterthought. 'Its secrets will be revealed to us in due course, Omnissiah be praised.'

ACT ONE: EMERGENCE

CHAPTER ONE
779.973.M41

THE VOX-TRANSMITTER WAS wretched with interference, so Falka hit it again.

'Keep doing that and you'll break it,' said a deep and sonorous voice behind him.

When Falka turned, his smile was broad and bright enough to light up the whole mine. 'Jynn!'

He seized the woman in a bear hug, lifting her off the ground. Even in her environment suit, she felt the steel of his girder-like arms.

'Easy, easy!' she warned, mock-choking.

Falka put her down, ignoring the questioning glances from the rest of the shift. Riggers, drill-engines and borer-drones advanced towards the darkness of the vast ice-shaft like an army. They were accompanied by menial servitors and heavy-set chrono-diggers. Like Falka and Jynn, the human contingent of the labour force wore bulky environment suits to stave off the cold and make the twelve-hour cycles possible.

'Where's your rig?' asked the big man. He'd stripped back the thermal protection on his arms, revealing faded gang-tats and wiry grey hair. 'I didn't see it.'

Jynn pointed to a docking station, one of many in the massive ice cavern. Like most of the mining vehicles it was squat, decked out with plates and protective glacis and only partially enclosed. A crew of three menials and a pair of chrono-diggers stood around it awaiting her return.

'She's all mine,' she said proudly, adjusting the thermal-cutters, flare-rods and chain-pick fastened to her tool belt from when Falka's bear hug had dislodged them.

A klaxon sounded and an array of strobe lamps filled the cavern with an intermittent amber glow. They started walking.

'You look good,' said Falka a moment later.

Jynn gave a wry smile. The ice concourse underfoot crunched as they moved. It was hard-packed by industrial presses to create a serviceable roadway for the mine entrance. Most of the light was artificial, though some natural light filtered down from the bore hole above them at the entrance's threshold.

'What I mean,' Falka struggled to say, 'is it's good to see you back at the ice-face. I thought after Korve, you might–'

'Honestly, Fal, I'm fine,' she said, brushing a strand of errant hair behind her ears and pulling down her goggles.

Falka did the same – close to the vent a fine spray of ice chips saturated the air. Environment suits managed the worst. Get one in the eye and you'd know about it, though.

'Just with the 'quake and all that…'

She stopped and glared at him. The other workers flowed around them to their riggers and crews. The first few cohorts had already begun descent.

'Seriously, Falka – just drop it. Korve's dead and that's it.'

The big man looked distraught. 'Sorry.'

She lightly gripped his shoulder. 'It's all right. I under–'

'Rig-hand Evvers,' a shrill, imperious voice interrupted.

Jynn had her back to the speaker and groaned inwardly before she turned. 'Administrator Rancourt,' she replied politely.

A hawkish man, trussed up in thermal gear and flocked by a retinue of scribes and aides, approached them. Despite the cowl drawn up around his small head and the padded mittens he wore, the administrator still shivered.

'I had not expected to see you on shift,' he said, fashioning a poor smile. It was meant to convey warmth but only exuded his awkwardness.

'Nor I, you…' she muttered.

'I beg your pardon. I'm finding it hard to hear under all of this.' He gestured to cowl and thermal coat.

'I said it's rare to see you, administrator… at the ice-face, I mean.'

Rancourt moved in close to Jynn.

'I've told you before,' he said. 'You may call me Zeph.'

Falka broke his stoic silence to grunt.

Rancourt's gaze moved to the giant. 'And Rig-hand Kolpeck. Don't you have shift to go to?'

'We both do, administ… ah, *Zeph*.' She tugged lightly on Falka's arm, urging him to join her.

The big man looked like he'd rather stay and squeeze Rancourt's neck, but he followed anyway.

'Of course, of course,' the administrator blathered, shooting a dark glance at Falka. 'I have much work to attend to. In the Emperor's name,' he added, pretending to look at a data-slate proffered by one of his toadies.

'May His glory watch over us all,' Jynn replied.

Heading in the direction of the vent, the air suddenly felt as if it were actually getting warmer.

'He still stalking you, then?'

'Leave it, Fal. I can handle it. He's harmless enough.'

Falka grunted again. He was prone to doing that. 'Eyes and ears,' he said, peeling off towards his rigger and crew.

'You too,' said Jynn, diverting to her vehicle. She'd put one boot on the boarding stirrup when the concourse trembled. She slipped, snatching a holding rail to steady herself. A second tremor shook some debris from the roof. More violent than the first, it sent men and servitors sprawling.

'What the feg was–' she muttered over the vox-bead.

A high-pitched keening cut her off.

She fell, the intensity of the sonic burst forcing her to press her palms to her ears. 'Throne!' Jynn gasped, grimacing against the auditory pain.

The keening became a hum, throbbing at the back of the skull, but at least she could stand. Around the ice cavern, the walls were shaking. Sections of the ceiling rained down on the labourers in a cascade. The cries of one man ended abruptly when a slab of permafrost crushed him.

Jynn staggered. It was just like with Korve. Memories came flooding back, but she suppressed them, focussed on surviving instead. 'Not yet, dear heart,' she muttered, finding some resolve. 'Not yet.'

Falka was on his feet too and rushing over to her.

'You hurt?' He had to shout to be heard above the ice-quake.

Jynn was about to answer when a massive cold cloud ripped through the vent in a bright white bloom. The rig-hands closest to the shaft were shredded by the host of shards within the cloud. Snow crystals fogging the air were tainted a visceral red.

A burst of hard, emerald light followed, refracted from the angular descent shaft beyond the vent. Shouting echoed from the icy dark, injured and desperate men trying to control some unseen catastrophe. The shouts became cries, and then screams. There was something else too... a sort of discharge, as of an energy beam or perhaps a heavy generator.

The winches slaved to the adamantite descent lines at the vent threshold started to retract. Someone was coming up.

'We have to get out,' said Jynn, then with greater urgency as the emerald light issuing from the vent intensified. 'All of us – right now!'

Falka nodded.

'No!' she cried, seizing the big man's arm as he made for the vent.

He looked back at her nonplussed. 'People are down there, our people. They might need help.'

Jynn was shaking her head. 'They're gone, Fal. This way, come on.'

'Wha... but...'

'They're *dead*! Now, come on!' She heaved and he followed, reluctant at first but then with more conviction. Something was scurrying up the shaft. It sounded like a horde of giant, mechanical ants.

The first of the rig-hands from below made it to the ice cavern. He was dead. Men screamed, terrified, when

17

they saw the flesh of his partly flayed corpse. Surgical, precise, horrific – it was as if the layers had been stripped anatomically.

More followed, equally gruesome.

Jynn and Falka were running, shouting at anyone who would listen to join them, yanking environment suits or shoving them bodily. *Down tools and flee.* This was not a rescue; it was a full scale evacuation.

She found Rancourt cowering behind a rigger, getting his aides to peer around its armoured flanks and provide him with updates. Several of his entourage were dead, one from fright when the keening blast had struck; another to the sudden avalanche from the ceiling.

'Get up!' She seized his collar and pulled. 'Get up! These people need guidance. The surface must be told what's happening down here.'

'What *is* happening?' he shrieked, unwilling to stand at first, casting fearful glances towards the vent where the emerald glow was now spilling into the ice cavern.

Jynn looked over her shoulder, still hanging on to Rancourt's suit. 'Falka!'

The big man gently moved her aside and threw the administrator over his shoulder.

'Unhand me! I am an officer of the Imperium. Release me at once!'

'Shut up.' Falka smacked Rancourt's head into the rigger just hard enough to leave him dazed.

Then they were running again. The remnants of the administrator's retinue followed without need for coercion.

The exit shaft and the rail-lifters were just a few metres ahead. The light from the surface was like a soothing balm as it touched Jynn's sweat-slick face. She glanced back.

Several more rig-hands from below had made it to the ice cavern. Though they were far away and her view was unsteady on account of her fleeing for her life, she made out... *creatures* attached to the miners. The rig-hands were thrashing and squirming. Eventually they fell and the swarm dispersed, silver beetle-like creatures the size of Falka's clenched fist, leaving a flensed corpse in their wake.

'God-Emperor have mercy,' she breathed.

Larger, bulkier shadows were reaching the end of the vent shaft. A coruscating emerald beam lanced from the darkness, throwing a spider-like creature into sharp relief. Like the beetles it was metallic, but almost the size of a rigger. The beam, fired from one of the creature's mandibles, struck a fleeing rig-hand and atomised him. The afterimage of the man's flayed skeleton was seared into Jynn's retinas just before it collapsed into ash and she looked away.

'Move, move!'

They raced into the nearest rail-lifter. About sixty rig-hands had joined them on the access plate, and Falka gunned the engine as soon as they were all aboard.

Jynn gazed to the distant surface as the heavy winches began to drone. She willed the oval of light from the ground-zero bore point closer.

Below them, the other rail-lifters started up – fifteen in total, all screaming, engines hot, towards the upper world.

One of the cables snapped, lashing wildly with the sudden slack. A beam from one of the spiders had severed it. Rig-hands screamed as they plunged to their deaths. Others, clinging on, could only watch in horror as the beetles already scaling the shaft wall sprang from their perches and landed amongst them.

Jynn saw a few of the miners let go and embrace death by falling rather than face being flayed alive.

The hard drone of a warning klaxon sounded from farther up the shaft. The oval of light was becoming a rectangular strip, narrowing by the second.

Rancourt, having recently regained consciousness, put away his command-stave. Falka saw him do it and rounded on him.

'What are you doing? The others will never make it.'

The administrator's pupils were dilated, his eyes wide and haunted. 'Those th-things…' he stammered. 'They can't be allowed to get out.'

'Bastard!' Falka punched him, a solid blow to the chin that put Rancourt back on his arse, and then ripped the command-stave from the administrator's trappings. 'Show me how to stop it,' he said, bearing down on him, threatening more violence.

'Leave him,' Jynn wrenched the big man's shoulder. She had a strong grip and made him turn.

'You're defending this worm?'

'He's right, Fal.' The sides of the shaft blurred past and the displaced air snapped at Jynn's hair.

Falka shook his head. Those men and women were his friends. 'No!' He was about to beat down on Rancourt again when Jynn smacked him hard in the chest with the flat of her hand. It didn't hurt the big man but it got his attention.

'He's right,' she said again, continuing in a small voice when she looked below – her mind tried to blot out the carnage and horror. 'We can't let them get out.'

Falka's grimace became a snarl as he pounded at the holding spar with impotent rage. 'Hold on,' he growled, moving towards the engine. 'We're about to breach the surface.'

The rail-lifter cleared the slowly closing shaft doors and after a few more metres broke into the pale Damnosian sun. Another miner called Fuge kicked open the exit ramp and the sixty or so survivors pounded it across to the arctic tundra of the upper world.

Though the sun was shining, an icy wind brought a chill and kicked up slurries of snow and frost eddies. The barren wastes of Damnos had never looked so bleak.

There was no need for conversation. What could any of them say, anyway? So the sixty survivors made for the distant comms-bunker, marching in file, heads bowed against the wind and ice. Behind them the shutting of the shaft door was like a death knell for the hundreds still trapped within.

850.973.M41

THERE WAS STILL no word from Damnos Prime, and the Valkyrie gunships Lieutenant Sonne had deployed from Secundus to investigate were also quiet. It didn't take a soldier's instincts to realise that something was wrong.

'We're experiencing a full communications black-out in the northern regions all the way to the Tyrrean Ocean, colonel,' he gave his report to Quintus Tarn. The commander of the Damnosian Ark Guard peered over steepled fingers into the shadows of his operations chamber. His mood was pensive. Leaning on the desk with his elbows, he hadn't stirred the entire time Adanar Sonne had been in his presence.

Behind the colonel a planetary map showed the location of each and every manufactorum, drilling-station, mining complex, refinery, labour-clave and outpost on Damnos. Unlit lume-globes represented the stations that Kellenport, the planetary capital, had lost touch with. Precious few of the globes were lit.

The wave of darkness emanating from the north reminded Adanar of a slowly creeping shroud. 'We picked up a group of refugee mine workers from one of the outposts near Damnos Prime,' he offered.

Tarn looked up at Adanar for the first time since he'd entered the room.

'How many?'

'Thirteen, sir.'

'Are they saying anything?'

'I don't know yet, colonel. They were picked up by a patrol. Apparently, they'd been trekking across the tundra for several weeks. Administrator Rancourt is amongst the survivors,' Adanar added.

'Inform the lord governor and bring them all to me as soon as they arrive at Kellenport.'

'Yes, sir. Is there anything else?'

'Do you have a wife and child, Lieutenant Sonne?' asked Tarn. The colonel was staring right into his eyes.

'Er, yes… Yes, I do.'

Though Tarn smiled, his eyes were despairing black gulfs.

As if seeing them for the first time, Adanar noticed the stubs of tabac in a silver tray to the commander's left; on the right was a vox-unit. Its message received light was flashing silently.

'Is something wrong, sir?'

'Listen,' Tarn answered simply.

He broke the steeple of his fingers and replayed the vox-message blinking insistently on the unit. The opening segment was fraught with static, natural interference on account of the distance and the weather conditions. Slowly, a voice resolved through the auditory crackle.

'...*found something, sir...*'

Adanar recognised the hard timbre of Major Tarken. He didn't know the man personally but his reputation preceded him as one of the most lauded combat veterans amongst the Ark Guard.

Colonel Tarn tapped a rune on the vox-unit and a grainy hololith issued from a projector-node. It took a few seconds to synch to the audio. Major Tarken appeared in jagged resolution.

'Image-servitors accompanied the platoon,' the colonel explained unnecessarily.

Major Tarken was speaking to the picter. '*The manufactorums at Damnos Prime were silent, but there is definitely something here.*'

The view swung downwards at the major's request, revealing several skeletal remains.

'*Could be labour serfs or rig-hands...*'

Adanar caught Tarn's hooded gaze. 'Was this a live feed?'

'Up until about twenty minutes ago.'

The picter swung up again. Panning left and right, it showed Tarken's men advancing in echelon formation. The sound kept cutting out, succumbing to crackling interference or the occasional hiss of static, but it seemed quiet. Mist from the cold exuded off the walls in a fine veil. Tarken's kit and that of his men was wet with the moisture, and crusted from it flash-freezing.

'*...moving into the main drilling area now...*' Tarken was whispering and brought up his lasgun. Somebody shouted from up ahead, a scout off-picter.

'Where was this?' asked Adanar, utterly enrapt on the hololith.

'Dagoth Station, three hundred kilometres north of Secundus at Halaheim.'

A flash on the pict was too bright to be static. Some-one had started firing.

'*Contacts! Contacts!*' Tarken was running and the whir of the servitor's tracked impellers could be heard as it shifted gear to keep pace with the major. Though largely stable, the additional momentum made the image blur and haze. The whine of lasguns was getting louder over the audio, too.

Adanar leaned in closer. Tarken had reached his front-line and was taking up a position behind some riggers evidently in for repair. Around thirty men adopted sim-ilar postures and hunkered down. Farther ahead, men were shouting. The scouts were discharging weapons and Tarken was trying to raise their sergeant on the vox.

Something garbled came over the vox-return, twice fil-tered for Adanar's ears and totally indiscernible.

The picter was still shaking, although the servitor had stopped behind the major.

'Can we steady it?'

Tarn didn't answer. He was fixated on the hololith.

Something was appearing through the mist. An emer-ald glow coloured the fog suddenly, as if tainting it. Shots from the scouts ended with its arrival.

'*Holy Throne…*' Tarken was levelling his lasgun over the makeshift barricade. A beam snapped out of the dark, ugly and green, and one of the riggers was shorn in two. '*Holy fegging Throne! All weapons, bring them down!*'

The chamber lit up with over thirty las-bursts. Tarken's troopers went to full automatic, draining their power packs with an abandon and urgency Adanar had never seen before in professional soldiers.

The things coming out of the fog, they were… *night-mares*. It was the only word Adanar could think of to describe them. Huge, broad-shouldered skeletoids with strange, glowing carbines attached to their arms. Energy coursed up and down the wide tubular barrels and was expelled in bright lances of dirty emerald.

They moved like automatons, neither speaking nor slowing as a barrage of las-bolts hammered them.

'Increase fire!'

The picter zoomed in, blurring the image at first but then focussing in on one of the metal skeletons. Its eyes blazed with a terrible fire, suggesting a crude sentience that chilled the lieutenant's blood even removed, as he was, from the firefight and the moment.

Adanar saw the creature jerk spasmodically as it was struck by countless las-shots. It must have taken over ten well-placed bolts to down it. Chunks of metal flew off its carapace body, fused rib-plate and punctured presumably vital systems before it fell.

The picter lingered. Horrified, Adanar watched the broken components slowly reknit as las-fire raged around the creature's prone form. Wires snaked across the ground finding other wires and, like sewn flesh, drew the shattered pieces together. Metal became as mercury, dissolving into liquid before being drawn to the torso as if magnetised. Impossibly, the skeleton rose intact and fired its terrible beam weaponry again.

'...all back... Fall back!'

Tarken stood up to order the retreat. The vox-man next to him was spun by a glancing hit from one of the beams. Half of his face and right shoulder were missing, simply stripped down to glistening bone.

It was more rout than retreat.

Major Tarken took a hit to the chest. His carapace armour dissolved on contact, so too his uniform and under-mesh, his skin and flesh and bone. A hole opened up in his back, what remained of blood and innards cauterised before Tarken crumpled in a dead heap.

The image-servitor was the last to fall. Unarmed, Adanar assumed it presented the lowest level of threat to the creatures.

Just before the report ended a looming skeletal face filled the screen. Bale-fires smouldered in its eye sockets and spoke of unfathomable hatred.

A squeal of binaric or something like it keened through the speaker. Adanar winced and recoiled. When he'd opened his eyes a split second later, the screen was dead, frozen on the skeleton's face.

The lieutenant was sweating, his heart racing in his chest. He licked his lips. They were dry and his voice croaked at first, 'What are those…?' He coughed, clearing his throat and tried again. 'What are they, colonel?'

A figure emerging out of the darkness behind Tarn had Adanar reaching for his laspistol. He only relaxed when he recognised Magos Karnak.

The tech-priest's timbre was as cold and unforgiving as Adanar imagined the skeletons to be. 'Ancient and terrible, and they are here, lieutenant.'

'What the hell is that supposed to mean?'

Tarn interjected, switching off the hololith and stopping the dead-air audio feed. 'It means they have come for us, for this world.'

Adanar bit back his anger – he was only reacting to his irrational fear. 'With respect, sir, that explains shit-all. What's going on?'

'The lord governor has been informed,' said Tarn, 'and is being secured in a Proteus-class command bunker with his generals as we speak. He intends to conduct operations from there.'

'Very wise, sir, but what precisely are we dealing with here?'

'The *Nobilis* has been contacted and is adopting geo-stationary orbit above the capital.'

Tarn was talking as if he'd lost it. Adanar wanted to shake him. 'Sir!'

'They are coming to Kellenport, Sonne. I sent over fifty thousand men to Damnos Prime and Secundus, and all the stations in-between. All of them, our fleet at anchor in the Tyrrean – dead, all of them.'

Adanar nearly choked. '*What?*'

Karnak advanced into Adanar's eye-line, the whirr of his tracks drawing a scowl from the lieutenant.

'That scrambled piece of binaric was a data-burst,' the magos explained. 'There was a message encoded within it. Based on a proto-Gothic linguistic system, it was easy to discern the meaning. My xeno-linguistic savants took approximately thirteen point two-six minutes to deci-pher it.'

'Are you looking for praise, magos?'

'No, I am merely suggesting that the simple encoding was deliberate. They *wanted* us to hear it.'

'Hear what?' asked Adanar.

Colonel Tarn activated a different message spool on the vox-unit. After a few seconds of charged silence an unearthly voice issued from the speakers. It resonated with age and archaic menace, as if drawn from the grave or the depths of a planet-eating black hole.

We are the necrontyr. We are legion. We claim dominion of this world… Surrender and die.

'Throne of Earth,' Adanar could only rasp. He found his composure again after a few more seconds. 'Surely, it means surrender *or* die?'

Karnak uttered a sombre reply. 'No, Lieutenant Sonne, the translation is accurate.'

'In the Emperor's name, what are these things?'

'Death, lieutenant – they are death. Adanar,' said the colonel, getting to his feet at last. 'Take your family and get out of Kellenport. Go south. Do it quickly, before it's too late.'

020.974.M41
Aboard the Nobilis

THE BRIDGE WAS frantic with activity.

Captain Unser barked orders at his command crew from a gilded throne inlaid with operation-gems and picter-slates. 'Get me firing solutions on those war cells, now!'

Naval ratings scattered as Unser's flag-lieutenant cracked the whip of his tongue in relaying the captain's commands. Far below the sub-command dais, servitors slaved to control-pits worked tirelessly to manoeuvre the ship, responding to the dictates of their helmsman; others processed and relayed back firing information, making minor weapons adjustments that would be fed down to the gun-decks.

'Melta torpedoes at forty-four per cent, my lord,' said the flag-lieutenant, Ikaran.

Unser's eyes flashed in the sepulchral gloom of the bridge. The long scar he'd earned whilst posted in support of the Plovian VI Imperial Guard looked like a vertical grin on the left side of his face. 'Give 'em another dose, sir.'

Ikaran relayed the orders and the message bled down through the ship to the gun-decks.

Unser smiled, his mouth pulling at the injuries that chronicled a life that had only ever known war.

He loved this. He absolutely… *Loved. It.*

The *Nobilis* was invincible. A capital ship, the largest in the line, Dominator-class – it was an expression of Unser's undeniable will and righteous anger. Dread enemies had come to Damnos, unearthed from the very bowels of the world. Though he had not seen them up close, Unser was determined to send them back to whence they came, turning them into the corpses they already resembled.

'Torpedoes away, lord,' said Ikaran.

'Bring it up.'

The bridge picters delineating the forward arc of the command dais came online. They showed a view of realspace and the half hemisphere of southern Damnos. Bright, blazing contrails invaded the vista as the torpedo payload sped earthwards.

Unser leant forwards, revelling in the power. 'And in three... two... one–'

A series of bright blooms lit the world's surface from the massive impacts. The *Nobilis* was at the cusp of the mesosphere and close enough to see the effect of the incendiaries on the ground.

Ikaran had his hand to his ear, a comms-officer on board ship reporting back to him.

'Hits on eighty per cent of targets, lord.'

Unser allowed himself to sit back. He gripped the arms of his command throne like a triumphant king. 'Another barrage, if you please.'

THE AIR WAS hot and sweaty on the gun-decks. Thousands of crew and hauler-servitors scurried in packs as the order came down from the bridge.

Overseer Caenen applied the lash to increase their efforts.

'Sweat and blood, dogs,' he drawled, bawling above the heavy drone of the engines and loading machinery. His hellish gaze followed the ammo hoppers, hoisted by teams of swarthy, soot-stained men, and glowered. 'The cap'n wants another, we give him another!' The lash cracked out again and the crews of torpedo tubes five through ten picked up the pace. All down the port-ventral aisle of the *Nobilis's* gun-deck, the scene was the same. Overseers urged their crews with threats and cajoling, just like any good Navy men.

In less than three minutes the next barrage of torpedoes was prepared, the tubes locked, their deadly cargo primed for launch.

A wave of green 'ready' runes flickered down the hot darkness of the gun-deck. Vox communication went to the gunners who angled the tubes mechanically from their firing nests according to solutions provided by the bridge. All was in harmony, the perfect machine with the men of its crew its blood and sinew.

Caenen leapt down from his pulpit, stepping on a servitor's bent back so he didn't have to use the stairs. He grunted when his boots met the deck in a heavy *thunk*, berating a man for getting in his way and punching out another as he moved to a viewport.

The tiny aperture afforded a limited view of realspace, but enough to witness a torpedo barrage. Tearing open the iron hatch, Caenen wiped the grime and warp-frost from the many-layered plascrete protecting them all from the void and simply looked.

To the overseer, a bombardment was a thing of beauty. Even the many slummer-whores he had bedded, in spite of his scars and his lack of hygiene, paled. She, the *Nobilis*, was his true mistress... and the bitch had quite a slap in her.

When the launch tubes failed to vent, Caenen frowned. He wiped at his heavy breath where it had fogged the viewport, but he hadn't missed it. The tubes

were still full. He was about to start shouting and bawling again, ready to apply his boot to the fegger who'd
screwed him, when a dense, ultra-concentrated beam
speared from the surface.

'What the shi–'

WE ARE INVULNERABLE.

The thought was a comfortable one and Captain Unser
was enjoying this feeling of pre-eminence when the
weapons failure rune on his command-slate spoiled it.

'Mister Ikaran, report!'

The flag-lieutenant had his hand to his ear again, getting information from the comms-officer. 'A jam, lord.
We'll have to repack and acquire new firing–'

The massive energy spike raging across all of the pict-
screens on the bridge arrested Ikaran's recommendations.

'Lord, our shields will be–'

'Impossible,' breathed Unser, sitting up so he might
defy his imminent death more staunchly. 'They don't
have... Up here... we're invinc–'

A bright flare of emerald light filled the bridge, blind-
ing the crew and scorching their flesh despite the
plascrete shielding on the viewports. The *Nobilis's*
shields capitulated in seconds, one after the other, and
the once mighty vessel's armour was sheared away like
parchment by the necron beam. It impaled the bridge
and lanced the heart of the ship. Plasma drives erupted
in conflagration, sending roiling firestorms across all
decks. Munitions and artillery cooked off in the blast,
killing thousands. The main breach caused by the
beam's hungry trajectory resulted in several more sub-
breaches – crewmen, equipment, entire bulkheads and
sub-decks were vented into the void, flash-frozen.

* * *

IN THE GUN-DECKS, Overseer Caenen didn't even have enough time to curse before the torpedo wall was ripped away and the entire gunnery crew, all two thousand, three hundred and fifty souls, burned to death before being expelled into the cold night of space.

LORD GOVERNOR ARXIS had not always been in the business of politicking. Unfortunately, it was a necessary evil when running a world of the Imperium. Such a task required a strong hand and a firm belief in the Emperor. Deviation from the Creed could not be tolerated; the people lived to serve His greater glory and the glory of mankind.

Arxis was once Imperial Guard, a general no less, and now he sat amongst his generals, the trappings of politics forgotten and the familiar mantle of soldier resting firmly upon his shoulders.

It was comforting.

The news he'd just received about the *Nobilis* was not.

'Throne, the entire ship? In one attack?'

Field-Marshal Lanspur nodded sombrely. 'Captain Unser bought us some ground, possibly even some time with the barrages the *Nobilis* was able to make, but the ship is dead, my lord – all twelve thousand, three hundred and eighty-one souls.'

'Merciful Emperor…' Arxis was staring into space, finding it hard to comprehend what the necrons had done. He looked up at his commanders. The sixteen men arrayed around the metal table in the Proteus bunker looked back with carefully neutral expressions.

'The astropathic message?'

'Has been sent,' replied the governor's choirmaster, a robed adept called Fava who was in charge of all interstellar communication to and from Damnos. 'We got it out just before the blackout.'

Though most short-wave vox transmissions were still in effect, anything longer range, certainly off-world communication, was utterly dead. The necrons had some kind of jamming shroud fouling it.

'Then we should pray to the Golden Throne that it reaches allies quickly. For now, we marshal what defences we can.' Arxis was about to address his master of ordnance, a short, pugnacious man who was loyal like a bloodhound, when a dull scraping sound stopped the words in his throat and altered them. 'Did you hear that?'

The scraping was getting louder, resonating against the metal inner walls of the bunker.

Several of the governor's military staff nodded.

Sytner, his chief bodyguard, drew a pistol. 'Sire, we have to move you. Now.' He said it forcefully but without panic. Sytner had been a storm trooper, serving in the same regiment as Arxis back in the day. The lord governor trusted the stocky man, recognised the urgency in his tan face, and nodded.

Beneath them, the ground trembled. Sytner stepped in, pushing the lord governor behind him and tipping the table back with one hand. Like the pillars of termites that formed in Damnos's arid zone, a column of metal-flecked earth spiralled upwards from the ground. The bunker floor was several-centimetre-thick ferrocrete, but the tunnellers bored through it anyway.

A beetle-like creature, silver-backed and dirty with earth, poked out at the apex of the pillar. Sytner shot it with his laspistol, pitching it onto its back, legs twitching.

'By the ice-hells, what...' Gaben-dun leaned in for a closer look. The pillar erupted in front of him and in seconds the master of ordnance was swarmed with the

33

beetle creatures. He fell writhing, the weight of the diminutive necrons bringing the big man down, and screamed.

'Throne of Earth,' gaped the choirmaster, seeing moist bone poking up from the chitinous mass assailing Gaben-dun. 'They're *eating* his flesh!'

'Out! Out!' shouted Sytner.

Lanspur and four of the other commanders had also drawn sidearms and put themselves between the carnivorous beetles and the lord governor.

'Open fire!' snapped Sytner and the crack of las filled the chamber along with the stink of fyceline.

Silver beetle-creatures split in half and spun off the corpse. A few las-bolts even pierced poor Gaben-dun, though the master of ordnance was little more than a sack of slowly dissolving meat by now.

When they were done with their first kill, the swarm converged on the rest.

Sytner and his fellows were soon shooting at the ceiling and the walls as the beetles scuttled towards them without impediment. A larger tremor shook the chamber and the room just as they were retreating into the bunker's annexe.

A vox-unit switched to open frequency crackled to life, adding to the confusion. Frantic reports came over the speakers from the outside: of the walls being compromised; of the enemy inside the defences, seemingly appearing out of thin air; of high-pitched beam weapons and the screaming of their victims.

Arxis clenched his fists impotently as the floor caved in completely, taking Lanspur with it, and a much larger insectoid lumbered into view.

Men were being flayed alive outside…

One creature, its carapace glistening silver and

suggestive of an arachnid construct, became three. Sytner's las-bolt caromed ineffectually off the hide of the first. Its mandible claw snapped out and severed the man in two. To his credit, Sytner didn't scream.

The choirmaster did, just as his face and torso were melted off by the second spider's beam-spike. It started as a death-shriek then ended in a wet gurgle of sloughed flesh and matter.

The rest of the command staff didn't last much longer. Scarabs claimed them – the lord governor could think of no better way to describe the beetle swarms – or the arachnids butchered them.

Arxis was alone, surrounded by foes, trapped by the illusory protection of his own Proteus bunker.

He had time to kneel before he died; a prayer to the Emperor on his lips and the barrel of a laspistol to his temple.

When he squeezed the trigger, the weapon groaned and failed. Exhausted during those first frantic moments, the power pack was out.

Arxis closed his eyes before the claws took him.

CHAPTER TWO

IT WAS GOOD fortune that placed the Ultramarines within the vicinity of Damnos. Although it would later be questioned what exactly was *good* about it. The desperate astropathic message delivered with Lord Governor Arxis's seal of verification was deciphered quickly by the sightless adepts aboard the *Valin's Revenge*.

Its captain, the dauntless Sicarius, had no compunction about ordering the vessel and his vaunted 2nd Company to the beleaguered world with the utmost haste.

The strike cruiser translated in-system amidst a debris field. Tracking augurs identified the stricken shell of the *Nobilis*, a vast Navy capital ship. The *Valin's Revenge* was undoubtedly smaller and lacking the same level of firepower, but it was also more manoeuvrable and boasted one of the most lethal payloads known to the galaxy.

Helmsman Lodis, long-serving of the Chapter, drew the vessel in close. In the void, the engine surges, the slight amendments to heading and bearing, might have seemed glacially slow but they were not. Whickering gauss-beams from the necron arc-obliterators on the ground, many kilometres long, tried time and again to skewer the strike cruiser. Each time Brother Lodis manoeuvred the *Valin's Revenge* out of harm's way or used the debris to ward them. Shields flickered with the glancing impacts, several minor hits were confirmed by the damage crews but still the ship drew closer, coming in line with Sicarius's perfect assault vector.

Hunks of the *Nobilis*, floating listlessly through the void, presented a serious threat to the strike cruiser's integrity. Volleys from the vessel's laser batteries sheared the larger sections in half. The lesser pieces of debris merely rebounded off the *Valin's Revenge's* armour.

It was a feat of bravura that finally allowed the exact attack point to be reached. Ventral drop pod bays vented in seconds, like tiny arrowheads launched from an unseen bow. They sped towards Damnos in formation, bearing Angels of Death and slim hope to the populace.

Finally capitulating under the necron gauss barrage, the shields broke down and the *Valin's Revenge* sustained a critical blow. Its payload delivered, Helmsman Lodis was content to retreat into the void, beyond the range of the guns, and lick his wounds.

For now, at least, Sicarius and his brothers were on their own.

DEEP PERCUSSIONS SHUDDERED through the walls of the drop pod.

The gauss-streams were getting closer. Warning runes flickered across the control console, urgent and red. Despite the thickness of the ceramite arrowhead in which the Space Marines were cocooned, the internal temperature was rising, not just with the heat of re-entry but from the proximity of the necron's anti-aircraft cannonade.

Sicarius was unmoved.

'Hold to your purpose, Lions,' he addressed his command squad. Except for Veteran-Sergeant Daceus, the rest of the nine-man retinue was masked by their cobalt-blue battle helms. 'We roar!'

The engine drone forced his shout into a bellow. The captain's retainers voiced a reverberant war cry as one. It was a sound to stir Sicarius's Talassari blood.

None would ever eclipse the Second, they were pre-eminent amongst the Ultramarines. Even Agemman's First were looking over their heavy-armoured shoulders.

His wide eyes flashed like stars as he roared again. 'Victoris Ultra!'

The reply was in mid-repeat when the gauss-beam clipped them, shearing away a portion of drop pod. Part of Brother Argonan went with it, most of his right shoulder and a chunk of torso. The blood vacating his body in the high-velocity pressure release of the pod vented like red streamers through the breach.

'Apothecary,' said Sicarius, donning his helmet and nodding to the only one of the squad armoured in white.

Brother Venatio leaned over to the stricken Argonan, unclasping one of his grav restraints to do so. Situated alongside him, Veteran-Sergeant Daceus instinctively seized the Apothecary's cuirass to steady him.

Punching a hole through Brother Argonan's gorget and chestplate with his reductor drill, Venatio quickly removed the sacred progenoids within and secured them in an ampoule-chamber mag-locked to his belt.

'Remember him,' Sicarius told his warriors. The wind

had built to a shriek inside the compromised drop pod. Outside, visible only through the ragged trench in the hull, the world blurred like smeared paint. 'Avenge him,' the captain concluded.

His gaze flicked to a series of read-outs on the control console. Their trajectory was still sound. The metres to planetfall clicked past on electronic tumblers at a fearsome rate.

'Twenty-eight seconds and counting, High Suzerain,' Veteran-Sergeant Daceus announced, using one of Sicarius's many honorifics.

The physical testament to his many deeds was plain for all to see in the medals and laurels that bedecked his armour. Sicarius was a warrior born but he was also not one to shy from ostentation.

'Bolters and blades ready, sergeant,' he growled, gripping the hilt of the sword of Talassar. Tempest Blade was its name. Even Sicarius's weapons had laudations.

'Hot hands and ready swords!' barked Daceus to the rest.

Snap-slides from bolters being primed filled the noisy drop pod interior. Flames were tearing off the point where the gauss-beam had glanced them and ended Argonan's life. None aboard gave them notice. All eyes were on the embarkation hatch.

LIKE THE THUNDER-SMITE of a storm god, the drop pod touched down and sent impact cracks webbing across the surface of Damnos. It was one wound amongst many the planet had suffered.

A pneumatic pressure hiss preceded the exit ramp slamming down. Seconds later Sicarius was bounding through it, cape flaring, Guilliman's name on his lips.

He speared a necron warrior, half-cooked by the drop

pod's incendiary flare. Another nearby had rapidly self-repaired and was advancing with automaton-like implacability. Sicarius pummelled its torso with a blast from his plasma pistol. Breaking into a run, he got close enough to behead it. The green bale-fires in its eyes guttered and died.

Behind him, the hard *chank-rattle* of bolters sounded as Daceus and the others opened up. Energy beams, viperous and emerald green, streaked through the smoke before Sicarius's retinal scanners could resolve a better view. A gauss-beam scudded over his pauldron, stripping it back to naked ceramite with the barest touch.

The necrons' bale-fire eyes appeared in the gloom like dead stars. The few they'd destroyed around the drop pod were just part of the vanguard.

More were coming.

THE THANATOS FOOTHILLS loomed in the distance like bad omens. The drop pods had got them as close as they could.

The ground running up to the snow-crested mounds was over three kilometres of debris-choked mire. Fanged by ice shards and dotted with arctic sink-holes, it was treacherous.

Scipio Vorolanus ate up the metres eagerly, his 'Thunderbolts' keeping pace alongside him and in spread formation. He checked the dispersal on his retinal display. A series of ident-runes showed good separation and fire-arc discipline.

'Move!' he said into the comm-feed, spurring his warriors as one.

Through the smoke-fog and the dust palls from the sundered refinery complex, shapes were moving ahead of them. They strode, slow and purposeful. Whickering emerald gauss-beams preceded them.

A grunt of pain, an armoured silhouette crumpling to Scipio's extreme right signalled a hit. Brother Largo's rune went to amber as the tac-display in Scipio's helmet registered a serious injury.

Just a few more metres…

A long line of silver-grey, flecked with pieces of ceramic, opposed them. The necron fire was a relentless barrage now. Another Ultramarine battle-brother fell to its fury.

+Halt!+

Scipio was stunned into obedience by the figure running just ahead of him. The word resolved in his mind rather than his comm-feed, a psychic impulse that could only be defied by one with sufficient will.

Varro Tigurius dropped into a crouch, gauss-beams flashing against a kine-shield the Chief Librarian had raised around him.

'Get to cover. Hunker down!' Scipio ordered, slamming behind a shattered wall in the gutted remains of the half-destroyed refinery.

The place was a grim mortuary, littered with the bodies of Damnosian labourers and indentured Imperial Guard troopers. There'd been a battle here, a hard-fought one that had ended badly for the human natives.

Scipio barely gave them a second glance. It had not always been so. Black Reach and the many hard years that followed had changed him.

Fifty metres of spar-studded, wire-drenched courtyard stood between the Ultramarines and the necron firing line. Tigurius had brought the Space Marines to a sudden stop behind a ragged barricade before the final charge.

Peering through the gauss-laced haze, Scipio engaged

the comm-feed. 'Specialists to point, on Vorolanus.'

Brothers Cator and Brakkius moved up, crouch-running, a few seconds later. Scipio clapped Cator on his shoulder guard. 'Plasma and meltagun at either end, brothers.' Both nodded as one, taking position at the edges of the wall.

Chips of rockcrete and semi-flayed plasteel slivers forced Scipio to duck.

'What are we waiting for, brother-sergeant?' asked Naceon.

Scipio had his eyes on the courtyard – there was more than merely war-churned earth beneath its shattered flagstones – and didn't look back.

'For thunder and lightning.'

Telion had taught him when to wait and when to strike; the Master Scout's expert tutelage and influence, presently engaged in other war zones, would be missed on Damnos. Scipio gestured towards Tigurius, a couple of metres ahead of them. 'Watch and be ready.'

A coruscation of electricity suddenly wreathed the Librarian's ornate battle armour and he pressed one gauntleted palm to the ground. Instantly, the azure energy banding him leapt into the earth and ripples of psychic force went searching through the no-man's-land.

Like gruesome marionettes jerking to horrific un-life, the necron 'flayed ones' sprang from their ambuscade. They'd been buried just beneath the surface of the earth, poised to attack the Ultramarines as they charged. A minefield of sorts, but one littered with an animate and deadly enemy rather than merely explosives.

Two of the ghoulish creatures juddered and expired from Tigurius's lightning arcs, the flayed human skin draped across them like cloaks and cowls burning off in a noisome flesh-smoke. Several more came on, having lost the element of surprise, but slashing with razored finger-talons anyway.

Scipio roared, 'Space Marines – unleash death!' The flare of his bolt pistol framed the hard edges of his crimson battle helm in jagged monochrome.

A plasma bolt took one of the flayed ones in the chest, annihilating mechanical organs and processors. The necron collapsed in a heap, quivered and then phased from existence as if it had never even been there.

Another sloughed away under the beam of Cator's meltagun. Despite the rapid self-repair engines of the necron's advanced mechorganics, the damage was critical and it too was teleported away.

Naceon had leapt the barricade, full-auto adding thrust to his battle cry. 'Ultramar and the Thunderbolts!'

Impact sparks riddled the onrushing necron, jarring but not stopping it. Naceon saw the danger, bringing his bolter's combat-bayonet low to block, but was too late. Finding the weak points of Naceon's armour joints, the flayed one punched several fatal wounds into the Ultramarine before slicing open his gorget.

Naceon's head rolled like a dud-grenade into the dirt.

'Guilliman and the Temple of Hera!' Scipio invoked a blessing as he cut into the metal clavicle of Naceon's killer. The chainsword bit deep and jammed.

An expressionless silver rictus, stained with blood, reared towards the sergeant. A bolt pistol burst took off the necron's left claw-hand before it could slash him. Scipio then butted it, snapping the creature's neck so its head lolled at an unnatural angle. He thumped his chainsword's activation stud again, muttering a quick litany to the machine-spirit within, and it churned to life. Dropping his pistol, Scipio drove the blade two-handed clean through the flayed one's body and out the other side. As he stepped back, ready to strike again, the two mechanical halves slid diagonally and fell in opposite directions.

Scipio had barely recovered when a second necron was advancing upon him. Without his bolt pistol, he adopted a rapid defensive stance.

The flayed one exploded before it could engage, sparks and machine-parts flying like frag.

A pair of hard eyes, glowing with power and set in an ice-carved face, regarded him.

+*Take up your arms*+

Scipio gave a curt nod of thanks to Tigurius, his soul ever so slightly chilled by the Librarian's gaze, and retrieved his bolt pistol.

There was little time. The flayed ones were vanquished, Brakkius and Cator were finishing the wounded at close range, but the line of gauss-flayers remained.

Scipio waved his squad forwards after Tigurius. Catching the Librarian's battle-signal on his retinal display, he opened up the comm-feed again.

'Squad Strabo. Bring fire from heaven.'

Hidden behind the wreckage of a refinery tower, ten bulky figures arrowed into the air on plumes of fire. The roar of their ascent jets made the necrons look skywards. Half of the creatures switched their aim, but the gauss-stream was too late and not nearly enough.

Hit from the front by Tigurius and Squad Vorolanus, and from above by Assault Squad Strabo, the necron firing line disintegrated leaving the Ultramarines the victors.

In the aftermath, Tigurius eyed the distant Thanatos foothills. The forbidding arc of necron pylons and the long noses of gauss siege cannon blighted the horizon line. Sustained particle whips and focussed energy beams bombarded the city of Kellenport relentlessly.

'They will be well guarded,' counselled the Librarian, without acknowledging Scipio's presence but answering his question before he'd even asked it.

'We'll need a way to breach their defences,' Scipio replied. Behind him, his squad and that of Sergeant Strabo secured the battle-site.

'A dagger rather than a hammer,' said Tigurius. 'But not one wielded by the hand of a Space Marine,' he added cryptically, turning his attention onto the sergeant. 'Does something trouble you, Brother Vorolanus?'

Scipio shifted uncomfortably in his armour, wishing he hadn't removed his battle helm.

'No, my lord,' he answered, truthfully. *Nothing, except your psyker's interrogation.*

Tigurius smiled and it was, at once, a deeply incongruous and unsettling gesture.

'Perhaps it should be,' he said, and left Scipio to plan the next stage of the assault.

Brother Orin was at the sergeant's shoulder before he could reply.

'We've secured the battle-site, my lord.'

Scipio re-donned his helmet. 'Retrieve Naceon's body and replenish ammo. We advance,' he replied, left to wonder at Tigurius's meaning.

THEY SAW IT as a star-fall from the heavens. All who manned the Kellenport walls, their tired bodies and weary souls crying out for succour, knew it for what it was. No mere meteor shower, although celestially that was how it first appeared.

No, it was salvation. Or so they all hoped.

Adanar Sonne surveyed the dispositions of his troops on the city battlements. They'd lost much of the outer ground beyond the core. Several of the defensive walls had fallen, those ringing the heart of the city. Ferrocrete, armaplas and adamantite had been made a mockery of by the necron flayer technology. The horrors it could inflict upon flesh and blood were even worse to behold.

The necrons had some kind of device, a phasic-generator the tech-priests had postulated. It had allowed the bulk of their awakened troops to teleport directly behind the Ark Guard's defensive positions. Fortified walls, bunkers, fields of razor-wire – they were no impediment to the mechanised advance of the necrontyr. Isolated pockets of resistance in these outer zones, 'the wasteland' as it had come to be known, fought still. Their lasgun reports diminished to the same ratio that the emerald flash of gauss-flayers increased. Soon they'd be silent and the metal host would come for the survivors cowering within the city's core.

Adanar could make out the remains of the lord governor's Proteus bunker in the snow-choked battlefield. How they had managed to extract him was unknown, but he was rumoured to be alive, albeit comatose and in critical condition. The body of Tarn, the former commander of the Ark Guard, lay amongst the corpse-tide. Their icy graves were barely settled when the necrons had begun marching over them. Tarn had been a brave man, and honourable. His rearguard action had allowed Adanar to lead the bulk of the troops behind the inner walls of Kellenport, all the way back to the western gate and the Courtyard of Thor. It was only delaying the inevitable but it gave them all a few more hours to contemplate their fate.

A sea of metal horrors extended all the way to the

horizon line, their bale-fire eyes adding to the chill colonising the hearts of the men. In the distance, arcane pyramids, newly unearthed, hove into position. Every burst of infernal light from their cores seemed to bring fresh monsters into the fray. This legion of death would not be denied, but despite his fatalism Adanar would not yield without making a fight of it.

Behind him, the dense thud of *uber*-mortars and long-cannons could be heard. Their reports, though loud and earth-shaking, had started to pale in comparison to the necron barrage. Slowly, they were being drowned out.

We are all drowning… in our fear. Death, slow and terrible, has come to my world and there is no escaping it.

Adanar flinched reflexively as another of the artillery stations was sundered. A vast cloud of smoke belched across the Ark Guard platoons waiting in the Courtyard of Thor to fill the inevitable breaches in the wall.

Lasgun fire rained from the battlements, a steady shriek of energy that the necrons waded through as if it were nothing but an insect swarm. Shielded by bunkers, hunched below plascrete bulwarks or hastily erected barricades, the Ark Guard were holding out. For now, at least.

Rotational guns – las and autocannon, heavy stubber and bolter – slaved to a rail network, spat muzzle flashes into an alien darkness. Not only had the necrontyr brought a comms shroud to blanket the regions before them, they had summoned an unnatural shadow too. Running hot on its tracks, Adanar watched a team wheel an autocannon in position only for it to be vaporised by necron heavy fire before it could shoot. Ammo buckets attached to the platform went up in a fiery cascade, shredding the crew and several more Ark Guard nearby. Below, platoon sergeants saw the hole and ordered more men into the gap.

'Sir.'

Adanar was dimly aware of someone addressing him. The voice became insistent. 'Commander Sonne.'

He glared at Besseque, his aide. The man was shorter by a head than Adanar and had his cold-coat buckled all the way to his chin. His goggles were perched on his hooded head and covered in rime-frost. Shivering, Besseque saluted before going on.

'Acting-Governor Rancourt has just been on the vox. He wants a battalion sent to the capitolis administratum. He says if the area outside the walls can be cleared then an extraction from the Crastia Shipyards will be possible.'

Adanar fought the urge to strike Besseque, but it wasn't the messenger's fault. He cursed the day that Rancourt returned from the ice wastes alive.

'Request denied,' he answered flatly.

The capitolis administratum was an isolated bastion out in the wasteland. From his vantage point on the wall Adanar could discern its troops fighting hard against necron aggressors. Somewhere inside, Zeph Rancourt had secreted himself, deep within the governmental chambers. Perhaps that was where they'd moved Arxis to, as well.

Mercifully, only the lesser necron constructs were harrying the bastion's high walls. Wave after wave of scarab creatures assailed the Ark Guard platoon and the capitolis storm troopers charged with its defence, but they were holding. The necron war cell diverting its attention in the bastion's direction suggested that situation was about to change.

'It's a suicide mission,' Adanar muttered, and brought

his attention back to the broader killing-fields.

'What should I tell the acting governor, sir, he won't–'

'Tell him to feg off for all I care, Besseque! There are no more men, no spare battalions. It's ov–' Adanar caught himself before he went too far. He lowered his voice, just for the aide. 'It's over, Corporal Besseque. This world is our tomb.'

Slowly, Besseque nodded and backed away. The hollow anger in Adanar's eyes was reflected in the corporal's fearful pupils.

Adanar didn't watch him go. He returned to observe the assault. Hard to see, as a sudden snowfall shawled the more distant defensive walls, but a line of shattered tanks punctuated the outer marker of the city where they'd first tried to meet the necrons. The enemy had annihilated the armour columns with perfunctory ease and then used their swarm creatures to gut the machine innards of the Imperial tanks and convert them into more necron warrior constructs. How foolish the humans had been to think anything other than hiding behind the walls of the capital would extend their lives, albeit fractionally.

'How much of a fool,' whispered Adanar. He rubbed his figure over a locket-charm chained to his wrist. There were two picts nestled inside, memories of the wife and child now slumbering beneath the Damnos earth like so many others.

'I'm sorry,' he said, ghosting the air with his breath, the din of the battle all around him receding. He felt the scar on his face, the ache in his shoulder and back from when he'd tried to save them. When the hab had collapsed and… and…

Adanar shut his eyes.

Tarn, the poor dead fegger, had been wise to tell him

to flee with his family. A pity Adanar had not heeded him.

'I'm sorry,' he echoed, talking to the phantoms in his mind. He wiped away a tear, crystallised on his cheek, and the battle rushed back. They were stretched. He needed more men. Once the phasic-generator was in range it wouldn't matter. Not long now. He'd be with them soon enough.

Some of the Ark Guard in the courtyard were pointing at the sky.

Adanar followed their gestures and saw... *comets*. Armoured comets, cobalt blue and streaked in flame, emblazoned with an icon he had seen depicted in tapestries and triptychs if never in real life.

Ultramarines.

The Space Marines had come.

WHEN ORDERED TO join the gate-guard, a soldier surrendered all semblance of control and accepted his fate was no longer in his own hands. Even firing a weapon was pointless. Engaging the enemy was impossible. The first moment a gate-guard would know of the enemy was when that enemy was bearing down on him, breaching the very portal he had sworn to protect.

Falka accepted the duty grimly. He never trembled like the other men did when the earth shook and the gate shuddered from artillery impacts. He gripped his lascarbine, felt the reassuring weight of the ice-pick tugging at his belt loop, and waited. He thought of Jynn, lost in the ice storm. It seemed like years, but in reality it was just months. She'd got them out of the mine and died an ignominious death for her bravery. Sometimes, the Emperor's sense of humour was a cruel one. Falka's last sight of her had been the ice bank collapsing, Jynn and a dozen or so others falling to the abysmal white of the frost-gale.

Now all he had was the gate. He had lived, she had not. It would count for something, Falka decided. He'd seen, first-hand, what had happened in the outer zones – 'the wasteland'. Ferrocrete and plasteel were no barriers to these creatures, these *necrons*. They filled the air with their threats, their promises of annihilation and domination, and there was nothing the Ark Guard could do. This was a menace that could materialise through walls or *inside* bunkers. There was no place on all of Damnos to hide. So, it was with a certain irony that Falka regarded the western gate.

When the phasic-generator, an arcane device spoken of in fearful whispers by the men, got close enough or attained enough power, they would be tooth to nail with the necrons. Flesh against metal, the humans did not stand a chance.

'You were the lucky one, Jynn,' muttered Falka, and the sadness plucked at his stomach, making him feel sick.

'Trooper Kolpeck.' It was the gate-sergeant, a hard-edged brute called Muhrne. 'Save your prayers until they're at the gate.'

'With respect, sir,' Falka replied, 'it won't matter a shard. They'll pass the western gate and be on us without warning.'

Muhrne nodded sagely. 'So, like I said: save your prayers.'

Falka laughed before his eye-line was drawn to the sky and he saw the stars falling, setting the clouds aflame.

THE DROP PODS hammered into the earth with concussive fury. Adanar watched a wave slam into position around the capitolis administratum, burning scarabs off the walls with the displaced heat of their re-entry. Slab-sides like the edges of an arrowhead crashed open with a hiss of venting pressure and a missile barrage disgorged from within. Tiny explosions, combining to form much larger ones, erupted throughout the necron ranks in close proximity to the bastion. Adanar had expected Space Marines; instead he got a fusillade that was punishing the enemy hard with automated precision. The defenders, pushed close to the brink of defeat, rallied at once. Redoubled las-fire spat from the walls adding to the carnage.

Adanar's vicarious exultation was short-lived as the phasic-generator came into range and so too did the necron warrior cohorts. Several war cells translated *through* the Kellenport walls and fell upon the vanguard Adanar had positioned in front of the Courtyard of Thor. A strange sensation emanated from the newly-arrived enemy, something brought on by the effects of the generator's recent activation. The world spun vertiginously and Adanar was forced to cling to the battlement for support. He heard screams, echoing through the fog of sudden dislocation, and assumed several of the Ark Guard stationed on the wall had fallen.

'Sergeant,' he began, spitting out the word through gritted teeth.

Sergeant Nabor was on his knees, blubbering like an infant with his hands over his ears.

It had affected the entire garrison.

Adanar tried to move, thinking he was stepping back when in fact he went forwards. He reached for his laspistol, hoping the sudden discharge might return his senses, but grabbed for the empty air on the left side of his belt, instead of the holster on his right.

'Throne of Earth,' he garbled, as an errant trickle of blood wept from his nostril and touched his lip. The copper tang was intense, almost acidic.

Below, through his tunnelling, kaleidoscopic vision, the vanguard was being slaughtered.

A voice, inhuman and metallic, resolved on the breeze.

Heed my words for I am the Herald and we are the footsteps of doom. Interlopers, do we name you. Defilers of our sacred earth. We have awoken to your primitive species and will not tolerate your presence. Ours is the way of logic, of cold hard reason; your irrationality, your human disease has no place in the necrontyr. Flesh is weak. Surrender to the machine incarnate. Surrender and die.

Adanar found his laspistol – it was as if it'd been placed in his trembling grasp – and pressed it to his forehead.

'Surrender to the machine incarnate,' he echoed macabrely. 'Surrender and die.' A thought, so small and insignificant he barely felt it, entered his brain and he paused for a few life-saving seconds. The trigger pull never came.

The comets from heaven crashed home, flooding the plaza beyond the walls with cobalt-blue angels, and the terrible sensation abated.

Weeping openly, Adanar put down his gun and praised the Emperor.

'Thank you, my loves,' he sobbed, rubbing at the locket-charm. 'Thank you.'

Mustering his resolve, ignoring the fact Sergeant Nabor had forcibly evacuated much of his brainpan across the battlement, Adanar issued the order to open the western gate and empty the Courtyard of Thor.

The tide had turned.

CHAPTER THREE

Aboard the Valin's Revenge *prior to drop pod assault*

SCIPIO KNELT ON the assembly deck, blessing his weapons before launch. Less than fifty metres away row upon row of drop pods waited, cinched in their launch tubes.

'As I anoint this holy bolter with these words of benediction, so too do I commit myself, body and mind, to the service of the Emperor. I swear by Guilliman's blade and for the glory of Ultramar that Thy will be done.' Holstering his bolt pistol, Scipio drew his chainsword from a sheath on his armour's power generator and pressed the still blade to his forehead. 'Make my hand into a ready sword; let my faith and certainty of purpose be my shield. For I am Adeptus Astartes, Ultramarine, pre-eminent of all Chapters. So swears Lord Guilliman.'

'So swears Lord Guilliman,' echoed a deep voice behind him.

Scipio smiled and turned, sheathing his weapon. 'Didn't think I'd see you again so soon, brother.'

Iulus Fennion had a face like a slab of carved granite

and displayed about the same amount of emotion. He clasped Scipio's proffered hand and tiny cracks sprang out from the corners of his eyes in what could have been amusement.

'A dangerous mission into the Thanatos Hills,' Iulus replied, all business. His square jaw and flat nose shifted like a mountain crag as he spoke, and the stubble on his chin and head reminded Scipio of grit rather than hair.

'Is that concern I hear, brother?' Scipio asked, releasing his grip and patting his fellow sergeant on the shoulder.

Iulus shrugged, pretending to run a final check over his wargear. 'A statement of fact. As part of the main push to relieve Kellenport, I won't be there to watch your back.'

'I can think of no better to perform such a task, either,' Scipio replied with genuine bonhomie. 'Or perhaps it's you that's in need of protection.'

Iulus grunted something when the pair were interrupted by a third figure.

'Brother-sergeants.' Praxor's greeting was friendly enough, but a chill entered the air at his arrival nonetheless.

The three clasped vambraces in the manner of the old way once favoured by Macraggian battle-kings.

'A glorious campaign is in prospect,' said Praxor Manorian. 'Our Lord Sicarius will bring many laurels to the Second this day.'

'Cast off your politician's mantle, Praxor,' growled Iulus, finding the other sergeant's vainglory distasteful. 'It is war, plain and simple.'

'There is more than mere soldiery at play here. We need to be seen to be supporting our captain.'

Scipio snorted. He hadn't seen Praxor in many weeks – he originally believed he'd been secluded in the practice cages, but later discovered he was involved in senate dealings concerning Calgar's eventual successor. 'Support for what? Sicarius's elevation?'

Praxor looked nonplussed, his thin face taut like wire. Together with his silver hair, the sergeant had the haughty cast of a statue. He was certainly inflexible enough when it came to Ultramar politics. 'Yes, what else?'

Iulus shook his head, 'We three have debated this point at length, and I still maintain it is unfitting talk for warriors. Agemman is First, therefore he sits at Lord Calgar's right hand. I vaunt Sicarius as much and as readily as any in the Chapter, as any in the Second, but the law of ascendancy is what it is.' The grizzled veteran folded his arms as if that were an end to it.

'Just because you have a uniquely simple view of matters does not mean everyone else has, Iulus,' chided Praxor. 'Every victory, laurel and laudation we garner for the Second brings us closer to our rightful place, at the head of Calgar's table.'

Bored of the debate, one that had been waxing and waning for over a century, Scipio began inspecting the seals on his power armour. 'There is no struggle, save that devised by your imaginings, Praxor,' he said dismissively. 'You've been spending too much time in temples with the legates, senators and magistrates instead of on the battlefield. I liked you better when you were a slave to the battle-cages. At least that improved your bladecraft.'

Iulus laughed, a rare concession to humour for him, but Praxor returned a serious expression. 'It is no trivial matter, Scipio. Our Chapter's future and who shapes it

is of the utmost importance to all of us.' He relaxed a
little, realising he was being goaded. 'And besides, the
struggle is plain to see.'

Scipio frowned, bidding Praxor to clarify.

'Or did you not see Helios in the mission briefing?
Him and four others of the First – Agemman's watchmen.'

'You see conspiracy and spies where I see only fellow
battle-brothers–'

'They are not alone,' interrupted Iulus, pointing further down the deck where three mighty Chapter
wardens stomped into view.

The drop pods meant to convey the Dreadnoughts
were slightly larger than the rest and designed out to
accommodate their bulk. Ultracius, Agnathio and venerable Agrippen – veterans all, formerly battle-brothers
but now warriors-eternal entombed within sarcophagi
of ceramite. Their mechanised shells were festooned
with honour gilding and reliquaries, purity seals and
oaths of moment. Each bore the sigil of the Ultramarines proudly and was armed with a brutal array of
weapons.

'Agrippen is First, is he not?' said Iulus, rubbing at the
rough texture of his chin as he considered what it must
be like to fight for the Chapter as a Dreadnought.

'Aye,' uttered Praxor darkly. 'He is.'

'You'll turn us all into company separatists with this
talk, brother,' Scipio warned. 'It's not fitting.'

Praxor turned on him, flint in his eyes and ice in his
voice. 'Eventually you'll need to find your loyalties, Scipio. The Second fight and die as one.'

Scipio smacked away his brother's coaxing hand
before it touched his shoulder. 'No, we the *Chapter* are
as one. Politics be damned.'

'It is for the good of the Chapter that I speak!' Praxor was clearly becoming exasperated. As if remembering where he was, he lowered his voice. 'And by supporting our captain, we are achieving that aim. There will come a time when political schism is inevitable. You won't be able to hide behind your indifference then, Scipio. Your hand will be counted as will every other sergeant and captain's.'

'Then I hope that day is long in the coming, brother. For it holds no interest for me.' It came out harder than Scipio had intended.

Praxor's expression went from animated to one of res-ignation. 'As you wish.' He saluted, somewhat crisply, and stalked away to find his squad. By now the assembly deck was thronged with battle-brothers from the Second. There were elements from other companies too: specialist forces the Ultramarines would need to face the necrons. Praxor only had issue with those warriors from the First, perceived as a threat by the paranoid brother-sergeant.

'He craves the captain's validation still, even after all this time,' said Iulus. 'Space Marines have long memo-ries and pride the same as any man.'

'I would see Praxor's pride lanced swiftly before it overtakes his reason.'

Iulus only nodded.

Scipio scowled at Praxor's back as he departed. 'He's a fool.'

'Perhaps.'

A raised eyebrow gave away Scipio's surprise. 'You agree with him?'

'I am a soldier, brother. I care not for the politics of advancement. Calgar will appoint the right successor, I trust in that. But I'm not blind, either. Agemman is looking over his shoulder, and Sicarius has his gaze fixed on what's ahead of the First Captain. Power struggles are inevitable in any organised structure – they don't need to be a bad thing, either.'

'You sound more like a Salamander, all tedious pragmatism and fatalistic acceptance.'

'Better to accept what you cannot change and learn to adapt than rail against the immutable and end up wasting time and effort.'

Scipio gave the facial equivalent of a shrug, indicating his interest in the matter was at an end. 'Battle calls, brother,' he said. Squad Vorolanus was gathering around their drop pod, awaiting their sergeant. 'May Guilliman guide your hand and the Emperor shield you.' His gauntlet slapping Iulus's pauldron made a dull ring before he turned away.

The hard-faced brother-sergeant seized Scipio's forearm, stopping him.

'Those heavy guns,' he said, releasing his grip. 'They won't be easy to knock out, even with Lord Tigurius at your side.'

'It is I who'll be at *his* side, Iulus.'

Scipio hadn't seen the Master of Librarians throughout the muster but somehow felt his presence. Varro Tigurius was formidable in the psychic arts – to take to the field with him was a great honour, but also a source of trepidation for the sergeant. What misgivings might he uncover in Scipio's turbulent mind?

Iulus brought him back. 'Even still, you'll be far from the rest of us.'

Confusion creased Scipio's brow. Did Iulus doubt him for some reason?

'The necron pylons *will* be destroyed, brother.' His eyeline strayed to the distant figure of Antaro Chronus as he inspected the Ultramarines armour. 'Rest assured of that.'

The master tank commander would not be deployed with the first wave, but Thunderhawk transporters stood ready on the launch bay for when the enemy beam weapons were silenced and passage opened for the Predators, Whirlwinds and Devastators in Chronus's arsenal.

'I don't doubt it. Antaro's cannons will be a welcome friend in a sea of foes when you do.'

'What is it then? All this evasion.' Scipio's eyes narrowed. 'It's not like you.'

'I give you counsel, that is all,' Iulus said plainly. He paused, as if deciding how and if to proceed. Good advice given at a bad time by a friend was always harder to hear; it was even harder to give. 'You are becoming like him.'

Scipio's face stiffened. It had lost much of its youthful exuberance over the last century, only the close-cropped hair remained the same. 'More allusion. Are you sure that's not Praxor Manorian under all that grim and sturm?'

Iulus didn't return Scipio's smile.

'I am my own man, Iulus.'

'I don't doubt that.' The sergeant had his hands up in a plaintive gesture. 'But these creatures are not ork, nor are they eldar or even Traitors...'

'I know what they are, brother.'

Warning sirens were sounding, signalling the imminent drop pod assault.

Further counsel from Iulus Fennion would have to wait.

Sicarius, ever the last to walk the assembly deck, ever the first out onto the battlefield, had just arrived with his Lions. The captain and his command squad strode with an imperious air about them. As they closed on their drop pod, the slab sides of the inverted arrowhead grinding open to allow them access, Sicarius spoke. 'Glory to the Second,' he roared, a broad grin splitting his patrician jawline. He lifted the Tempest Blade and its edge glittered in the half-light. 'Let's give them a taste of Guilliman's wrath.'

The necron cannonade had begun outside the thick walls of the *Valin's Revenge*. The rapid manoeuvres by Helmsman Lodis and the close proximity of the blasts resonated through the hull and shook the assembly deck.

Sicarius laughed it off, even as he was enjoying the bellowed affirmations of his men.

'I am my own man,' Scipio repeated, watching Sicarius and the Lions of Macragge climb aboard their drop pod. It was something he and Iulus should also be doing.

'Just watch yourself, brother. Promise me that at least.'

Scipio nodded, not liking the hint of anxiety in Iulus's eyes. They clapped pauldrons, their brief disagreement forgotten, and made for the drop pods.

It would be a long time before they saw each other again.

WHEN THE LIONS were in their positions and the access hatch was closing, Sicarius's expression changed. Swathed in shadows, with only the internal lumes of the pod interior to light it, his face took on a much darker cast.

'These revenants are not like the greenskins,' he warned. 'The warriors outside this covenant are Second Company – there are none better – but they require steel and fire, not cold hard facts. Let the tactica briefings give them the knowledge they require to do their duty. You, my Lions, are *chosen*. You, as I do, will know what we face on the Damnos soil.' Sicarius looked to his second-in-command.

Veteran-Sergeant Daceus narrowed his eyes. He swept his gaze across the other eight Space Marines in the drop pod. A countdown timer had begun. Intermittent vox-chimes signalled the imminence of launch; the shuddering impacts felt against the hull conveyed its urgency.

'There have been few reported sightings, let alone engagements with these creatures. We, the Second, have yet to lock blades with them but they are a foe unlike any other. Your tactica briefings are inloaded to your retinal displays – I suggest we all analyse that data during launch. Their technology, resilience and ability to self-repair are all in there.'

The vox-chimes were getting closer together as the countdown started to reach its final cycle.

'There is no drill, no amount of training or physical honing that can prepare you for this foe,' he went on. 'Preparing for the unknown, adapting to face the unforeseen scenario, it is what we Space Marines excel at. We are not the Guard, mere men, who would balk and pale in the face of this enemy. We are Ultramarines, but our mettle will be tested here – yours, the valiant Lions, most of all. To be chosen means something. It is more than honour, it is responsibility. Inspire your battle-brothers, for we will need inspiration and visible courage this day.'

Each of the warriors present met Daceus's hard eyes. Vandius, their Company Banner Bearer, wore a determined expression – his duty was to keep the standard of the Second aloft. Gaius Prabian, as Champion, was charged with keeping Sicarius alive and allowing him to lead the line – Daceus didn't envy him, but there was steel in his eyes and aggression. Of the others, all showing grim resolve and ready violence, only Venatio remained carefully neutral. The Apothecary knew his task would be hardest of all and it carried the most weight – in his hands was the future of the Chapter, the harvesting and safeguard of the gene-seed.

'Trust in the Codex, and in your captain,' Daceus concluded. 'Through that we will triumph.'

'You all know my mind,' said Sicarius. 'Know this, also: I do not want this fight. I desire to gild our banner with victory, to elevate our station, to glorify our Lord Calgar and the Chapter. But our chances of victory here, on Damnos, are almost none. We will do what is needed, because it is asked of us and as Adeptus Astartes it is our solemn calling, but we are stepping onto a dead world.'

He thrust out a clenched fist.

The move was immediately mirrored by every warrior in the drop pod, until ten spokes of ceramite formed a wheel of brotherhood around the interior.

'Courage and honour.'

The words were returned to Sicarius, spoken with stern conviction.

The vox-chimes reached a long sustained whine. Launch engines were burning outside the drop pod. The bays opened in unison. There was a sense of weightlessness, then of gravity pulling them downwards through the atmosphere. Temperature gauges rose; so too did the sound of the necron guns.

The liberation of Damnos had begun.

CHAPTER FOUR

IULUS ISSUED A series of orders using Ultramarines battle-sign and his squad tightened around him in a defensive cordon centred on the drop pod. Sicarius and his Lions had landed ahead of them. Somehow, impossibly, even their transport was more eager than everyone else's to close with the enemy.

Necrons were thronging the plaza. Hot beams from their gauss-flayers turned the accumulated snow to slush that detonated wetly beneath Iulus's armoured tread.

'Dense separation, suppressing fire,' he bellowed, voice grating through his vox-grille. Iulus seldom wore a battle-helm, preferring for his squad to see his face and the fury therein, but on this occasion he was glad of it. The snow-fog occluded the view. Retinal sensors built into his helmet lenses overcame that easily, the reddish blur of the unique necron heat signature readily discernible in his field of vision.

Staccato bolter fire, clipped and precise, rewarded the many training drills he'd put the 'Immortals' through during his tenure as their sergeant. Several of the automatons jerked and bucked against the bolt storm before collapsing into the snow-slush.

'Advance and execute,' he continued.

The Immortals moved on their sergeant's lead, charging up to the stricken necrons. Three battle-brothers hung back as the others went ahead of the enemy casualties. The loud *crack-bang* of single headshots and the sonorous report of a phasal shift filled the air.

Iulus had read the Tactica briefings extensively. Nothing barring critical system damage would prevent a necron's ability to self-repair. He was taking no chances.

'Report,' he barked into the comm-feed.

'Eliminated, brother-sergeant.' Three identical replies came back before Iulus's squad were reunited. The dense *chud-chud* of a heavy bolter, unleashed by 'Guilliman's Hammer', Tirian's Devastators, sounded from the left. It was paired off with another weapon, the two cannons giving off intermittent barrages that overlapped at the beginning and end of their ammo cycles. The *foom* of missile tubes provided a low chorus to the percussive refrain of the bolters. Explosions, hazy through the mist, bloomed. Snow and frag spat in diagonal bursts. It was brutal, but in the distance necrons were rising from the carnage.

'Temple of Hera.' Iulus had moved ahead of the Devastators, but caught the flare of muzzle flashes and the fading contrail of expelled smoke in his peripheral vision as they advanced. There was little to no cover on the plaza, the necrons had levelled it with their cannonade, but that was why Space Marines wore power armour – ceramite battle-plate was all the cover they needed.

From the right, Brother-Sergeant Atavian brought up a second squad of Devastators, the Titan Slayers. Their weapons brought swift death to the mechanoids. Even the necrons' enhanced repair ability couldn't save them from the searing beam of a lascannon or metal-sloughing effects of a multi-melta. Iulus stayed close to Atavian, advancing in an oblique line. Engage, take ground, engage – enacted as if on the training ground.

The first few raiders had been the exploratory elements of a vanguard. The reddish heat signature blurs on Iulus's retinal display suddenly increased as the Ultramarines reached the shadow of the first of Kellenport's defensive walls. It was overrun and the sound of desperate Guardsmen fated for death resolved on the breeze like a requiem.

Spreading out, the necrons had enveloped them. Bolters tracked and fired to compensate, relying on advanced targeting sensors – the mist was so bad that the enemy were literally appearing as if from nowhere, and in numbers.

'Brother, my flank has been compromised.' It was Atavian through the comm-feed in Iulus's helmet.

'Close up battle-formation, there are more necrons than we first believed.'

An affirmation rune flashed on Iulus's retinal display. The tac-icons representing the Devastator squad started to move closer to the Immortals. Iulus noticed there were several red markers that remained static.

Squad Fennion and the two Devastators – they were the rearguard. Glory belonged to others.

'Take and hold the ground.' Those had been his orders during the mission briefing. Thirty Ultramarines to keep a simple esplanade from the enemy. It had seemed like overkill; now, Iulus Fennion wasn't so sure.

A swarm of beetle-like creatures droned out of the fog, mandibles champing.

The Immortals turned with battle-honed efficiency and cut them down. Brother Galvia cried out as one of the creatures clamped onto his forearm. Iulus stepped in and excised the mechanoid with his chainsword. A stamp of his armoured boot ceased the beetle's squirming after it was removed. A bolter salvo exploded another with mass-reactive fury before it could refashion itself and attack anew.

'They're hard to keep down,' breathed Galvia. 'I've never seen such–'

A gauss-beam skewering his shoulder and upper torso cut him off. Iulus reached for Galvia, who grunted and slumped to his knee. Blood-stained slush spattered his armour viscerally as he fell hard.

The wounding preceded a fusillade of gauss-fire as the necron vanguard force tried to pin them. Enfilading beams streaked across the trio of Space Marine squads diagonally while more of the drone beetles pressed an assault from the front. Iulus had one arm under Galvia to support him; with the other he wielded a whirring chainsword with menace. He swatted the first scarab-like creature, cracking its carapace but not disabling it; a second he carved with a heavy downward swing. A third latched to his vambrace but he was able to shake it off and crush it under his boot.

Another dug into his back, gnawing at the power generator. Emergency icons flashed up on his retinal display warning of an imminent energy drain. Iulus reached for the creature but staggered when a pair of scarabs fastened themselves to his pauldron. He cried out as one attached itself to his battle-helm. Below, Galvia screamed in agony and frustration.

'Aristaeus!' The comm-feed was wretched with inter-ference. The creatures were slowly disabling it.

The low *whoosh* of pressure-release and the acrid stench of promethium filled the air as Iulus and Galvia were consumed by fire. Aristaeus had kept the aperture of his flamer narrow. Both Ultramarines emerged from the conflagration blackened but otherwise unscathed. Smoking, burning scarabs writhed about on the scorched earth. Iulus crushed one underfoot before dis-patching the others with a desultory burst from his bolt pistol.

He waved Aristaeus forwards. 'Bring the heat.'

The Ultramarine had lost his battle-helm in the fight and wore a scarred grimace instead. His eyes became hateful slits as he unleashed the full fury of his flamer.

The swarm died in a nucleonic storm and Iulus was readying to advance when his retinal display was over-loaded by a beam hit to his eye. He cried out, dropping his chainsword so he could rip his helmet off before it corroded through and the gauss-flayer started in on his face, but still held onto Galvia.

The battle-helm hit the ground with a dull *thud* and rolled, the right ocular lens partially dissolved, the ceramite around it bare and raw.

'Set me down,' Galvia mumbled. Even lying on his side, an unknown number of internal organs ruptured, he triggered his bolter. The swathe of shells found sev-eral marks and the scarabs exploded aerially like flak.

Iulus resisted the urge to touch his injured face. It hurt but pain-suppressing chemicals were already flooding his system to fight the pain and keep him fighting.

With the gauss-fire intensifying around them, forming an almost lattice-like web of emerald, any ordinary sol-dier would have retreated. Bolt pistol blazing as he stooped for his chainsword, Iulus's order demonstrated that Space Marines were no ordinary soldiers.

'Hold the line and return fire. In Guilliman's name!'

The Ultramarines were dauntless, but so too were the implacable necrons. One side would have to break. The low booming voice, rendered through a vox-caster, decided which side that would be.

'For Chapter and the Lords of Ultramar!' The assault cannon of Brother Ultracius whirled into a blur of muzzle flare. Out in the cloying snow-fog, Iulus saw necron raider constructs torn apart. Instantly, the gauss enfilade lessened.

Ponderous but redoubtable, the Dreadnought had taken a little longer to reach the hold-point than the rest of the rearguard. It had been a long few minutes before his arrival but now the veteran warrior had arrived, Iulus knew the tide was with them.

'Defend the line; maintain it until the veterans of the Second can join you.' It had been a sound plan and one that suited the sergeant's intractable nature.

What was more, Ultracius was not alone.

'I am the warrior eternal of my Chapter. Long live Macragge and the Empire of Ultramar.' Where Ultracius was bombastic and glorifying, Brother Agnathio was unshakable and pragmatic. He moved with the slow but inexorable purpose of a glacier, his multi-melta scything the distant raider formations with impunity.

'Spread and engage,' bellowed Iulus, taking advantage as the necrons faltered, 'slow and exacting.'

He nodded to Agnathio who had pounded up alongside him.

'Good to have you with us, Venerable One.'

'I am the avatar of my Chapter's will. I serve eternally.' The Dreadnought's mind was not as lucid as it had once been. Agnathio knew not what year, what conflict he was embroiled in, only that he fought for the glory of the Ultramarines. A part of Iulus relished the simplicity of that existence as much as another part pitied it.

'For Ultramar.'

'Aye, for Ultramar!' The multi-melta sang its shrieking refrain again, spearing the necron constructs that were moving to engage them at closer quarters.

Tirian's gravelly voice came over the comm-feed. 'They're adopting more aggressive protocols.'

'They react,' said Iulus, 'as if directed. These shells are automatons with only hate and fell technology to animate them, but a will is at work here. Engage and destroy.'

Iulus felt his grip on the esplanade tightening. Despite the change in tactics, the necrons would not prevent him making a fist and holding the ground indefinitely. It was then, as the rearguard was fanning out and punishing the necron vanguard, that two things happened almost simultaneously to change the complexion of the battle.

First, the massive gates behind the Ultramarines opened and a human Guard force poured out, lasguns flashing. Second, a larger and much more densely packed necron cohort emerged from the fog ahead. They were bigger than the raider constructs and more heavily armed. Iulus was forced to reassess the internal boast he had made. His fist had become an open palm, clinging with fingertips. The tide had shifted again. Instinctively, the Ultramarines closed ranks. Even the Dreadnoughts paused in the face of this latest threat.

'Bring them down,' Iulus roared as the necron elites unleashed a gauss-storm of terrifying potency. 'Give them nothing!'

Estimating thirty of the hulking necrons and factoring in the remnants of the raider constructs that were still operational, Iulus made a quick assessment of their odds. His conclusion was muttered defiantly. 'We need more men.'

THE SKY ABOVE Kellenport was wracked with incandescent thunder. The city was a distant silhouette, leavened only by the flash of explosions.

Scipio wanted to be there, alongside his brothers Iulus and Praxor, but that was not his lot in this war. Instead, he was crouched in a slowly melting mire of slush and hard earth, peering through a pair of magnoculars.

'How does it look, brother-sergeant?' asked Largo, flat against the escarpment on his armoured chest.

Power armour didn't really lend itself to stealth missions, it was too bulky and better suited to more direct engagements, but without any of the Tenth to reconnoitre the Thunderbolts were being used as de-facto scouts.

'Busy,' Scipio grumbled. He handed Largo the magnoculars for a look. He was bearing his earlier injury well, the sergeant noted. Barely a flinch when Scipio had forced him to twist and reach for the scopes.

'Their picket lines look thick even without magnification,' added Ortus, sighting down the barrel of his bolter. Despite the fact the Ultramarines assault force was still several kilometres away, he could tell that the war cells protecting the pylons and gauss-obliterators were numerous. He had a good eye for that. Ortus spent most of his training allocation on the firing ranges. He could deploy his weapon like a sniper rifle, so accomplished was his aim.

'Find the leader and you have my permission to take

the shot,' replied Scipio, before shuffling backwards down the ridge on his stomach. Part of their scouting task, as well as assessing the level of resistance, was to find the necron hierarch commanding the force. Imperial tacticians, those that were privy to the threat of the necrontyr, had postulated that rather than being unfeeling automatons the necrons actually adhered to a series of 'protocols' not that dissimilar from a servitor's. Their logic-engines were far more advanced, of course, but by removing the sentient will that guided it, a war cell would resort to secondary functions. Their tactics would become less adaptable and more predictable. Such a disadvantage made them easier to defeat and increased the likelihood of a full scale 'phasal retreat'. These were all theories, however. There wasn't enough battle-data yet recorded that allowed any firm conclusions to be drawn concerning potential necron weaknesses.

Tigurius obviously thought the reasoning was sound – Scipio agreed – and so charged his 'scouts' with finding the hierarch leading the cell defending the artillery. So far, they'd had little luck in doing so.

Largo was putting the magnoculars away when he asked, 'How will we breach it?'

'Not this way, that's for certain.' As he was returned to the present, Scipio brought to mind the densely thronged access routes through the hills to the necron artillery. As well as the ubiquitous raider constructs, there were larger elites and even semi-ephemeral ghosts patrolling the enemy picket lines. They'd formed concentric rings around the mass of heavy cannons in the centre. While the ghosts phased in and out of existence, the raiders and elites stood still and unspeaking like metallic sentinels. Scipio suspected they would wait like that until the galaxy burned and the universe itself ended, if commanded to do so. At least orks bickered, even the alien tyranid chittered and the Traitor hordes exalted and chanted: these soulless machines just stood in abject silence. Despite Scipio's Adeptus Astartes hypno-conditioning, it was unnerving.

'Perhaps a diversionary attack to draw out the bulk of their troops, allowing Strabo and Ixion to neutralise the guns.'

Scipio shook his head at Largo. 'There's too many and they won't move. That's a defensive force, whatever protocol it's operating on will keep them from coming at us.'

He'd seen enough of the necrons, their mechanistic idioms, their logic-engine style tactics to know that they couldn't be coaxed or goaded. Only a certain and direct imperative would force the mechanoids to alter their battle-routines. Somehow, the Ultramarines attacking the Thanatos Hills had to find it. If executing the necron leader was the key to that, there was still a lot of work to be done.

His eyes narrowed when he spied a rocky promontory overlooking the artillery. 'How does that look to you?'

Largo went back to the scopes, magnifying to enhance the view. He scowled. 'Impenetrable.'

'No route through the terrain?'

'We need gunships and speeders,' Largo replied.

'A pity they are locked down aboard the *Valin* then,' added Ortus.

With the necron cannonade still in operation, not only was Kellenport subject to constant bombardment but Antaro Chronus could not deploy his tanks and any aerial support was denied to the Ultramarine spearhead.

'What are your orders, sergeant?' asked Largo after the silence started to become uncomfortable.

Scipio's expression was foul with frustration. 'Return to camp. Then we go deeper. There has to be a way through those pickets without taking them head-on.'

SCIPIO FOUND TIGURIUS alone, looking out onto an ice expanse. Snow flurries chased each other across the barren tundra like arctic devils, whipped into sudden frenzy by the wind.

There was a rime of frost coating the Librarian's cheeks, nose and forehead but he seemed not to notice. Though his eyes were open, he was locked in psychic trance. It took Scipio a few seconds to realise before he fell into respectful silence and waited.

'The direct approach to the Thanatos Hills is denied to us,' Tigurius said without even turning around, 'and we have yet to locate the force leader.'

Scipio suddenly felt quite redundant in the face of the Librarian's prescience. 'Is it *that* easy to read my mind?'

Tigurius faced him, wiping at the crust of frost veneering his features. 'Your mood anyone could read.'

'Transparent too. I must attend to that upon our return to Ultramar.'

'I admire your optimism, Brother Vorolanus. You think our victory here is certain?'

Scipio tried not to balk before the Librarian's penetrating gaze. He didn't think Tigurius was interrogating him psychically but couldn't be sure. 'Far from it. These creatures are like nothing we've ever faced. I also believe our sternest challenges are to come.'

Tigurius nodded. 'Yes, I–' He collapsed before he could finish.

'Master!' Scipio sprang to the Librarian's aid. He was clutching his head and screaming in mental agony.

The air was filled with the scent of burning and Scipio

noticed rivulets of arc-lightning spilling from Tigurius's eyes. His power armour was hot with psychic energy. Tendrils of smoke were coiling off every plate of ceramite. Seizing his force staff, the Librarian tried to anchor himself and channel some of the energy away.

Even through his gauntlets, Scipio was feeling the heat. His fingers smouldered but he clung on to Tigurius in spite of the pain.

'Master,' he hissed through clenched teeth. Below them the Ultramarines assault force was readying to move out and unaware of the unfolding crisis.

Just as Scipio thought he could hold on no longer, the baleful energy that had gripped Tigurius slowly started to dissipate. In a few seconds it was over and the Librarian could stand unaided.

'They know we are here,' he gasped, a wisp of smoke escaping from his mouth into the cold air. 'And what we intend to do.'

Scipio looked to the direction of the enemy cohorts, though they were far away. 'How will they respond?'

Tigurius looked him in the eye. It disturbed the sergeant to see the obvious disquiet there. 'Nothing. They will do nothing.'

Frowning, Scipio asked, 'What?'

'Because they believe our efforts are in vain, that there is no possible way for us to achieve victory.' Tigurius licked his lips and for a moment Scipio thought he might stumble again when he gripped his shoulder. 'I touched their minds. Fathomless, ancient, they think this world is their own. They want to reclaim it, to eradicate its population, to annihilate us. Damnos is doomed.'

'You… you *spoke* to them?'

'One of their number, part of the hierarchy,

communicated with me. He called himself the Herald. But I saw something else, a fragment of the future.' Tigurius's respiration became elevated, and he clenched his fingers into claws as he fought for recall. 'It's like trying to grasp a wisp of cloud... The truth eludes me, brother. A dark pall is clouding my prescience. Another of their kind...' The Librarian wrinkled his brow, seeking an appellation. 'The Voidbringer. He is the one we are looking for.'

'And this glimpse of the future,' Scipio asked. 'How does it bode for us?'

Tigurius's voice rang with the forbidding timbre of prophecy. 'Ill, brother. It bodes ill for all of us.'

PRAXOR WAS EXULTANT. Fighting by his captain's side, he felt empowered. His squad, the 'Shieldbearers', had fought hard to stay within striking distance of the Lions. Praxor had never seen such purpose and fury from the Second's pre-eminent warriors and Sicarius's retinue. To be counted one amongst them, to become one of the High Suzerain's inner circle, was one of the brother-sergeant's most fervent desires.

'Guard against pride, brother,' Iulus had once coun-selled him. He sounded like Orad. But the Chaplain was long dead and Praxor's ambitions very much alive. It wasn't pride so much as idolisation and that fact – one the brother-sergeant was ignorant of – was precisely why the senators of Macragge, indeed the Masters of the Chapter, debated Sicarius's tenure so furiously. His apparent growing cult of personality was regarded as vulgar by some, as Invictus reborn and a return to the glorious golden age of the Ultramarines by others. Some in the Chapter, the oldest campaigners, felt the sons of Guilliman had been diluted by the breaking of the

Legions. The many subsequent Founding Chapters all held allegiance to Ultramar but were autonomous otherwise.

Agemman, as captain of the First and with therefore the largest number of veterans in his company, was in the ironic position of recognising the importance of heroes like Sicarius but at the same time being wary of his popularity. He wanted the old days, just not ushered in by the Grand Duke of Talassar.

'Advance with all speed, stay with the captain!' Praxor was running and his squad ran with him. They moved in a 'V' formation, bolters blazing. Kill-shots were few, but the objective was to bust through the packed necron vanguard and strike deeper into the mechanoid ranks like a spear.

They had bypassed the first defensive wall already. Sicarius had studiously ignored the pleas for help and deliverance from the stricken Guardsmen still battling to hold it, his face undoubtedly a mask of hard indifference, focussed on his mission. To do otherwise, to give in to compassion, would be the end for all of them. At least, that was what Praxor believed.

A necron construct sprang out the fog, seemingly materialising from the very air. It glided in tandem with three others; no, it wasn't gliding, the moves were almost serpentine, like a snake reared to attack. It was supported by a long, segmented tail that ended in a broad barb like a scythe. Its torso was equivalent to the raider constructs Praxor had already dispatched on their charge through the breach in the first defensive wall, but its arms ended in razor talons. There was something incorporeal about it, as if it were only partially in the material realm or somewhere between solidity and necron phasal shift.

Acting on instinct and too close to fire, Brother Vortigan swung at it with his bolter's bayonet. The monomolecular blade should have carved into it, but slipped through the creature as if parting vapour. Like a whip, the tail lashed around and speared Vortigan in the neck. The talons found weak points in his armour between plastron and greave. The Ultramarine spewed a film of blood into his helmet that speckled the lenses before he fell.

Praxor cried out Vortigan's name and swung at the same time. His power sword crackled, as if reacting to the creature's nature, and he clove off a limb. Then he drove the point of the blade through the wraith's gear-like intestine and it shuddered and phased out.

The other three were in amongst the Shieldbearers, whose charge had now faltered to a stop. Krixous was down, his forearm severed, but still lived. A melta blast from Tartaron maimed another wraith, sending it back to whatever abyss spawned it. The other two weaved in and around the slow-moving Space Marines, who swung and fired with little effect. Praxor was reminded of the gorgons of old Calth, cave-dwelling harridans that could turn men to stone with a glance. Such was the necrons' speed, it appeared as if the Shieldbearers were indeed petrified.

Praxor rallied them quickly, ordering them to corral the creatures and bring them to Tartaron's meltagun. Another died with its living metal turned to mercury, the fourth the sergeant dispatched himself with a determined thrust of his power sword.

Agony lanced Praxor's shoulder and he realised there was a fifth wraith he had not accounted for. Its barbed tail sent Tartaron sprawling before he could fire, whilst the creature jerked and twisted around the clumsy bolter shells railing at it. The troopers were of no consequence. It wanted Praxor. Only the sergeant's blood would do. He'd dropped his bolt pistol. He heard it skitter across the ice before he lost it in the mist. With a grunt Praxor shrugged off the talons and managed to half turn before the tail barb cut his legs from under him. He fell hard onto his back, a flicker in his retinal display indicating the power to his armour had been briefly compromised. It returned with a whir of servos, and the piston-grinding swipe of his power sword was too slow for Praxor. A flick of the wraith's talons sheared his vambrace and forced his fingers to part. Like the bolt pistol before it, Praxor's blade spun away from his grasp and he was suddenly weaponless.

'Shoot it!' he growled, determined to show the mechanoid his unswerving hate before he died.

Bolter shells crashed around it, but were like exploding flares for all the damage they caused. The wraith phased through the bursts, advancing on the Ultramarines sergeant who was crawling away on his back.

'You'll have to work it for it, scum.'

The necron seemed willing to oblige, darting forwards on its tail with talons primed.

A shock of lightning bent its skull-head at an awkward angle. It tried to turn when the bolt hit again. Only it wasn't lightning, Praxor realised. It was a power mace. A crozius arcanum.

Trajan bludgeoned the wraith until its restorative programming kicked in and it phased out. Where the necron's face was skull-toothed metal, the Chaplain's was gimlet-eyed bone studded with platinum service bolts.

'Arise, brother,' he said with a deep, silken voice utterly unlike his predecessor's, 'for the Chapter finds you wanting.'

Praxor ignored the Chaplain's proffered hand. His power armour's systems were fully operational again. 'I can stand unaided.'

'A pity your pride didn't keep you on your feet,' Trajan snarled. He regarded the Shieldbearers. 'These creatures are fleshless abominations. They are an affront to the machine-spirit and cannot be allowed to live. Purge them all and let faith guide your holy bolters!'

Then he was gone, lost to the snow-fog as quickly as he'd arrived.

'I can see why Sicarius wanted him,' said Tartaron, his tone wry. It swiftly changed to contrition. 'I'm sorry, sergeant. My aim should have been better.'

Praxor clapped his pauldron. 'We live, don't we? Your aim was sound. Get Brother Krixous and follow on my lead. Captain Sicarius is not far ahead.'

'Are you still with us, Brother-Sergeant Manorian?' It was Daceus through the comm-feed. The veteran-sergeant was only metres in front of them with the Lions, and waving the others on.

Contrary to his initial beliefs, the point of the spearhead had been slowed to a man. Beyond the first wall, the battlefield was thronged with the necron vanguard. Praxor made out the black ceramite of Trajan nearby. The Chaplain was everywhere it seemed, singing litanies of hate against the alien and the abomination, as he swung his crozius. Squad Solinus, 'The Indomitable', formed an honour guard around him.

'He prefers his warriors to carry the Victorex Maxima,' said Tartaron with disdain.

Praxor's eyes hardened. 'They are the heroes of Telrendar, brother. Would that the Shieldbearers be so vaunted.'

'Apologies, brother-sergeant,' Tartaron replied, head bowed.

'Come on. We are missing the battle.' Praxor ordered them forward, but within he was burning with envy at the honours garnered by Solinus. At Damnos then, that was where they would earn their laurels and perhaps even Elianu Trajan would find the Shieldbearers worthy of his company.

In the wastes, little more than rubble and accumulated ice, Agrippen had continued his irresistible advance. Spider-like constructs the size of attack bikes had impeded him, but the great warrior had battered them aside with his power fist, swathing the remains in glowing-hot promethium from the flamer attached to his wrist. A vast ball of plasma tainted the ice-storm cerulean blue as the last of the spiders was engulfed and destroyed. After it was done he came to stand shoulder-to-shoulder with Sicarius, the old juxtaposed against the new.

'To the captain, for the glory of Ultramar!' The Dreadnought's augmented voice was lucid and powerful. Rare amongst the Chapter, he was one of few veterans of old that still remembered who he was and what time period he was fighting in. With Agrippen not being one of the Second, Praxor had been surprised to learn the warrior-eternal was part of the force led by Sicarius. Perhaps the captain desired to show solidarity towards the First or maybe he wanted Agemman to hear of his prowess from one of his most loyal and forthright warriors. None could doubt the word of Agrippen – it was spoken with thunder and the weight of ages.

The breaks in combat were brief, but a patch of open ground had formed at the site of the spearhead's last victory. Sicarius occupied a half-ruined promontory overlooking the wastes. A shell of some manufactorum or perhaps a lectory – it didn't matter. The structure's blasted plateau, the burnt-out remains of a second floor, was stable and expansive enough to allow the captain and all his officers the benefit of its vantage. It also offered a moment to take stock and reanalyse as the Ultramarines squads regathered for a fresh offensive.

'We should hold here, my lord,' advised Agrippen from the ground floor below. Broad and strong it might be, but even if the Dreadnought could have reached the second floor his mass would have crushed it. 'Our forces in the Kellenport plaza can reinforce us.'

Sicarius surveyed the distant battle lines, the drifting smoke and emerald flash of the necron guns. To his right, the capitolis administratum still stood. It was isolated but now ringed by a defensive cordon of Deathwind drop pods.

'How long will their payload last?'

'Another few minutes, captain,' Daceus replied. 'Guard forces are en route to liberate the acting governor and his staff.'

'Largely irrelevant, brother-sergeant,' said Sicarius. 'The leaders of Damnos are spent, just like their armies, but without those missiles cleansing our flank we'll become exposed and forced back.' He shook his head, looking down on Agrippen, 'Advice noted, brother, but we advance. Let the rearguard hold our lines.'

'My lord.'

'Yes,' Sicarius had removed his battle-helm to wipe the sweat from his brow. His eyes were as hard as sapphire and belatedly Praxor realised it was he that had spoken and that the captain's gaze was fixed on him.

'The mechanoids have cut off our way back.' He pointed east, to where the vanguard had flowed behind them like the living metal from which the necrons were infernally constructed. 'Our forces are split in two.'

'Then it is fortunate we do not turn back, isn't it, sergeant?'

'I–' Praxor was wrong-footed. Sicarius already knew, and didn't care. Vortigan was dead, Krixous at least was being tended by Brother Venatio – his stump in place of a hand was swathed in pinkish gauze and bandage. His Larraman cells had clotted the blood quickly but there was still some residual fluid. The casualties amongst the Second were rising, though. How many more would fall in this insane gauntlet they were running?

'Do you know what a gladius is, brother?'

'Of course, my lord, it's–'

Sicarius nodded. 'Yes, and I trust that you know. I trust that you can wield bolter and blade, that you can lead your men and inspire them to greatness.' He put his hands on Praxor's shoulders like a father to a son. He sheathed the Tempest Blade to do so. The weapon was still humming eagerly despite the ferocious tally it and its wielder had reaped. 'So too must you trust me.'

Praxor bowed his head, 'I meant no offence, Lord Sicarius.'

'Chapter Master Calgar is your lord, I am your captain. That is all the loyalty and deference you need afford me. Remember the gladius?' He nodded as Praxor did, their eyes meeting. Sicarius let the sergeant go and mimicked a thrust with his hand. '*We* are that gladius, driving at the heart of our enemy.'

'But the mechanoids have no heart, brother-captain,' chimed Daceus, to facilitate his leader's point.

'And so they must be fought another way. The necrons respond to one thing, and one thing alone,' Sicarius said. 'Punishment. If we hurt them enough, they will yield. To do that we must bring their masters out into the open. *They* are the heart. Spear that and the machine will fail. I want these creatures to notice me. I want them to recognise my wrath as a threat to their existence. Achieve that and Damnos has a chance.'

So moved, Praxor fell to one knee, his power sword held across his body. 'I am honoured to serve by your side, Grand Duke of Talassar.'

'Then you had better stand, for we shall press on, find the command node and bring glory to our Chapter.'

The Lions roared with their captain. So did Praxor, but as he was getting to his feet he noticed that Agrippen stayed silent. The time for reflection was over. A large necron war cell was resolving out of the mist and heading for them.

Sicarius grinned ferally. 'In Guilliman's name, and for Talassar. War calls us, brothers…'

As one they replied, 'We shall answer!'

FALKA WAS SECOND through the western gate after Sergeant Muhrne, running on pure adrenaline. Most of the Ark Guard behind him didn't want to die, nor did they want to fight. If anything, it was fear and mad fatalism that drove them into the wasteland. A part of Falka hoped it was the cobalt-blue angels that had suddenly arrived in their midst compelling the men, a smaller vestige of him dared to believe that some spark of bravery and pride still burned within Damnos.

'We shall not surrender!' he heard Sergeant Muhrne bellow. 'On, on, on!' he roared.

As they closed on the battlefront, Falka was glad he would meet his death head-on and not trapped behind a gate waiting to be crushed by fallen masonry or vaporised by a faceless necron artillery barrage. At least this way he could be proud when reunited with his ancestors, he could look Jynn in the eye and say, 'I died with

honour, defending our world.' He hoped he would see
her again soon, but was determined not to waste his life.
It would be worth something to these mechanised bastards.

The Ark Guard were four hundred strong when they
left the Courtyard of Thor, just under two battalions.
Ominously, the western gate was closed behind them.
The resonant din of it being sealed broke some of the
men who turned and ran back, pounding against the
metal impotently with their fists. The commissars on
the battlements put them out of their misery with precise pistol shots and the wailing ceased. Not that the rest
of the Ark Guard could have heard it. The shattered
plaza drowned out the noise with the cacophony of war.
Not just any conflict though – this was Space Marine
warfare, and it was brutal.

Falka marvelled and balked at the Angels of Death.
They were as resolute and indefatigable as the necrons.
When he and the rest of the Guardsmen had managed
to get two hundred metres from the gate unscathed, he
dared to hope that with the Space Marines' help they
might yet save Damnos. Necron warriors, turning their
baleful gaze upon the humans at some proximity warning within their machine brains, crushed that
assumption quickly.

Muhrne was the first one Falka noticed. The pugnacious sergeant couldn't even scream as the gauss-beam
flayed him. Metal and cloth became particles, skin and
flesh turned to dust, organs liquefied until there was
nothing left of Muhrne but a charred skeleton. Even that
cracked apart when it hit the ground.

Falka ducked instinctively, though it was really just
luck that spared him during that first headlong charge.
Charred skeletons were exploding all around him as

the necrons exposed the weakness of the human form so horrifically. He was shouting, incoherent and wordlessly, but it kept the fear down. He also realised he had yet to fire his gun, so intent was he on running the length of the plaza. Falka checked the load and hauled the trigger. His first shots went wide and too fast. He was still running and needed to conserve his ammunition. Keep going at that rate and he'd be out in a few seconds. The barrel flash, though ineffective so far, brought attention. He dived behind a rubble pile, thanking his saints as the gauss-beam careened away without killing him. Falka took a second to realign himself and was moving again. He had about twenty others with him. Judging by their shoulder patches, they were from several different squads. The gauss barrage had scattered them; the Ark Guard's discipline and coherency broken in seconds.

'What do we do?' one man asked.

It took Falka a few moments to realise he was talking to him. He wished Jynn was there, fighting by his side. She was a warrior; at least her natural instincts suggested it. She would have been an asset to the Ark Guard.

'A hit, even glancing, from those flayers and we're dead men,' said Falka. He tried not to let the fact that so many were hanging on his words disturb him. He slapped the hard flank of the ruin they were hiding in. It wasn't much, just the worn-down footprint of a defensive barrier. Each man was crouched low, keeping out of the gauss-beams streaking above them.

One man, Falka didn't know his name – he was a professional soldier, not a conscript from the mines like himself – rose a fraction to wipe his brow. An emerald flash filled the ruins and the nameless man slumped down without his head, the ragged neck stump cauterised. Two of the others had to be restrained from fleeing before Falka could continue.

He looked down at the decapitated corpse grimly. *That's the fate that awaits us all.*

'Stick to the cover, what little there is. And make for the Angels. The Space Marines will protect us.'

'We've been sent to our deaths,' one lad sobbed. His helmet didn't really fit him. Falka took off his and gave it to the boy. It wasn't a much better fit but it seemed to galvanise the lad.

'Aye, and we'll meet it on our feet, defending our people like heroes of Damnos.' He reached over and patted the boy on the shoulder. 'All right, son?'

The lad nodded. The lasgun looked awkward in his hands. Falka turned away, unwilling to see his fear any longer.

Crawling to the edge of the barrier, he waited until the whine of gauss-beams diminished and then risked a look over the top. Through the mist and carnage, he saw a squad of Space Marines giving battle. They'd abandoned the sanctuary of their landing vessel – it looked like an inverted spear-tip with its sides split open and laid flat on the ground. A black scar surrounded it, slowly obscured by falling snow.

Warriors from heaven, indeed.

Falka tried to turn that realisation into hope.

'Come on,' he shouted to the men. 'With me!'

CHAPTER FIVE

It was cold in the ice cave, but it came from more than just the temperature. There was a chill that emanated from inside, a hollowing of spirit and resolve that would kill her far quicker than a drift or even being crushed beneath an avalanche of compacted snow. It pressed against her body. She felt its weight against her torso and her left shoulder. Her legs she could no longer feel. Her bored-out heart was simply numb.

I am dead, she realised. *I am dead – my body simply doesn't know it yet.*

It was black inside, not white at all, underneath the snow. She knew it must be a cave that she'd broken through to, because of the quiet. No screaming, no weeping or mewling. The moaning had stopped too. It had started out as belligerent anger at their situation and a refusal to accept it. Then it became doleful. In the end it just *was*. She was ashamed to admit that she missed it.

I am dead and that's why I am cold.

Then she saw a light, a tiny pinhole that turned her black world into powdery grey. Noise followed, a sort of shuffling then a scuffing. Finally, she realised it was digging. *Something* was digging her out.

She panicked, but she couldn't move. Vaguely, she remembered snapping on the distress beacon and how stupid that decision had been, even born of desperation as it was, given what stalked the drifts.

I wish I was dead. The digging sound was getting closer, it became a wet scrape and a hard rasp of metal chipping into ice as the hole widened and her world lightened with every stroke.

Why can't I will my body to accept that I am dead?

Her fingers trembled, and she realised she could move them. They seized the pick half-frozen to her belt and leg.

If I am alive, then I will fight...

The edges of the hole collapsed as they were torn away by sharp metal blades and her dark world expanded exponentially.

Then you'll be the dead one.

She tried to shout, but her larynx was dry and frozen stiff, so all that came out was a choking rasp. In her mind, her fingers freed the pick and brought it down on the creature's head, buried it in its skull. But her arm didn't respond. All she could do was grip the haft, and that wasn't nearly enough. She couldn't even fight. She could only submit, and it was this that bothered her the most. When the blades were done, the shadows of them loomed over her, blotting out her newly-risen sun. Faced with the sheer terror of it she found her voice, and screamed.

Jynn awoke.

* * *

THE CHAMBER WAS bathed in a sickly emerald glow. The light came from channels and conduit lines describing esoteric runes, sigils from an elder age lost to history. It limned bulky sarcophagi and weather-grained tombs, rubbed to mirror sheen by the action of the elements. They had been underground for a long time. Sleeping. They didn't know what imperative had woken them, what pre-programmed scenario had activated the resurrection protocols of the tomb spyders, but they were conscious again – the long dream was over and vermin were abroad in their dominion.

The Undying sighed, though he had no breath to expel from his mechaorgans, nor did his fleshless torso heave. It was affectation, a piece of extant learned behaviour that persisted in the cold existence of the now. He had trouble remembering that, differentiating between what *is* and what *was*. They all did; all except the Architect.

'Your logic-engines are functioning without imparity.'

It was a statement of machine-fact, not a question. The Undying did not question, he did not need to. He was knowledge, aeons and aeons of it. He was pre-eminent but he was also still in a pseudo-torpor. The scarabs refashioned his beautiful mechaorganic body, re-attaching his limbs and re-energising his weapons, while the tomb spyders tended to his revivification casket.

The Architect made a slight bow. The sound of shifting servos and gears within his unseen workings testified to it. 'You are still weak, my lord. Your strength is returning, though.'

'The others are waking too.' The Undying's machine-voice was deep and resonant, but not on account of the resurrection chamber. His baleful eyes narrowed to fiery slits as they regarded each of the four portals that led to the upper echelons of the tomb in turn.

'We live,' said the Architect. 'Do you remember me, master?'

The Undying nodded slowly. 'So many lives,' he muttered.

'We have awoken to interlopers infesting our sacred realm.'

The Undying's reply was a bellicose rumble. 'Excise them.'

'I am waking the rest of the royal house. We shall be one again soon.'

'I desire to move, to command the legions. My sky-chariot–'

'Has long since turned to dust and memory,' the Architect interjected. He did not touch the Undying, for that was to invite his overlord's wrath, but his tone was conciliatory. They had all lost so very much to gain so very little.

Our flesh for metal, our veins and blood for circuits, our very being sacrificed for the machine.

Some felt it more than others, which was the real reason why the Architect was in attendance. The Undying would not fully awaken for several hours, but other, lesser lords would.

A flash of translocation lit the grand tomb chamber. When it abated, the Architect was in a different room. Using his chronomancy, he had descended several levels in a nanosecond. The catacombs were dank and sealed. It was fear. Fear of contamination that drove the necrons to such lengths. And for good reason.

A shriek of anguish broke the silence in the catacombs but none of the insects toiling slowly and methodically gave it heed. The Architect merely looked towards the sound, his long lamellar cloak fashioned of bronze sigil-ingots clanking as he moved.

Another revivification casket had opened behind him. Now he faced it, he saw the awakened lord within. This one was ripe with putrefaction, the decaying flesh that swathed it long since turned to rot.

The Architect glared. His real name was Ankh the Herald of Dismay, a title self-appointed. He would need to cow this one. Rabid and disillusioned, he would need to direct him quickly and forcefully if he was to be of any use. Unlike the Undying and the other dynastic nobles, Ankh did not fear the flayer disease. He had many arcane items to protect him. Caution was still wise, though – he took a step back.

Ankh stretched to his full height, making the most of his cryptek's skull panoply and brandishing his rod of office like a threat. His appearance was that of a skeletal, metal-skinned sorcerer. There were devices about his person, amulets and speculums, star-compasses and fathomless orbs. A vial of liquid adamantium attached to his belt by an ornate chain contained his predecessor; the mirror of the speculum trapped another of his would-be usurpers a nanosecond out of synch with the rest of reality.

'Do you remember who you are?'

This one gibbered, hunched as if broken, as it looked on with fervent eyes. For a second, Ankh thought the tomb spyders had revived him too early and that the scarabs would need to deactivate him again. The doubt passed when the lord spoke.

'My robes,' he said, holding up the flaps of skin draped about his metal frame, 'they are wretched. Where is my tailor?' He paused, staring at his bone-that-was-not-bone limbs and blood-stained torso. 'Where is my flesh! My skin!' He wailed, then just stopped.

Ankh glared, patient. Revivification was not easy.

'Wait,' said the other. 'Wait...' A deep melancholy affected his voice, though it was still the timbre of the mechaorganic. 'Waaaaiiiit...' he rasped, almost like a sigh. 'Oh, how I miss the flesh.' He caressed the putrefied skin layering his body, pulled down the flesh-mask over his rictus countenance. Emerald orbs of hateful desire burned through the ragged human sockets.

'You are Sahtah, the Enfleshed,' Ankh told him.

'Am I a butcher, a skin-surgeon?' Sahtah asked, looking up and brandishing the razored talons that replaced his fingers. Inadvertently, he'd snipped several pieces of skin from his grisly mantle and they hit the floor of the chamber with a soft thud.

Ankh's eyes flared brighter. They were like fire-tempests of sudden excitement.

'Yes.'

The forbidding tones of the Undying echoed inside his skull from the mind-link to the grand tomb chamber. 'The fourth is due. The royal hierarchy is incomplete.' He was saying it by mechanised rote, still not fully lucid, but even in his millennia-spanning dementia, the overlord was right.

Ankh shifted back. He arrived and scrutinised another part of the chamber where the shadows were darkest.

'He comes...'

The darkness shifted, coalescing like the formation of a black hole into something of substance. It came with a susurrus of sound like air vacating the lungs of a corpse, only much longer and louder. Flaps of parchment, pieces of old cloak materialised on an unfelt breeze. A figure stepped from the penumbra, whole and imperious. It clanged the butt of its staff against the metal floor and with each percussive blow stepped forwards until a lord of metal and night-shrouds was revealed.

Where the Architect's jaw was angular, almost pointed, this one's was square. His brow was heavy and he bore an icon stamped to his forehead. Ankh could not recall its meaning. Though less than the others, he too had lost much during transition.

'Why am I summoned?' the arrival demanded. 'The fleshed are reinforced with their armoured saviours, the genebred ones.'

'Flesh cannot prevail against metal,' droned the Undying in a moment of slow-returning lucidity. 'Hearts and minds of mortals cannot endure against the machine.'

'As you can see,' said Ankh, gesturing to their overlord, 'our master is waking. So too are the other cells. The royal house must form, Tahek.'

The shrouded lord snarled. 'Address me as Void-bringer, cryptek.'

'Tahek Voidbringer, you are summoned,' said Ankh with unnecessary ceremony. He fed a crackle of power through his staff but failed to goad the other lord. 'An enemy has arrived on our world. It fills our resurrection chambers with the plebeian and thins our scarab hive.'

'They are in my midst?' asked Voidbringer.

'Plotting to eliminate our pylons and gauss-obliterators. I theorise they plan to deploy further reinforcements from the vessel we struck in orbit.'

'I will slay them, then.'

Only the voice of the Undying stopped Voidbringer from turning and merging with the darkness. 'No.'

Ankh took over again, herald in every way. 'You will continue with your primary mission. Defend our artillery.' His eyes narrowed, partly in pleasure at the rage emanating from Tahek, partly in anticipation of what was to come. 'Sahtah the Enfleshed will hunt them down. He has need of a new skin.'

From a small black crystal attached to his body, Ankh projected an image of the lower catacombs where he'd been a few seconds ago.

Voidbringer glanced at Sahtah with disdain. 'I need no help.'

Sahtah was an outcast in necron society, a noble who had become little better than a beast. Proximity to other lords was strictly forbidden, the possibility of infection real and abhorrent. None amongst the royal house wanted to be cursed as a flayer.

Ankh drew Tahek's gaze. 'Focus on your task,' he said. 'Bring the night.'

The necron's eyes narrowed, a pair of tiny flames inside two pools of abject night. 'I obey,' he rasped, his voice disappearing into the shadows as did the Voidbringer himself.

Ankh turned to Sahtah in the image-cast. 'Your servants await you,' he said. 'Follow them. They will lead you to the surface.'

Sahtah looked around at the disembodied voice in the chamber. His confusion was forgotten when he saw the other flayed ones approaching.

'So ripe,' the Enfleshed marvelled, regarding a pair of hunchbacked necrons skulking into the wan light of the catacombs. He reached out for their capes of skin but retracted his claws – the mirror of their own – not daring to touch, shamed by his own rotten rags. 'So fresh. A slave's attire should not eclipse that of his lord.'

The flayed ones bowed to him.

'So, renew your robes,' uttered Ankh, adding resonance to the voice that Sahtah was hearing, 'with the flesh of our enemies.'

Like a hound let slip of its master's leash, the Enfleshed leapt from his revivification casket and scurried after the slaves as they went to hunt.

The image phased out and Ankh put the crystal away.

'I long for proper sentience again,' groaned the Undying.

Now he and the Architect were alone.

Ankh considered the motions of the scarabs and tomb spyders, perceived the ethereal presence of his wraiths as they patrolled the deeps of the tomb. More and more cells were awakening. With the first hierarchy at full strength, the rest of the royal house and with them the entire legion would not be long in waking.

'Our numbers multiply. It will be soon, my lord.'

'I long...' the Undying moaned again, trailing off when his mind fell into oblivion again.

'We are legion,' said Ankh, partly to himself. With a gesture, he summoned a column-shaped node from the resurrection chamber floor. When his skeletal fingers closed on the icon inscribed at its apex a tiny coruscation of lightning fashioned a web-matrix between them and bathed Ankh in its light.

On the surface, several levels up, projection nodes churned into position; the activation runes delineating display dais lit up.

The Herald spoke and his graven image was broadcast to all who still lived on Damnos.

ADANAR FELT AS hollow as the clanging of the western gate when it was shut. He heard the flat reports of the commissars' pistols as they brought down the deserters. He closed his eyes when he thought of the four hundred who'd left the Courtyard of Thor. He doubted they'd last long against the necrontyr but someone had to go and get Rancourt – the administrator-turned-acting governor was the closest thing to Imperial authority left on Damnos. Not including the Space Marines, of course, but theirs was a different remit.

Adanar doubted he'd ever even meet them. What consequence was he to them? What were any of them? The Emperor's Angels were as cold and aloof as the necrons. The only difference was the Space Marines weren't trying to eradicate them.

The people needed a figurehead – Zeph Rancourt, loathsome as he was, had to fulfil that role and bring some sort of stability to Damnos. Kellenport was the last city on an unremarkable world, but it had to have unity if it were to survive.

Adanar recalled cheering at the sight of the azure arrowheads streaking through the heavens. People were praising the Emperor for their deliverance, for the saving of Damnos.

The Space Marines were formidable. They could do what no ordinary man could. They could turn certain defeat into victory, but these creatures… they were even a match for the Angels of Death. And all the while the emerald artillery barrage went on unabated.

'Send four battalions down to the Courtyard of Thor to replace our losses,' he said to the air. He'd forgotten Sergeant Nabor was dead, slumped in a pool of his own brain-ooze.

Adanar raised Corporal Besseque and gave the order down the vox. He also tasked him with getting another sergeant to help man the walls and relay instructions to the other officers.

'And get a message to Acting Lord Governor Rancourt. A force is on its way to bring him back to Kellenport.' Adanar had wanted to add, *and the safety of its walls*, but couldn't bring himself to lie that heinously. He was about to request a status report when a hololithic image materialised in the smoky haze over the battlefield. Adanar recognised the voice of the Herald of Dismay.

Your saviours are not angels sent to deliver you. There is no deliverance. We, the necrontyr, reclaim this world. Your saviours cannot stop us. We are not creatures of flesh and emotion, but of circuit and reason. We are the machine, and the machine will not be denied.

The hololith, rendered in grainy emerald, crackled and faded. It left a pall of despair in its wake. Adanar could almost sense the collective groan of the men under his command.

Hope, so cruelly given, was being snatched away. He could feel it.

'What have I to be thankful for?' he asked, remembering the premature celebrations while the artillery barrage raged all around him. He regarded the fire-blackened streets, the shattered plaza, the collapsed towers and ruptured domes of his city. 'What have any of us?'

SMOOTHING THE THINNING hair of his greasy scalp, Rancourt paced the floor of the medi-bay for what felt like the hundredth time. He had wanted position, power and all that came with it, but not in these circumstances. He was lord governor in everything but name, a de facto potentate, but of what? A rock, a fegging rock soon to be extinct or declared *excommunicate xenos* by the Imperium.

'Am I not a dutiful servant?' he asked the recumbent form on the medi-couch next to him. The room was bare and stank of sanitation fluid. It was tiled and besides the couch contained a single chair that Rancourt had yet to sit in. A chrono on the wall above him no longer functioned. Wouldn't matter it if did; he'd lost all sense of time. Ever since the mine, ever since…

He crushed the thoughts, not wishing to relive the days after that, the bitter struggle for survival in the ice wastes.

'Oh, Throne…' he murmured, pressing his hands hard against his forehead in an effort to push out the memories. 'If you'd have seen what we had to do. If you'd–' He stopped suddenly when his gaze met that of Lord Governor Arxis, laying on the medi-couch. 'You… you bastard! Leaving me with all of this. I don't want it, I tell you. I don't, but I can't give it back, can I? Can I?' He tossed the chair and it cracked several tiles when it landed, bending a leg.

Rancourt's fists were clenched and he was about to pound on Arxis when he stopped and caught his breath. His arms, so full of nervous anger just moments ago, fell to his sides. Instead of lashing out, he leaned in and spoke softly into the lord governor's ear.

'Help me,' he pleaded. 'Tell me what I'm supposed to do.'

A knock on the door made Rancourt start and he straightened, wiping away the tears on his face. 'What is it?' he snapped, turning to face Sergeant Kador who'd just entered.

'We've just received confirmation that we're moving you to the Kellenport wall, my lord.'

Rancourt shrank back as if stung. He stopped when he touched the medi-couch and could go no further. 'Is it safe?'

'Safer than the capitolis at this time,' answered Kador a little ruefully. 'The Space Marines are here, my lord, and they are reclaiming the outer defences, including this bastion.'

'Then I should stay, shouldn't I?' Rancourt was nodding. It looked like he was trying to convince himself. 'If the Adeptus Astartes are my protectors.'

'They won't be staying. Once we have the outer walls, Commander Sonne has vowed to garrison them again so our saviours can press the assault and liberate our world.' Sergeant Kador outstretched his hand. 'You need to accompany me, my lord.'

'Very well,' Rancourt replied, not entirely sure. 'What of Lord Governor Arxis? How do you plan to move him?'

Kador frowned. 'I don't understand.'

'It's very simple, sergeant,' Rancourt replied in exasperation. 'How do we get him from the capitolis to Kellenport?'

'We don't. He's dead.'

Rancourt was about to protest when he looked around. The room was bare. All the equipment, the life-preserving machines were gone... because they were no longer needed. The lord governor hadn't survived his injuries in the Proteus bunker.

'Of course... Yes, I will leave now. Lead on, sergeant.'

IULUS WIPED THE sweat off his brow with a heavy hand. Despite his advanced physiology, the wound he'd sustained in his shoulder was slowing him. Ahead of the squad, Agnathio led the line. His armoured bulk bore the worst of the intense gauss-barrage. A fusillade of beams staggered the Dreadnought and Iulus willed the venerable one to endure it.

Slamming a fresh clip into his bolt pistol, Iulus released a tightly controlled burst. The hulking necron in his sights bucked, sparks cascaded off its armoured body, but it came on undaunted. Galvia and Urnos added their bolters to their sergeant's barrage, but to little effect.

Still firing, Iulus levelled his chainsword at the seemingly invulnerable necrons. 'Throw up a wall, brother.'

Aristaeus opened up his flamer, bathing the front line with a wave of super-heated promethium. Implacable, the mechanoids just ploughed through it, their bodies trailing with tendrils of fire and smoke.

'Oath of Hera,' breathed Galvia. 'They are unstoppable.'

Somewhere in the distance las-beams stabbed into the flames, but they were as insect stings to the monstrous automatons.

Iulus realised the Guard had engaged the enemy, but discounted the humans as an asset almost immediately. The Second were alone. He was determined they would triumph. It rested on the necron elites. Break them and the plaza was won.

Iulus grunted. 'Tough, but not inviolable. Close the gap and intensify.'

His Immortals advanced in Agnathio's shadow, crouched low and widely dispersed, but stalled as the warrior eternal faltered. His armour, his mighty sarcophagus that had endured for centuries over countless campaigns, was slowly being eroded.

'Venerable One. We need to move!'

Agnathio levelled his multi-melta and sent a blast into the necron elites. It cut one of the mechanoids in half and it phased out.

Iulus rallied his warriors. 'See! They are not indestructible.'

A second necron lost a limb but incredibly self-repaired, its living metal reflowing and its wires re-stitching before Iulus's very eyes.

'Mercy of the primarch…'

Agnathio was not to be denied and strafed the line. The wounded mechanoid was only partway through its regeneration cycle when a salvo of mass-reactive shells from the Dreadnought's storm bolter tore it open. Balefires dying in its eyes, the necron phased out.

'I serve the Chapter eternally!' Agnathio was about to advance again when a plume of fire exploded from his motive servos. Haemorrhaging smoke and machine-fluid, one of his trunk-like legs seized.

A cry was ripped from his vox-emitter as a raw, burning line jagged up his sarcophagus. Visceral matter was leaking from the wound and Aganthio's agony resonated around the plaza.

Iulus felt a tremor of disquiet. He had never seen the Dreadnought hurt before. A small part of him hadn't thought it was possible that he would ever witness such a thing.

'Brother-sergeant,' Agnathio's speech was broken and fizzed with static, in part from the damage done to his vox-emitter and part from the pain he was enduring. He even had to fight the din of the gauss-assault to be heard. 'You must take… the gate alone, brother. I can go no further.'

The gate? Then Iulus realised. Agnathio was back at Chundrabad, where he had fallen over five millennia ago when he was a mere battle-brother.

Iulus had no time to reply. A piece of armour plate was ripped from the Dreadnought's shoulder, flung shrapnel embedding in the sergeant's pauldron. Agnathio turned in the direction of his aggressors, unleashing a salvo from his storm bolter. It was to be his last as the weapon attached to his power fist burst apart in a cloud of exploding ammo. Like a pugilist that had taken too many beatings, Agnathio jerked and rocked as the blows rained down.

Iulus had seen enough. He pressed the comm-bead in his ear and spoke into his gorget vox-grille. He might have lost his battle-helm and with it the retinal display, but he could still command.

'Brother-Sergeants Tirian and Atavian, bring hell and fury!'

A barrage hammered from either flank. The sharp tracers and missile contrails blended together furiously as the Devastators concentrated fire on the hulking elites.

A storm of hot frag exploded in the necrons' midst but they came on implacably. Their numbers had thinned but they merely closed ranks and drove at the Ultramarines, laying down an emerald curtain of fire. Some of the casualties were rising, picking up their slowly reconstituting bodies and rejoining the rear echelons.

The Ultramarines had to get close, make certain of their kills. Iulus tightened the grip on his chainsword.

'Immortals! Hand-to-hand. Engage and destroy!' He ran headlong at the necrons, ignoring the gauss-beams glancing off his armour.

On his right shoulder, Urnos was struck in the chest and pitched off his feet. Iulus lost sight of him in the rush. 'Low and fast.'

Nearby, a terrible thunder shook the frost-caked earth as Ultracius joined them. A spew of assault cannon shells ripped a ragged hole in the elites, interrupting their fire pattern and allowing Iulus and his squad the precious seconds they needed to close the gap.

His first swing was like striking the bulkhead on a battleship. Sparks churned into the air but the blow left little more than a scar against the necron's torso. Up close the elites were even bigger, dwarfing even the

Space Marines. Iulus ducked beneath a swing of its gauss-blaster. There was strength in the attack and even used as an unconventional bludgeon, the weapon was potent. A burst of fire raked the sergeant's left side but it only stripped away paint and surface armour. He rammed his bolt pistol into the creature's neck cavity and pulled the trigger.

Spitting shards of metal opened up a dozen shallow cuts on his face but the necron's head came away, leaving behind a sheared spinal column. Iulus kicked it over with an exultant roar before it phased out.

'Taste the fury of the Immortals!'

A savage blow to his solar plexus cut his victory short. He felt his armour plastron crack and struggled to breathe before his multi-lung kicked in to take up the slack of his collapsed organ.

One of the hulking necrons regarded him curiously. 'You are not immortal, flesh-thing. They are before you. They are your doom.'

Chainsword screaming, Iulus swung, but the mechanoid blocked with its arm and butted him.

Groggy, he shook it off.

Around him, he was acutely aware of his squad fighting hard with bolter and blade. Somewhere in the dense throng of the necron elite, Ultracius was avenging the crippling of his fellow Dreadnought. A heavy necron form was tossed into the air before landing back down into the melee and disappearing.

Ultracius was relentless. 'Guilliman watches over us. Do not be found wanting in his hallowed sight!' The assault cannon shrieked and a half-dozen mechanoids were ruined, their shattered bodies flung into the closing mist.

Iulus took a blow against his wounded shoulder and

felt the bone crack. His guard was split in two and fell away uselessly. He brought his chainsword around for another swing, this time ramming the blade where the necron's innards should be. The creature pulled the blade away, losing skeletal fingers to the chain-teeth, and brought its gauss-blaster up one-handed. With a feral shout, Iulus severed the weapon where it was conjoined to the necron's wrist and rammed the sword in again.

Iulus rejoiced as he drew out a modulated scream from the monster, but it came on undeterred.

'Desist. Your efforts are futile.' Bereft of its gauss-blaster, the hulking mechanoid smashed the Ultramarine's shoulder repeatedly with its wrist-stump. The other hand closed around Iulus's throat with three clacking digits. Its grip was incredible and the sergeant felt his trachea being crushed immediately. Without his battle-helm, the seal between it and gorget was compromised and his throat was exposed. The necron had analysed this weakness and exploited it.

Mag-locking his bolt pistol – its clip was spent and he had no room to insert a fresh one – Iulus took a two-handed grip on his chainsword and drove it deeper. His sight was darkening as his air supply dwindled to a trickle.

He spat a last, defiant breath. 'Die, you soulless dog.'

Then the darkling world closed around him and Iulus felt his fingers slipping on the chainsword, losing their grip on the haft and his life.

FALKA WAS IN charge. He didn't know how, but he was. At least fifty men, most of the paltry survivors from the four battalions, were looking to him for orders. They'd left the flattened ruins behind them and had made it to a second line of broken-toothed defences. From here he'd formed the fifty into a firing line and got them to man the still-operational heavy guns behind the barricades and in the hollowed-out pillboxes. The bunkers and walls were prefabs, set up by Commander Sonne just before the *Nobilis* was destroyed and their hopes with it. They hadn't lasted long; the garrison behind them a few seconds longer. Now, what was left provided scant cover but it was better than nothing.

'Keep your head down and your lasgun charged,' Muhrne had said during basic training. Falka missed the tough old bastard already. His bones were ash by now. It didn't seem a just fate for such an honourable man.

'Feed the cannon,' he shouted at a heavy stubber team down the line, 'and watch for jams. Keep the barrel cool,' he bellowed at another working a tripod-mounted multi-laser. 'Don't let it overheat. It overheats, and you're dead.'

Throne, he even sounded like Muhrne. Maybe his spirit was alive and well, and fighting the battle through him. Falka hoped so.

He'd found a pair of magnoculars clutched in the cauterised limb of some dead officer. The rest of the soldier's body was gone, presumably atomised by the enemy gauss-flayers. The battling Ultramarines weren't far, but the scopes allowed Falka to get a good look without needing to be up close and personal. With the Emperor's Angels in their midst, the necrons had stopped shooting at the Ark Guard. Falka wanted to keep it that way… at least for a while.

Through the scope's infra-red – conventional vision was largely useless for detailed observation in the snow-fog – he saw the Space Marines had committed to close assault against a wedge of necron warriors. Even the

Angels looked diminutive compared to these hulks, but they had some kind of towering war machine to even the odds. Falka caught only glimpses of the gargantuan machine, swinging fists and shredding necrons with its fearsome cannon at close range.

The other Ultramarines were not faring so well, ill-suited to hand-to-hand combat against such heavily-armoured opponents. They fought valiantly, though, and Falka felt a swell of courage fill his breast. Lowering the scopes, he eyed the open ground between the barricades and the melee. Narrowing his vision, he reckoned on thirty metres. He let his lasgun sag on the strap around his shoulder – it was almost out, anyway – and hefted his ice-pick.

Damnosian permafrost was hard. It didn't break easily, especially in the deep caverns beneath the surface. Falka had once seen a man swing at the ice-face and miss. Instead of burying the pick-blade in the meat of his thigh, he'd sheared his leg off completely. It was so sharp it went straight through the bone.

Across the blasted esplanade, another group kept up a constant las-barrage. Falka nodded to his vox-man. 'Tell them to give it everything.' Then he growled at the others crouched around him, his makeshift command squad. 'I'm going over into *that*,' he said, meaning the frenzied melee. 'I won't ask any of you to come with me.'

Eighteen hard-faced men, some soldiers, some conscripts, drew blades and picks grimly.

Falka smiled. 'That's what I hoped you'd say.' He shouted to the gunners. 'Keep firing but try not to shoot us.'

Then he vaulted the barricade and ran towards death.

* * *

THEY WERE IN deeper than before, hunkered down in a tight defile with thick ice-shawled rocks hugging their shoulder plates. Scipio scowled as the frostbitten crags scraped his armour. He'd wanted to pare the powered suits down for better manoeuvrability, remove all but the body armour and leg greaves. Tigurius had forbidden it. The necrons were too dangerous, their technology too advanced, to go up against without full protection.

Behind Scipio a heavy *clank* echoed down the gorge as Largo slipped and cursed. The noise was carried away on the howling wind but his finger slipped into the triggerguard of his bolt pistol anyway. The necron patrol below continued without pause. Whatever sensors or auspexdevices they possessed were being foiled by the weather and the altitude just like the Ultramarines' scanning gear.

Scipio glanced over his shoulder. 'You eager for a fight, brother?'

Largo held up his hand, signalling contrition.

Ortus, who was a metre behind him maintaining rearguard, smiled thinly. He scoured the way they'd come through his bolter sight. The falling snow was settling over their tracks nicely. After a few seconds of intense and still interrogation, he nodded to Scipio.

Crawling on their stomachs, heads low against the arctic wind riming their features with tiny spines of hoarfrost, they moved on.

After the initial recon had drawn a blank, Scipio had been forced upwards. Somewhere across the sheer-sided cliffs that bent around the necron artillery like a crooked spine was a rocky canal. He was intent on finding it. The Ultramarines needed a way to bypass the defensive cordon, something the necrons had overlooked. Being isolated from the main battle group in the mountains was risky. Pressing on beyond the outer marker Tigurius had provided could even be considered reckless, but the mission demanded Scipio locate a route through which to assault the pylons and gauss-obliterators.

Ducking into a natural alcove, he raised the other squad members on the comm-feed. '*Venetores*, report.'

With Naceon's death earlier, it left the Thunderbolts with nine. To tackle the mountain, Scipio had broken them up into combat squads of three. Unconventional as far as the Codex was concerned, but small groups would serve the Ultramarines' purpose better.

After Black Reach, Telion had told him that the Codex was not a book of strictures, nor was it meant to be an inflexible and comprehensive tactical manual.

'It is our primarch's wisdom,' he'd said, 'distilled for all of us to utilise as we see fit. Some in the Chapter are old and hidebound, but as Adeptus Astartes we must adapt. The spur that does not bend before the sudden storm will surely break, Scipio.'

So it was they reconnoitred in threes.

Cator's voice came through the feed. '*Thracian*, this is *Venetores*. Nothing so far.'

It was followed swiftly by the deep timbre of Brakkius. '*Retiarii* has found something. We are fifty-three metres east of *Thracian's* position.'

Scipio opened up the feed to all three combat squads. 'Converge on *Retiarii*. Confirm.'

A pair of affirmation chimes sounded in the sergeant's ear. Waiting for the last of the necron column to disappear from sight, he waved the others on.

* * *

'ONE OF YOURS?'

They were standing in a shallow valley. The snow blustered overhead but they were well shielded from the wind. A necron lay dismembered in the valley basin. Attached to each of its limbs, skull and torso was a tubular device wrapped in wire. A faint veneer of snow was building on top of the body parts, slowly obscuring it. Scipio looked down at the mechanoid as he addressed his battle-brother.

Crouched next to the corpse, Cator shook his head.

Vermillion Cator was known in the Thunderbolts as an expert at fashioning booby traps. All Space Marines possessed some level of fieldcraft that allowed them to make improvised grenades and other simple snares, but Cator was often described as *gifted*.

Brakkius gave the torso an experimental kick. 'Why hasn't it phased out yet?'

Cator answered. 'Because it's still alive.'

A flurry of movement saw Ortus raise his bolter into an execution position.

Scipio waved him off. 'Easy there, *Torias Telion*.'

Ortus stood down, but kept his weapon ready.

Scipio looked at Cator. 'How?'

The other Ultramarine was prodding the tubular devices with his combat blade. 'There's an electrical charge running through these wires, attached to a powerful battery.' He tapped the tube itself. 'A strong magnet is keeping it from reforming.'

'It foiled the self-repair system?'

Cator nodded. 'Yes, but it's designed as a form of torture rather than being useful on a military level.'

Scipio pressed further. 'So it can't phase out because it's not sustained critical damage and it can't self-repair on account of the opposing magnetic poles keeping its components apart?'

'Precisely,' Cator said, getting up.

Brakkius shook his head at the meticulousness of it all. 'Who did this?'

'That, my brother,' said Scipio, 'is the *real* question.' He exhaled, thinking. 'I want a deeper spread – a hundred metres.'

Cator cleared his throat. 'Sir, this far into enemy territory – are you sure?'

'Someone or something else is out here with us and I want it flushed out. We can cover more ground separated.'

Showing his obedience with a salute, Cator broke away east. Brakkius went west.

Scipio's combat squad carried on north. When they were moving out, he nodded to Ortus. A single bolt shot, baffled by the wind and the valley depth, rang out a few seconds later as the Ultramarine got his wish.

CHAPTER SIX

Aboard the Valin's Revenge, *forty-seven years after the*
Black Reach Campaign

IT HAD BEEN a long time since Scipio had visited the
reclusiam. The chamber was dark, lit by guttering can-
dles ensconced in the mouths of votive cyber-skulls.
Flickering firelight seemed to animate their grisly features.

'I have been your Chaplain for over a year and this is
the first time I've seen you in the Emperor's presence.'

Scipio finished his benedictions, stood and turned to
face the speaker.

Elianu Trajan was standing opposite, framed by the
reclusiam's narthex. The arch was inscribed with holy
rubrics and catechisms, and there was a stylised effigy of
the primarch at its apex to bring it all together.

Scipio bowed. 'Brother-Chaplain.'

'Brother Vorolanus.' Trajan, like Scipio, was dressed in
a supplicant's robes. His were black to match the hue of
his battle-plate and had a cowl in lieu of a helmet. His
crozius mace hung from a hook attached to a thick

leather belt and his Chaplain's rosarius fell to his broad chest suspended from a gilded chain.

Aside from the tools of his office, Trajan did not favour ostentation. Devotion was another matter and his simple power armour was festooned with purity seals and scripture parchment, oaths of moment and votive chains.

He waited in silence, not moving.

Scipio felt suddenly uncomfortable. 'Do you wish to ask me something, Brother-Chaplain?'

Trajan's eyes were penetrating. Embers seemed to smoulder behind the pupils.

'Just this – *why*?'

'Why what?'

The Chaplain's eyes hardened, and the embers became a sharp flame conveying his annoyance.

'I am not one of your battle-brothers, nor am I a fellow sergeant. I am your Chaplain, Brother Vorolanus, and won't tolerate games. Answer the question.'

Scipio's mouth became a hard line. Despite the fact he'd been with the company for over a year, Scipio had not yet found an accord with Trajan. Where Orad had been quiet and reflective, Trajan was direct and exacting. He bullied faith, rather than preached it. A supreme warrior, as fiery and zealous as any Chaplain Scipio had known, but hard to like.

'I have observed the requisite devotions…'

'Just not in my sight. Chaplain Orad served this Chapter with distinction. His death was a tragedy, as are the deaths of all true sons of Guilliman, but I am here now and I alone minister to the purity of this company.'

Scipio's gaze narrowed. He tried not to make a fist.

'What are you suggesting?'

Trajan smacked him hard across the cheek, and the

shock of it felled the sergeant to one knee.

'I don't *suggest*. I decree and act,' he snapped.

Scipio found the crozius pressing on his shoulder as he went to rise.

'Stay down,' Trajan warned, 'I am not finished.'

The Chaplain's face glowered behind the shadows of his cowl. 'Your captain and I have known each other for many long years. He speaks highly of your actions on Black Reach, as does Master Telion, so I shall assume you have yet to show me the same qualities that inspired praise in them.'

'If I displease you, I apologise.'

Trajan rapped Scipio hard on the shoulderblade, drawing a scowl from the sergeant's mouth and blood from his body.

'Don't mock or pander to me, Brother Vorolanus. You are already testing my wrath.'

Scipio's teeth were gritted. To strike a fellow son of Guilliman was heinous if done without just cause; to strike a member of the Chaplaincy under any circumstances was unconscionable. He bowed his head, allowing the anger to subside.

Trajan continued. 'Your disaffection has been noted, as has your absence from my ministrations. I will not tolerate it. Orad's ways are not my ways. You will learn to value them and venerate me as your spiritual leader. Are we clear on this, Scipio?' Trajan dug the sharp edge of the crozius into Scipio's flesh to help make his point.

Scipio maintained his position of penitence and nodded.

Trajan nodded back. 'Being a sergeant carries certain *expectations* that you will meet. Now,' he added, lifting the crozius. It left a bloody trail. 'I go to the battle cages. You should work that anger out. Meet me there once

you're done here, if you wish, but regardless let this be
the last time we exchange words.'

Then he was gone, headed to the training deck.

Scipio never joined him.

'WHAT DO YOU think that is?'

Ortus was pointing at something in the distance – a
series of large, pyramidal silhouettes.

'Designation: *Monolith*.' Largo had the scopes and was
using them to get a closer look. 'And something else.' He
handed the magnoculars to his sergeant.

Through the elliptical lens, Scipio saw the three
monoliths that Largo had identified. They were moving
ponderously, levitating just above the ground on an
anti-gravitic energy pulse. Slab-sided, metallic and
inscribed with necron runes they looked more like
mobile obelisks than battle tanks. Scipio had yet to see
one in combat. Given their fearsome weapons array and
eldritch crystal power matrix, glowing at the pyramid's
summit, he had no wish to. A portal of light shimmered
in the front arc of each monolith, emerald like the
gauss-technology and rippling as if fluidic. Even without Mechanicus indoctrination, he knew this was some
form of energy gate.

The other machinery Largo had pointed out was larger
and of a similar design. It was some kind of *alpha*-
monolith. Lightning arcs crackled between it and the
other lesser pyramids, suggesting it as a sort of power
node.

'Looks like a capacitor, something to focus the firepower of the other war machines.' He gave the
magnoculars back to Largo.

Ortus's face was grim. 'Moving away from the artillery,
too,' his jaw hardened, 'bound for Kellenport.'

Scipio was already on the move again. 'It gets us no closer to breaching the defensive cordon around the heavy guns. Tigurius can relay a message once we return to camp with better news.'

The comm-feed in his ear crackled.

'*Thracian*, this is *Retiarii*.'

'Go ahead, Brakkius.'

He was whispering. 'A necron static outpost. Forty-two metres north of our position.'

'Status, brother?'

'Hunkered down and undetected. We have eyes on six targets, Raider-class construct.'

'Swarms?'

'Negative, sir.'

Scipio muted the link and turned to the others. They were proceeding across a narrow pass and had pressed their bodies against the cliff wall. Heavy snowfall effectively whited-out their armour, forming a natural camouflage.

'Why would the mechanoids garrison an outpost? It makes no sense.'

Largo's broad forehead creased with thought. 'Unless they are defending something.'

'But not artillery,' said Scipio.

Largo smiled and nodded. 'A way into the mountains.'

'Precisely.' He racked his bolt pistol's slide, checking the load. Enough for a skirmish.

'I'm tired of skulking in the ice and wind.' He un-muted the comm-feed, telling Brakkius to observe and wait, then he raised Cator and gave him the coordinates so the Thunderbolts could converge on the outpost's position.

Scipio gave a feral smile before they moved out. 'Brothers, we have our opening.'

* * *

SCIPIO CLENCHED HIS fist as he listened to Cator's report over the comm-feed.

'*Venetores* delayed. Route impassable. Doubling back.'

'How long?'

'Approximately twenty-two minutes, brother-sergeant.'

Shaking his head, Scipio eyed the necron garrison. Just as Brakkius had said: six raider constructs, no heavy guns, elites or swarms. Six of Second Company against the mechanoid foot soldier. Scipio didn't want to wait any longer. The outpost could be reinforced or they might miss their assault window.

'Ortus.' Scipio pointed to a shallow ledge behind a cluster of boulders.

The Ultramarines were below the outpost, hiding in the basin of an ice trench. Sharp crags further obscured their vantage point. The ledge was slightly off-centre of a narrow gorge that fed up to the necron bastion – a functional obelisk-like structure with a small chute at the summit, its sides like the petals of a partially open flower – and offered a clear line of sight for Ortus's deadly aim. Rivulets of frozen meltwater swathed the path up to the structure. Scipio thought he saw faces beneath the ice and wondered briefly what it must be like to have human limitations, to be at the mercy of the elements. Slain by the fickle nature of your own world – it was dishonourable.

Ortus got into his firing position immediately and was already sighting his bolter as Scipio outlined the rest of the plan.

He utilised battle-sign. *Retiarii* would attack from the road, drawing the necrons out and into Ortus's crosshairs. *Thracian* would flank, low and quick, and attack once the garrison was committed.

Telion had often extolled the virtues of 'divide and

conquer' as a strategy. It enabled a smaller force to out-manoeuvre and outgun a larger or better defended one. Here, Scipio intended to split the necrons' attention by first having them focus on Brakkius's squad, then Ortus and finally his own.

Scipio reckoned on an estimated total engagement time of thirteen seconds.

He didn't consider another of Telion's maxims, however: 'Always assume the enemy knows something you don't.'

CHAPTER SEVEN

Praxor saw the Stormcaller a split second after Sicarius.

They had known one of the minor necron lords was present in the vanguard; the further the Ultramarines had forged beyond the Kellenport walls, the more that emerald lightning had cracked the sky open.

It was a harbinger, this one, and a billowing tempest preceded him.

'Twilight falls upon Kellenport and all of Damnos,' uttered Agrippen, his booming voice as deep as the necron thunder.

A stricken tank company, one of the Guard's last few on Damnos, fought valiantly in the wastes but they were alone and engulfed by the eldritch storm. Searchlights mounted to their cupolas strafed the darkness, trying to lock onto targets, but this was no ordinary twilight. There was no way to penetrate it. *Creatures* writhed around in the lightning and the wind, at once solid and incorporeal. Praxor had fought the wraiths before and nearly been killed. What chance did human men have against such things?

He watched with narrowed eyes as the gale overtook the battlefield and pressed in on the Ultramarines. Even the steel plate of a Leman Russ battle tank was no proof against the ghost-like necrons who phased *through* their hulls. Praxor could only imagine the horror of the crews within as they were slain.

The cobalt giants were unmoved, both by the storm and the futile plight of the armoured company. Slowly, the rattle of pintle-mounts subsided and the flash of muzzle-flares decreased. Even the churn of turrets and the booming report of their cannons became silenced.

'They are beyond our aid, brother.'

Standing at Praxor's side, Trajan's face was a grim and emotionless mask of sculpted bone as he placed a conciliatory hand on the sergeant's shoulder guard.

Praxor wanted to shrug it off. Elianu Trajan was colder than the Damnos arctic wind. He let it linger, though, using the moment to observe the battlefield.

Kellenport's defences were based on a series of three octagonal walls. Each was punctuated by several towers and fortified bunkers. Each had three gates: south, west and north. The east side of the city – and it was a vast megalopolis – was completely sealed off, its byways filled, its roads mined and razor-wired. Between each wall was a stretch of land. They had once been districts: commercial, residential, military and religious. Now they were ruins; ash and debris flattened in the necron advance, crushed in the sprawl of war.

From his Tactica briefings, Praxor knew the Damnos naval asset, the *Nobilis*, had bombarded some of these outer regions with torpedoes before it was destroyed by the artillery in the Thanatos Hills. The then lord governor had balanced the collateral damage against the severity of the blow it would strike against the necrontyr. No doubt it had bought them some time, and such desperate courage was hard to ignore – without it, the Ultramarines might have landed on a world already subjugated by the soulless machines. But ultimately, it had not saved them and condemned thousands to plasma-death.

Their charred corpses paved the roads and haunted the ruins now, despite the eager snowfall that sought to blanket them with its white veil.

To reach this point, at the threshold of the third defensive wall, Sicarius had led them on a killing spree. Large sections of the necron primary awakeners, as they were designated by Imperial codifiers, had been destroyed but nothing remained as testimony to it. This fact gnawed at Praxor, making him feel the death of Vortigan more acutely.

When we are slain, we stay dead. The necrons merely disappear. How do I know I am not fighting the self-same enemy over and again?

Perhaps that's why Trajan had singled him out for benediction first. It was the only reason Sicarius had attacked already – he desired the blessing of his Chaplain. Perhaps Trajan *knew* of Praxor's doubts. He had a gift for it, he of the Black, spotting the chinks in a warrior's armour of faith.

Praxor's expression was firm. 'I am resolved, Brother-Chaplain.'

The armoured company was all but obliterated from sight now. The small pockets of Guard fighting desperately around the vestiges of the city's defences were gradually being eradicated by the meticulous enemy. Once they were finished with the humans, the necrons would focus their full attention on Second Company. Sicarius had been right to strike hard and strike swiftly.

Praxor heard the captain speaking as he was anointed by Trajan.

'We stand as the lonely bastion, the last resistance of an Imperial world.' He stared into the ever-expanding void of necron-fuelled night, his helm in the crook of his arm so his charges could see his noble countenance. His gaze was unswerving like steel, his purpose violent and obvious. 'It was settled in the halcyon days of the Great Crusade, when gods walked amongst us, by our ancestors and the progenitors of our Chapter. Let us not falter in their sight, nor allow the blood they shed for Damnos to be in vain.'

He drew the Tempest Blade – a storm to match a storm – and singled out the necron lord in the midst of the lightning. Replacing his battle-helm, Sicarius growled into the comm-feed.

'Follow me into the stygian night and let no fleshless horrors stay the fury of the Second. *Victoris Ultra!*'

The storm proper had reached them at last. It broke in waves of dense black cloud, roiling in a spectral wind. Lightning cascaded from the sky, emerald green and as unnatural as those who harnessed it. An otherworldly zephyr whipped at the captain's cape and crest. It stirred the purity seals and oath parchments on his armour.

Sicarius charged. The Tempest Blade ignited with a fire redolent of older, greater days.

The others followed, ready to fight and die.

Praxor's doubts, his misgivings about the indestructible foe, vanished in the face of Sicarius's bravura and dauntless courage. Basking in the reflected light of a true hero, he cried out until his lungs burned and the air turned hot with bolter-fury.

They all did; every glorious one of them.

'Victoris Ultra!'

Praxor stayed close to the captain and his Lions, using the resplendent glow of the blade as a beacon. He made to speak but the hellish wind robbed him of his voice. He tried again, bellowing to the Shieldbearers. 'Keep to the sword.'

Upon entering the maelstrom, the comm-feed had died. It wasn't wracked by static interference – it had simply ceased to be. A shroud had been cast over them and all within was deafening silence. Except it wasn't, not quite. The wind whipped and billowed, so loud it shrieked. Voices, cold and mechanical, hollow and pleading, manifested on the chilling breeze. Flecks of earth and pieces of debris churned about in the night-black storm the necron lord had weaved.

A heavy flash overloaded Praxor's retinal display as bolt-lightning forked earthwards in a jagged trajectory. One of the Lions was struck, lit up in cruciform like a human torch. He shuddered, emerald energy wreathing his body, before he crumpled in a smoke-drooling mess and never moved again.

Brother Halnior was dead.

A second bolt arrowed through the night, and ripped a ferocious line in the blackness. It cratered the ground then leapt into Etrius.

A flare, magnesium-bright, saturated the storm cloud edging it in white. At its core was Etrius. The Ultramarine was lifted off his feet, the lightning tendrils like a puppet-master's strings animating him jerkily.

A low *foom* battered Praxor's auditory canal and he was pitched into the air with the sudden shockwave. Time slowed in that terrible moment. His arm, going to shield his eyes, moved as if through gelatine. His legs, flung away from the blast, moved with all the purpose of sodden sand struggling through the neck of an hourglass. Belatedly he realised Etrius's spare ammo had exploded. It turned him into a fireball.

Hitting the ground hard jolted Praxor around and time rushed back, urgent and filled with smoke and agony. Hurrying to his feet, he tackled his battle-brother out of the inferno.

Etrius lived, but was barely able to nod as he left his ruined bolter behind. He pulled a bolt pistol from his weapons belt and nodded again to show he was ready to fight on.

But the lightning arc wasn't done. Four more times it struck the earth, tearing holes in the ice and scorching the ground. No one else was felled by the blasts, but it seared battle-plate and cut blackened scars into shoulder guards. The Ultramarines' impetus had been slowed.

The wraiths detached themselves from the darkness as if it were an entity and they its cellular defences. Serpentine and sinuous, they advanced on the Ultramarines with a terrifying grace and fluidity.

'Brother-sergeant.' Krixous pointed with his mutilated stump.

Praxor followed it to where Brother Vandius valiantly upheld the company standard. The banner was stilled, heavy as if soaked with rain, though the wind raged around it.

Buffeted by the gale that failed to lift the Second's banner but hammered everything else, Praxor urged, 'Fight on, brother. Courage and honour.'

Something as close to fear as a Space Marine could experience tainted Krixous's voice. 'How is that even possible?'

Trajan's vehement dogma tore through the storm and

his doubt. 'Our glory is more than the hallowed cloth of a standard. It is blood and sinew, heritage and valour – virtues these soulless aberrations know nothing of. Wars are not won by cold machination and the calculus of metal. Victory is achieved through heart and flesh-made courage. We are Guilliman's heirs, his noble sons. Honour his legacy!'

He held the crozius aloft and it burst into azure flame, banishing the darkness around it. Three wraiths recoiled from its brilliance, revealed in the shadows. Trajan brought the power mace down upon the skull of one, crushing it and sending the vile thing back to the unholy cradle that spawned it.

Praxor drove at one of the others, swinging his power sword in a lethal arc. It was a master blade, forged by the Chapter artisans, crafted from the purest metals and imbued with an indomitable machine-spirit.

It passed right through the creature as ethereal as smoke. The wraith resolved a moment later and its long talons cut Praxor's bolt pistol in half as the Ultramarine made to fire. He cast the ruined weapon aside as his fist closed on a useless trigger and took his sword in a two-handed grip, feeding more power to its monomolecular edge.

'We are defiant!' he roared, mustering righteous anger. 'The scions of Ultramar!'

The wraith was unmoved and attacked with whipcord, preternatural speed.

An instinctive parry warded one talon strike, a frantic block fended off a lash of the wraith's whip-like tail. He had yet to strike a blow. Hard-pressed, Praxor fell back a step.

'Only forward, brother-sergeant.' It was Daceus. The formidable veteran was leading the line. He bellowed to the Lions, 'Forge a path for the captain!'

Somewhere ahead of the wraiths was the Stormcaller. Sicarius meant to meet him in combat and do what he was born to do – end lives.

Daceus seized a wraith in his power fist, but it squirmed free before he could clamp his fingers together to crush it and was lost to the storm. To his right, obscured by the mist and shadows, Honourable Gaius Prabian fought with sword and shield like the Macraggian battle-kings of old. The Company Champion moved with relentless purpose, a match for any of the serpentine wraiths. He severed necks and sundered bodies, his mind and body as one, his weapons an extension of his martial will. As Daceus and Gaius Prabian drove them, the other Lions sent salvos of fire into the night, tearing the blackness to strips.

Sicarius advanced in the killing ground they made, slaying when he had to, searching for his prey when he didn't.

In those few frantic moments, Praxor's world contracted into microcosm where only his Shieldbearers and the Lions existed, surrounded by the night. Silhouettes ranged in the shadows still, bellowing oaths or yielding screams, but they were indistinct and phantasmal. Somewhere in the dark were Trajan and Agrippen. The faint corona of the Chaplain's crozius was yet visible spitting righteous fire, while the Dreadnought was a hulking nightmare limned emerald against onyx-black with each lightning strike.

Of Brother-Sergeant Solinus and the Indomitable, there was no sign.

Praxor hoped they fought on still. Without his bolt pistol, he drew his gladius and battled with two swords instead. The wraiths still lingered at the edge of his vision, distracted by the march of Sicarius and his Lions.

Perhaps the Stormcaller was reacting to an imminent threat to his life, such as it was, and recalling his revenants.

Brandishing his power sword, Praxor roared a challenge. 'Here, machine!'

Twisting its head on a strange, segmented neck, the wraith regarded him as a predator to prey. Coiling first, like a snake, it attacked.

With his gladius Praxor batted away the first talon thrust, following up with the power sword and hacking off the necron's wrist. A burst of shells from Etrius's bolt pistol strafed its torso and skull-face, angering it.

Tartaron impaled it with a thrown spear of rebar he'd found amongst the debris. Somewhere along the line, his meltagun had been rendered inoperative. While the creature was still squirming, Praxor removed its head. Permanent phase-out was instantaneous.

Keeping pace with Sicarius and the Lions was a feat. When a second wraith emerged from the shadows, Praxor lunged – first gladius then power sword – to gain ground. Both blows missed but Krixous hammered it with a bolter salvo, steadying his aim on his ruined stump. Praxor carved the wraith open as it staggered, before Tartaron and Etrius each rammed a gladius into its neck cavity. It jerked once, the balefires in its eyes flaring with impotent fury, before phasing out.

Krixous had his eyes on the sky, 'Emperor's grace...' he breathed, 'Look!'

All eyes went to the heavens where dozens of wraiths swirled and twisted like the denizens of some black infernal sea.

Praxor levelled his gladius in an order to fire. 'Bolters!' he cried, and the air was torn apart by explosive, mass-reactive death.

Some of the wraiths were drawn by the attack, swimming effortlessly in and out of phase, with only the viridian orbs of their eyes a constant.

'Hold them off.' Praxor knew they must give Sicarius time to find and kill their lord. 'By Guilliman's sword!'

The wraiths engulfed the Shieldbearers. Talon-blades and tail-barbs became a ghostly blur as the necrons swept amongst them. Their rending tools cleaved and cut.

Brother Belthonis was dragged into the storm, the hard bangs of his bolter stolen on the air. Skewered through the torso and neck, Brother Galrion crumpled spitting blood. His vambraces shredded, Brother Hexedese screamed the primarch's name as a spear-like tail punctured his plastron and he fell.

'Form shield around me!' Praxor urged his warriors to rally, and the Shieldbearers closed ranks like an armoured laager, firing in all directions. They were an island of cobalt in a hostile black ocean surrounded by a shoal of pitiless killers. Images flashed before Praxor in the chaos: Daceus crying hell and fury; Gaius Prabian, colder and more clinical in his kills than the machines; Venatio, stooped over the body of Galrion. Through the blood-soaked blur, one resolved brighter than all the rest.

Sicarius...

The Grand Duke of Talassar had found his prey. He angled his blade, energy bleeding off the edge in a pearlescent haze. Answering, the Stormcaller brandished his staff. Alien sigils ran along the haft and it crackled with emerald lightning. Moments later, their weapons clashed in incandescent fusion. Above, the thunder bellowed in empathy. Every emotion, every blow and counter-blow was described in the storm-wracked sky.

For a machine, the necron moved more swiftly that Praxor gave it credit for. He caught only snatches through the frenzy of his own battle, but heard the lightning crack time and again. The duellists became shadows in the harsh light of its afterglow, lit in stark monochrome.

It lasted only seconds. With a shout of triumph, Sicarius cut the Stormcaller's staff in half, sending a backwash of energy through him, and then decapitated the creature with the reverse blow. The necron lord's head didn't even have time to hit the earth before he disappeared, leaving behind the malicious resonance of his passing.

The storm went with him, evaporating as if carried on a strong wind, light replacing dark like a sudden breaking dawn. Lightning ebbed, thunder subsided. Even the wraiths melted away, returned to their master's side. In the centre of it all was Sicarius. He leant on one knee, heaving breath into his body.

The lightning had struck him more than once – the smoke coiling off his scorched armour was testament to that. In spite of the obvious pain, he rose and with straightened back and head held high lifted the Tempest Blade.

'Victoris Ultra!'

Relief and exultation blending as one glorious emotion, the Second – Lions, Shieldbears, Indomitable and all – gave voice that echoed their captain.

Desolation surrounded them. And more than one of Guilliman's sons had returned to their primarch's side in the Temple of Correction on Macragge.

Vandius's banner stirred again, rippling on an arctic breeze.

The necron vanguard was defeated.

Though of exultant mood, a small kernel of Praxor felt hollow at the victory. Over half his squad were dead or maimed; Sicarius's maddened rush at the enemy the reason for it. Solinus's squad had suffered too, though not nearly as badly.

As he watched Apothecary Venatio add the gene-seed of Hexedese to that of Galrion and Vortigan, Praxor could not help but question.

'Only in death, Brother-Sergeant Manorian.'

Trajan again, the ever-vigilant shadow of Second Company. 'Duty is all we have, brother.'

Praxor nodded.

'Yes, my Chaplain.'

At least Belthonis had lived, though he was badly wounded. He might walk, but fight? Given their position, he had little choice with either. Venatio would have to patch him up and make him last for however long he could.

Agrippen met the sergeant's gaze, stoic and unreadable within the armour-eternal of his sarcophagus, and within Praxor felt an accord.

Suddenly the presence of the First on Damnos, Agemman's watchmen, seemed all too necessary.

ACT TWO: SALVATION

CHAPTER EIGHT

Macragge, two years before the Damnos Incident

PRAXOR WAS ENRAPT as he listened to the senators' endless debating.

Watching from a seat at the back of the auditorium, Iulus frowned and was glad of the concealing shadows cast in the wake of the late Macraggian sun.

Attired in robes of various hues and ostentation, he found the senators over-fond of their own voices, prolix for the sake of it. Their arguments did not interest him. He had come for Praxor.

Helots roamed the hall, plying the officials with drink and sustenance, while lexicographical servitors dictated every spoken word on clacking scriptoria. The debate had been going on for several days. It did not appear as if any resolution were in sight.

Iulus noticed other Adeptus Astartes in the throng, company spokesmen and the aides of captains. Daceus was there. The veteran-sergeant looked strange with a stump of arm instead of his power fist. It was rare to see the Lion without his battle gear. He looked as enthralled as Iulus felt. So too was Helios from the First. His demeanour appeared keener but no less exhausted at the endless procrastination.

Politics was not Iulus's strong suit. He believed in what he could touch and fashion towards war, but the Chapter needed solidity too and so its future was given to the politicians to argue over. Not that their opinions *really* mattered. It was the illusion of diplomacy. Only one man could end the debate with any real authority and finality, and his throne in the auditorium was empty. He wasn't wasting his time listening to this.

Deciding Praxor was too involved to disturb, Iulus headed for the battle-cages alone.

He met Scipio, waiting for him in training fatigues and wielding a blunted rudius.

'I saw Praxor at the senate council again,' he said as he began stripping off his armour. A pair of serfs came to attend him, but Iulus waved them away. 'I am capable of donning my own training garb.' He glowered and sent the serfs scurrying.

Scipio was sketching test swings with his rudius. 'Why do you terrify them, brother?'

The corner of Iulus's mouth twitched as he set down his cuirass. 'Because it's enjoyable.'

Shrugging, Scipio made two arcs, switching from one hand to the other, before ending on a low thrust.

'Serious, eh?' joked Iulus. His armour was stowed and he picked up a rudius himself, gauging the weight and heft.

'I have to be when sparring with you, ox.'

Iulus snorted, mimicking the beast Scipio had likened him to.

Then he swung.

Scipio blocked expertly, moving aside and allowing the blunted blade to roll down and off his own. His riposte was a sharp jab that Iulus swatted down before he backed away and said, 'We have not spoken of it since it happened.'

Scipio leapt and swung an overhead blow that staggered Iulus at first but the sergeant got his footing quickly and rammed his shoulder against his opponent, denying him the room for a follow-up. Scipio grimaced as he tried and failed to match his friend's superior strength, 'Spoken of what?'

Iulus felt Scipio move, turning his momentum against him. He checked his stance, bracing his legs wider, and pivoted on one foot to parry the reverse swipe aimed at his shoulder blade. The rudii *clacked* loudly around the cage.

'Orad.'

A hail of blows rebounded against Iulus's blade and he was hard-pressed to defend against them. He had to back away, fending off each fresh attack, his options for a reply diminishing with every blow. It bordered on frenzied.

Like a pugilist against the ropes, he went in close, seizing Scipio's torso in a wrestling move and heaving him back to reassert some distance. Scipio came back undaunted and swinging. He carved elaborate approach swings in the air and Iulus had to use his full concentration to anticipate his opponent's strike pattern. He blocked and feinted, but could find no counter.

Scipio was relentless. And silent, until saying, 'What is there to speak about? He is dead. That is the likely fate of us all in the end.'

He aimed a punch, which Iulus deflected easily with his meaty forearm. He could sense his battle-brother tiring. Anger, when misused during battle, was as much

137

an enemy as a friend. He asked, 'When did you become so fatalistic, Scipio?'

Their blades locked, one pressing against the other. Scipio's face was a mask of aggression.

'I am merely being realistic.'

He took a two-handed grip. It forced Iulus onto the back foot, but he then rolled on his heel and allowed Scipio to lunge forwards into mid-air. Using the flat of his blade, he smacked Scipio hard on the back of his neck.

'I don't think you're angry at me, brother.'

Stung, Scipio turned with murderous eyes and flung his rudius like a throwing dagger. The move almost fooled Iulus who was forced into a desperate block that sent the weapon spinning loose. It was a hair's breadth from his neck and causing serious injury.

Iulus threw down his rudius a second later and punched Scipio hard in the jaw. He recoiled but didn't retaliate. Shame supplanted anger as he realised he'd broken a sacred trust.

Iulus was breathing hard; they both were. 'You want to fight for real, bring armour and chainblades next time, but don't expect to walk out of this cage.' He moved in close, his voice deep and full of menace. 'You'll need to be carried out.'

Scipio's face was a hard, defiant line.

'Bout over,' he said, and left.

When Scipio was gone, Iulus sagged and wondered at how he had failed to see his friend's degeneration and pain. He slammed his fist into the cage wall, stretching the metal into a perfect mould of his knuckles. Then he picked up the rudius and performed training rotas until he was sore and burning, and all the frustration had vented away.

* * *

The wise say, just before you die, that your life and all its achievements pass before you in a blur of enlightenment.

Iulus recalled the words of the ancient Macraggian philosophers he'd been forced to endure as part of his neophyte training. On his back in the dirt and bloody snow, he found issue with that belief. There was only an encroaching darkness and the dense thunder of pumping blood in the ears. There was no epiphany, no glorious moment when a golden halo beckoned or cherubim sang of his deeds in archaic verse.

It was copper-stink, it was hot fading breath and the futile knowledge that he had been found wanting in the face of his liege lords of old.

As the necron's grip ever-tightened Iulus railed against his fate, too obstinate to accept it. He wanted to scream his defiance but even that was denied him. He'd pushed the chainblade as deep as it would go, dragged it around organs that were not organs, but still the necron endured.

Then the pressure lifted.

First his sight returned, like a fresh dawn after a moonless night. The blood stopped rushing quite so loudly and mortally after that, and was replaced by a hard insistent *clank*. Something that looked like a spear-tip jabbed out of the necron's left eye socket. Then it happened again and again. Before it phased out, Iulus was dimly aware of a human clinging to the creature's back and hacking for all his worth. The ice-spike's final blow punctured the necron's forehead, dead centre, and it flickered from existence.

The human, a conscript by the look of his uniform, landed heavily but on his feet.

He grinned at Iulus. Behind him, there were other conscripts hacking with blades, picks and axes. 'I have saved an Angel,' he said, and offered his hand.

Iulus got to his feet, ignoring the human's aid because his weight would have toppled him and he didn't want his saviour to suffer that indignity. 'Who are you?' he asked instead.

The necron elites were defeated. The entire war cell had phased out, removed tactically from the battlefield by their masters below and abroad.

'Kolpeck,' said the human. He sketched a salute, but it was awkward and rough. 'Falka Kolpeck.'

Iulus liked him already.

HISTORY WOULD NOT remember the deeds of the Damnos Ark Guard in the liberation of Kellenport. They would fail to record the courageous actions of the four hundred souls who ventured beyond the western gate from the Courtyard of Thor to certain death. Sicarius and his glorious Second would be the heroes and for them alone the laurels of the battle attributed.

But Iulus Fennion would always know the full truth of it.

He regarded the bedraggled remnants of the Ark Guard that had fought and died in the 'wastes' alongside the Ultramarines and felt… *surprise*.

Ever since Ghospora City back on Black Reach, over a century ago, he had known humans had mettle. To fight greenskins from behind barricades and fortified battlements was one thing; to charge headlong into hand-to-hand combat with necrons was something else. Perhaps these hundred or so soldiers before him were suicidal.

They were mainly miners, he decided, Damnosian labourers pressed into service as a last act of a desperate world to shore up its decimated armies. They'd just returned from the capitolis administratum bastion with the acting lord governor. With the Deathwinds' payload depleted, it was no longer safe and he was to be secured within Kellenport.

Word had come through Daceus from the front. Sicarius was pressing on into enemy-held territory, to Arcona City and the Zephyr Monastery. He'd requisitioned forces from the rearguard, both squads of Devastators and Brother Ultracius. Kellenport was won, but he wanted to keep it that way.

According to Tactica briefings, Commander Sonne had over fifty thousand Ark Guard at his disposal; a large part of the planet's remaining population. Iulus was given the unenviable job of galvanising them and ensuring they held the line and the ground already won.

Agnathio could not make the long walk. The damage done to his motive functions had reduced the mighty warrior to an undignified shuffle and until a Techmarine could be tasked with conducting the correct rituals and rites to effect repairs, he would remain so. The Dreadnought joined Iulus's command and the brother-sergeant was glad of his presence and his wisdom.

Presently, he had one ear to the recently restored long-range comm-feed.

'Brother.' The return was crackly and broken, but Iulus recognised the voice of Praxor. 'I'm sorry that you've been left behind.'

'It is no matter,' Iulus replied. 'My duty is to the captain and the Emperor whatever form it takes. How goes the battle farther out?'

'Tough.' It was rare for Praxor to be so upfront and honest about the severity of the fight ahead. He was usually possessed of the same vainglory as their captain.

Iulus wondered what had changed.

'You lost battle-brothers?'

The voice that came back over the feed was quieter, almost hushed, 'More than I'm comfortable with. The Shieldbearers are at barely half-strength.'

'We always knew this war would be arduous. Galvia and Urnos were wounded but we are inviolable still.' He was referring to the fact that ever since they'd been formed, the Immortals had yet to sustain a casualty. That feat might be put sorely to the test on Damnos.

'I only wish you were fighting by my side, Iulus,' said Praxor, his mood oddly candid. 'I have need of your counsel and temperance.'

'Guilliman willing, we will all survive this campaign to fight another in the primarch's name.'

'Or die in the prosecution of it.'

Iulus nodded without trace of regret or denial. 'If that is his will, then yes.'

Praxor left a pause as if agreeing with his fellow sergeant then asked, 'Any word from Scipio?'

The activation runes on the portable hololith projector were flashing. Iulus needed to cut this short. 'None, but there is another comm shroud over the Thanatos Hills.'

'May Guilliman watch over him.'

'And all of us. Courage and honour, brother.'

'Courage and honour.'

Iulus cut the feed. Troopers were filing in from the western gate, more Ark Guard. There were twenty thousand men with heavy cannon and servitors. The majority looked like the conscripts arrayed before Iulus in the reclaimed 'wasteland' in front of the first defensive wall.

The hololith unit flickered to life, a grainy blue three-dimensional image suspended in mid-air through a projector node, and Iulus looked away from the marching men.

'Lord Fennion.' It was Commander Sonne, from somewhere within the Kellenport city-bastion. He gave a crisp salute but his eyes appeared haggard, his face drawn and his uniform bedraggled.

'I am a Space Marine sergeant,' Iulus corrected him, nodding in recognition of the salute, 'so you may refer to me as such. I am no one's lord.'

'Duly noted, sergeant. I want to convey my deepest appreciation for your efforts in liberating Kellenport. You have saved many lives with your actions and all of Damnos expresses its gratitude to you, our saviours.'

The words were there, but the belief was not. Sonne did not think his life or the lives of his people were saved, nor did he regard the Ultramarines as saviours. Iulus saw a broken man before him, one that was going through the motions and had all but given in to fatalism.

'Further hard work is needed, commander. We have only stalled the necron advance, not stymied it completely.'

'I am at your disposal, as are my men. I've already sent the twenty thousand requested to the wastes.'

'You might want to reconsider naming that zone,' Iulus advised.

Sonne nodded, mildly chastened. 'Of course... Yes. It was the Courtyard of Chronus before the desolation. So it shall be again.'

'Chronus it is,' said Iulus. 'Our tank commander will be pleased.'

Sonne didn't understand the reference, but acknowledged the remark with another nod anyway.

Iulus went on. 'Your thirty thousand will defend the

city-bastion whilst the other twenty will be split evenly garrisoning the defensive walls. The third wall we mine and give up to the enemy.'

Sonne went to object but Iulus cut him off. 'We're already stretched and defending three walls will spread us too thinly. Our focus shall be on the first two walls, the first as a fall-back point for the second and then Kellenport city-bastion as our last redoubt.'

Sonne looked ashen at that last remark. If they lost Kellenport then it was over. For everyone.

'You push on for the outer territories?' he asked, a rare glimmer of hope in his tired eyes.

'Captain Sicarius is driving the spearhead purposefully, yes.'

As Iulus understood it, the 'spearhead' was actually a series of daring raids. The necron vanguard had been beaten, a tiny respite bought for the Kellenport defenders, but the mechanoids would return as soon as they'd calibrated for fighting against the Ultramarines. Iulus nearly said as much to Sonne but chose to stay his tongue. Perhaps some of Scipio's old empathy was rubbing off on him. But that had been a different version of his friend. Something, the death of Orad he suspected, had hollowed out that optimism and replaced it with a core of ice. He'd half heard of an altercation with Praxor in the past, something prior to Damnos, but had no wish to pry. The business of others was precisely that. Iulus knew his duty and how to do it to the best of his ability. He had gifts, the legacy of his Chapter brothers flowing in his veins, and he meant to honour that with each and every one of his actions.

Iulus only half-watched Commander Sonne's salute, his mind on other things as the hololith shrank back into the projector node.

'Don't let it consume you, Scipio,' he said to the wind, shifting his gaze to the Thanatos Hills where the necron barrage continued unabated. 'Don't give in to reckless hate, brother.'

Aristaeus loomed behind him; Iulus could hear the warrior's careful tread.

'Break up the squad,' said the sergeant, 'and distribute it around the separate battalions.' He regarded the one hundred survivors from the battle for the plaza, the renamed Courtyard of Chronus. Falka Kolpeck was standing in the middle, their de facto leader. 'These ones are with me.'

IT HAD BEEN so long since he had hunted.

For a moment he was skin and bone again and it was blood, not oil and circuitry, that flowed through him. The wild lands of his birth stretched as far as he could see and the hooting of cattle and herd-beasts called into the umber evening. The sun was dipping and he felt its warmth fading on his cheek. The coarse grain of his antique phase-rifle was a reassuring presence in his hand. The wind, ghosting through the hills and across the plain, touched his exposed skin with chilling tendrils.

As quickly as they came, the sensations bled away again and left numbness and sorrow in their wake. The sun did not warm him, the wind was as dead as the bloodless arteries of his mechanised body. No rifle identified him as a noble plains hunter, instead a pair of gruesome talons betrayed him for what he was – a monster.

Sahtah the Enfleshed groaned inwardly. Even as the tundra rushed by in a blur of greyish white, as his slaves followed his lead, he was not placated. Funnelling into a deep gorge, he paused before the carcass of a dead herd-animal. Its flesh steamed with recently exposed entrails. Sahtah plunged his talons inside, turning them incarnadine with the beast's spilled viscera, hoping…

'Why can't I feel it?'

He rounded on his slaves in a sudden fury. 'There is no heat from the blood, no kill-stench. Where is it?'

Powerless to answer his demands even if they wanted to, the flayed ones merely stared and waited. Their flesh-cowls were rank with putrefaction but stirred a pang of jealousy in their lord.

'I want my robes!' Sahtah raged. His synthetic voice could only simulate his anger. In a quieter voice, he added: 'I want my body.'

His instincts told him the genebred humans were close.

'Soon I will have it,' he promised. 'Soon I will be enfleshed again.'

CHAPTER NINE

BRAKKIUS LED RETIARII up the slope. Brothers Renatus and Herdantes kept low behind their squad leader, weapons up. As soon as they were spotted a strobe of emerald gauss-fire lit up the snow and ice. It was answered by bolter fire that incapacitated one of the raiders but didn't render it inoperative. Before Brakkius and his troops were retreating the downed necron had already begun to self-repair.

Despite the lack of lasting damage, their attack provoked the reaction Scipio was hoping for. Three of the six raiders left the obelisk and went after Brakkius.

Two hard *bangs* from Ortus took one of the mechanoids in the side of the skull. It crumpled into a heap, shuddered and phased out. Another shot exploded a raider's shoulder and left it unable to shoot.

The crossfire was working. It drew the other three necrons out. Scipio and Largo had already sneaked into position before Brakkius's attack and were about to flank them when the sniper fire stopped. Scipio was about to give the attack order when he hesitated and looked over to Ortus's vantage point, wondering why he'd stopped firing.

'Brother, report,' he snapped into the comm-feed. Then came the screaming from back down the slope. It sounded like Renatus.

'Brakkius!'

The reply was frantic. 'Under attack, sergeant...'

Scipio had moved out of the gorge and couldn't see back down the path because of the slope's sharp incline. He caught muzzle flashes, though, and knew the weapons that made them were turned away from the obelisk.

'In the ice. Beneath us!'

Largo was ready to move. 'What do we do?'

The raiders were laying down a thickening curtain of fire. Their slow, methodical advance would get them to the edge of the path and looking down on the gorge in a few minutes. Then Brakkius would face enemies to the front and rear. Scipio swore loudly. He still had no sense of what was attacking Brakkius in the gorge but he suspected it was the same foe that had neutralised Ortus.

'We fight!' Scipio came up off his haunches like a jack-hammer and thundered half a clip into the nearest raider. Battered, the necron turned and unleashed a swathe of gauss-beams. Scipio took one in the leg that staggered him, but he kept on running. Just behind him, Largo provided support fire and tore the raider's chest open with a series of precise shots. It phased out, leaving four and whatever was in the gorge.

A claw broke through the ice at Scipio's feet, answering that question, and locked onto the sergeant's ankle. Instinctively he shot downwards at his assailant, carving

up the ground into jagged chips. Pitiless eyes glowed
emerald through the glossy filter of the ice before dying
into embers and then voids as the creature phased out.

It was not alone.

Scipio cursed again, realising there *had* been faces
beneath their feet but not of Damnosian natives, not
any more – they were necrons, flesh-wrapped night-
mares that tunnelled and burrowed like mechanical
insects. Brakkius fought the same foes. Ortus had been
claimed by them. This was a trap, but one of the
necrons' making, and Scipio had blundered right into it.

'Sergeant Vorolanus!'

The ice broke apart at Scipio's feet and he was dragged
downwards, Largo's warning echoing behind him. He
kicked out and made a solid connection, ceramite hitting necron metal. For want of a better strategy, he
jabbed his chainsword into the ice-slush where the half-
fleshed horrors were slowly emerging. Sparks fizzed and
died as they hit the ground, cascading off whatever Scipio's blade was locked against.

Talons. The creatures had long, curved talons just like
the ambushers they'd met and destroyed at the
Thanatos Refinery. Scipio cursed himself for a fool. He
had rushed to engage without properly gauging the lie
of the land, but he was an Ultramarine with his brothers beside him – all was not lost. He swung his bolt
pistol around, sending two shells into the ice just as a
lance of pain shot up his leg where the flayed one had
impaled him.

A second broke free of the ice and loomed over him.
Scipio yanked his chainsword free and parried a blow
that would have slashed open his neck.

'Hell-kite!' Two more shells put down the invisible
aggressor still lodged below, trying to emerge; a swing of

the chainblade ripped open the cabling and servos around the other necron's torso. It fell back, stunned, but was self-repairing.

'Brother!'

Largo had his own problems. Three more flayed ones had pulled themselves free of the ground, like corpses come back to life to revenge themselves on the living. Largo sent tightly controlled bolter bursts into their ranks in an attempt to slow them but ammo was low and any damage caused wasn't severe enough to take out the necrons permanently.

The fight in the gorge was fading too. The intensity of fire from *Retiarii* was lessening, which Scipio took to be a bad sign. Brakkius could be dead. When the raiders reached the edge of the gorge, he surely would be.

Time was slowing. Fate had caught up with Scipio Vorolanus. It had witnessed his reckless abandon, his selfish fatalism that had grown like a cancer in the years since Orad's death and decided to make him pay for it.

Scipio railed. 'This is not the end!'

The flayed one he'd maimed was getting up. He swung the bolt pistol around to finish it but the trigger *chanked* empty. Powerless to intervene, still half buried under the ice where his spare clips were pinned against his belt, he watched.

Metal flowed like oil, running on the surface of the tundra. Wires and cables reattached themselves, weaving viperously across the ground, re-establishing function to vital systems. The spinal column severed by Scipio's blow caterpillared towards the half-wrecked torso, dragging abdomen and legs with it. Metallic fusion occurred quickly and vigorously – only the necron's cape of skin showed any lasting damage.

'Breath of Guilliman,' he spat through clenched teeth,

looking heavenwards for divine intervention. 'Can't they just stay dead?'

Largo had run out of room and ammunition. He hauled Scipio from the ambush-pit and onto his feet. Back-to-back, they faced six flayed ones, a match for any warrior of the Second. The raiders had their own mission and closed on whatever was left of Brakkius and *Retiarii*.

Scipio slammed his last clip into his bolt pistol; Largo let his spent bolter sag on its strap and drew a combat blade.

'If I had known, Largo…'

'We would have still followed you, brother-sergeant. Only in death.'

Scipio nodded grimly. 'Only in death.'

A smoke contrail *foomed* across the Ultramarines' eyeline, making them turn. It lit up the closest flayed one in an incendiary burst, tearing the creature into fragments. A pair of grenades followed in its wake. They emitted a low hum before attaching magnetically to a second necron. The explosion was hot and deafening. Frag showered the Space Marines' armour. Disregarding this new element to the skirmish for now, Scipio and Largo broke apart and were about to engage the enemy when a bola whipped around a mechanoid's neck and took off its head in the resulting firestorm.

Three necrons phased out in under a minute. The raiders were turning, reacting to the change in engagement dynamics. Three las-beams pinned one, shredding leg joints and the chamber on its gauss-flayer; a thrown axe embedded in a second. Laced with explosives, it was blasted apart like the flayed ones.

Sensing the swing in their favour, Scipio cut down another mechanoid with Largo applying the killing stroke with his combat blade. The two raiders and flayed ones that remained, their forces so brutally punished, phased out.

In their wake, Scipio observed their saviours. His enhanced eyesight picked out their shadows in the snow-kissed crags above. They wore ice camouflage and had powder beneath their eyes. Even their guns were swathed in bleached-white rags and painted to blend in with their surroundings.

'Show yourselves,' Scipio addressed the half-darkness. 'In the name of the Emperor's Adeptus Astartes.'

Slowly, the hunters, or whoever they were, came down from their vantage points. They were well-armed. Scipio saw a tube launcher, heavy-gauge lascarbines, grenade lanyards and several improvised explosives amongst their battlegear. Every one of them carried an ice-pick too. It was this, and not an axe, that been utilised earlier.

As they emerged into the light at last, though it was a fuliginous twilight that shadowed the gorge and the plateau at its summit now, a band of grizzled men were revealed standing amongst the Ultramarines. Scarred and as hard as the permafrost beneath their feet, Scipio knew guerrilla fighters when he saw them.

He nodded to the one who looked like their leader. A thick beard covered the lower half of his face and there were strange tattoos marking his cheeks and forehead. He wore several ragged scarves and his nose, ears and around the eyes were red with overexposure to the cold. Bandages, several layers thick, served as gloves. A tattered cloak that might once have been a storm coat fluttered on a solemn breeze.

Though Scipio towered over the man, he didn't flinch or appear intimidated.

He looked down, extending a hand. 'We are in your debt.'

Besides taking a firmer grip on his lascarbine, the man didn't respond.

'The trap wasn't meant for you,' said a confident voice from higher up in the crags. It was a woman, moving slowly but expertly through the rocks. She was attired like the others but Scipio noticed a ribbed bodyglove beneath her scarves and cloaks. It reminded him of some kind of environment suit, albeit non-functional. Reddish hair, dried out and rough with the cold, peeked from beneath a furred hat. A pair of goggles, their lenses tinged a pinkish hue, hung around her neck.

Piercing jade eyes appraised the Ultramarine, taking in the curves of his armour, his sheer size and power, as she approached him.

'They're after me.' Stopping a few metres away from Scipio, she spread her arms wide. 'All of us.'

Pointing to the obelisk, she added, 'Communication tower, Emperor knows how it works. The Herald uses it to speak to us.'

Scipio frowned. 'Herald?' He recalled Tigurius's traumatic connection with a creature of the same name.

'He is their voice,' she explained. 'Don't see many towers this far out. Must be expanding.' The woman came closer, deciding she could trust the warrior, and held out her hand. 'Jynn Evvers.'

Scipio took it out of politeness, being careful not to crush her delicate fingers, and was surprised to feel some iron there. 'You're hunting them.'

'Why do you think they want to catch us? Got close too until you Angels arrived from on high.' She turned in profile, revealing a string of the self-same tattoos down her neck as on the bearded man. They weaved like a strand of chromosomes. 'This is my crew: Densk, Farge, Makker...'

The names were unimportant to Scipio, though this Jynn related all eighteen of them. Each man and woman nodded, smiled or returned grim indifference to the Ultramarine sergeant. Densk was the bearded one. He later discovered the man had no tongue – he'd lost it due to frostbite. He also later found out that there had once been more of them... lots more.

'We should move,' she concluded at the end of the introductions. 'The metal-heads will be back soon.'

Scipio exchanged a glance with Largo – this must be the guerrilla's term for the necrons. Out the corner of his eye, he noticed Brakkius emerging from the gorge. He was limping. Herdantes cradled a wounded arm. Between them they dragged Renatus.

Largo went to go to them when Scipio placed a hand on his shoulder. 'Find Ortus,' he murmured.

'Captain Evvers!' One of the guerrillas, a woman called Sia, was watching the perimeter. Her warning was met by the priming of lascarbines and an immediate dispersal of the human forces amongst the crags.

Scipio was mildly impressed – he'd seen squads of storm troopers that were only a little better disciplined. He didn't move, though. An auspex chime revealed the identity of the new arrivals to him.

'Stand down,' he said, seeing *Venetores* led by Cator run into view. 'They're with me.'

The guerrilla fighters eased off but only when Evvers gave the signal. Scipio's opinion of them improved further. He surreptitiously battle-signed to Cator that the humans were allies. *Venetores* were back amongst the others in short order after that.

'I'm sorry, brother-sergeant,' said Cator, speaking for

his combat squad. 'Doubling back cost us a lot of time.'

Scipio waved away his contrition. 'I should have waited, brother. And now...' He gestured to the carnage that had hurt the Thunderbolts.

'What happened?'

Brakkius and the rest of *Retiarii* joined them.

'We were ambushed,' said Scipio. 'In the gorge and up here.'

Largo returned but shook his head when he met his sergeant's gaze. Ortus was gone.

'Venatio is back with Captain Sicarius. His legacy is lost to us,' he said.

Scipio gritted his teeth, not liking the options. 'We can't get him back across the mountains.'

Largo was shaking his head again. 'It doesn't matter. There's nothing left of him.'

Now Scipio made a fist. He was trying hard to rein in his anger. He turned to the woman, Evvers.

'How close is your camp to here?'

'Not far.'

'Do you have medical supplies?'

'Some.' She looked worried, as perturbed about unfolding events as Scipio was.

'Take us there.'

Largo put a hand on Scipio's vambrace. His eyes counselled caution.

'What choice do we have? What else would you have me do, Largo?'

He let it go, but wasn't quite done. 'What about the mission?'

'Without a way through the mountains, there is no mission. Ortus is dead already, so too Naceon.' Scipio looked to Brakkius and his men. 'I won't lose another. Not senselessly, not like this.'

Largo nodded.

'So, your camp.' Scipio asked Evvers. 'Where is it?'

IN THE END, Jynn had no choice. She didn't want to bring the Space Marines to the encampment, for one thing their presence would attract the metal-heads, but how could she refuse? It had been a close call whether to intervene on the Ultramarines' behalf, and as they wended through the mountains a part of her had begun to regret that decision.

Of course, the superhuman warriors would make excellent protectors but the humans had survived so far without them and Jynn had no desire to change that, plus she couldn't be sure that protection was the Space Marines' primary objective. They were death incarnate and being close to such beings would only invite the very spectre of mortality into their ranks.

As they climbed higher, up the steep ice-daggered slopes and brittle crags thick with snow, she wondered about their leader. From listening in on the Space Marines' hushed exchanges, she gathered his name was Scipio and he was a sergeant. Jynn knew about as much as most Imperial citizens did about Space Marines, which was precious little. To her, they were warriors of myth, Angels sent on wings of fire and wielding fists of thunder and lightning.

Such impressions were romanticised, of course, little more than cultural extrapolations from tapestries, statues and galleria. The truth was there before her. These were super-men, for sure, but they were fallible and could be killed; they weren't the untouchable immortals that some claimed them to be. Jynn would have been in awe of them, she felt, if her spirit had not been so embittered by the war.

The memory of Korve, her long-dead husband, came into her mind as they crested another high and the drifts thickened. What started out as a light dappling of snow upon her shoulder and head became a deluge that swathed Jynn's entire body. She slipped on a patch of ice and nearly fell. Reaching out, she braced herself on a rocky spur that felt smooth to the touch and realised it was Scipio.

'Be careful, Captain Evvers,' he warned, setting her upright again.

She nodded a curt thanks. 'It's Jynn,' she said. 'My name, I mean. It doesn't seem right that an Angel of the Emperor should call me "captain". It doesn't seem right that anyone should.'

'You carry the rank well... *Jynn*.'

She prodded the Ultramarine's plastron. 'And you are Scipio?'

Scipio looked down at her pointing finger, debating what to do about it. In the end he merely answered the question. 'I am Brother-Sergeant Vorolanus, yes, but you may call me Scipio. You very probably saved my life and that of my squad, so you've earned the right.'

She snorted derisively, echoing, '*Earned the right*, eh? Come on,' she turned and moved on. 'We're close.'

THEY REACHED THE encampment in a few more minutes. It was high up and well shielded from the necrons' attention. The guerrillas must have had engineers and technicians amongst their group, for they'd erected bafflers to thwart the mechanoids' sensors.

Scipio counted six more men at the camp; one was a medic, the other looked like the individual responsible for the sensor jamming array.

Largo appeared at his sergeant's shoulder and spoke in

a low voice, 'Our comm-feed is down, should we…?' he indicated the bafflers; slim, flanged antennae jabbed into the ground like a spear. Looking at them, Scipio realised the entire encampment, even its rough tents and boxy generators, was portable. He wondered how many times the guerrillas had been forced to move since the occupation and how long it had taken them to realise they needed to.

'No,' he held up his hand, flat with the palm down, 'leave it. The comm-feed is no use to us out here, anyway.'

They followed Jynn Evvers, the guerrillas bleeding off from the main group to talk with their comrades and help explain why cobalt-blue Angels were in their midst. Scipio ignored their awed glances. Only the medic seemed unmoved.

'Medical tent,' Jynn supplied as they passed it.

Scipio gestured for Brakkius and the injured to peel off and get some attention. He held Brakkius's forearm as he was leaving and looked to Renatus. 'How bad is he?'

'Sus-an membrane coma. Only Venatio can bring him out of it.'

'Get him inside and see what can be done for his wounds.'

Brakkius tried to mask his shock. 'We're leaving him?'

'Better that than drag him through the mountains. He's safer with the humans. We come back for him, brother.'

Satisfied that Brakkius understood, Scipio let him go and caught up to Largo who was waiting a little way ahead. Cator, Garrik and Auris had stayed behind to watch the entrance. The humans had sentries but they were not Space Marines and Scipio trusted his Thunderbolts above all others.

Defensively, the guerrilla camp left a lot to be desired, amounting to little more than a few clustered tents, some razor-wire barricades and a handful of tripod-mounted heavy stubbers. Not enough to seriously deter a necron attack but then he supposed that was why they had the bafflers. It was meant as a place of shelter, somewhere to regroup and rest, not a fortress.

'In here,' said Jynn, without looking back.

Scipio left Largo outside. He was alone with the female guerrilla leader in what he assumed was her operational base. There were hanging charts and maps, a simple sleeping bag in one corner and a butane lamp kit turned off in the centre of the space. Low burning lumen rods dangled from the tent's internal guy ropes and provided the only light source. The lowing breeze that had started to pick up nudged the rods. As the shadows moved, more makeshift bomb and grenade combinations were revealed here and there. Someone had set up an improvised table and there were more maps and charts on it.

'Found a lot of patrols on our forays inland,' Jynn explained. She turned on the lamp kit and rubbed her hands next to the warmth. She looked over her shoulder at Scipio. 'You generate a lot of heat, don't you?'

The Ultramarine shrugged, as much as he could whilst wearing full power armour. He knew she was right but heat or cold was of no concern to one such as him.

'We could have used some of your generators in the early days.' She started to unbuckle her kit and peel off the bodyglove. 'Certainly makes doing this a lot easier.'

Jynn had her naked back to him as she changed out of the sodden kit into something dry. 'Good thing about having fewer mouths to feed,' she said ruefully. 'It means there's plenty of extra rags to go around too.'

The tattoos on her neck went down her shoulder and across her back, all the way to the base of her spine. Despite her nakedness, Scipio didn't avert his gaze. Jynn seemed unconcerned about it.

She called. 'Densk!'

The bearded one from earlier came in, silent on account of his missing tongue. He stalled a little when he saw the Space Marine but moved around him to Jynn's side.

'Lamp's hot,' she said. 'Three marks.'

There was a metal prong next to the lamp. Densk took it and proceeded to burn the three marks Jynn had requested. To her credit, she barely flinched.

When he was done, Densk dabbed some gauze with counter-septic on the wounds and left the tent just as he'd arrived.

'Those scars,' Scipio ventured when Densk had gone. 'What do they represent?'

She arched her neck to look, touching one of the higher tattoos. 'Kill-marks,' she said. 'One for each metal-head I've ganked. Everyone alive in this camp has them.'

Scipio counted at least seventeen kill-marks. He'd seen Chapter veterans do something similar on their armour.

'Three from the ambush. Yours is the highest tally, am I right?'

Jynn taped fresh pads of gauze over the burns. She struggled to reach the lowest one. 'Could you assist me?'

'I'm no Apothecary,' Scipio replied, but came forwards and applied the last of the tape. He had to be careful; his gauntlets were ill-suited to delicate work, especially field medicine.

'Thank you.' Jynn stepped away, shrugged on a fresh bodyglove then an overcoat, and faced him. Her eyes were like shards of glass. 'Yes, mine is the highest tally. And I'll see it doubled, tripled until everyone one of those mechanical bastards is dead.'

Scipio recognised something in her demeanour. It was like looking into a mirror. The bitterness, the impotent anger. He wondered whom she had lost to make her this way.

'You've buried many comrades-in-arms?'

'No, but I've seen friends and colleagues die. And I've lost family too – my husband, but not to the necrons.'

'My condolences,' he said, even though he didn't really feel the compassion of the words. He eyed the maps and charts, particularly the ones on the table. 'You know these mountains?'

Jynn laughed but it was without humour. 'We've been dying and surviving in these crags for over a year. Yes, we know the mountains intimately.'

Scipio walked up to the table. There was a marker to one side and Scipio used it to circle the Thanatos Hills. 'And here,' he added, drawing an arrow to represent the Ultramarines' desired angle of attack on the necron artillery that would bypass their defensive cordon. 'Do you know of an approach through to this region from this heading?'

Jynn studied the map for a minute. She smiled at Scipio. 'Now you'll owe me two.'

He eyed her curiously. 'You are not like most humans I have met.'

'Most humans haven't seen the things I have or endured what I've had to.' Sitting down on a crate, she started to field strip her weapons. 'Do you know how many times I've died out here in this arctic hell. Well, almost died?' Jynn held up four fingers. 'Makes you think about your existence a little differently.'

Though his expression was neutral, Scipio marvelled at her confidence. There was something about this woman, something great and indefatigable. Whatever her attire or current disposition, she was much more than she appeared to be. It wasn't disrespect, Scipio didn't feel that. It was fearlessness and a determination that made Jynn Evvers stand out amongst the human flock. Such a thing was rare and usually reserved for generals and great war-leaders with names like Macharius, Creed and Yarrick. She was just a miner turned guerrilla fighter but her charisma and presence were undeniable.

'Two? How so?' Scipio asked eventually, willing to play along.

Jynn took the marker and jabbed it into the centre of the Ultramarine's circle. 'We're the answer to your prayers, Angel.'

CHAPTER TEN

THOUGH HIS MORTAL faculties had long since been surrendered, Sahtah the Enfleshed could still find prey. Other senses guided him now and though he didn't fully understand the instincts of his machine brain, he learned to embrace them.

Ice and snow were forming on his body, masking it against the all-consuming white. Scraps of delusion impaired his emerald vision. Images from a past he no longer fully remembered flicked back and forth like visual interference. The arctic mountains became high dunes; the tundra below, a desert plain stretching for leagues. There were cities, so small they were just specks, and carrion birds wheeled in flocks framed against the hot afternoon sun.

Sahtah longed to bask, to feel the sun's warmth against his neck and back, but his nerves were dead, his form cool and aberrant. Ever since biotransference it had been that way. Somewhere in the process, perhaps during the *long sleep*, his engrammic circuitry had been damaged. It was difficult to discern present from past, old from new. It hurt Sahtah's mind and made him want to scream.

The encampment had first appeared as an enemy village with high stockade walls and a wooden gatehouse. Now he saw it for what it was; a cluster of tents and the promise of new 'robes'.

He crouched and let the arctic storm smother him and his wretched companions. There were chunks of half-chewed flesh, the rime of dried blood around the flayed ones' mouths where they'd gorged themselves.

'We are ghouls...' Sahtah told them, though they didn't answer.

They would circle the camp and avoid the genebred warriors at first.

Sahtah wanted blood. He wanted skin.

Oh, how I hunger...

FUGE CLAPPED HIS arms around his body for what must have been the fiftieth time. It was doing no good. Even the many layers of storm cloak, his padded jacket and bodyglove, couldn't keep the cold out – it was insidious. The storm had worsened. Visibility was almost nothing. He looked at the magnoculars, sitting next to his freezing feet in the tent, and decided to ignore them. Captain Evvers was quite strict – scan the perimeter every fifteen minutes – but Fuge was too numb to move. What good would they do anyway? The Space Marines were protecting them now. He'd seen them, walking back and forth like animated statues, unperturbed by the cold. Not everyone was so hardy. Fuge didn't see why he couldn't just find a warmer tent and a sleeping bag to crawl into.

The sentry was still bemoaning his poor luck when he noticed something outside the tent, maybe fifty metres away. It was hard to tell – the snow was thick and the wind was tossing it around like a maelstrom. Fuge reached for the magnoculars.

His goggles were fogged with an icy sheen, but he didn't bother clearing them when he pulled them down off his face so he could peer through the scopes. Training the magnoculars fifty metres distant, he tried to discern what he thought he'd seen earlier.

'Definitely something...'

His voice trembled, teeth chattering as he spoke.

The wind was really howling now, making even thoughts hard to hear. It tugged at Fuge's thermal layers, slipping in through the gaps, chilling him.

Through the greenish resolution of the scopes, he thought he saw something... *burrowing*. He knew of iceworms that roamed the northern tundra – it was the closest thing he could think of to describe what he was seeing. But this was the mountains. No ice-worms up here.

Fuge zoomed in and worked the focus. Thirty metres out now. Just as he was about to raise someone on the vox, the wind kicked in, tearing his coat loose, and he dropped the magnoculars.

Scrambling at his feet – the fear was on him now for some reason – Fuge picked them up but only got the scopes halfway to his face when he felt a hot burn in his chest. He looked down and saw a metre of sharp metal jutting from his body. Lifting his head was an effort but when he managed it he met the gaze of his killer. Two emerald green orbs regarded him as a god would an insect. They flared, ignited by an infernal desire.

'Your flesh is mine,' the thing promised.

165

So frozen was he with terror, poor Fuge didn't even scream as he was flayed alive.

ANKH WATCHED AS the last of the Undying's limbs were finally attached to his body. The venerable necron shone with an unearthly lustre, gilded and ochroid as befitted his station as overlord.

It had taken time and many repair constructs to revivify his master.

As if a sudden power surge had granted him life, the Undying's eyes flared brilliant and terrible.

'Stormcaller is dead,' he uttered.

'He has returned to us, my lord,' Ankh replied. 'All must return in the end.'

'Architect,' said the Undying. His mental functions were still slightly addled by his aeons of slumber. 'I am whole and desire to exact vengeance.'

'Our forces have resorted to retreat protocols. It may be some time before Stormcaller and his vanguard can be resurrected.'

'I have the means of resurrection,' the Undying assured him, 'and the tools of death.' In his hand he clutched a brutal war-scythe, its blade coruscating with energy.

He exhaled breathlessly as the last of the scarab swarms reknitting his body retreated into the hidden alcoves of the chamber. The Undying's revivification casket opened and the overlord strode out imperiously. His heavy footfalls *clanked* as they hit the metal floor.

Ankh bowed deeply in the manner of the old courts. 'You are resplendent, my liege.'

The Undying glowered at him. 'Send your drones, Architect. Retake the ground that the Stormcaller lost.'

Wrong-footed, Ankh stumbled a little. 'I... my lord, our war cells are still reviving. All our repair constructs are needed to bring them online. It will only be a matter of–'

'No. Send them now. Activate the monoliths and bring our legions into the city of the fleshed. I am awake and will not suffer the degradations of these interlopers any further.'

It was pointless to protest. The Undying was all and everything; Ankh was a mere cryptek at his whim and command. True, he had dominion over the scarabs and the tomb spyders. He could make them all cease with but a simple command, but the Undying was not an overlord to deny. His wrath might see Ankh destroyed and another set in his place. He had worked too long, too hard as Architect to allow that to happen. 'As you wish, overlord.'

The Undying did not wait for confirmation. At some invisible, mechanised signal an aperture opened in the ceiling of the resurrection chamber. At the same time a band of light delineated a circular disc in the floor that began to rise. The overlord rode the levitating disc all the way out of the chamber, bound for the surface.

Ankh was linked to the tomb like no other in the hierarchy. He felt its movements, knew the position and condition of every scarab, tomb spyder and wraith that made up its dedicated cohorts. Through them, he was interfaced with the hundreds of thousands still slumbering, still self-repairing and gradually coming online, that made up the necron war cells.

With the repair constructs occupied elsewhere that process would take exponentially more time to complete. Ankh made the calculations in a nanosecond. In the next he retasked the swarms to attack the city above.

Izarvaah was not a subtle creature; he shared many traits with Tahek. He would gladly march his immortals and his warriors into the jaws of enemy guns, convinced of his own inviolability. Cloaked by lightning, his eldritch darkness swarming with wraiths, he assumed he was untouchable. At least one amongst the genebred saviours had disproved that belief.

Ankh was not so foolish or arrogant. His ways were cunning. He resolved to use a different method of attack.

But first he would chill their hearts and make their mortal bodies tremble. The Herald of Dismay extended his skeletal fingers and summoned the invocation node.

Unlike the Stormcaller, he would not fail.

SICARIUS SURVEYED THE battlefield ahead. Just like at Telrendar, Selonopolis and Ghospora, he looked every inch the hero. Cape flapping in the breeze, his patrician face open to the elements, he was Invictus, Cestus, Galatan – a true inheritor of Guilliman.

The forces from Kellenport Plaza had joined his spearhead. Sicarius had summoned their sergeants. Standing amidst the ruins of an Imperial temple, Praxor was amongst them.

This was an ill-fated place, he decided. It had none of the glory or culture of Macragge. Even Calth, its upper atmosphere wretched with poisonous fumes, had spirit. These were a broken people. Damnos should be defiant, yet the humans cowered in their last remaining city, their lord governor in hiding and their military commander unwilling to leave the safety of his walls. Praxos thought of the sacrifices already made and wondered if the Damnosians were a people worth saving.

Daceus intruded on Praxor's dark thoughts, and he was glad of the interruption. Never far from his captain's side, the veteran had a pict-slate clutched in his hand and showed it to Sicarius. It was a geographical map of the immediate area, radiating several kilometres from the Ultramarines position.

'Since the defeat of their vanguard, several necron phalanxes have started to converge on us,' said Daceus.

The initial defeat of the Stormcaller had immobilised the necrons under the lord's immediate command. The Ultramarines found them holding their ground where they stood, unwilling or unable to press. It made them much easier to neutralise. At first, it seemed as if the necrons were in retreat but soon other forces, those attacking distant areas of the city, were rerouted. Another necron command node had taken over. It regarded the Ultramarines as a threat it could not ignore, or tolerate.

Sicarius glanced at the slate, but only cursorily. His attention was on the horizon where the necrons could be seen in the distance manoeuvring and amassing. There were thousands.

'A cut from the gladius's blade has got their attention, then.' He smiled, but Praxor thought it had an indulgent, ugly quality about it.

A storm was rolling in, coming off the mountains. Low drifts were already curling across the tundra. Soon it would develop into a blizzard.

'Even if Guilliman were still with us,' offered Daceus, 'we cannot fight them all.'

Sicarius stepped down from a rocky plinth where he'd taken vantage.

'And yet, we shall still engage them. The weather turns, worsening still. We'll use it to our advantage.'

His sergeants were arrayed before him in a semi-circle. The Lions, along with Daceus, stood apart. Trajan stuck to the shadows, divorced from the rest but ever watchful. In the background, towering over them all, was Agrippen. The other Dreadnought, Ultracius, was with the squads waiting outside the temple ruins.

The venerable one's modulated voice rumbled, 'Our odds of victory against such a force are miniscule, brother-captain.'

Sicarius bowed to Agrippen's obvious wisdom. 'We are still the gladius, Ancient, and our thrust has barely pierced our enemy's armour. With the application of greater force, we will penetrate flesh and organs.'

Agrippen shifted and his servos churned as he moved his massive bulk. A few of the sergeants stepped out of the way to avoid being crushed. 'You mean to strike the heart.'

Sicarius was pugnacious. 'I mean to cut it out. The necrons come for us. We are a threat that they must neutralise. I shall turn that mechanised response against them.' He pointed to the silvered legions mobilising in the Ultramarines' direction. Pyramidal structures shadowed the horizon too, but they seemed to be locked on a less direct route. 'These are creatures of cause and effect. Whatever we do to them, they react accordingly.' He clenched his fist. 'It is a *weakness* that we can use against them. Force is met with greater force. Apply it in the correct place and the enemy will render its heart to us. That is when they are vulnerable.'

Brother-Sergeant Solinus spoke up. 'Tell us where you wish us to strike, captain, and it shall be done.'

Nodding approvingly at his commanders, Sicarius pointed to the slate at the core of the necron force. 'Here, right in the middle. With everything we've got.' He pointed the fingers of his left hand, making them into a blade. 'This,' he said, 'is the necron line. It is predictable, industrious. Here,' he added, making a fist with his right hand, 'we are. Our heavy guns will get their attention. We'll emulate their tactics and hold the line. The necrons, realising they possess overwhelming firepower, will simply advance towards us.' The bladed hand moved closer to the fist. 'When the storm rolls in it will obscure our positions and mask our true intent.'

'What is our *true* intent, captain?' Praxor asked, not yet seeing the wisdom of this plan.

Sicarius smiled and made the fist into two fingers, which he then proceeded to move around his other hand to the tips of the fingers. 'While our Devastators and Dreadnoughts hold their attention, you and I, brother, and the Indomitable–' Sergeant Solinus nodded humbly '–will attack their flank, cutting a hole through to their very heart.'

Praxor was unconvinced but chose to keep his misgivings private. He was not Sicarius and did not see battles as his captain did. It was his duty to obey and fight to his utmost, for the Second, for the Chapter and Lord Calgar.

Sicarius picked up his battle-helm that was sitting on a broken stone tablet nearby, indicating that the tactical briefing was over. He faced Trajan, clasping the crested helm under his arm. Sinking to one knee, he said, 'Chaplain, bless us as we go to war.'

Behind Sicarius, the other sergeants followed their captain's example and kneeled before Trajan. Praxor was amongst the last. Agrippen met his pensive gaze before the Dreadnought too bowed, as much as he was able, to the Chaplain.

It was a deadly gambit that Sicarius proposed. The Second had already lost so many.

Praxor's slain battle-brothers rose foremost into his mind. As the Shieldbearers, they had been at the

forefront of countless engagements for company and
Chapter but they had never been as badly mauled in any
action as they had on Damnos.

I am my captain's sword, Praxor reminded himself of
the oath he had sworn upon elevation to the Second
and the rank of sergeant. *I am his will and blood, his fury
and his courage.*

But as Trajan's shadow fell over him and he closed his
eyes to receive benediction, Praxor couldn't banish his
doubts entirely. All of the catechisms and liturgies
known to the Chapter couldn't do that.

AFTER BENEDICTION, SICARIUS dismissed the other officers.
Ahead were the ruins where he planned to make their
stand. By the time the Ultramarines had reached them,
he reasoned that the storm would have already begun to
impede visibility. Once in position, the attack would
have to come swiftly.

The Lions were already moving to the centre of the
battle line. Daceus was the last to leave.

Sicarius called out, 'Brother.'

Daceus stopped and turned. Like no other in the Second he wore his veteran status with the pride of a
hard-won battle-scar. He had lost his left eye in a previ-
ous engagement – a bionic one replaced it – and his left
arm was gloved by a formidable power fist, another relic
earned during an earlier campaign. His face was a knot-
work of scars and scabbed flesh. His laurels and purity
seals were as abundant as the chips and grooves in his
well-worn armour.

He had always been at Sicarius's side and the captain
trusted Daceus above all others. He also confided in him.

'Back aboard the *Valin's Revenge*, just before planetfall,
I was wrong.'

'Sir?'

'I said our chance of victory here was almost none. I was wrong.'

Daceus frowned, wondering what had changed.

'They are automatons, brother. They cannot function properly without leadership. When I struck down the leader of their vanguard, the others capitulated. It affected them, *tactically*.'

Daceus nodded, remembering, 'And unlike green-skins, these revenants are all cast into specific roles. One does not simply supplant the other.'

'Exactly. If I can incapacitate their principal command node, it will send shockwaves throughout their war infrastructure. They will be crippled.'

Daceus's eye narrowed as he thought about it. 'An impossible victory.'

'Attributed to the Second,' Sicarius concluded for him.

'Agemman's position would be tenuous after this.'

Sicarius's demeanour hardened instantly and he straightened as if insulted. 'I serve the Chapter and its glory, Daceus, as do we all.'

The veteran-sergeant bowed, reprimanded. 'Of course, captain. We are the inheritors of Guilliman. His legacy is the torch by which we light the darkness of the galaxy.'

'You sound like Elianu.'

'It is one of his sermons, or a part at least.' Several affirmation runes flashed up on Daceus's retinal display. 'The battle company is in position. We move out on your order.'

Sicarius donned his helmet. It clamped to his battle-plate with a hiss of pressurisation. His voice was full of grit as it came through the vox-grille. 'Then make ready. Glory awaits us, brother. Guilliman is watching.'

CHAPTER ELEVEN

THE WATER FELT cold but it did nothing to revive Adanar
as he splashed his face.

He was in the bombed-out ruins of ex-Commander
Tarn's operations chamber. It looked quite different now
from how it had been less than a year ago. Much of its
superstructure was exposed, like the metal innards of
some dying beast. The wounds from the necron gauss-
artillery went deep. Parts of the chamber were little more
than rubble. Blank map screens, thick with dust, reflected
Adanar's grim face. He had aged twenty years since the
invasion, or at least that was how it appeared to him.

Fresh water from the ice caverns below Kellenport's
bedrock was still being pumped into the facility, and
Adanar stood bent-backed over a dirty basin in the corner of the room. He surveyed it despairingly. Tarn's old
desk was broken, the two halves slumped in the centre
where a chunk of debris from the ceiling had cracked it.
Occasionally the walls shook – most of the paintings

and tapestries had fallen and been crushed underfoot by the incessant necron bombardment. Statues of former nobles and Ark Guard officers, once standing proudly in alcoves around the chamber, lay shattered and discarded. *So much for glory, now.*

An overwhelming weariness overtook him. The weight of it sank Adanar to the ground, one hand limply grasping the edge of the basin when he fell. Fumbling around in his uniform jacket, he found his service pistol and set it down on the floor. Then he unwound the chain from around his wrist and took the locket-charm in the palm of his left hand.

'How much more must I give?' he asked.

The two picts inside of his wife and child couldn't answer.

'Why didn't I flee? Why didn't I send you away?' The fingers of his right hand brushed against the laspistol's grip. 'Say I've done enough…'

He was abruptly aware of someone watching from the broken archway into the room. An ashen-faced Corporal Besseque was standing there staring.

'Commander Sonne?'

'What is it, Besseque?'

The corporal ventured a few steps into the chamber. 'Sir, the– are you all right?'

Adanar growled at him, tucking his possessions away again and getting to his feet. 'Make your report.'

'The Space Marines have signalled they are in position.' He pulled a data-slate from the folds of his padded jacket. Besseque shivered as he did it – the water was still being piped in to the city but the heating was out. It was almost as cold as it was on the wall in the operations chamber. 'I have the dispositions here. Our defences are ready, sir.'

Adanar ignored the proffered data-slate. 'What good do you think they will do us, corporal?'

Besseque was genuinely confused, 'The Space Marines, sir. They are a cause for hope.'

'They cannot protect us.' Adanar's bile was really flowing now. All his grief, his sense of impotence and futility, it came out toxically. 'We cannot even protect ourselves.' The chamber was rocked by a close artillery impact outside but both men managed to keep their feet. Adanar slapped the wall where the dust and debris were still rolling downwards. 'What use are defences if our enemy can merely pass through them? What good are guns if our foes stand up again after we've killed them? What use is hope, Besseque, tell me that!'

Another tremor hit the chamber as the necron bombardment increased. A chunk of debris parted from the ceiling and struck Besseque across the forehead preventing his reply.

As the corporal fell in a heap, Adanar picked himself up and ran to him.

'Besseque!'

A heavy contusion marred the corporal's forehead, spreading like a bloom of purple ink across his skin. The cut was only shallow. It left a thin trail of blood but Besseque was dead. An internal haemorrhage had killed him instantly. The data-slate he'd been carrying slipped tamely from his lifeless grasp.

Exasperated, Adanar sat down cross-legged next to the corpse. He laid one hand on Besseque's still chest. It was ridiculous. The horrors of the invasion, the bombardment – all the things the corporal had survived only to be killed by a chunk of rock, and not even a large chunk at that.

Adanar threw back his head and laughed. He laughed uproariously until his throat was dry and his eyes stung from the tears. All the while, the room shook and the necron guns thundered.

ADANAR MET RANCOURT on the stairwell. The acting lord governor was shadowed by Sergeant Kador, who looked less than thrilled with his posting.

'Commander Sonne,' he said, slightly tremulously, 'I am glad I've found you.'

Adanar moved past him, and Rancourt went with him walking at the commander's shoulder. 'What is it?'

'I have been trying to get a meeting with you. Your aide – Becket is it? – was supposed to inform you.'

Adanar took the stairs two at a time. They led up to the battlements. He was making it deliberately difficult for the Imperial official. 'He's dead.'

Rancourt let out a little gasp. Adanar had to begrudgingly give him credit – he was keeping pace. 'Dead? The necrons killed him? Are they inside our defences?'

Adanar stopped halfway up the stairs and glared straight ahead. 'No, acting governor, he's back there.' He thumbed over his shoulder. 'A rock killed him.'

'A ro– A what?'

Adanar faced him, 'A piece of debris fell from the ceiling and he died.'

Rancourt peered upwards, as if expecting a similar fate. 'What did you want?' Adanar pressed.

When Rancourt saw the undisguised contempt in the commander's eyes, he reacted. 'Respect, firstly. I am an agent of the Imperium, the highest authority on this world. And I–'

'No,' Adanar replied flatly. 'You are not.'

Rancourt practically screeched at him, '*I am the lord governor!* I demand–'

Shaking his head, Adanar interjected. 'You are not.

You are acting governor and your authority at this time is meaningless. I will grant you a guard detail, but your demands will not be met.'

Kador's face darkened further at the news.

Rancourt grasped the commander's lapels. 'Let the Adeptus Astartes fight. That is what they were made for. We should make all haste to the Crastia Shipyards and evacuate.'

Adanar looked down at Rancourt's scrawny fingers. He let the commander go.

'Secure your evacuation, you mean.'

Rancourt made a plaintive expression. 'As the lord-gov– as the *acting* lord governor,' he corrected, 'I should, by Imperial dictate, be amongst the first, yes. But–'

'Look around you, Rancourt. Look at the skies. What do you think those tremors are that shake the walls? What are you listening to when the air booms? It's not thunder, not in any natural sense, anyway.' Adanar leaned in close. His alcohol breath wafted back at him. 'The necrons control the skies. They fill it with emerald death. Even if we could reach the Crastia Shipyards, even if they were still standing, we would not get off the ground. Our vessels would be destroyed before they even breached the upper atmosphere.'

Rancourt knew this. Despite his actions to the contrary, he wasn't a stupid man, just a desperate one. He seemed to shrink with the realisation that Adanar was telling the truth. His voice quivered like a child's. 'But I'm afraid…'

At first, Adanar regarded him with disgust – this was the lord governor of Damnos, the one the people looked to for leadership – but then he only felt pity.

'We all are,' said the commander and carried on up the stairs.

* * *

'I HAVE NEVER fought beside an Angel before.'

Iulus's attention was focussed on the battlements. His command was the second wall, the one farthest from Kellenport bastion, the heart of the last city on Damnos. The third was well mined and booby-trapped. He credited Commander Sonne – he had drilled his men well. They had marched from the western gate and assumed the positions on and around the walls as Iulus had instructed.

His keen eye for tactical dispositions picked out gunnery nests, heavy stubbers on pintle-mounts, bolter emplacements and lascannon at enfilading points around the wall. The lines of Ark Guard were not thick but they were steady and every man, woman and child capable of doing so carried a lascarbine, autogun or shotgun. The Damnosian armouries were bare. Everything they had was on the walls or in the courtyards and it was pointed at the killing-fields where the necrons would come. He had named the courtyard below Xiphos, on account of the fact he liked the weapon. It was a cutting, thrusting blade and in the Terran dialect meant 'penetrating light' or something close to that – he was no expert in translation. There had been overly much darkness and not enough light on Damnos. The name was a fitting one, he decided.

As if only just realising he'd spoken, Iulus raised an eyebrow at Falka. 'What did you say?'

The trooper was alongside him, part of the Ultramarine's retinue, his 'One Hundred'. 'I said: I've never fought beside an Angel before.'

Iulus returned to surveying the defences. 'I am not an Angel. I am a soldier, like you. Why must you humans constantly over-venerate?'

Falka laughed. It was a deep and wholly honest

sound. 'Me, a soldier? No. I'm a rig-hand, a miner. Have been all my life.'

Iulus looked at him askance. 'Then you do a convincing impression of a soldier. I had not thought humans capable of such reckless courage as you showed. Do you crave death? I have witnessed men commit suicide in battle in similar circumstances to this.'

Falka shook his head. 'No. I want to live but think I will probably not, at least not for much longer. I lost… a friend, and I want my death to mean something so that her sacrifice will too.'

Iulus considered that before resuming his vigil.

'Those studs in your head,' said Falka a few seconds later. 'What are they for?'

Iulus touched the tips of the platinum studs with his gauntlet. He was almost reverent. 'They signify a century's service to the Chapter.'

Falka whistled. 'So, you're over two hundred years old?'

'Yes, though I have not really thought about it before.'

'Are you immortal then?'

'No, I don't think so. Long-lived certainly, thanks to the gene-science of the Emperor, but not immortal.' Iulus kept his gaze ahead, as if drawing inspiration from the silent desolation of the killing-field. 'Ours is a violent calling. Death is an inevitable fact of our existence. I'm not sure if an Adeptus Astartes's mortality has ever been put to the test. I cannot think of one that has ever died of old age. That would be a failure of our warrior purpose, I think.' Iulus angled his neck to look at him. 'You ask a lot of questions, human.'

'Just nervous, that's all,' Falka replied. 'We all are.'

Iulus took a moment to look around the battlements and the Courtyard of Xiphos below. Haunted faces came back at him, with hollow eyes and empty hearts. A revelation struck him. The defenders were not merely guns and bodies, they were people and within they had already lost the battle. He had mistaken fatalism for fortitude, acceptance for resolve.

'Trooper Kolpeck,' he said, still scanning the frightened crowds. 'How can I galvanise these men so they will fight for me as you did in the Courtyard of Chronus?'

Falka followed the Ultramarine's gaze as it swept the walls and ground below.

'Inspire them,' he said. 'Give them something to fight for.'

Now Iulus stared at the trooper, nonplussed. 'There is no greater honour than to serve the Emperor in battle, and die in His name.'

'We are a courageous people, proud too, but we have long been without hope.' Falka rubbed the hard stubble on his chin, seeking the right words. 'Tell a man enough times that all is lost and his world is doomed, and he'll start to believe it.'

As if prompted, the image of the Herald of Dismay flickered in the sky over Kellenport.

Heed the edicts of the necrontyr, your doom is at hand. Your efforts are in vain. Abandon this futile defence, abandon hope and the–

The heinous image vanished, consumed by an explosion that destroyed the invocation node from which it was being broadcast. There were dozens of others erected throughout Damnos but this one was the closest to Kellenport, within sight of its walls. A stunned silence greeted its demise.

Iulus handed the rocket-tube back to one of the conscripts on the battlements. They had precious little ammunition and a part of him, an old part, regretted the waste of materiel, but it was worth it.

'That's enough negative propaganda for one war,' he told Falka. 'Hand me the vox.'

A trooper carrying a boxy vox-caster scurried over to the cobalt giant who had turned to address the stunned masses. It crackled loudly and there was a squeal of static before Iulus's voice came through.

'I am Brother-Sergeant Iulus Fennion, of the Ultramarines Second Company. I am warrior-born, clad in the Emperor's metal, bearer of his wrath. You have been under the boot of your oppressors for too long. It ends. Here. Now. On these very walls. In this very courtyard. My brothers and I will bleed with you, and through blood will buy back your freedom. Do not surrender this world without a fight. Show these horrors that you wear the Emperor's metal too. Show them our faith will not be daunted.'

Iulus drew his chainsword. All of Kellenport, the warriors on the walls and in the Courtyard of Xiphos – his battle-brothers included – were listening.

'Damnos shall not yield,' his voice grew in stature and power. 'We shall not yield!' He thrust the blade aloft and everyone who heard him cheered. Their fear and anxiety, their long-held despair and heart-gnawing grief came out in a cathartic flood of noise. It resounded off the walls and the barricades. It was a call to arms, an affirmation of belief that they all had needed to hear.

'How was that?' he asked Falka when the noise had finally subsided.

He took the receiver-cup – a little dumbstruck – and gave it back to the trooper with the vox-caster. 'Stirring.'

Iulus looked stern as he about-turned to face the battlefield again. 'Good. Now I expect them to fight.'

* * *

WORDS, JUST WORDS that was all they were. Even when spoken aloud and with purpose by an Angel of the Emperor, Adanar could not deny the fact. His faith had been crushed long ago under the tenement rubble that killed his wife and daughter.

He wanted to be uplifted, to believe there was anything else but death for the people of Damnos, but he couldn't.

Corporal Humis, his new aide, stepped into his peripheral vision. 'I can hear cheering.' He was standing at Adanar's shoulder and turned towards the commander. His face was full of hope. It could get a man killed, hope. It could hollow him from the inside out and he wouldn't realise he was dead until he dared to hope again. By then it was too late, he was already a walking corpse, a shadow waiting for some hell to claim him.

'It is just a false dawn, Humis, that's all.'

The corporal licked his lips. He'd been Adanar's aide for less than an hour. 'Perhaps a few words would steel the troops on this side of the wall. Perhaps a rousing speech–'

'There'll be no speeches. There'll be no hollow words.'

'But, commander... Why not?'

Adanar fixed him with a withering gaze, and as Humis looked into his dead eyes he understood.

'Because I won't lie to them, corporal. I won't lie.'

CHAPTER TWELVE

IT HAD BEEN aeons since the throne room had enjoyed attendance. It was a dust-clogged ruin now, its lustre dulled, its ostentation tarnished and decrepit.

Old statues lined the alcoves, clutching ancient glaives, their appearance skeletal and overly regal. Sickly luminescence emanated from the geometric sigils carved into the floor and walls, the chamber's only light source. Their emerald glow limned the throne. It was immense, set upon an oval dais and wrought of gold or some superior mineral compound that looked like gold. Rune-sigils marked its every surface.

Ankh toured the dilapidated halls and anterooms with an air of detachment. It did not surprise him that the Undying avoided this place now. It was a reminder of a long-dead age, of a former life. Sahtah bemoaned his loss of skin and blood like a crazed, hungry dog but he was not alone in that malady. It was an affliction that clawed at every necron, at least those whose memory engrams still functioned with lucidity.

He flickered out of time for a moment, bending the chronology of the universe and mocking its laws with his advanced science. Ankh was back in the revivification chambers again, the lowest catacombs this time.

Malady.

The forming of the word in his subconscious had brought something to mind, something aberrant. He regarded the humming caskets of the destroyers. This cancer, the one which the destroyers represented, was everywhere amongst the necrontyr. Ankh would have pitied them if he were still capable of such an emotion. Nihilistic, fatalistic and possessed of the conviction that their sole purpose was to eradicate, the destroyers were a breed apart.

Madness flowed through their mechanised arteries, fed the electric impulses of their cables and hard-wiring. This was the fate of all necrons. They butchered their bodies, removing limbs and replacing them with repulsor platforms, tesla beams and gauss-cannons – all the better to destroy, all in the service of the destroyers' only creed: annihilation.

Delusion was common, as was a false sense of pre-eminence.

It was at times like these, when confronted with the realities of their existence and its potential corruptions, that Ankh felt the necrontyr's fall most keenly.

Virus plagued them, more insidious than any disease of mortal flesh. They had exchanged their humanity for bodies of metal, their sinews for servos, their individuality for servitude and base sentience. They had done all of that and still they were not immune to corruption. Little wonder that so many of Ankh's kind were angry or insane.

He would revive the destroyers soon.

Tens of thousands of caskets lined the catacombs. The tomb went deep into the world's heart and many levels were surrendered to the revivification chambers. Of all the constructs, the destroyers numbered the greatest. A dull glow emanated from every runic archway to every sarcophagus. To a non-machine mind the vista would be incomprehensible, stretching into infinity in all dimensions.

The role of the destroyers in this conflict was assured and predestined – he had already witnessed it with his own cold, dead eyes. Ankh just wanted to look upon them and remember the shared doom of his damned race.

Another flicker of chrono-dislocation brought him back to the throne room. His true business was here, now that he'd satisfied idle curiosity. The effect of translocating was disconcerting. It pulled at the strands of Ankh's sense of reality. For a moment, he tried to recall what this place was like before biotransference. But the images in his subconscious mind were far from vivid.

Despite the stability of his memory engrams, he found recollection a little difficult to come by sometimes. He was a master of the elements, a chronomancer, a phantasmal manipulator, a walker between universes, but still he could not always grasp the thread of his former existence. In fact, the more he tried the more it unravelled until he realised his grip on the days before the long sleep was eroding, inexorably.

He regarded a cracked mirror of polished jet along one of the walls. Faces swarmed in and out of focus within its reflective surface. It was not Ankh, nor was it several beings. Rather, it was just one, trapped inside the stone a fraction out of time like the cryptek in his speculum. Ankh liked this particular torture most of all.

He uttered, 'Awaken.' It was more than just a word; it was a command, a mechanical imperative that put balefires in the eyes of the statue-guardians. The lych-like creatures arrayed through the hall came jerkily to life. Rimes of filth cracked open as their slow-moving joints stirred. Dust motes spilled from their servos and webs of gossamer parted from their cabling like torn funerary shrouds.

'We serve the royarch,' they chimed as one.

Standing in the centre of the hall, within the protective cordon of a ceramic sigil-totem inscribed in the floor, Ankh was surrounded.

He bowed. 'I am the Architect, the royarch's vassal and extension of his will.'

The guards did not react. Instead they stood with their pole-armed glaives straight against their armoured bodies, pommel down against the floor.

'Your apotheosis is at hand,' Ankh declared. He drew a portal with his staff in which a vision of Damnos was projected. It showed the walls of Kellenport, occupied by the fleshed and their genebred saviours. 'Our world is overrun and the royarch calls you to war.'

One of the lych-like guards stepped forwards. He wore a circlet of tarnished gold around his forehead and his shoulder guards were cracked pieces of super-hardened ceramic – this was the leader. He raised his war-glaive and cut through the portal-image, banishing it.

His eyes flared with millennia-old anger. 'We obey.'

LARGO LISTENED TO the wind as he kept vigil over Renatus. His wounded battle-brother was deep into sus-an membrane coma now and would not easily be revived. It was a regenerative measure, triggered in extremis when a Space Marine was so badly injured that he could fight no further. Much of Renatus's armour had been removed so he could be examined properly. His power generator, helmet and plastron were nearby, laid out reverently by Herdantes. There were blade marks in the ceramite, as long and thick as one of Largo's gauntleted fingers. They were a killer's marks, aimed for the weak points and targeting vital organs. Renatus had survived by virtue of being Adeptus Astartes, but only barely.

Largo hadn't witnessed what happened in the gorge but suspected it was bad. Herdantes was on the other side of the tent, lost in shadow and catalepsean sleep. Another hour and it would be Largo's turn. The other Ultramarine hadn't spoken about the ambush. There'd been little time and too much blood. Brakkius had left the tent earlier, in need of air and an opportunity to stretch his injured leg.

Outside the medi-tent, the storm was building. Largo didn't like it. He didn't like being stuck in this camp with the humans and so far away from the rest of their battle group. He didn't blame Scipio. He was Largo's sergeant, as brave and resourceful a Space Marine as he'd ever known, but there was no denying the necrons had them reeling. He wanted, bitterly, to strike a blow.

'I will watch him,' said the medic. His name was Holdst, a man of middling human years but with a world-weary air that made him hunch. 'If you need to rest, like your comrade.' He glanced at Herdantes.

'I need no rest. I am a Space Marine.' It came out harder than Largo had intended, but he wasn't sufficiently moved to apologise.

'Of course,' said Holdst. He'd been washing the blood off his hands and carried a pinkish rag that he used to dry his fingers. 'There's nothing further I can do for him, though.'

'I understand. The Chapter thanks you for doing your duty to the Emperor.'

Holdst lingered and set down the rag.

Largo looked at him.

'There is more?'

'This was my world that has become a wasteland. I had a family, a life. I am angry too.'

For a human, Holdst was remarkably perceptive. Largo was about to respond when Holdst turned around at a noise behind him. It was hard to see what had got the medic's attention, the tent was poorly lit and his body was in the way.

'Fuge?' he said at first, then, 'Merciful Thro–'

Four blades punched through Holdst's back and lifted the medic off his feet. His legs were already spasming as the thing wearing Fuge's face stepped into the tent and the light. Largo was up, his bolter loose.

'Herdantes!'

The other Ultramarine snapped awake and armed himself.

Twin muzzle flares tore open the darkness, filling it with fire and noise.

Poor Holdst was shredded. The man was already dead when Largo and Herdantes opened up at the ghoul inside the tent with them. Bolter shells exploded against its tough carapace but failed to slow it. The creature sprang, its body swathed in bloodied flesh flayed from one of the sentries, and landed on the bench supporting Renatus.

Largo drew his gladius, afraid he'd hit Renatus if he kept on shooting. In his peripheral vision, he saw Herdantes turn and spray wide as another flayed one ripped through the tent lining and came scurrying inside. The blast pitched the necron off its feet but it was followed by another and another.

Largo kept going. Renatus was in danger. A fifth creature emerged on his flank and he was forced to engage. A swipe of his gladius parried its talons wide of the mark, leaving them to scrape the ceramite of his leg greave, before Largo triggered his bolter point-blank and blew a hole in the flayed one's torso.

'Herdantes. Our brother!'

Seeing the danger, Herdantes was moving. He punched one necron in the jaw, stunning it, before bounding onto the slab where Renatus slumbered. The necron crouching over the wounded Ultramarine was different to the others. There was a gleam of malicious sentience in its eyes and its trappings were more elaborate.

'*Fleeessshhh…*'

It hissed at Herdantes. Its teeth were gummed with blood and viscera. There wasn't time to lift a gladius as a swipe of the necron's talons ripped Herdantes's armour open and sent him sprawling.

Largo reacted to his brother's cry of pain and converged on Renatus. But he was too late to stop the creature lopping off Renatus's head and bathing in the bloody fountain projected from his neck stump.

'No!'

A flayed one tried to stop him, but Largo rammed his gladius into its neck all the way to the hilt. A second he gunned down with the last of his ammunition, before discarding both weapons and leaping for Renatus's slayer, his hands curled into strangling claws.

The creature wearing Fuge's face punched both talons into Renatus's lifeless body, hoisted the dead Space

Marine onto its back and, pumping its legs, sprang through the roof and out into the night.

Largo's fingers closed on air and he cursed again.

Herdantes had been finishing off the last of the flayed ones in the medi-tent but saw what happened. There was something akin to fear in his voice. 'It will defile him…'

Largo roared through clenched teeth, took up his fallen bolter and ran outside into the storm.

THE CAMP WAS in chaos. Screaming merged with sporadic las-fire, half-heard through the wind, as Scipio rushed from Jynn's command tent and realised they were under attack.

He tapped the comm-feed in his ear, scanning the darkness for threats. 'Brothers! Thunderbolts! Report!'

Cator's voice, crackling with the weather interference, came through first. 'Something got through the gate… went under… everywhere… Engaging!' Percussive bolter fire cut him off. Scipio saw the muzzle flashes in the distance. Several more came from the direction of the medi-tent and he was torn.

'Largo!' he shouted down the feed. Silhouettes crossed his vision, the guerrillas were running back and forth as they struggled to fight an enemy they couldn't see. Scipio almost shot one of them on reflex. 'Captain Evvers,' he called behind him. 'Marshal your troops before my brothers and I cut down them down by mistake.' She was on the vox in her tent, trying to find out what was happening.

Her reply was cut off by the voice of Largo, loud and urgent in Scipio's ear. 'It's got Renatus! It cut off his head, sergeant. It took him.'

First Naceon then Ortus and now Renatus – this war is exacting a heavy toll.

Scipio crouched in the lee of another tent. The tripod guns had started rattling. Someone was panicking. 'Largo, repeat. You're not making sense.'

'It took him,' said Largo – his breathing was hard, he was running and angry. 'I'm getting him back.'

A skin-draped horror emerged from the gloom before him and Scipio realised at last what was attacking the camp.

He ran at the flayed one, thumbing the activation rune of his chainsword.

There was a hollow *prang* and a cascade of sparks rained down onto the snow as blade met talon but Scipio would not be denied. He aimed a punch at the creature's neck, followed by a blow that cut through its clavicle and severed a clutch of cabling. It crumpled and Scipio finished it. Instant phase-out told him he'd done it right.

Jynn Evvers came running up beside him. She was armed and kitted out for a sudden departure. 'We're overrun.'

Scipio's eyes were on the darkness. 'They're here for us.' Shadows cast in the camp's portable floodlights swivelled in all directions. It was like trying to catch smoke. A dozen gun battles were happening at once but most of the guerrillas were firing at shadows. Or each other.

Jynn sounded rueful. 'I know.'

Before Scipio could respond, Brakkius joined them. His cooling meltagun suggested he'd had a recent encounter.

'Necrons have tunnelled into the camp and bypassed the sentries.'

'How many?'

Brakkius shook his head. 'Hard to tell. Could be as

many as twenty, possibly more.' He clapped the stock of his weapon. 'I took out two, but there are skirmishes breaking out everywhere.'

'Have you seen Largo or Herdantes?'

'No. I went back to the medi-tent but they were already gone.' He met Jynn's questioning gaze. 'I'm sorry, but your medic is dead.'

Her face tightened into a hard line as she suppressed the grief. That wouldn't serve her now.

Brakkius focussed his attention back on his sergeant.

'We can't mount an effective counter-attack in these conditions. What are your orders, sir?'

Nodding, Scipio said, 'Signal the squad, all Thunderbolts to regroup at the command tent.' He turned to Jynn. 'Your men, too, Captain Evvers. Bring them all here, what's left of them. We're falling back.'

Scipio broke into a run, away from the command tent.

'Sir, where are you going?' asked Brakkius.

He looked over his shoulder, his face determined. 'After Largo. He'll ignore the order. He wants revenge for Renatus.'

'How do you know?'

'Because it's what I'd do.'

'Wait!' Brakkius pulled a spare bolt clip from his belt and threw it over.

Scipio caught it, nodded and ran off into the night. The snowfall thickened in his wake, smothering him from sight as if he'd never even been there.

Brakkius raised the others on the comm-feed.

SCIPIO'S BLOOD WAS up. He was crouched low against the wind, using the falling snow to mask his advance through the camp, but all he really wanted to do was unleash his anger. One clip, given up by Brakkius, was all he had – that, his chainsword and his gladius – he'd need to make every one count.

He headed for the medi-tent, hoping to pick up on Largo's trail. The camp was relatively small and should have been easy to navigate but the battle was spilling over its borders into the mountains beyond and the weather conditions were impeding even his superhuman senses. The guerrilla fighters had trained in this arctic waste, they'd fought and survived the environs but even so they would be blind in this blizzard. Their screaming punctuated Scipio's every thought. He blocked it out, focussed on finding Largo.

Can't lose another. Not this way.

The medi-tent was empty, aside from the carnage. Even the medic's corpse was gone, though Scipio discerned bloody drag marks in the snow.

What kind of automatons are these things?

He found Herdantes a few metres away. He was slumped against a rock, veiled in snow and holding his ruined chest so his organs stayed inside.

'Brother-sergeant,' he rasped. The frozen air from Herdantes's mouth was blood-flecked, suggesting internal bleeding. Even his Larraman cells were struggling to form clots. 'Opened me up,' he continued, moving his hand for a few seconds to show the red crater in his torso. 'But I killed it, sent it back to whatever hell spawned it.'

Scipio wasn't sure what that place was or if the necrons could even *be* killed. He knelt beside Herdantes, assessing the damage. 'Where's Largo?'

Herdantes went to speak but the blood in his throat only gurgled. He pointed to the darkness just outside the camp instead. It was north, deeper into the mountain range. Scipio narrowed his gaze and made out the jagged silhouette of a frozen peak.

'Are you armed?'

Herdantes nodded wearily. His breath was coming out in ragged gasps. Patting the bolter on his lap was difficult. 'Half a clip.'

'Use them wisely. I'll return,' Scipio promised. A group of guerrilla fighters appeared out of the blizzard and he waved them over. 'Get him up, regroup at the command tent.'

The storm was so loud, the humans just nodded.

Scipio left them and headed for the jagged peak.

LARGO WAS HUNKERED down behind a cluster of snow-caked boulders, staring into a sheer-sided rock face above. He glanced over at Scipio as he crouched next to him.

'It's up there,' he whispered, nodding to the fathomless darkness.

The blizzard was getting worse. It made following Largo's gesture almost impossible.

'I see nothing,' Scipio hissed

'It's there. It's got Renatus. Look...' Largo unclasped his bolter's targeter and gave it to the sergeant.

Scipio lined the crosshairs over a plateau above. The night-vision scope picked out the shoulders and spines of massive rocks in the darkness. He tweaked a dial on the sight to heat-tracking. A muffled red shape resolved as the image went from hazy green to grainy blue. It was moving. There was another shape in front of it, though its red glow was less vibrant.

Renatus. Scipio suspected the dead Ultramarine's generator was providing most of the heat trace.

'It took his head, brother-sergeant. Tore it off in front of me.'

Scipio scanned the area through the targeter. A chasm

fell away a few metres beyond the boulders, explaining why Largo had given up pursuit. A fragile ice escarpment led to the edge of the precipice which was thorned with dagger-like crags.

He brought the crosshairs back up to the plateau again, gauging the distance the necron had climbed. The fact they were capable of such feats surprised him. 'Where is your squad, brother?' Scipio asked.

Largo was nonplussed.

'Where are your brothers?'

Largo looked behind at the snow-shrouded encampment.

Scipio still had his eye on the plateau. Something was happening. 'We cannot indulge in personal vengeance, Largo.'

'Renatus–'

The sergeant cut him off. 'Is dead. But the rest of your battle-brothers still live. We're– *Move!*'

Scipio dropped the targeter and thrust Largo aside as the necron landed between them. It had vaulted the chasm.

Both Space Marines were on their feet quickly with weapons drawn.

'Circle it!' Scipio shouted. He began strafing along the necron's flank, drawing its gaze, as Largo went the other way to blindside the monster.

It tracked Scipio's movements, like an alpha predator tracks a threat. Scipio levelled his chainsword, but kept the movement slow. His bolt pistol was at his side ready.

It was a *ghoul*, this thing. Ropes of skin clung to its skeletal form and great tranches of flesh swathed its back, fashioned into a cape or robes. Blood crusted its muzzle and thicker visceral fluids drooled through the cavities in its structure, hanging off cables and congealing over wires. Its face was the most disturbing aspect of its appearance, for it was a mask of flesh. The human called Fuge had been butchered for his skin and this creature had taken his face whole, robbed the man of the only thing left to him in death – his identity. Even so, the mask was breaking, stretched too thinly across the necron's gruesome visage, and patches of gore-streaked metal showed through. As the flayed one glared at him, Scipio saw a piece of chewed skin tear and fall to the ground.

'A face…' It spoke with sepulchral madness, trembling with anguish. 'I had a face. Give me my face…'

Scipio realised it wanted *his* face or anyone's. It was the only reason it had jumped from its perch. It had decapitated Renatus and lost his face. Now the wretched creature wanted another.

Only Scipio's psycho-conditioning stopped him balking in terror.

Largo could wait no longer. He'd drawn his gladius – with only the necron between them, he might hit Scipio with his bolter – and leapt at the creature.

With viperous dexterity, the flayed one parried the blow and stabbed Largo in the shoulder. It drew a shout of pain from the Ultramarine.

Scipio launched his attack a second later before the necron could injure Largo further.

Again, the creature moved with preternatural swiftness, coiling its body around to slash at the brother-sergeant. The talons missed Scipio's neck by a finger-width and he stepped back, warding off the monster with a chainsword thrust. It smacked the weapon aside, chain-teeth spitting sparks but doing little else.

Largo attacked again, slowed by his wound. He managed to land a blow on the necron's shoulder but it *pranged* off as if striking adamantium. The resulting shockwave ran up Largo's arm and into his shoulder, numbing it.

'*Flesh…*' A jagged wound ripped open Largo's face, drooling blood.

The blizzard was worsening and enveloped the combatants in a swirling maelstrom.

Scipio's shout was almost robbed by the wind. 'It's not working. Follow me, brother.' He peeled off from the attack, making for the escarpment.

'What are you doing?' asked Largo, taking off after Scipio.

'Do you trust my judgement, brother?'

'You are my sergeant.'

That was all the answer Scipio needed.

Behind them, the necron turned. Despite its fluidity in combat, when not under imminent threat its insanity seemed to slow it down. It took a few seconds to realise its prey was running, then it sprang into the air with a dense crunch of servos and landed on the boulders, squat like a skeletal gargoyle.

'*Flesh…*' it hissed, filled with a terrible yearning. '*I need it…*'

Backing slowly towards the escarpment, Scipio could feel the ice cracking under his weight. This was no ordinary necron, he realised. It was one of the masters, a superior construct. Within a few seconds of the engagement, Scipio knew the chances of the two of them defeating it were slight.

'When an enemy seems unbeatable, do not attack it head-on,' the sage words of Telion came back to him. 'Instead, devise another strategy that turns its strength into a weakness and balances the odds.'

It was massive, a hulking monster of a necron. Judging

by its size and the strength behind its blows, Scipio reasoned it probably weighed more than him and Largo combined. He remembered how it had leapt from the plateau, the power in its servos, and saw the raw need in its eyes to take their skin.

'Are you ready, Largo?'

They were barely a half-metre from the edge where the escarpment curled like a clenched finger and was at its weakest.

Largo nodded.

The flayed lord's shoulders were heaving up and down with the movement of its chest. It had no lungs, no way of dragging air into its body even if it needed to. It was emulating a remembered behaviour.

Scipio was reminded of a rabid dog. He'd holstered his bolt pistol, and pulled out his gladius as he called to it. 'You want our faces,' he said, drawing a shallow cut across his cheek with the blade. 'Come and take them.'

The flayed lord threw back its head, emitting a shriek of machine-noise, and sprang off the boulders.

Scipio waited until it reached the apex of its jump and then shouted to Largo. 'Now!'

The Ultramarines threw themselves aside a split second before the necron crashed down in their wake. It whirled around when it realised its prey had gone, skin-robes flecking the snow with blood and matter.

Cracks veined the ice, but the escarpment held.

Largo had rolled onto his back. 'It's not breaking!'

'Give it some encouragement,' Scipio bellowed.

Largo unleashed his bolter against the cracking ice. The effect was instantaneous.

A massive chunk of the escarpment sheared away from the rock face and took the flayed lord with it. Their last image of the creature was its hellish eyes, blazing, thwarted.

Largo got up and punched the air. 'Ha! Bastard!'

Scipio grabbed his shoulder. 'Now we go.'

Both gave a last look to the plateau where Renatus's headless corpse was lying unmourned, without honour. The destruction of the flayed lord would have to do as tribute.

Then they ran back towards the camp and the command tent where Scipio hoped the rest of his squad were waiting.

THE SUN WAS warm against his tanned skin. It felt good to be out in the mountains, alone and unshadowed. Sahtah couldn't remember the last time he'd been climbing, he couldn't remember...

He couldn't remember...

...*Anything*.

Reality came crashing back like a cold wave. The sensory illusion faded and he was clinging to the rock face again, his talons lodged in the sheer-sided wall of the mountain. Sahtah had been broken for a moment, but his mechorganic body had healed him. He blinked, though it was an android interface rather than a physical one – he had long since surrendered his eyelids. Even during the long sleep he had not closed them. His awareness during those aeons had been fleeting, confusing, as if he were only partially alive and a passenger in someone else's body.

He didn't know how far he'd fallen but the ice-gorge was dark and deep. The spines of rocks scraped and broke against his body. His robes were being torn. Sahtah moaned, climbing faster, but the damage only worsened. A false sense of urgency filled him. He wanted to be out of the chasm and back amongst the peaks. Reaching the lip of rocky plateau, he pulled himself up and found the feast he had left behind.

It had no face.

Sahtah wanted a face. The one he wore now was virtually gone; his robes were in tatters too. He regarded the semi-armoured carcass lying in front of him.

It would have to do.

When he saw the glistening ribbons that bound it, the redness inside, the pallor of its succulent organs, he was overcome. Like the ghoul he knew he was but inwardly reviled, Sahtah sprang onto the corpse and continued to feed. And as the red matter inside splashed across his borrowed face and drizzled down the cage of his ribs and amassed in his joints, he was visited by such horrific visions.

Flesh palaces resolved in his ancient mind, infinite realms devoted to the skin. Corpses hung from hooks and ringed the vaulted ceilings on chains like gruesome chandeliers. Blood ran in rivers, thick with viscera and carrying chunks of bone. Piles of offal, threads of muscle and intestine formed incarnadine sculptures that decked the stinking halls. And everywhere the feast of the flayers went on indefinitely, lost to madness, lost to flesh.

Sahtah threw back his head and emitted a keening that reverberated around the mountains. It signalled his desire, his terrible anguish and the certain knowledge that he was damned.

In the distance his slaves heard the call of the master and echoed it.

'WHY HAVE THEY stopped fighting?'

Across the encampment, the flayed ones had shuddered to an abrupt halt. As one, they squatted in the dirt and growled – a dirge of machine-noise that hurt Jynn's ears.

Only the Space Marines seemed unaffected. The one Scipio had called Brakkius was standing stock-still and peering into the darkness. He moved at some unseen disturbance ahead – Jynn had no idea what – and signalled to the others who had recently joined them.

'Is it Scipio?' she asked.

Brakkius regarded her as a disapproving mentor would his student. His eyes were two ovals of blood-red. *'Brother-Sergeant* Vorolanus is still absent.'

Clearly the cobalt giant didn't approve of first name familiarity.

'Who then?'

Jynn's question was answered when three of her guerrillas emerged from the blizzard supporting one of the Ultramarines. His injuries looked bad but he was walking, albeit with help.

'Herdantes…' There was an edge to Brakkius's voice, an undercurrent of suppressed anger that frightened her. She also felt something else at the sight of the stricken Space Marine.

She realised it was anxiety.

For Scipio.

At Brakkius's command, two Ultramarines went to their wounded comrade and took his weight off Jynn's men. The three guerrillas looked exhausted when they finally reached her.

'The metal-heads are no longer killing us,' said Sia. She had a small cut on her forehead and the arm of her jacket was slashed, but otherwise she was unharmed.

'Glad you made it,' said Jynn, exchanging a brief embrace with all three of them. Of the twenty-four guerrillas she'd started with at sun-up that day, only nine remained before the night was out. Doc Holdst was amongst the tally of the dead. It was hard to be grateful for anything when confronted with such wasteful loss.

Jynn turned to Brakkius. His attention was on the Space Marines dragging the one called Herdantes to the command tent. 'We need to move. My people, or what's left of them, are all here.'

Brakkius didn't bother to look at her. 'Mine are not.'

She tugged on his vambrace to get his attention. It was like trying to move a mountain. Brakkius didn't shift. Jynn went on anyway. 'Look, those monsters have stopped for whatever reason. Maybe they're fallible after all and there's a malfunction in their wiring or something – I don't care. I've lost nearly two-thirds of my people and the rest of us won't last much longer once those metal-heads come around again. We have to move!'

This time Brakkius met her gaze. It was impossible to tell through the lenses of his battle-helm but she hoped there might have been a measure of respect in his eyes. He held her gaze for a few seconds before looking back at the darkness.

Another Space Marine approached him and stopped by his side. 'Herdantes is badly wounded.' He glanced at Jynn. 'The human is right, we must leave this place.'

'I won't leave him, Cator. You go – lead the others back to Lord Tigurius if you can. I'm staying.'

Brakkius resumed his vigil.

In the end, Cator didn't have to decide. Two more cobalt giants came running through the blizzard.

Jynn recognised Scipio – the other one she'd heard him call Largo.

Now they could go.

'I'm pleased you're alive, Jynn Evvers,' said Scipio upon reaching the command tent.

'So am I.' It was a truthful answer at least. She was about to say more when the low growl emitted by the dormant flayed ones grew into a shrieking cacophony. Several of Jynn's men were sick, some wept openly. It took all of her resolve not to break down too.

'What is it?' she asked, her hands pressed to her ears.

Scipio exchanged a knowing look with Largo and said, 'Time for us to leave.'

He recognised that sound and as they fled back down the mountain, headed for what she assumed was an army of Space Marines somewhere below, she heard Largo mutter to himself.

'It's not dead.'

CHAPTER THIRTEEN

FEAR SATURATED DAMNOS. It permeated its air, its rock and ate away at its people like a cancer. Their screams, their plaintive moaning, their abject grief was an urgent throb at the back of the Librarian's mind.

Tigurius was a supreme psyker, the most accomplished of his Chapter, perhaps of any Chapter. There were others with power, of course: hooded Ezekiel, enigmatic Vel'cona, dreaded Mephiston. All were masters of their art but Tigurius was of the Ultramarines, the purest of all Space Marines, and his abilities were prodigious. Even so, he struggled to find a path through the necron shroud and the fear they propagated.

His mind had touched that of the necrons. It found only infinite darkness and endless hate. There was something buried in that well of nothingness, a warning; he felt certain of it. Without knowing why, he realised it was important and that by not seeking the truth of that vision he would be allowing some heinous evil to pass. Tigurius had fortified himself, performed the many rituals and psychic mantras designed to steel his mind against any potential aggressors. The Herald was strong, far more potent than he had first realised. Tigurius resolved that this time he would be prepared.

Inscribed in the ice with the pommel of his force staff were three concentric rings. Double-banded, he had also wrought sigils of warding and aversion to bind them together. Tigurius crouched down in the centre, his eyes closed, and tried to ride the darkling waves of his subconscious.

Everlasting night filled his mind, the fearful voices of the humans pushed to the fringes and no longer a distraction. He went deeper and fashioned a psychic beacon that he attached around the Hood of Hellfire like a halo. Still, the darkness would not yield. Landscapes resolved below him as he soared across Damnos as a mental projection of himself. It was grey and bland, the life had left it.

Was this a vision of the future? Was he witnessing their ultimate failure?

Something glowed up ahead and Tigurius soared towards it. Psychic winds buffeted him, tried to throw him off course and dash him against the rising mountains on either side. He renewed his efforts, making his body into an arrow that sliced the air apart and cut through the tempest.

For a moment, a tiny light shone below him but it was fleeting and quickly snuffed out. The glow ahead intensified, turning from a phosphorescent white into a sickly emerald. Too late, Tigurius realised the danger he was in and tried to flee. The light became a blazing green orb that reached for him with the tendrils of its light.

One caressed the Librarian's arm and pain, hot and incandescent, fed into his body. His heart was thundering, a dull ache filled his head and a keening wail deafened his thoughts.

Must return...

All his efforts were focussed on getting back but something was stretching the psychic landscape below, reshaping it so the distance became lightyears instead of leagues. Behind him, the baleful sun rose further and its tendrils grew with its influence.

They lashed at the Librarian like the appendages of some ocean-borne beast, a kraken or leviathan of old. Tigurius was forced to weave and pin wheel and dart as the sparrow eludes the eagle. Though he had not moved from his chosen spot since the vigil began, he still felt the physical exertion of his efforts. Mind and body were concomitant aspects of most beings – one affected the other. At that moment as he angled through the mental sky, his mind was being put to the sternest test and it visited that self-same tension upon his body.

Back at his vigil point, Tigurius had blood in his mouth and a tremor in his limbs.

Maintain focus...

Below, grey mountains and cities became monuments of emerald and obelisks of necron devotion and servitude.

Death...

The wind promised a certain end should he let the green light touch him.

Only light can outrun light and in so doing bend the laws of time. That revelation prompted a response. Tigurius fashioned his arrowing form into a beam, pure and focussed and so thin it left the baleful sun in its wake. The crouching form of his physical body loomed before him, solace for his mind at last.

Tigurius came to swathed in a feverish sweat. It took a moment to regulate his breathing, another to ensure he had awakened in the physical world and this reality he inhabited was not merely verisimilitude.

The vision was beyond his grasp. It lay behind the emerald sun and the Herald was preventing him from seeing it. With that obstacle alone, Tigurius might have triumphed but combined with the darkness shroud, it was near impossible. He did witness something, however. The snuffed-out light – it was a glimpse of the future. Prescience was guiding him to something, some event yet to transpire. It must be close; otherwise he would not have seen it. Somehow, the keening he had heard was a component of that possible future.

Like the vision, he knew deep down that it was important. That he must act. Though his limbs protested, Tigurius got to his feet and let his instincts pull him. The mountains beckoned. Drifts that had yet to fall upon the lower regions swathed the peaks in a storm. He headed upwards, leaving his battle-brothers behind. They were deep in the valley, monitoring the Thanatos Hills. Urgency governed the Librarian's step – there was no time to summon the other Ultramarines, no time at all.

PRAXOR ADVANCED THROUGH the ruins slowly and carefully. He crushed something underfoot and looked down.

It was a bent piece of flat metal, frozen solid and cracked down the middle. Frost-edged letters were described on it in Gothic script.

'Arcona City,' said Etrius. His voice was low and sombre as if he were touring a mausoleum.

In many respects, he was.

Praxor assembled the fractured letters into a more meaningful arrangement and nodded. Kellenport really was the last human bastion on Damnos.

The Ultramarines line was well dispersed. Each of the cobalt giants kept a wary eye on the way ahead, watching the ruins for hidden threats. According to reports, too many had already fallen to necron ambush. Sicarius led from the front, as he always did, his Lions of Macragge alongside him. The stretched battle line was a deliberate strategy from the captain. Not only did it make it easier for the Ultramarines to pick their way through the rough ground, they'd also present a harder target for the mass fire of the necrons. Once the storm hit, it would present the illusion that a larger force was arrayed against them too. Engagement would happen soon, but they kept the pace even so Atavian and Tirian could keep up.

The Devastator squads occupied one end of the line. Heavy bolters and plasma cannons were low-slung on their cumbersome rigs. Too weighty for a human to bear alone, the Space Marines hefted them with relative ease. The missile launchers and lascannons, being shoulder-mounted, were pointed down and steadied by the gunner's other hand. Ponderous but implacable, the Dreadnoughts marched with the Devastators. Their cannons were simply a part of their bodies, whirring and auto-targeting as they scanned the immediate area. As soon as battle was joined, these heavy guns would close ranks and present a concentrated volley of fire to hold the necrons' attention.

Just as Sicarius had predicted, the storm was rolling in. It began a half-kilometre back, the incessant ice flurries getting thicker and faster by the minute. There came a sweeping veil of finer snow in their wake, fogging the air and veneering the forlorn ruins still further.

Praxor moved on. 'Tactica briefings suggest there was a garrison here at the start of the war,' he said to Aristaeus down the comm-feed.

'There was... before the city was left to rot in the wake of necron victory. Look at the earth banks around the ruins, brother-sergeant.'

Praxor did. What he had initially mistaken for emplacements and earthworks, he now saw for what they truly were. Fused by ice to the very bulwarks they were sworn to protect were hundreds upon hundreds of Guardsmen, frozen forever in the moments of their deaths.

The necrons had turned this once proud Imperial city into a bombed-out mess. It was a grim place now, inhabited by ghosts and their terrified memories. Had he been anything other than Adeptus Astartes, Praxor might have quailed at this realisation.

'Apparently, Arcona was once a key city on Damnos,' added Aristaeus.

Praxor's mood was as cold as the weather. 'Looks like every other ruin on this hollow world.'

They were making steady progress across a roadway that had suffered least in the bombardment. Only part of its surface was cratered and it was still navigable. The quiet gave Praxor too much time with his thoughts. Even the thickening snowfall failed to smother them and he railed against the doubts plaguing him.

I am Adeptus Astartes. I am without fear, unaffected by doubt!

His misgivings weren't so easily silenced, though. Captain Sicarius was an incredible warrior, the greatest Praxor had known. In his presence, a warrior of

Ultramar felt invincible, became capable of feats even a Space Marine would think impossible. He had… an *aura* about him that was undeniable. Yet he was relentless, even reckless. Heedless of casualties or cost, he would pursue his plans and vendettas until they were achieved or he was dead. In a perverse way, it was this obsessive, mercurial nature that made him the hero he was. It was also why he garnered voices of dissent within the Chapter.

Praxor was torn. He had not believed he'd ever think this way, but here on Damnos… this was beyond what the Second had ever faced before. He was not superstitious but Praxor couldn't deny the sense of foreboding that was building steadily within him. He didn't like the sensation; it felt almost treasonous.

Less able to pick their way through the denser rubble, the Dreadnoughts had shifted position in the battle line to walk along the roadway. It brought Agrippen close to Praxor and he nodded to the ancient warrior when he joined them.

Ahead, the Lions grew distant as they forged off with their captain. Sicarius was ever eager to be the first to battle and kept a close counsel with his command squad. Save for Argonan, who had died in the landings, he had yet to lose a single one of his chosen Ultramarines.

'They are a breed apart from the rest of us.' It came out more ruefully than Praxor had intended.

'And yet you aspire to join their ranks.'

Praxor glanced at Agrippen but the hulking Dreadnought was unreadable. The words simply emerged from his vox-speakers as fact. 'No. I am proud to serve as the sergeant of the Shieldbearers. It is my honour and oath to the Chapter.'

'I don't doubt it, brother. But I know your service record. You and the Shieldbearers are almost always leading the line, the first into any engagement, always at the forefront of our assaults. Some of a more cynical nature might suggest you were trying to prove something.'

Insulted, Praxor's voice took on a hard edge that he was careful to monitor in the face of the venerable Agrippen. 'Only my unswerving loyalty and dedication to the Ultramarines.'

'Do you think that is in question, brother?'

'Is this really the time for such a conversation, on the cusp of battle as we are?'

'Tell me of a better time to discuss honour and courage than before going into war against our enemies,' said Agrippen. 'But you are avoiding my question.'

Praxor left a long pause. He did not find the answer easy. 'Perhaps. There are times when I have questioned.'

'At Ghospora, a campaign over a century old.' It was a statement, not a suggestion.

'You of all of us, venerable one, should know that time is immaterial when concerning matters of honour.'

'Aye, I do. It displeased you that your captain left you behind?'

'It stunned and humbled me,' Praxor admitted. 'It felt as if I were being punished, though I did not know why.'

'Humility is as important a lesson as learning how to wield a gladius properly or fight in squad with your brothers.'

Praxor nodded and saw the wisdom in the Dreadnought's words.

The roadway was coming to an end. They were deep into Arcona City now and the drifts were coming down in swathes. Even through the blizzard, Praxor could see the necron phalanxes manoeuvring to intercept them. It wouldn't be long.

'Before we go to battle, I must ask you something, Agrippen,' Praxor said, voicing his mind as he had wanted to since they'd made planetfall.

'Speak. I shall answer if I can, brother.'

'Are you here to watch for Agemman's interests? Is what they say in the senate true?'

'As all should do, I serve the Chapter alone and my Lord Calgar.' Agrippen was stern but there was no hint of reproach in his modulated diction. 'I possess the wisdom of centuries and all I see are two great heroes, dissimilar in method but equal in courage and honour.'

'In the senate, I have heard talk from Agemman's ambassadors of Sicarius overreaching himself.'

'He is daring and innovative,' Agrippen conceded.

'But there is concern that this will go too far and of the consequences when it does.'

'And how does our Lord Calgar respond to such concerns?'

'He is not present. His voice is absent from proceedings.'

'And what does that tell you, brother?'

Humbled again in the time it takes to field-strip a bolter, Praxor decided he would speak less to Dreadnoughts in future. Their logic was as redoubtable as their armoured bodies. 'That I should not listen to Chapter politics.'

'And what do you think, Praxor Manorian? Do you think Cato Sicarius, your captain, overreaches himself?'

Praxor's gaze went to the Lions out of reflex. Sicarius was as fine a warrior and a captain as there was in the Chapter. Perhaps he was even the best they had.

'Until now, no.'

'And now?'

'He does things, formulates tactics and executes plans that I could never even conceive of.'

'That is why he is captain of the Second. It's why his legend will endure long after he is dust. But you haven't answered my question again.'

Praxor bowed his head. His answer was forestalled by Sicarius's voice blasting over the comm-feed.

'Ultramarines! We are engaging!'

CHAPTER FOURTEEN

Sporadic gauss-fire erupted across the ruins, forcing the Space Marines to hunch over. It kicked up snow and fragmented rubble but missed the Ultramarines who advanced steadily, returning fire. Bolter flashes lit up the icy gloom in retaliatory bursts and spread the necrons' aim across the line so that no one part of it was ever under heavy barrage.

A blanket of snow and ice rolled over the battlefield, carried by a biting wind. Neither necron nor Ultramarine felt it, their metal bodies and their armour protecting them, but it made targeting more difficult.

'Holding positions!' shouted Praxor, prompted by a rune-signal on his retinal display. The Shieldbearers adopted firing postures. Farther up the roadway, the Lions had slowed to allow the rest of the company to catch up.

Sustained bolter fire came from the more advanced tactical squads, punctuated by plasma bursts and missile expulsions. At the end of the line, the Devastators unleashed their guns. A heavy bolter salvo filled the air with the dense *chug-chank* of high-velocity shells. Missiles boomed from their tubes. Plasma and lascannons spat incandescent death in a series of bright lances. The storm made it difficult to tell easily, but the necron frontliners were being torn apart by the fusillade.

'Keep it up,' ordered Daceus, shouting between bolter bursts. 'Make them pay for every damned step.'

It was as intense as any battlefield Praxor had fought on. His warrior-spirit soared. The line was dug in well, spread thin and hurting the necron phalanxes. But they were not like most enemies and could absorb a lot of punishment. Even obscured by the fog, their numbers were staggering too.

'Seems we have poked the nest,' offered Krixous.

'And they respond to the threat,' Praxor replied, pointing. He opened the comm-feed. 'Captain, monolith rerouting on our position.'

He saw Sicarius turn towards the floating pyramid of living metal moving slowly into a flanking position.

'Maintain fire,' he said. 'We need to draw them on.'

But the necrons had stopped advancing and occupied static positions. A small cohort of elites had joined the raider constructs, their heavier fire swelling the barrage.

Praxor registered a couple of hits on his tactical display but so far no red icons. Several Space Marines were at amber status – injured but still effective.

Elianu Trajan added his voice to the battle, 'Repel them, brothers. Bring down the soulless xenos, hated in all its forms. Do not relent. There is no forgiveness, no quarter. Guilliman is watching!'

He couldn't see the Chaplain – the fog was too thick now – but Praxor noted his position on the tactical map, accompanying Atavian's Devastators. He was advancing swiftly: soon he'd be with the tactical squads. Praxor could almost feel his wrath already.

'POUR IT ON!' yelled Daceus. All the while the shadow of the monolith was getting closer. Still the necrons took the hammering, refusing to move, refusing to commit their command nodes to the fight.

'Do they know our plan, captain?' he asked over the clangour.

Sicarius was adamant. 'Impossible. They are not engaging because of the monolith.' Daceus heard the snarl behind his captain's battle-helm. So far, the captain's objectives were eluding him. The storm was worsening, though. Visibility was weak to poor. If they were going to break off then now was the time.

'We need to destroy that thing. Do you still have your melta bombs, sergeant?'

Daceus let off a burst of bolter fire then nodded.

Sicarius holstered his plasma pistol. 'Give them up.'

Handing them over, Daceus said, 'What are you going to do?'

Mag-locking the additional melta bombs to his armour, Sicarius replied, 'Take out that monolith. Gaius, I'll need your blade.'

The company champion bowed his head. 'I am yours to command, my lord.'

'Captain–' Daceus began.

'It is my duty, sergeant,' he said, and his posture took on a nurturing look. 'I know you would throw yourself into the hells of the warp for me, Daceus. You are more than merely my sergeant – you are my ally, my friend.'

Daceus saluted by slamming his fist against his chest-plate. 'Courage and honour, Cato.'

'Courage and honour, Retius.' It had been many years since the two had exchanged first-name greetings, and never before on the battlefield. There was something about it, and this war, that Daceus did not like. It felt significant in a way, an ending of sorts. It did not portend well.

Sicarius showed none of his sergeant's misgivings. 'You have command. See the plan out.'

Then, together with Gaius, he ran into the fog.

PRAXOR SAW TWO cobalt figures running from the Lions' position. With the adverse weather, he couldn't be sure who they were.

'Brother-sergeant?'

'I don't know, Etrius. Maintain fire.'

Sergeant Daceus's voice crackled over the feed. 'All flanking forces, converge on the Lions' lead. We move now!'

The rest of the command squad broke off from the battle line, headed in the opposite direction to the pair of Ultramarines.

'Temple of Hera,' breathed Praxor. 'It was Captain Sicarius.'

'Guilliman's breath, what is he doing?' asked Krixous.

Though he was saying it, Praxor could still not quite believe it. 'He is living up to his legend, and going to destroy the monolith.'

Etrius was incredulous. 'Alone?'

The reply sounded hollow even to Praxor. 'Gaius Prabian is with him.'

'Make their sacrifice a deed of honour!' boomed Agrippen, plasma cannon pulsing. 'He is Cato Sicarius, High Suzerain, Captain of the Second and Master of the Watch. On this field, he is Guilliman's sword; we are *all*

Guilliman's sword.' The Dreadnought had regrouped with the Devastators and was intensifying fire along with Ultracius.

Praxor found his purpose refocussed after the ancient warrior's words. Sicarius's reckless bravery would not be in vain. In his retinal display, he saw Indomitable was moving. Not to be outdone by Sergeant Solinus, Praxor led the Shieldbearers after them. As they joined up with the Lions, his gaze met Trajan's.

'He has the courage of Invictus and the guile of Galatan. Banish your doubts, brother-sergeant.'

They were moving too swiftly for a long reply, so Praxor merely nodded. Still the necron phalanxes weren't moving, content to hold and defend while their ponderous war engine got into position. If the monolith managed to open up its power matrix in a singular beam-pulse, the plan was finished. Broken off from its phalanx, the machine was fairly isolated but attacking such a thing beggared belief.

'Stay on me! Move as one!' Daceus was keeping the line intact, marshalling the tactical squads into position so they could prosecute Sicarius's plan.

They deviated far from the roadway, which was now wholly occupied by the Devastators and Dreadnoughts. The necrons' reaction to the barrage was feeding more mechanoids into the grinder. Their supplies were endless, their sense of self-preservation obsolete, despite the strange cries that came from each mechanoid as it was struck down. Phase-outs were happening constantly but just as many of the creatures self-repaired and returned to the fight.

The Ultramarines couldn't win by sheer weight of arms – they didn't have enough battle-brothers.

'Any eyes on the command node, yet?' Daceus had

drawn them to halt, out of the firing line and approaching the flank of a necron phalanx exchanging fire with the Space Marine heavy guns. The storm was so thick now, they could only see through their retinal senses or magnoculars.

Solinus was at the scopes, scanning the silver horde. 'Nothing from here.'

On the opposite side, Praxor also returned a negative.

'We need to get into them, force their hand,' said Daceus. He opened the feed. 'All heavies advance and resume fire.'

Praxor watched the line move up through the fog. Agrippen and Ultracius anchored it with Tirian and Atavian's Devastators in the middle. The necron casualties intensified. And with slow inevitability they started to shift.

Daceus grinned ferally, 'That's it, you xenos scum...'

But the attack would still be stalled if the monolith couldn't be destroyed, and without Sicarius they would have little chance of eliminating a necron overlord.

Praxor looked to the looming pyramid. Its capacitors were wreathed with emerald lightning, preparing to fire. It would need to be soon.

'KEEP LOW, BROTHER.' Gauss-beams flashed overhead, forcing Sicarius into a stooping run.

Gaius Prabian kept his combat shield up and close to his body. Several blasts had already skimmed off its surface.

The power armour of both Ultramarines was pitted and scored from where they'd run the necron gauntlet. Ahead, the shadow of the monolith finally reached them.

It was immense, a horrifying testament to the

mechanoids' power. In truth, Sicarius believed the necrons to be much more than mere robots. They were something else entirely. Something ancient.

Although Arcona City had been pummelled into dust during the necron invasion, some ruined structures were still standing. Using the fog to cover their movements, the two Ultramarines skirted around to the monolith's flank. Its gauss-arc projectors were patrolling the immediate vicinity but looked incapable of firing whilst the machine was feeding energy to its crystal power matrix. Close up they got a chance to see the shimmering unreality of the monolith's surface and the eldritch sigils engraved upon it. Truly, this was an engine of evil.

Sicarius noticed the crystal at the pyramid's summit start to glow brighter as the capacitors fed it power from their lightning field. Its power matrix was coming on-line.

A small retinue of raider constructs protected the monolith, moving in step with it, their weapons ready but not yet firing. In his time as a warrior of Ultramar, Sicarius had prosecuted many tank ambushes. An armoured column was a fearsome force in battle; its guns were powerful and its resilience potent against all but the heaviest weapons. But it was also relatively slow and cumbersome. Surgical strikes by squads bearing armour-busting grenades were deadly to tank formations. This monolith was no tank, and Sicarius suspected its strange surface would be resistant to most weapons, but he was determined to at least neutralise if not destroy it utterly.

A commando move such as the one he was about to attempt didn't exactly follow the strictures of the Codex but then Sicarius had his own way of interpreting

Guilliman's writings. He hoped the primarch would approve of his ingenuity and bravura.

'Champion,' he said, resting a hand on Gaius's shoulder guard as they crouched in the ruins and peered out at the passing monolith, 'you are my unsheathed sword.'

Gaius nodded slowly, his eyes on the raiders. There were only five of them. He ignited the blade of his power sword and it hummed hungrily.

Before he let him go, Sicarius added, 'Beware that portal at the front. Only Hera knows where it might lead you. Courage and honour.'

Gaius growled back through the vox-grille of his ornate helm. 'Courage and honour, my lord.'

The two then split apart, Sicarius headed around what appeared to be the rear of the monolith and Gaius engaging from the front.

The Champion vaulted the ruins and cried, 'For Ultramar!'

TURNING AS ONE, the raider screen opened fire with their gauss-weapons. Gaius Prabian was an experienced warrior. As Champion he had slain countless warlords, alien potentates and demagogues. Before Damnos, he had never engaged necrons. Held in an aggressive gladiatorial position, his combat shield absorbed much of the mechanoids' fire and enabled him to run and defend at the same time. Several beams lanced his shoulder guard and greaves, but he ignored the damage runes flashing on his retinal display. Perhaps realising hand-to-hand combat was inevitable, the closest of the raiders stopped firing. Instead, it brandished its gauss-flayer like a club, intending to cut the Ultramarines Champion apart with its barrel-blade.

Gaius's shield broke skeletal teeth and snapped the

DAMNOS

ULTRAMARINES

2ND COMPANY

PICT DATA 22893/DD/35
NECRON WARRIOR
ACCESSING DATA:
DATA RUNE N244 ACTIVE//
PROCESSING....DISPLAYING
THREAT STATUS: HIGH
WEAPON DATA: UNKOWN GAUSS TEK
ADVISORY: DISENGAGE/DELTA TEK

ULTRAMARINES GROUND FORCES
Battle Group: Salvation

Led by Captain Cato Sicarius, this portion of the Ultramarines' strike force was tasked with the liberation of the only surviving human city on Damnos, Kellenport.

Command Squad 'Lions of Macragge'. Full strength honour guard of Second Company captain. When not under Sicarius's direct orders, led by second-in command Sergeant Daceus.

Chaplain Trajan. Spiritual leader of the Damnos force and successor to the late Chaplain Orad.

Brother Agrippen. First Company Venerable Dreadnought representing the support of Captain Agemman on Damnos.

Brother Agnathio. Dreadnought who once fought at Chundrabad in 141.M36, stayed behind at the defence of the Kellenport walls.

Brother Ultracius. Dreadnought who fought in the Pyra Crusades, advanced to join Sicarius once the landing zone was secure.

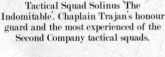

Tactical Squad Solinus 'The Indomitable'. Chaplain Trajan's honour guard and the most experienced of the Second Company tactical squads.

Tactical Squad Manorian 'The Shield Bearers'. Vanguard fighters who were at Captain Sicarius's right-hand throughout the Damnos Campaign.

Tactical Squad Fennion 'The Immortals'. Led the human defenders in defence of the city walls and formed the conscript veterans, the 'One Hundred'.

Devastator Squad Tirian 'Guilliman's Hammer'. Anti-infantry specialists who fought at the last stand at Arcona City.

Devastator Squad Atavian 'The Titan Slayers'. Anti-tank specialists responsible for the destruction of several key enemy targets, including necron monoliths and heavy destroyers.

Battle Group: Heaven Strike

Led by Chief Librarian Tigurius, this portion of the Ultramarines' strike force was tasked with the destruction of the necron artillery situated in the Thanatos Hills.

Tactical Squad Vorolanus 'The Thunderbolts'. Reconnaissance and scouting specialists who unlocked the assault vector into the Thanatos Hills.

Drop pods were utilised to deploy the entire Ultramarines ground force and included a number of unmanned Deathwind variants.

Tactical Squad Octavian 'Swords of Judgement'. Second Company's pre-eminent marksmen and one-shot kill specialists.

Tactical Squad Vandar 'The Victors'. Led by the youngest and least experienced tactical squad sergeant, who is also recipient of the Iron Halo.

Assault Squad Ixion ' Macragge's Avengers'. Re-tasked by Sicarius to shore up the main assault and neutralise necron destroyer squadrons.

Assault Squad Strabo 'The Heroes of Selonopolis'. Re-tasked by Sicarius to shore up the main assault and disrupt necron infantry cohorts.

Chief Librarian Tigurius

Leader of the Thanatos Hills battle group, Tigurius is also the Chief Librarian of the Chapter and Master of the Ultramarines Librarius.

DAMNOS
PLANETARY MAP

Mandos Prime – Geothermic fusion stations under the purview of Mechanicus Magos Karnak suffer critical failure after increased seismic activity, heralding the xenos invasion.

Damnos Prime – Several manufactorum sites of Damnos Prime are utterly destroyed by the necron advance. Ark-Guard forces are unable to meet the threat and swiftly eradicated.

Halaheim – All hands at Dagoth Station at Halaheim are massacred. A pict-cast caught by a servitor drone escapes ahead of the comm shroud but only foments greater anxiety in the surviving Imperial resistance.

Tyrrean Ocean – Upon crossing the largest water mass on Damnos, the necrons drain much of the ocean into an extra-dimensional sinkhole, turning it into a barren wasteland. All fighting vessels still operational are beached, their crews slaughtered.

Damnos Secundus, Tertius, Southern Polar Bastions, Fourth-Bloc Mining Station – Attacks break out across multiple locations. As the necron comm shroud moves southwards, military coordination between Imperial Guard regiments is rendered impossible. Resistance is quickly crushed.

Zephyr Monastery – All priests, serfs and helots, together with relics, basilica and all religious icons, are lost in a single necron energy pulse.

Arcona City – Secondary Damnosian settlement is subdued, its army decimated, within hours of the necron's arrival. Scattered damage reports indicate heavy and sustained bombardment.

Thanatos Refinery – Total destruction of refinery complex by a necron splinter force moving into the Thanatos Hills for purposes unknown. Area suffers from a total comms blackout more pervasive than experienced previously.

Kellenport – The last major city of Damnos is besieged by an immense necron force. Despite the presence of the battleship *Nobilis* the city is swiftly overrun and Imperial forces retreat into the inner bastion walls.

Crastia Shipyards – Remaining star-port is rendered 'out of commission' and overrun by subterranean necron forces. All efforts to retake ended with failure. Fate of garrison stationed at Crastia: unknown.

necron's corded neck as he thrust it into the creature's face. The head was hanging by a piece of cabling at an odd angle when the mechanoid crumpled. A second creature Gaius cut down with his power sword, slicing through weapon barrel and then the necron itself. The wound was catastrophic and it phased out. The third and fourth were dispatched by fierce sweeps of his blade – the air hummed and crackled as the weapon bisected it. The fifth he battered with the shield. He was a force of will, a deadly guardian intent on his mission. All three necrons phased out. He stalked over to the last, the one he'd injured but not quite enough. Already, the necron's broken neck was repairing itself. Gaius slammed the edge of his shield against the cabling that was holding the mechanoid's head to its body, severing it.

'Stay dead,' he spat, and the last of the retinue phased out...

...Only to return, or so it appeared, through the portal – five more raider constructs, carbon copies of the first. They moved slowly, resolving first as dark shadows in the pooling emerald light, then as actual beings of metal and hate.

Gaius Prabian faced them down and, touching the blade of his power weapon to his forehead, saluted.

No, he had never fought necrons before. It was to be a challenge.

'I am the unsheathed sword,' he vowed, and charged.

A BATTLE TANK had flanks, it had hatches and tracks, it possessed weak points and was forged of metal in a foundry – this monolith was something else. It had no aspects, save perhaps the front and that was only because the emerald portal suggested it together with the direction it moved in. The flanks or rear were merely faces of the pyramid, constructed of some dark pseudo-metal, a substance that didn't appear entirely corporeal or, at least, constant. Looking carefully, Sicarius could see the sides of the monolith rippled, their hue changing in the light like oil upon water. He wasn't even certain that an explosive charge could be attached to its surface, let alone destroy it. Priming a melta bomb, he eyed the gauss-arc projectors. The cannons protruding from the machine swivelled and turned to draw a bead on him and Gaius Prabian but they were powerless as a defensive measure whilst all the monolith's energy was being used to unleash the crystal power matrix.

That situation wouldn't last. Sicarius slammed the first charge against the flank of the machine. It took hold and stuck there. Then he attached another. And another. He planted four melta bombs in total, all of his and Daceus's supply.

A pulse rippled down the side of the monolith as they went off, expelling intense microwaves that the machine seemed to absorb and nullify. Ordinary metal would slough and corrode against a melta bomb, but the material comprising the monolith was much more resistant.

Despite its alien resilience, the combined explosive fury of Sicarius's melta bombs would not be denied and the captain shouted his approval as something in the machine died and it floated slowly to the ground. At its peak, the crystal faded as the charging of the power matrix was forcibly aborted.

'Brother Gaius,' Sicarius ran around to the front of the machine in time to see his Champion destroying the last of the retinue. Even the emerald portal was dormant, revealing bare metal behind it. With its structural integrity damaged, the necron monolith became nothing more than a monument, inert and powerless. At least for now.

'Should we enter?' Gaius pointed his sword at the area where the portal had been. It seemed he intended on cutting their way inside.

'No. We return to the others. We don't know how long the war machine will be offline. Let's make the most of it.'

Mission achieved, they headed back to the line.

Behind his battle-helm Sicarius smiled. Perhaps there was glory to be had on Damnos after all.

SICARIUS'S RETURN WAS heralded with restrained joy. There was no time for celebration. The Devastators and Dreadnoughts were taking a lot of fire. With the monolith neutralised, at least for a time, the others had to press the attack from the flank and cut into the necron horde.

The captain of Second Company lifted his Tempest Blade into the air as the mechanoids advanced into a position where the edge of their formation was exposed.

'There is still no sign of the command node,' Daceus warned.

Sicarius was not about to be denied. 'We can wait no longer.' He slashed his sword down. 'Ultramarines, attack!'

IT WAS INFECTIOUS. Praxor felt the groundswell of strength and righteous anger first in his feet, then his legs until it infused his entire body. Sicarius was the source of that power, he was certain of it. In his presence, it was as if a halo of inner fortitude surrounded them and made them capable of the deeds of legend.

'I am my captain's sword!' he swore, power sword tearing open the first necron in his path even as his bolt pistol shattered a second. All of his doubts, his notions of Sicarius's vainglory, were banished from his mind in that single attack. In their place came an utter certainty that they would triumph; that Cato Sicarius would lead them to glory.

He had never fought harder, neither had the warriors around him. Together with the Lions of Macragge, the Shieldbearers and the Indomitable ripped into the necron flank and sundered it. They were several ranks deep, mechanised limbs and appendages tossed like metal refuse, before the Ultramarines slowed.

'Come to me,' he heard Sicarius rage at the heart of the battle. 'Face me now!'

The captain searched the silver horde for the command node but still it would not present itself. Row upon row of endless necron warriors did instead. The Tempest Blade was reaping a heavy tally, but it could not slay them all. Even the mighty Cato Sicarius could not achieve that feat.

Praxor glanced behind him. They were slowly being surrounded. Even now, some of his warriors had formed a rearguard with battle-brothers from Solinus's squad. In a matter of moments, they would be enveloped.

Trajan was at the front with the Lions, spitting curses and litanies. He would never surrender – he was, in every way, Sicarius's Chaplain. But it occurred to Praxor that there was now a certain futility to this plan. Without sight of the necron overlord the Ultramarines were effectively attacking an infinite production line of necrons. In that, there could be no victory.

In the end, it was Solinus that was the first to break.

'We should retreat,' he said, defending against a flurry of attacks before replying with one of his own. 'There is no glory in this, for Damnos or the Second.'

Smashing necrons with his crozius, Trajan was quick to silence him. 'Hold to your purpose and the orders of your captain. Fight for the glory of Ul–'

A necron blade in his gorget cut the diatribe short. Trajan blasted the creature with his bolt pistol, before dismembering it with his crozius, but could not remove the metal wedged in his neck armour.

The circle of Ultramarines was getting tighter. They were back-to-back now, their gallant charge stalled by the sheer amount of resistance facing them.

Sicarius turned to Daceus. 'Signal the other squads, close and concentrate fire on this part of the line.'

'Our brothers might be hit also, lord,' suggested Venatio. The Apothecary was holding his own, as gifted a warrior as any of the Lions.

Sicarius was quick to counter. 'It's worth the risk. Daceus, give the order.'

'Should I order the Dreadnoughts to engage, also?' came the veteran's gruff reply.

'Negative, they won't reach us in time.' Sicarius sounded angry. 'This isn't working. We're disengaging.' It wasn't an easy decision but the captain of Second didn't like lost causes, nor did he like admitting to them. He opened up the comm-feed to the flanking force. 'Cut a hole through them. Fall back.'

DESPITE HIS DARING actions that neutralised the monolith, despite goading the necron horde into being outflanked, despite everything the plan had failed. Sicarius needed something to strike; something to attack and kill that might make a difference. He could not do that slaying endless hordes of mechanoid warriors. Though it was difficult to admit, he had underestimated the necrons and their forces. He

NICK KYME

resolved not to do so again. He needed greater numbers.

Victory was possible; he felt it in his heart. It could be won at the tip of his Tempest Blade, but for now it eluded him.

Cutting his way back through the necron ranks, one hand dragging an injured Brother Samnite of the Lions, an unpleasant taste filled Sicarius's mouth. It was at once acerbic and unfamiliar.

It was defeat.

IN THE CHAOS of the melee there is little time for thought. Instinct takes over. It is a part of every Space Marine's genetic coding; it is the reason for his existence, his purpose and God-Emperor given duty. War is not just their craft, it is their sacred calling.

So it was for Praxor as he fought his way back through the horde that had slammed around the Ultramarines like a vice. The warriors of Ultramar had sprung the ambush but they were the ones caught in the necrons' trap. These things, with their cold logic, their calculating processes, could not be fought like an ordinary foe. And they were endless; at least, it felt that way as Praxor's shoulder burned with the continuous hacking through living metal.

Trajan punctuated his every blow with grating vitriol. The Chaplain had removed the metal sliver from his neck, or rather it had phased out along with the necron it belonged to, but it had left him with a razored harshness to his voice. If anything, it only made his wrath even more imposing. These realisations would come upon Praxor later, after the maddened fight to break out of the necron phalanx was done.

Punching through the other side, mechanoids exploding dangerously around them with the heavies' suppressing fire, an ordered retreat was put into effect. Veteran-Sergeant Daceus was first out, battering his way through with his power fist. He marshalled the line, setting up a fire base of bolters to open the gate of the trap for the others. Slowly, the Ultramarines emerged. Mercifully none fell, but Samnite was injured and so too were three of Solinus's men. Praxor had been spared more casualties.

The mist thickened further still, enabling the Ultramarines to make a tactical retreat without pursuit. Sicarius was the last to leave the fight. His reticence to do so and his rage were almost palpable.

In truth, all of the Ultramarines felt it.

'Retreat to the line,' he snarled when they'd put some distance between the phalanx. He caught Daceus up. 'Have the Devastators and Dreadnoughts begin a staggered retreat. We're withdrawing from Arcona City.'

Snow and fog swallowed the Ultramarines. It took the necrons too, who merely continued their implacable advance. They already had forces headed to Kellenport, a phalanx of monoliths. Some of the other phalanxes would reroute there too.

'Are we regrouping with the others?' asked Daceus. In the background, Venatio supported Brother Samnite. Gaius Prabian kept a wary eye on the fog as if expecting a necron to spring forth at any moment, but none did. The mechanoids had even ceased the gauss-barrage.

Sicarius sheathed his blade. He took a while to do it and for a moment Praxor thought he might plunge back into the fog and seek his prey anew. 'No, the necron artillery *must* be destroyed. I want heavy armour and the guns of the *Valin's Revenge* on these metal heretics. But the assault squads should be reappropriated. We need to attack and withdraw, disrupt their formations, strike at the weakest points. Heavy punishment hasn't worked, so we sting them with punitive raids instead.'

'Lord Tigurius won't be pleased, captain.'

Sicarius was remorseless, 'He will submit to my orders. The Librarian's pleasure is not my concern. Make it so, Daceus.'

The veteran-sergeant saluted, opening up the long-range feed as they began the march back towards Kellenport. He only got a few footsteps when Agrippen spoke up.

'Are we still trying to win this war?'

All eyes went to Sicarius who'd turned at the Dreadnought's voice to face him. He removed his battle-helm so the venerable warrior could see his eyes. 'Of course. If victory is possible then we must strive to achieve it.'

'Though I serve the Chapter eternal and would glorify it with every deed, I can see no victory here.'

It was a bold statement. Only Agrippen as one of the First and a revered Ultramarines veteran could have made it. The old and wise had ever had the right to challenge the decisions of the young and reckless.

'There is,' said Sicarius with finality. He replaced his battle-helm, the last part of his statement grating through the vox-grille. 'I will make it thus.'

Agrippen bowed. If he had any further doubts, he did not voice them but merely continued the march instead. Praxor had no idea if the Dreadnought was assuaged. When Agrippen had spoken up, he'd at first thought this was the moment when Agemman, through his venerable champion, would make his feelings known about the captain of Second. In the middle of a campaign, the timing would have been inauspicious but seldom were the moments when Sicarius could be brought to task.

The words, though not as inflammatory as they might

have been, lingered though. They resonated inside Praxor's skull, kindling the sparks of his own uncertainty. He wished they were not on the battlefield, though perhaps that was where the instincts to follow and obey were simplest to adhere to. Trajan was an iron-hard bastard but he was their Chaplain. His counsel would be greatly appreciated. In lieu of that, Praxor opted to be pragmatic. He organised his squad into the march, silently proud at their battle-conduct. It was a defeat, but the Shieldbearers had acquitted themselves well. Even still, it was hard fought for little to no gain. Heading out, he rotated his shoulder to work out some of the muscle ache.

'Should I summon Apothecary Venatio?'

Praxor winced as he snapped his dislocated shoulder into place. 'No, Krixous,' he said. 'It's just been a long time since I hurt this much after a fight.'

CHAPTER FIFTEEN

Aboard the Valin's Revenge, *two years and nine months before the Damnos Incident*

BY THE TIME Praxor left the battle-cages, most of his brothers had gone to their cells for nocturnal meditation. True, some still trained on the shooting ranges or otherwise occupied their minds towards the betterment of making war in the Emperor's name, but the way back to his dormitory was largely empty.

The Cullinar Suppression had gone well. A task force of Ultramarines, on direct orders from Lord Calgar himself, had been sent to the little known planetoid of Balthar IV to eradicate an uprising of the tau in one of its principal cities. Cullinar was wretched with xenos, who'd managed to sway a significant amount of the human population with their lies including much of the noble family that ruled it. All efforts by the Vardia Imperial Guard 15th and 18th battalions had failed to break the will of the xenos, whose influence had spread to neighbouring enclaves. Allow them to go unchallenged for much longer and a planet-wide seccession from the Imperium was in danger of becoming a reality.

The arrival of the Ultramarines put a stop to that. Breaking into fire-teams, they cleansed the avenues and excised the root of alien taint within three days. Not all of the Second had been chosen for the duty, which had also included elements of the First Company veterans and Tenth Company Scouts. Praxor had neither seen nor heard Torias Telion at the battle, but knew the Master Scout was behind enemy lines pulling the strings and blowing things up. He suspected the explosion that had swept in a firestorm through the sewer lines where Praxor had then led the Shieldbearers to kill the tau ambassador was caused by the invisible hand of Torias Telion.

Scipio had fought with the Master Scout at Black Reach. Most only glimpsed him in shadows or on the training fields, for Telion was a supreme mentor within the Chapter. Praxor admitted, shamefully, to a pang of jealousy on that account. He had bled with the Master Scout on Cullinar, but had never seen him. He had seen the Terminators, led by Helios, and was as impressed as he'd been on Black Reach when they'd joined bolter and blade together.

Sicarius had not led the assault; rather it was Agemman that had captained the battle force in a methodical cleanse and burn approach. It was painstaking and exacting, where Sicarius would have been direct and brutal. The war had taken longer, Praxor suspected, than it would have with Sicarius but the risks were less and the results almost guaranteed. He would have preferred to serve his liege-lord but Praxor was still ebullient after their victory, and celebrated by performing seven hours of training katas upon return to the *Valin's Revenge*.

Agemman's strategy was utterly unlike Sicarius's, though adherence to the Codex ensured certain basic similarities, but these were almost unnoticeable due to the way they were applied. The experience had led Praxor to consider observing some of the senate sessions when afforded the opportunity. They were headed back to Macragge for an official ceremony: Mikael Fabian, the captain of Third, and Master of the Arsenal, was to be honoured.

Ultramarines vaunted the successes of their Chapter; they did so proudly and in full voice. All who could attend would be expected to be there.

On his way across the flight deck where the Thunderhawks slumbered, their landing stanchions mag-locked to the ground, and mindless servitors toiled, Praxor saw another Space Marine.

He was also not wearing his power armour, but instead had a blue surplice with a cowl to hide his face. His bulk and manner marked him out as one of the Chapter.

'Brother,' he began in idle greeting.

When the Ultramarine looked up, he realised it was Scipio.

Praxor's mood hardened to steel in an instant. He had witnessed firsthand lately Scipio's disregard in battle. To Praxor's mind, there was a difference between insane bravery and just plain insanity. 'You are no longer in Venatio's care then.'

Scipio stopped in front of his old friend. 'I left the Apothecarion a few hours ago.' He looked Praxor up and down, noting the training fatigues and half-carapace he was wearing. 'I see you still live in the battle-cages when not at war.'

Praxor raised an eyebrow. He felt a challenge in his

brother's tone. 'And is that something to frown upon? Does it not make me a better warrior in the eyes of my captain and my Chapter Master?'

'It depends on your motives, brother.'

'And you suspect them to be less than admirable, do you, Scipio? It sounds as if you have decided my reason already and deemed it an unworthy one.'

'A selfish one, perhaps.'

Praxor licked his lips. It took all of his self-control not to unsheathe his rudius and smack Scipio around the head with it. 'You were in that sus-an membrane coma for several weeks so I shall allow for your behaviour. Do not forget your place, brother.'

'I am of sound mind, I can assure you, Praxor.' Scipio drew back the hood. His eyes were diamond-hard. He wasn't about to back down. 'And we are both sergeants. *You* perhaps have loftier designs.'

Now Praxor let his anger show. 'What is your issue, brother? Ever since Karthax you have carried your aggression like a clenched fist aimed at whoever or whatever displeases you. Is that anger now focussed on me?'

'Seekers of personal glory will only ever find the means to undo themselves,' Scipio spat.

'What is that supposed to mean?'

'They are the words of Orad. You should know them, brother.'

'What? What are you even doing here, Scipio? Were you awaiting my arrival so you could pick a fight?'

Scipio's mouth was a hard line. He gave nothing away, so Praxor was forced to continue without his participation.

He leaned in close. 'Do you know why I go to the battle-cages, why I seek to perfect my warrior-self? I shall tell you, Scipio, I shall do so because you and I are brothers, we are friends. I do it to become strong, in mind and in body. You cannot blame yourself for what happened. It was frailty that Karthax exposed. It was a tragedy, but one brought about through weakness.'

'So I have heard you claim… *several* times.'

Praxor frowned, incredulous.

'I awoke from my coma days ago.' There was a grating undercurrent to Scipio's voice. Whether it was caused by his ire or his injuries, Praxor didn't know. He went on. 'Venatio had me confined to the Apothecarion while my wounds healed–'

'A pity whatever damage was done to your head and humours was not also allowed convalescence,' Praxor interrupted. He was in no mood for Scipio's misplaced anger, but when he went to move around him the other Ultramarine stepped in his path. 'You are rash, brother. That's why you spent time on the Apothecary's table. I would counsel caution in your future actions.' He was no longer referring to campaigning, Praxor made that much obvious with his tone.

Scipio's blood was up, though. He would not be denied this reckoning, 'While my wounds healed,' he said again, 'I heard talk of Karthax and Orad.'

'I did not speak ill of him, brother.' There was a warning in Praxor's voice, one that suggested he did not enjoy the inference Scipio was making.

'Weakness, was it? Is that why he fell?'

Praxor clenched his fists. There was no avoiding this now. Tensions had run high between them for months. It had to come out; this was as good a way as any.

'You know the answer to that. Now,' he added levelly, 'do what you came here to do.'

Scipio roared and threw himself at Praxor. Anger

fuelled a rain of blows that battered the other Ultramarine before he could reply or throw up any defence. Still pumped and alert from the battle-cages, Praxor blocked a frenzied punch to the side of the head, deflecting it with his forearm before planting a jab in Scipio's stomach. An elbow-smash to follow crunched Scipio's shoulderblade and the combination was finished by a blade-kick to the ribs.

Scipio tumbled and rolled, grunting in pain, but got his footing quickly.

'You're still weak from the Apothecarion,' said Praxor, wheeling around Scipio's flank, forcing him to rotate. 'Let your wounds heal and we'll settle this in the battle-cages in the proper manner.'

Scipio shook his head. 'We do it now.'

Praxor scowled. 'You are a fool, Scipio. A slave to your emotions and your anger.'

'Are you afraid, brother?' The curled lip made Scipio's face ugly in the half-light. There was something dark inside his eyes.

Praxor shook his head – it *was* inevitable then – drew the rudius and tossed it aside. This was a fist fight. He would not dishonour it further by using a weapon, even a blunted one, against an unarmed combatant. 'You want me to break you, brother, I *will* break you!'

Scipio charged, but Praxor was quick to avoid his battering ram of an attack.

'Reckless...' He slammed a fist into Scipio's flank. A chop to the side of his brother's neck paralysed the nerves and sent pain sparks into his eyes. 'And ill-considered.'

They faced off, circling one another. Despite the inappropriate setting, the hangar deck made for a perfect arena. Their audience, the servitors, continued their labours without pause or regard. The long shadows of the Thunderhawks bathed the combatants in darkness. Scipio was breathing hard, belaboured by his injuries. Praxor had yet to break sweat.

'Where is the warrior Torias Telion has spoken so highly of?' he goaded.

Scipio came on again. He feinted, drawing Praxor's guard, and landed a heavy blow on the other sergeant's cheek. A head-butt brought white dagger-flashes to Praxor's eyes and he staggered.

'He's right here,' Scipio promised and hit him again.

Despite his earlier advantage, Praxor was being worn down by his brother's fury and was forced back a step. Sensing his superiority, Scipio leapt and came at Praxor with his fists linked in an overhead smash. Had the blow connected it would have probably shattered his clavicle but Praxor side stepped out of harm's way, punching Scipio hard in the gut with the same motion. The other sergeant grunted then choked as the air blasted from his lungs.

Expecting that to be the end of it, Praxor relented but Scipio whirled around and caught him with a wild hay-maker. He felt the bone crack and reeled at the force of the impact. An uppercut from Scipio's other hand glanced Praxor's chin. He had enough presence of mind to retreat defensively, so the blow was telling. Throwing up his arms, Praxor hit the side of Scipio's head with the flat of his hands, stunning him. Dizziness made the other sergeant sluggish and Praxor used it to his gain, blocking another all-or-nothing swing and driving a knee into his brother's stomach. Seizing Scipio's wrist, he bent it around and used his weight to push him down to his knees. The other arm he wrapped around the neck and squeezed.

'Yield!' He was breathing hard, partly from exertion, partly from anger.

Scipio still struggled.

'You've lost, brother. Give it up.'

Still Scipio fought. He made enough room for an elbow strike to Praxor's gut and drove it back hard.

Praxor grunted, hurt, but held on.

'Weakness,' he hissed between clenched teeth, spitting phlegm. 'Yes, you're right, brother. It was weakness.'

Scipio roared, anger lending him strength, but Praxor didn't let up. Rather, he pressed further.

'But who is weak, now?' He wrenched Scipio's neck when he tried to move. By now the air was being cut off to his lungs, though a Space Marine could last much longer than an ordinary man in a choke-hold – even one made by another Space Marine.

Praxor leaned in so he could speak directly into Scipio's ear, 'You are a patrician son of Ultramar, an inheritor of Guilliman,' he said, almost pleading. 'This does not befit your Chapter or your heritage. Don't dishonour that any further.' His grip lessened, allowing Scipio to speak, albeit in a rasp.

'I have no honour left.'

Praxor loosened his arm further. Scipio had stopped struggling now and hung like dead weight in his arms. 'What are you talking about?'

'Do you know what happened on Karthax?'

Praxor's eyes narrowed in confusion. 'A tragedy, the death of a hero – we lost Orad.'

'It was more than that. No one else knows… No one but the captain and maybe Daceus.'

'What happened?' A strange sensation was working its way up Praxor's spine as he asked the question. He couldn't quite place it; it had been a long time since he'd experienced the emotion or one similar.

Scipio's confession was delivered with sobs for a fallen brother. 'I killed him, Praxor. I killed Orad.'

'WE NEED TO move, now!'

Scipio was waving the human guerrilla fighters farther down the mountain pass, but his attention was fixed on the upper slopes behind them.

It was Largo who had spotted it, skulking in the peaks, concealed by the drifts. Not content with its feast, it still craved their skin and had come to claim it. What was more, the flayed lord was not alone – it had brought its cohorts with it. Like slavering dogs, ruddy with the life-blood of others, they galloped down through the icy crags on all fours. A wave of sheer terror had swept through the humans upon the first sighting. Men and women, those that were left of Captain Evvers's group, had fled wildly. One had even pitched off the side of the mountain in his haste to escape. The scream only lasted a few seconds before it was lost to the wind or snuffed by the razored flanks of rocks.

'What do we do?' asked Brakkius. He was kneeling down by the edge of the pass, bolter aimed at the peaks where the silhouettes of necrons were steadily gaining ground on them.

'Look how it moves,' added Cator, a little incredu-lously. These things were not merely the automatons the Ultramarines had first suspected them to be; they were so much more than that. 'An automaton should not be that agile.'

'We can't outrun them,' said Scipio, once all of the humans had passed him. 'So we fight.' He turned to Cator. 'Have Garrik and Auris get Herdantes back to the camp. Brakkius, Largo and I will hold back the necrons for as long as we can.'

Brakkius went to protest, as did Cator, but Scipio silenced them with a glance. 'See it done,' he said.

Neither Ultramarine would see their sergeant endangered but they were dutiful soldiers and followed orders.

Only Largo made no reaction. He still had unfinished business with the flayed lord – the blood of Renatus was on the fiend's talons and he would make it pay for that. He eyed the storm intently, tracking each shadow as it moved through the drift, a patch of grey on white.

'I'll return as soon as Garrik and Auris are on their way,' promised Cator. The others were at the front of the column, scouting the way ahead, all except Herdantes who was only able to limp alongside the guerrillas. His wounds were healing but it would take time. A ready bolter filled his grasp and Scipio didn't doubt his purpose, only his combat effectiveness.

'See that you do,' said Scipio, clapping a hand on his brother's shoulder. 'We'll need all the bolters and blades we can get.'

Cator saluted and set off down the pass in search of the others.

'That leaves the three of us for now,' said Brakkius, somewhat redundantly. He checked the load of his weapon – the ammunition count was low. Scipio saw it flash red in the darkness. He had a similar number of shells remaining in his pistol.

Largo wasn't watching, but breathed deeply. 'The air is crisp and clean. I like it up here,' he added. 'I think I will be happy to lay my gladius down in this place.'

Scipio didn't bother to reprimand him. It wasn't fatalism. Largo had simply come to terms with his probable death and embraced it. If anything, Scipio admired him for it. He racked the slide of his bolt pistol. 'Hold them off for as long as you can,' he said, the whipping wind adding drama and sorrow to his words. 'Let's give our brothers every chance to reach the sanctuary of the camp.'

Brakkius nodded. His weapon was already primed.

'Brother-sergeant,' he said. 'It has been an honour to cross blades and shed blood with you.'

'I could not be prouder of the Thunderbolts,' Scipio replied. 'You are my warriors, my brothers.'

'Courage and honour,' added Largo in a level voice.

Brakkius echoed him.

'And to the hells of the warp if we fail in this task,' said Scipio at the end.

Shoulder-to-shoulder, bolters ready, they waited for the flayed lord to come. There'd be no precipice to send it over this time, no cunning ploy to trap or destroy it. Scipio was as proud as any warrior of Guilliman. He was one of his patrician sons, something a friend had told him long ago – a shame it took his imminent demise to realise that. But he was not dragged down by hubris, either. He knew this creature had the beating of them. He avowed he would make it work for its feast. While there was blood still pumping in his veins and the veins of his brothers, there was hope. A keening cry split the rushing of the wind, giving it a sharp edge that felt as if it could shear steel. Death was coming.

It would reach them soon.

ANGER AND SHAME warred with excitement in the mind of the Enfleshed. Since his apotheosis, a need had arisen in his jagged psyche. It was a wholly unnatural hunger. He had railed against it at first, but now he embraced it and let it consume him.

If I am damned then so be it…

His slaves scurried on all fours like pack hounds on the hunt. He resisted the urge to prostrate himself like that; he was still a noble lord of the necrontyr despite how debased his form had become. He was not an animal yet, not quite.

He revelled in his agility, leaping rocks, darting around crags and racing down the icy slopes towards his prey. Flashes boomed in the darkness below, framing the gene-bred humans in orange, as they unleashed their weapons.

The Enfleshed felt no fear, only anticipation of the kill, of the skinning to come. His talons clacked and scraped of their own volition at the prospect.

Flesh…

It was as if his mind was being pulled apart, stretched taut in many directions at once – loathing, self-pity, feral abandon, ennui, self-satisfying sadism. He was Sahtah no longer; only the Enfleshed existed now.

One of the slaves was struck in the chest. The Enfleshed lost sight of it as it fell with a pseudo-scream. The storm of hot metal was intensifying the closer he came to the end of the slope. Something chipped his armoured shoulder, but he paid it no heed. To his left, another slave was destroyed. The Enfleshed smiled, or at least he did so in his mind – his rictus jaw was incapable of such expression – it meant more skin for him.

I shall devour you all…

He imagined hot blood coursing down his gullet, the succulence of ripe flesh rolling around in his mouth. It was intoxicating. A final thought penetrated the shattered remnants of his memory engrams as he leapt the final few metres to the kill,

I am lost…

The heavy shells burst hot and hard against his chest as the prey tried in vain to stop him, but the Enfleshed was not to be denied. His talons fanned in a killing arc, eager to eviscerate…

…when another figure emerged through the storm.

The light surrounding him was painful to the Enfleshed's dead eyes. The aura seemed to expand, washing over the others in a wave of azure. It was fringed by crackling bolts of power, coursing over a growing energy dome like vipers. It struck the Enfleshed mid-flight and threw him back.

A scream tore from the Enfleshed's throat and was echoed by his slaves who felt it sympathetically. Pain snapped at his nerves, some real, some imagined – though he couldn't tell one from the other. Blood, dried hard by the frost, cooked off his joints and servos in a ruddy haze. He tried to stand, poised to attack this new-comer and rend his face from his skull, but another bolt arced from the figure's fingertips – his eyes were alive with power – and now the Enfleshed felt fear.

His chest was torn apart, his living metal body slough-ing into slag. Sahtah, the Enfleshed – his head was so scrambled, he couldn't tell who or what he was any more – felt his memory engrams exploding one by one. Though he grasped at it with his melted talons, he could not seize his fading identity. Sentience shrivelled and turned to dust like bones upon a pyre. Slumping to his knees, Sahtah felt oblivion approaching. It stirred a final thought in his destroyed conscious, one that would echo for aeons.

Peace…

TIGURIUS REGARDED THE steaming remains of the necron lord with contempt as it phased out. His storm had van-quished the other flayed ones too and the mountainside was disturbingly empty barring where his psychic light-ning had scorched it.

He allowed the aura around him to fade and with the absence of the light, darkness swarmed in around them again.

'Your intervention is timely and most welcome, Lord Tigurius.'

The Chief Librarian turned at the sound of Scipio's voice. As he nodded, it took a moment longer for the fire in his eyes to die.

'I was travelling the Sea of Souls when I witnessed you in peril, Sergeant Vorolanus,' he said, motes of power still drifting from his lips and an unearthly resonance in his timbre.

Scipio bowed. 'We are glad of it.'

Tigurius looked beyond the brother-sergeant and his warriors. 'Who are these people?'

Drawn by the lightning storm, the human guerrillas and their Ultramarine escorts were standing a little farther down the path.

Scipio glanced over his shoulder where the humans had sunk to their knees before the Librarian.

'They are our saviours, Brother-Librarian.'

Tigurius eyed them curiously, unconvinced. 'Get up, all of you.' He turned back to Scipio. 'How so?'

'One amongst them can lead us through the mountains, bypassing the necron picket lines.'

Tigurius considered this for a moment, before answering, 'Bring the scout with us, the others we must leave behind.'

Scipio opened his mouth to protest, but the Librarian's steady gaze, latent with psychic power, stopped him. He nodded then gestured to the humans. 'Captain Evvers.'

A woman, the farthest forward in the group, who had now all got to their feet, looked up.

'You're with us. The others–'

'Are coming with me,' she said firmly, shaking her head. 'I won't leave them, not now.'

Tigurius glowered at her impudence. He released a little of his power into his eyes, which crackled with tiny lightning sparks. 'You will obey. This is not a negotiation.'

The one Scipio had called Evvers cowered a little but stood her ground. 'I need them. To get through the mountains. I need their skill. So do you.'

Tigurius didn't like it. Being beholden to one human was bad enough, to be argued down as well bordered on intolerable. 'I am tempted to ignite you like a flare, little human,' he said. Evvers looked like she might shrink from the threat but stayed steady. Despite her obvious frailty, she impressed the Librarian.

He laughed, as alien and unusual a sound as Varro Tigurius was ever likely to make. 'You have some courage in you.' He slammed his staff into the ground, 'Stay close. None of the Ultramarines here will be responsible if you fall behind.'

Evvers nodded. He could tell she was shaking and eager to be away from his penetrating gaze. 'Same goes for you,' she said, by way of rejoinder and went to marshal her troops.

'She is… *forthright*, brother-sergeant.'

Scipio nodded in agreement. 'I have never met a human like her.'

The drifts were lessening. Winds still howled around the peaks, chill and desolate. The storm wasn't done, it would come again.

Tigurius watched Evvers leading her troops down the slope. 'I saw into her mind. She carries much grief and anger, but believes she can master it and do what is asked of her.' He turned his gaze on Scipio. 'Do you believe it, too, Brother Vorolanus?'

Scipio's eyes narrowed. 'Do I believe what, my lord?'

'Exactly as I asked.'

'She will do her duty, as will I.'

Tigurius's expression was neutral, he gave nothing away. 'Then that is all any of us can be asked to do.'

'What else did you see, my lord, in the Sea of Souls?'

Scipio had been there when Tigurius had tried and failed to identify the darkness plucking at the edges of his prescience. He knew it had disturbed the sergeant and now he wanted assurances. But the Librarian couldn't provide them.

'Nothing.'

'There is no doom in our future then?'

'No, there is a tragedy to come but I cannot see it. A terrible will is blocking my prescience. For now, my eyes are blind, Scipio.'

The expression of the sergeant's face told Tigurius he had only enhanced his misgivings. That could not be helped. A lie would not serve him, either.

They left the slopes after that. The valley where the rest of the Ultramarines waited was not far. If what Scipio said was true and the humans could indeed find a way through the mountains and the necron defence line then victory was possible. The artillery could be destroyed and a foothold gained on Damnos all in the same move. Tigurius only wished he could grasp the thread of his disquiet. A sense of foreboding weighed upon him still. His psychic flight had done nothing to dispel it. The dark shroud over his thoughts was heavy and obscuring. Perhaps when the mission was done and the Voidbringer vanquished that veil would be lifted. He only hoped that by then it wouldn't be too late.

CHAPTER SIXTEEN

AFTER MONTHS OF continuous bombardment Adanar Sonne was used to the sound of the necron guns. They were a constant throb against the inside of his skull, a heavy-handed passenger demanding his attention. At the moment, the artillery was silent and it was the absence of their din that was unsettling him.

'It's like a lullaby, don't you think?'

Corporal Humis frowned. Not long after the Ultramarines had defeated the necron vanguard, a curious stillness had descended on Kellenport. The silence of the guns in the Thanatos Hills could mean anything. Perhaps the Emperor's Angels had destroyed them somehow and salvation would come from the stars in the form of an evacuation boat, or perhaps the necrons were merely preparing to unleash some greater horror. For now, the air was quiet... except for the screams.

'I don't understand, sir.'

'Of course you don't,' Adanar replied. He was using the

lull to tour the battlements, to check on their defences. Even if they were fated to die – and Adanar was certain this was the case – he would ensure they would go down fighting, in blood and fire. 'You haven't been on the wall as long as I have.' He turned to look at him. 'You don't come from Kellenport, do you, Humis?'

'I was stationed at the Zephyr Monastery, sir.'

Adanar smiled thinly. 'Ah, protecting the priests and their relics.' He carried on down the wall, saluting the officers blindly as he went. Humis followed in lockstep with his commander. 'Well your piety has got you this far, I suppose.'

Humis had no reply to that.

'So, what's left?' Adanar was all business again as he regarded the fire-blackened remains of the Kellenport artillery.

Consulting a data-slate, Humis said, 'Three *uber*-mortars and three long-nosed cannon, sir.'

'Earthshakers?'

'Yes, sir.'

'And what of the *Hel-handed*?'

'Still functional.'

Adanar nodded, satisfied. He already knew that the rail guns, cannon nests and emplacements were below thirty-five per cent. They were useful against infantry, but it was the really big guns that mattered – and they didn't come much bigger than the *Hel-handed*.

'Raise Sergeant Letzger on the vox,' he said. 'I want to see through the eyes of his god-engine.'

IT TOOK A further eighteen minutes to cross the battlements and meet with Sergeant Letzger. They passed strung-out squads of Ark Guard and conscripts on the way. All of Damnos, the remains of its entire population, had mustered in one last act of defence. The officers saluted, some even muttered greetings – many were just silent, contemplative of their fates. It seemed to Adanar that the army had thinned greatly since he'd last been around the wall.

A broad-shouldered, stocky man, Letzger was one of the few original officers to have survived the siege of Kellenport thus far and was the city's, and the Ark Guard's, gunnery master. Sweat-stained breeches, a pitted helmet strung with webbing and a flak jacket riddled with cigar burns painted a dishevelled picture of a man that Adanar trusted with his life.

'Commander Sonne,' Letzger saluted when he saw Adanar approach. His bare arms were covered in wiry black hair that failed to stop the Guard tattoos from showing through. His leather gloves were cut off at the ends, revealing oil-stained fingers. It didn't stop Adanar from shaking the man's hand after he returned his salute.

He appraised the cannon. 'How does she fare?'

The *Hel-handed* was a massive artillery piece. It was so big that it had to be built into the very foundations of the city wall and had immense recoil dampeners and impact compensators wrought into its leg stanchions. The column-like barrel was telescopic and segmented in four places. It required a crew of six men to fire it. A team of three was needed to rotate the barrel. Its firing platform was large enough for half a platoon of Ark Guard to stand on. Kill markings ran down the barrel, a source of pride as well as an illustration of Letzger's vengeance against the necrons that had invaded his world and murdered his friends.

Such engines were described as 'Ordinatus' by the Adeptus Mechanicus. This one had been fashioned and anointed by Karnak, but the tech-priest was no longer able to perform the rites of the Machine – he had died in the early weeks of the invasion. The fact that *Hel-handed* had kept firing without pause or complaint was a testament to the fortitude of its machine-spirit. There was not a day went by that Letzger did not thank it for that.

'Still operational, sir. The break in the bombardment has given us a little time to effect some minor repairs.' Letzger nodded to the work crews halfway up the barrel reaffixing plates and the servitors welding sections back together. 'She's holding.'

There was a tang of ozone in the air. Adanar tasted it on the back of his tongue. The smell was in his nostrils. It was preferable to the stink of death, at least.

'And the shield?'

Letzger breathed in. He genuinely enjoyed the acrid taste in his mouth.

'Still burning out my nose hairs, commander.' He smiled and his entire face seemed to crease up like an old rag. The stubble on his face was patchy and clumped with the movement of his features. Letzger really was an ugly brute.

Because of its size and importance, the *Hel-handed* was protected by a void shield. Such measures were usually only afforded for Titan god-machines but certain static installations like defence lasers and macro cannons also possessed them. With its sheer mass and destructive potential, the *Hel-handed* easily fell into that distinction. The void shield was the only reason it had not been rendered to scrap by the necron guns months ago.

'You've come to sample the view, I take it?' Letzger added.

Magnoculars only penetrated so far through the fog, but looking through the sights of *Hel-handed* was like peering through the eyes of a god.

'Only if it won't interrupt your labours.'

Letzger gestured to the machine behind him with a wide arm. 'Go ahead, sir. Her gaze hasn't wavered since the killing and death began.'

Humis balked a little at the gunnery master's words. Adanar allowed himself some private amusement – Letzger's pragmatism was infinitely preferable to the desperate hope of most of his officers. At least it was honest.

Mounting the platform, nodding to the crews who saluted him crisply, Adanar took up a position in the sighter's chair and looked through the *Hel-handed's* crosshairs.

Unsurprisingly, the view was fixed on the Thanatos Hills where the necron artillery was based. It was something of an unfair fire exchange but Adanar sensed the challenge was relished by Letzger's old girl. The arc of pylons and heavy gauss-cannons blighted the rugged horizon line. Several years ago, when his family was still alive, Adanar had trained in the Thanatos Hills. His barracks were based at the old refinery. That too was in ruins now, little more than a blast scar on the ground. So much was gone, never to return.

He squinted through the sighting lens, careful not to alter any of the gunnery master's measurements. He couldn't tell why the necron artillery had stopped firing but he did see something moving to the west. It was on the fringes of his vision through the scope. Adanar turned to Letzger.

'There's something out there.'

Letzger gave the reports back to his chief engineer and

took up the secondary sighter's seat. He peered through the lens.

'Eighteen degrees west,' he bellowed into the vox-horn. Several metres above him, a trio of crewmen rotated the barrel precisely.

Letzger adjusted the scope, tweaking it for focus. 'Clever bastards.'

Adanar had the same view but wasn't seeing whatever the gunnery master was.

'See the hill line?' asked Letzger.

Adanar nodded.

'Watch the peaks.'

Adanar stared. The drifts were blowing themselves out but despite that and the incredible range of the *Helhanded* it was still hard to discern detail. He *had* seen something earlier, though, so he tried to focus on that. His eyes narrowed and he smiled.

'They're moving.'

'Aye, it's no hill line out there.'

'Necron pyramids,' Adanar asserted.

'Trying to sneak up on us. Hoping we'd think the barrage was over and relax our guard.'

'How close do you think they are?'

Letzger made some adjustments, consulted instruments. He'd also lit a cigar and puffed on it enthusiastically.

'Too close.' He started yelling orders at the crews, shouting out coordinates. There was a flurry of action as his men reacted. Letzger left the sighter's seat and looked at Adanar.

'We need to get you off the platform now, sir,' he said politely.

Adanar matched the gunnery master's salute and left with Humis. They were heading back down the wall when he noticed something else that gave him immense displeasure.

'What is *he* doing on the battlements?'

Humis didn't catch on immediately. Adanar had to point him out before the corporal understood.

Rancourt was on the walls, his guard detail with him. It looked like he was trying to inspire the men, but was getting strange looks and wary salutes instead.

Adanar scowled and thrust out his hand. 'Get me Kador on the vox, right now.'

SERGEANT KADOR KEPT his voice low; the acting lord governor was only a few steps ahead of him and he didn't want to be overheard. 'He insisted, commander. I believe he wanted to do his part to galvanise the men.'

A stream of invective made Kador wince ever so slightly. 'I understand, sir.'

There was more, and the sergeant could see by Commander Sonne's hand gestures, as far away as he was on the battlements, that he was extremely displeased.

'I will do so immediately.'

The vox link was cut abruptly and Kador gave the receiver cup back to his comms-officer. His face was as hard as Damnos ice. 'Bring Governor Rancourt to me. Now.'

'NEVER LET IT be said that Lord Governor Zeph Rancourt sat idle while his people suffered.'

Kador thought he looked knowingly officious in his robes and suspected the only reason the lord governor had ventured from his quarters was in fear of the ceiling falling in on him. Upon hearing of Corporal Besseque's death, he'd been especially paranoid about that.

'Commander Sonne has ordered me to escort you from the wall, sire.'

Rancourt looked genuinely nonplussed, 'But who will inspire the men?'

'He assures me they are well steeled already, sire.'.

'Yes, of course...' His gaze drifted to southern gate. 'The Crastia Shipyards,' he said, 'they are a short march in that direction. With the cessation of bombardment, an evacuation might be possible.'

'Commander Sonne has ordered that no one is to leave the safety of the city.'

Rancourt returned his gaze to Kador. His expression was distinctly conspiratorial.

'A small mission from the city gates would likely go unnoticed.'

The sergeant's face was like stone. 'What are you suggesting, sire?'

'Nothing. Only that an enterprising officer might be well rewarded should he deliver an Imperial official from certain peril.'

Kador leaned in close, just to be sure there was no misunderstanding. The relish in the lord governor's eyes made him want to clench his fists. 'No one leaves the city. *No. One.* These are my orders, sire. The Crastia Shipyards have been taken. Even if there were a vessel capable of taking us to orbit, the area is likely to be swarming with the enemy. Necrons employ hidden snares. They have troops able to bore through earth. There's no telling what hazards we would encounter.'

The lord governor looked as if he might argue but Kador's glare placated him.

'Yes, of course. I was merely speaking hypothetically.'

'Hypothetically, sire, indeed.' Kador stepped aside, indicating the lord governor should make for the battlement stairs.

'You are a dutiful servant, sergeant,' he said as he passed.

'Thank you, sire.' Kador watched him go. Perhaps Governor Rancourt was right, perhaps the ceiling would fall on his head. He could but hope.

CHAPTER SEVENTEEN

A LOW RUMBLE ran through the earth below the newly christened Courtyard of Xiphos. Iulus felt it through his armoured boots, his greaved legs. In his core, he knew the necrons had found some fresh way to attack Kellenport.

He expected to see lumbering war machines, bipedal walkers, arachnid constructs or a host of other mechanical horrors pounding towards the walls. But no emerald beams scorched through the snow-fog that had rolled down off the mountains and swathed the world in dirty white. There were no ranks of blinking, soulless orbs as the phalanxes marched on the city. Even the necron communication-nodes were silent. It was something else.

Iulus scanned the third wall, the one that was mined with as much explosive as he could spare. The rumble beneath his feet grew deeper and heavier. Some of the men had to steady themselves on the battlements to stop from falling.

'Battle positions,' he bellowed. The order was relayed through the other Immortals. The entire defensive line, including the troops in the courtyards, tensed.

A Space Marine can exist in a state of heightened battle-tension for hours, even days. Their enhanced physiologies are genetically engineered to cope with even the most arduous mental extremes. For a human it is unbearable. Like a sinew pulled taut across a muscle it can only be strained for so long. Over-tense it and it will snap.

Still the tremors persisted.

The men looked fit to break.

Despite the absence of a vox-caster, Iulus's voice reverberated around the wall. 'Hold positions!'

Again, he searched the third wall. The proximity triggers were rigged throughout the ruins. There was no way the necrons could have bypassed them all. He searched the killing-field on which their guns were aimed and primed, despite the fact he knew no enemy could set foot there without first coming through the third wall. Where was the fire? Where were the explosions and the shrapnel storm he had laid for them? *Come on, come on... We shall unleash death upon you.*

'Where are they?' hissed Kolpeck, the normally stoic conscript showing signs he was on edge.

Iulus silenced him. 'They are close. Be ready, brother.'

He'd said it without thinking, by rote. Iulus didn't take it back. He could see instantly the effect it had on Kolpeck's resolve. He was emboldened. In another life he would have made a fine Space Marine, Iulus was sure.

'I am at your side, brother-Angel.'

'And I yours,' Iulus muttered. Breaking up his squad had felt unnatural at first. Iulus would still have preferred his brothers by his side but Kolpeck was a good soldier and a fine companion. He had never really thought much of humans before. This enemy they faced was enough to push an Ultramarine's resolve and strength to the limit and yet here these men stood, in defence of their homes, defiant to the last. Yes, Iulus was proud to stand with them and learn an important lesson about the depth of the human spirit.

Small motes of debris were shaking loose from the defences now. The Ark Guard in the gun nests had to hold onto their pintle mounts and tripods to prevent them moving and fouling their aim. Several troopers knelt, leaning against the wall for stability. Some prayed, making the sign of the aquila. Others locked arms with their comrades for mutual support.

'Like ice in your veins,' Iulus said to them, his abyssal voice carrying on the wind. 'Your spine and will as steel.'

A conscript with a rocket tube gestured into the whiteout fearfully. 'What if we cannot see them? What if they are already upon us?'

Iulus growled at him. 'Get hold of your fear, seize it and lock it fast. *I* will see them coming.'

Except he couldn't see them. Iulus saw no more than the frightened conscripts on the wall. How quickly a man's insane courage could corrode in the face of inaction, when confronted with the unknown. There were no horrors in the universe that could compare to what a man harboured in his own mind. It was a place where daemons and monsters reigned, where blades and guns were no protection. And it was here that a Space Marine was armoured the most.

But still, the humans held.

A cry echoed across the battlements. It was followed by the crack of splitting stone as part of the wall collapsed. Huge plumes of dust, grit and snow spewed up into the air like a frozen geyser just under fifty metres from Iulus's position. Men and materiel were swallowed in the cloud, their screams dampened by the crash of sundered stone.

In the other direction, another section of the wall fell, broken in two as if its foundations had rotted through or succumbed to rapid erosion.

Uncertain where best to turn first, Iulus reached for the vox. He was scanning the dust cloud for some clue of a necron attack, when Kolpeck left his position and raced for the ladder to the lower level.

Iulus shouted, 'Trooper, stand and fight!' He had no time to go after him. Something was happening to the wall but he was still ignorant of the cause. He eyed the third wall again, but the mines and explosives were intact. He heard no las-fire, no bolter bursts. Kolpeck had fled, climbed down the ladder and was racing down the stairs to the Courtyard of Xiphos.

So much for human courage, Iulus thought bitterly. Perhaps the war had broken the man. Cracks were usually hard to see until it was too late to shore them up.

At least the rest of the One Hundred were holding firm. He'd glared at them all when Kolpeck had run, defying them to move with sheer force of will. None did.

Putting the thought aside as he would a spent clip or blunted gladius, Iulus barked down the vox. 'Aristaeus.'

He was the closest Ultramarine to the site of the second collapse. Iulus himself was in command of the wall section where the first collapse had taken place.

Aristaeus's reply was riddled with static, the dust and grit muddying the signal even at close range. 'Nothing, brother-sergeant. I see...' The vox return crackled.

'Repeat. I cannot make you out, brother.'

'A hole, brother-sergeant. There is a vast hole opened up in the wall right down into the earth.'

Iulus heard screaming over the vox-return and could imagine the fates of those on the section when it collapsed. Aristaeus continued.

'I can see into its depths. There is…'

There was a pause as Aristaeus consulted his autosenses and cycled through his retinal spectra.

Iulus's patience was threadbare. They were under attack but he still had no idea by what or from where the next assault would come. 'Speak, brother. What do you see?'

'Darkness, only darkness.'

Crouched at the battlements, one eye on the dissipating dust cloud ahead of him, Iulus frowned. 'Is your retinal display malfunctioning? Tell me what you see through infra-red and night vision.'

'Nothing, brother-sergeant. It's just black, like oily cloud. Visual filters have no effect.'

'That can't be good,' said Kolpeck. The grizzled righand was out of breath and clutching a strange device in one hand. He'd obviously gone to retrieve it after the attack. It was based on a long metal spike with some kind of data-slate at the top. Iulus had never seen one before but its design suggested some kind of seismological mining tool.

'A soldier does not desert his post, Trooper Kolpeck.' His voice was stern but now was not the time for a long reprimand. He wanted to know what Kolpeck had found.

'I'm sorry, brother-Angel, but I was acting on a hunch,' he replied with a little less contrition than Iulus had expected. 'I told you, I am a miner not a soldier.' He brandished the seismological device. The data-screen was grubby with dirt and hoarfrost but a series of undulating lines were visible along three horizontal axis. 'They are *beneath* us.'

The three lines were depth markers. The last, therefore the deepest, was jagged with activity. Iulus saw what the necrons were doing. Undermining was a common siege tactic, well-used and perfected over millennia of war. Here the necrons had added a fresh element – they were using the darkness as a way to conceal themselves.

Iulus seized the vox, nearly crushing it in his gauntlet as urgency overtook him. 'Aristaeus, burn it! Burn the hole. The mechanoids have tunnelled underneath us!

'Pour everything you've got into that bore hole,' he shouted, running the battlements in long, metre-eating strides. 'Turn the cannon emplacements, fill it with hell and frag!'

Iulus got halfway to the site of the first collapse when the ground beneath him gave way and he was falling. Another bore hole had opened up in his path. Several of the One Hundred plunged to their deaths, unable to move in time. It was a dishonourable end for such brave men. Iulus reached out, his survival instinct impelling him to grab a chunk of rock jutting from the broken rampart.

He stared down into the abyss below and saw the darkness there that Aristaeus had described. Unhooking his weapon, he could almost sense the presence of alien minds regarding him and fired.

The bolt pistol scream resonated inside the bore hole, magnified as it rebounded off its sides. With the darkness cloaking the advancing scarabs, Iulus didn't realise he couldn't miss. As soon as the first creature was hit, the illusion faded and the blackness receded to reveal a chittering host of the things. They scurried up the walls, which were ridged with the burrowing action of whatever monster or device had hewn them, in a swarm. Their eyes glinted like tiny emeralds in the natural shadows of the circular cavern, mandibles champing.

When Iulus's bolt fire struck them, a stream of the scarabs exploded leaving burning contrails in their wake as they fell. He panned the pistol around, finger tight on the trigger, and left a muzzle scar across the open air. Still holding on one-handed to the piece of broken rampart, Iulus gave a wordless cry.

He could not kill them all. Even with the las-fire flashing down from above, the scarabs would soon breach the surface. He estimated there were hundreds of the things and for every one he destroyed, another four replaced it. His ammunition counter was burning to zero when Iulus noticed a large mound ripple through the undulating mass. Down to his last rounds, he switched targets and fired a close burst into the mound. The scarabs outside it were blasted apart like a piece of ablative armour revealing a much larger construct beneath. It moved slower than the others but its carapace was thick and absorbed the impact of the explosive bolt shells without pause. Iulus was debating whether to draw his chainsword and drop into the bore hole to kill the monster personally when it swung a gauss-blaster arm in his direction and fired.

The beam cut into the Ultramarine's battle-plate and he cried out. Armour shed like snake skin as the flaying effect of necron technology went to work and Iulus's leg greave was reduced to half-corroded mesh.

The pain was so severe he dropped his pistol. For a moment his grip wavered. Several more of the larger mounds were moving through the scarab swarm, which had almost reached him. Dangling off the edge of the precipice, Iulus realised it would mean his death to fall now. Eternal night reigned in the depths of those bore holes, as cold and unnatural as the creatures emerging from it.

A hand clasped around his wrist. Then another and another. Iulus looked up to see Kolpeck's straining face above him.

'Heave!' he yelled to the other conscripts – all from the One Hundred – that were trying to rescue their captain.

'At your side, brother-Angel,' Kolpeck said again through gritted teeth.

It took the combined efforts of four men to lift the Ultramarine even a small amount. They were all rig-hands, all strong men used to back-breaking labour in the Imperial mines beneath the Damnos ice, but none had ever worked so hard to lift something such a short distance.

It was enough for Iulus to swing his free arm around and grip the battlements with both hands. He pulled himself up as another gauss-blast speared the rock where he'd been hanging a moment earlier. The conscripts fell back as he emerged back over the top.

'Back! Fall back!'

Iulus turned towards the bore hole even as the conscripts started to retreat. He unclamped a pair of frag grenades from his belt just as the first wave of scarabs was spilling over the edge of the wall. Ignoring the smaller creatures, he tossed the explosives over the shiny bodies. A low boom came from beyond and below. The mechanoid spyder did not emerge and Iulus thanked the Emperor that his grenades had done their work.

He contemplated staying and trying to hold off the

scarab swarm coming at him – he had already drawn his chainsword – but decided to fall back with the others.

Kolpeck was just behind him, waiting for his captain.

'We need to get off the wall,' he said, bringing his las-gun to bear on the smaller mechanoids.

Iulus pushed the barrel down. 'Then do it. Marshal the One Hundred. Every man is to head for the Courtyard of Xiphos. We'll stand a better chance of holding them there.'

Kolpeck nodded and ran. He was already shouting orders at the men, ushering them downwards, organising them into groups.

Unclamping his last pair of grenades, Iulus tossed them towards the scarab swarm and jumped from the wall.

The explosion blossomed behind him, kicking up debris and broken scarabs as the Ultramarine landed hard on the Courtyard of Xiphos. From there he could see the wall was breached in no fewer than six areas, each sunken by a bore hole and now swarming with scarabs. Gauss-fire cracked from the spyders, stripping men to bone and ash.

'Heavy weapons, target the larger mechanoids. Bring them down!'

From across the courtyard, rocket tubes and heavy stubbers hammered into the spyders. They were tough and took a lot of killing, but they were falling. So too were the Ark Guard. A mass retreat was in effect. Even done in good order, the humans were still pressed on all sides. The walls were empty, apart from the dead. Several squads had been overwhelmed completely in the first few seconds of the breach, swallowed beneath the necron wave. Even their bodies were no longer there, the scarabs had stripped them from existence.

The first wall was behind him, and Iulus knew they would need to fall back to here if they had any chance of surviving, let alone repelling, the attack. A massive bore hole opened in the Courtyard of Xiphos, splitting flagstones and toppling shattered monuments. Men went with it, whole swathes of Ark Guard lost with a tortured scream. Iulus thought he saw something gargantuan surface from the depths. It looked segmented, almost centipedal, but was quickly swallowed by the unnatural darkness. Scarabs and spyders spilled forth in its wake.

'Incendiaries into the bore holes,' Iulus bellowed, pointing to the fresh attack point. 'Burn it down. Cleanse their route of assault.'

He saw Aristaeus, a rack of three promethium flamer tanks rattling on his back. He reached the circular crevice in the courtyard and threw the tanks in. Bringing up his boltgun in the same motion, he fired off a single round and a jet of liquid flame as thick as the pillars of Hera's Temple shot up from the bore hole.

The blast wave took Aristaeus off his feet but he was quick to recover and head for his sergeant. The other Immortals were doing the same, marshalling their troops with them, converging on Iulus as they sought to consolidate their forces.

Slowly, the squads came together. Stragglers were picked off easily by the scarab swarm but a concentrated wall of fire was ripping steadily from the Ark Guard now. At the orders of their Space Marine captains, they formed firing ranks and bathed the courtyard in hot las.

'Brother-sergeant,' Aristaeus reached Iulus's side and held out his sidearm, 'you seem to be without the Emperor's wrath.'

Iulus punched his chest, the air filling with las-beams

around him. 'Here is where I keep it, brother,' he said, but then smiled as he took the bolt pistol.

More Ark Guard joined the others massing outside the gates to the first wall – even the troops on the battlements had opened up with their weapons – and the rate of fire intensified. The scarabs and their larger, monstrous cousins had seemed infinite at first but now they were withering. None of them could penetrate the slowly retreating Imperial cordon. Even the spyders were pinioned by lascannon beams from the first wall battlements. But the necrons were tenacious and fed even greater numbers into the meatgrinder. Like a river of mercury swollen at its banks, they began to lap at the sides of the Imperial defences.

Several soldiers at the outer edge where the Ultramarines presence was weakest were dragged screaming into the swarm.

Iulus tightened the cordon further still but his troops were already shoulder-to-shoulder with their backs against the gate of the first wall. He sensed the tide turning, the sheer overwhelming force of the necron constructs tipping the balance. What had started out as an organised defence of hold and repulse was turning into a desperate last stand.

Behind him, there came the churning of gears as the mechanism to the gate was activated. It did not open wide but it was enough to admit a towering war machine into the Courtyard of Xiphos.

'The walls of Chundrabad shall never fall!' Agnathio's multi-melta tore a hot line through the scarabs. Men of the Ark Guard hurried from the Dreadnought's path as he bullied his way to the front rank. 'I serve the Chapter eternally!'

Though he moved slowly, his motive servos still

spitting oil and steam, when Agnathio reached the necron horde it reeled. So indomitable, so utterly relentless, the venerable warrior's example was followed by all. Together, they threw the scarabs back.

Agnathio had been joined by the rest of the Immortals and several platoons of Ark Guard who lent their fire to the Imperial barrage.

As if sensing the futility of their attack, the necron machines retreated like ants from a fire and withdrew to their bore holes.

The shooting from the Ark Guard was slow to relent. In the end it took all of the Ultramarines to bring the humans back down again. They had survived a terrifying ordeal and fear did not give up its hold on lasgun triggers easily. When the noise of the barrage died, a wintry silence swept through the Courtyard of Xiphos. Already, the drifts were covering the evidence that a battle even took place. There were only the half-flayed remains of dead Ark Guard, anyway; all of the destroyed necrons had phased out. It made for an eerie scene.

Iulus rested his hand on the still-hot shoulder casing of Agnathio's multi-melta. 'We owe you a debt, honoured one.'

Pride was not really amongst a Dreadnought's limited emotional responses. Agnathio was typically matter-of-fact. 'I am my Chapter's servant. I seek only the glory of Ultramar.'

'Well spoken, brother,' Iulus murmured, humbled by such stalwart courage and loyalty.

Brother Galvia had been one of the Space Marines from the first wall to come and bolster the beleaguered defenders. 'Do we return to the second wall and try to regarrison it?' he asked.

Iulus shook his head. The second wall was all but

rubble now, the bore holes had seen to that. It would be indefensible. He turned to Kolpeck who was crouching nearby, breathing hard while some of the men around him were puking out their nerves.

'Find as many of those seismographic staves as you can,' said Iulus. 'Plant them around this cordon, ten metres out.'

'I could take them as far as the second wall,' Kolpeck suggested.

'No. Ten metres, no farther. Do it quickly.'

Kolpeck saluted, gathering up some men he trusted, and went about his orders.

Iulus's face was grim as he surveyed the ruins in front of them. Aristaeus was by his side and must have seen his expression.

'Something wrong, brother-sergeant?'

'That was just a probing attack to test our strength,' he said. 'This isn't over.'

Iulus did not intend his words to be prophetic but as he said them there was a flash of emerald light around the rubble of the second wall. A crack had opened in the air itself. The drifts did not fall there. It was as if something had interrupted the very ebb and flow of nature. The crack widened and became a pool of light that expanded again into roughly the size of a large doorway. Within it, the emerald light rippled as if something very deep down beneath the pool was attempting to surface. Shadows loomed there. Iulus could not be certain but he thought he could make out a long, glowing corridor with the shapes of necrons marching down it, growing more distinct with every step.

Another portal opened up a few metres away. A third followed swiftly after that. Down inside the bore holes a chittering clangour arose as the scarabs returned.

On the battlements, some of the Ark Guard were pointing beyond Kellenport's walls. Officers were looking through scopes. Iulus could hear the larger guns rotating to fresh trajectories.

Some of the men were muttering amongst themselves. A few in the front ranks who could see the enemy emerging had turned and were trying to reach the gap in the gate, but it had already closed.

'Hold to your positions!' Iulus bellowed, revving the teeth of his chainsword. He levelled it at the trio of portals and the shadows coming through them. 'Death comes for us. It comes clad in metal and with engines instead of organs. We shall hurl it back, back into the abyss. Faith in the Emperor.'

The rallying cry was taken up by his brothers; some of the One Hundred, including Kolpeck, echoed it too.

'Faith in the Emperor!'

Emboldened, perhaps even shamed by the ragged band of conscripts, the rest of the Ark Guard stopped trying to flee and gave voice.

'Faith in the Emperor!'

As the shout of defiance echoed to nothing, Kolpeck, alone, could be heard.

'And in the name of our brother-Angel, Iulus Fennion!'

Iulus wanted to rebuke him, but then the Ark Guard and the conscripts resounded with, 'Iulus Fennion! Brother-Angel!'

Despite himself, Iulus felt a slight swell of pride. It lasted but a moment as the shadow of the monoliths loomed through the gaps in the wall and the necrons emerged at last.

'Keep your courage steady,' he told Kolpeck as gunfire filled the Courtyard of Xiphos.

* * *

LETZGER SWEATED LIKE a stuck pig. The gunnery crews had worked well; *Hel-handed* was ready to unleash her first salvo.

'Let 'em have it!' he cried into the vox-horn.

Even with the dampeners and compensators, the recoil from the cannon was immense. It shook its staging platform like the hand of an angry god, while the explosive shell fell like its clenched fist.

A huge cloud of dust and debris rose up from the strike point, obscuring the slow-moving phalanx of monoliths from view. It looked like a direct hit. Certainly, Letzger had made no mistake in his calculations. That heavy a missile payload... nothing in human creation could survive that.

Some of the gunnery crew were already celebrating. It was as much fear as it was exultation that fed their shouts and angry cheers.

Letzger stayed at the scopes, sweating. He was wearing plugs, but his ears still rang from the report of *Hel-handed*. She was a noisy bitch, all right, sometimes capricious, but he loved her and he loved what she could do.

Through the scope the smoke and dust was clearing. Ice and snow around the blast site had melted away to steam, adding to the obfuscation.

'Let me see it,' he murmured. 'Let me see your broken carcass.' He'd never fired on monoliths before; he didn't know what happened to them when they were destroyed. Perhaps they phased out too; perhaps he was looking for a ghost he'd never see.

The image resolved. Letzger sagged at his post and the men groaned in despair. It was still there. Three of the necron pyramids advanced towards Kellenport. Somehow, impossibly, he had missed. The crater was so large, its effect so awesomely powerful, he didn't know how. But *Hel-handed* had been fouled somehow.

Wiping away the perspiration on his forehead and lips, the cigar cinched between them no more than a smouldering nub, Letzger peered through the scopes more intently for an answer. He saw tendrils of darkness, coiling and twisting between the triumvirate of war machines. They appeared in synch, feeding off one another, boosting the terrible shroud that had somehow saved them.

The only mercy was that, for now at least, the monoliths were not firing their weapons. They had phased forces into the vicinity, but otherwise their power matrices were dormant.

For an experienced crew, it took six minutes to load, prime and fire an Ordinatus like the *Hel-handed*. Letzger prided himself that his men were the best. As he bellowed the orders to reload, he knew the old girl would be spitting fury in less than five.

As he watched the monoliths float towards them, in defiance of all natural laws of physics, he clutched the aquila bracelet on his wrist.

'Come on sweetheart,' he said, patting the gun. 'This time…'

ADANAR WAS RUNNING the battlements when the first shot from the *Hel-handed* rang out. He'd not got far, and even though he knew he was out of position, stopped to watch the magnificent weapon in action. The blast wave, felt even where he was standing on the wall, was invigorating. His heart sank to a cold and pitiless place when he looked through Corporal Humis's magnoculars and saw the monoliths were untouched. He'd always thought nothing would survive a blow like that.

From the Courtyard of Thor behind him, the *uber*-mortars and long-nose cannons churned out shells as if on a production line. With their subterfuge revealed, the necrons recommenced their barrage from the Thanatos Hills. As the emerald beams from pylons and gauss siege-cannon started up, Kellenport was under siege once more.

This time, however, the mechanoids were aiming for the walls.

A chunk of crenellation spumed into the air, trailing dust, grit and snow. Men went with it, broken and half-flayed.

Adanar ducked, grabbing Humis's jacket before he fell off the battlement like several others. The screams of the falling men didn't last long as they cracked against the ice-hardened flagstones of the square below.

'I've lost one aide today,' he said through gritted teeth, dragging the corporal bodily against part of the wall that was still intact. 'I don't intend on losing another.'

Humis was a little shell-shocked but otherwise grateful. He gestured to the blast-scarred section of wall. It gaped like an old wound, still festering. 'We are dead men out here on the wall.'

Adanar nodded. 'Agreed. All except the heavy cannon and gunnery nests are to drop below the wall to the lower level. The emplacements are dug in harder, that should give them some protection. For the rest: heads down and hunker down,' he added, as Humis got on the vox and started relaying orders to the officers spread throughout the defences.

The corporal put his hand over the receiver cup, though he scarcely needed to – the combined barrage from both sides was deafening. 'What about the troops in the Courtyard of Xiphos? They'll lose the support fire from the platoons.'

Adanar thought for a second. He ducked again, as did Humis, when another explosion rocked the wall. More screaming followed.

'Tell Sergeant Fennion he's losing his support and offer to open up the gates. He's a warrior-knight, so I doubt he'll retreat easily, but at least the Ark Guard can get behind shelter if the Ultramarines want a glorious death.'

Adanar could tell by Humis's expression that he'd shocked the corporal. 'I'm sorry, Humis. It's hard to see any hope amongst all this death.' Subconsciously, he rubbed at the locket-charm strung around his wrist. 'It's been too long since I've seen anything else.' Another blast shook Adanar from his reverie. 'Give the order. The Angels are not immortal, they'll either fall back or they'll die like heroes.'

CHAPTER EIGHTEEN

IT FELT STRANGE to be above the ground. So long he had dwelled in darkness, his thoughts lost in a timeless miasma without meaning. The long sleep had gnawed at the Undying. Even his name, his true name was denied to him. He was only the Undying now, an immortal king upon a decayed throne. Eternity was not the paradise he had hoped for. With every waking moment, as his lucidity returned to him, it became a terror instead.

How can I exist for all the long aeons of the galaxy? Will I not atrophy? Will my mind not erode to oblivion?

As a member of one of the necrontyr's royal houses, he enjoyed certain privileges. No servitude as an automaton for him. Though the Undying had lost part of his identity, he knew that much. Plebeians and nobles were separated by a gulf. Since the necrons had embraced metal over flesh, that divide had increased exponentially. Not only was freedom denied to the lower classes, so too now was true sentience.

Though tarnished and tattered, the Undying's vestments looked regal enough. As he'd left the tomb, eager to dispense death and annihilation, his lych-like guardians had found him.

Like their lord, they carried long war-scythes in silvered fists. As they bowed, he saw the flare of recognition in their eyes and knew these were no ordinary slaves.

'Retinue,' he had proclaimed. 'Summon my phalanx to war.'

Immortals had filed from the bowels of the tomb, rank upon rank recently armed and revivified. They were the Undying's honour guard. In the lowest levels, the very catacombs, the reviled spilled forth. Held aloft on humming repulsor platforms, the destroyers were a blend of necron and something else. Nihilism burned coldly in the depths of their eye sockets. Fused with gauss technologies, boasting cannons not limbs, they were amongst the tomb's deadliest servants.

The Undying felt an instant kinship with them, despite the fact that the house shunned such creatures. Their curse, the slow descent into madness and destructive desire, was a fate shared by all. The destroyers' presence was merely a reminder of that.

Lesser creatures joined the hovering gun platforms in legion, raider constructs and the flickering shadows of tomb wraiths. The latter were an obvious bribe. The Architect was trying to make certain of his position and influence.

That might have amused the Undying once but now, as he gazed out upon the frozen city of the humans, he only craved to vanquish. There was one out in the wastes who had defied him. He had led an attack and slain lords of his royal court. As the killing urge boiled up within him, the Undying vowed he would humble this worm. An arc of emerald fire raced up the war-scythe's blade in empathy of its master's rage, as he willed his forces onwards in the snow and ice.

They marched, their royarch at the forefront, and together their footfalls shook the earth. There were no war cries, no banners held aloft, none of the pomp and ceremony of other armies. The necrons were silent and implacable, their advance unstoppable. Nothing except total annihilation would do. And even then, the Undying's lust for carnage would not be sated.

'Let it all burn,' he growled, and in the balefires of his eyes it did.

ANKH SURVEYED THE cold black metal of the necron artillery approvingly.

Rows of pylons, once held in stasis and now dredged from the very earth, stood alongside static gauss siege-cannons. The latter were long, multi-barrelled monstrosities. Their flanks were wrought from the living metal of the necrontyr and pulsed fluidly in the half-light. The former were sickle-shaped turrets that spat death from their gauss-annihilators. A wash of emerald light bathed the ordnance with every discharge of their power. Lances of energy scored the sky, cutting into it with harsh green jags of light. Where the pylons fed continuous beams into the heavens, the siege-cannons throbbed with the drumming staccato of their salvos.

The earth trembled. Far into the distance, the human city was slowly rendered to dust.

Ankh joined another of his noble brethren, who was watching the barrage from the same icy ridge but with prideful eyes.

'Impressive,' the cryptek conceded.

Tahek, the Voidbringer as he demanded to be known, turned on the other necron lord like a jackal scenting prey. 'It is irresistible, world-slaying,' he snarled.

Black vapours surrounded the Voidbringer, the reason for his name. They roamed and twisted about his metal form, seething through the gaps in his ribcage, spilling over his skeletal fingers and out of the sockets of his aeons-dead eyes.

This was the Night Shroud, a piece of ancient necron technology that had existed since before the long sleep. Not only did it swathe the Voidbringer, it encircled his dominion too. Like some unnatural fog it rolled over the ground and between the artillery emplacements, foiling the efforts of the humans to target them with any certainty. It was not foolproof, some of the weapons had been destroyed in the ordnance exchange, but the Void-bringer's technology kept the damage to a minimum.

Effective as protection, it was when deployed as a weapon of terror that the Night Shroud truly excelled. During the taking of the Thanatos Refinery, Voidbringer had sent the darkness snaking through corridors, seeping into anterooms, infiltrating the hearts and minds of the crude human soldiery. Mortal fears amused him greatly. So primal, so instinctive, the horrors of the dark would ever plague the souls of the fleshed.

Tahek Voidbringer was powerful, Ankh knew this and it was the reason for his visit. He also knew of the Undying's malady. Despite his status, the long sleep had not been kind to him. Tahek was aware of that too and had set his ambitions to becoming royarch.

'The Night Shroud proved extremely useful,' said Ankh, showing his appreciation with a slight bow. 'The humans are trapped inside their stone cage.'

'Did you doubt it?' Voidbringer snapped. A crackle of

energy was fed down the haft of his staff but dissipated quickly.

Ankh went on, unperturbed. 'Your shadows blinded them to the machine host until it was too late. Their outer defences are in ruins, their forces driven back.'

'Yeeesss.' A fire burned in Voidbringer's eyes. It was as if he had discovered something in the cryptek's penitent demeanour. 'I know why you are here, *Ankh*.'

'To return your gracious favour, my lord.' Ankh bowed lower.

'*My lord*? Yes, that's right. I am of noble heritage and you...' Voidbringer's tone expressed his disdain, 'you are little better than a plebeian with certain... *gifts*.'

'I live to serve the necrontyr,' answered Ankh, carefully politic. Away from the tomb he was vulnerable. Although very unlikely, Tahek could decide to destroy him here and he'd be able to do little to stop him.

'You will serve me,' Voidbringer asserted. 'The Destroyer curse has him, does it not?'

'As lord, I bow to your wisdom. I am merely–'

Voidbringer seized Ankh by the chin, clamping his mouth shut and halting his reply.

'This pact we have made is a wise one for you, *Ankh*. The Undying is mad. He has succumbed, hasn't he?'

Ankh did not need to move his jaw to speak but the sound emanating from his vocal emitters was tinny and dull as it resonated through his metallic frame.

'As will we all.'

Voidbringer nodded slowly. 'The tomb is awakening,' he said, 'and other crypteks can be put to the task of weapon-making and revivification. Yours are not the only tomb spyders and scarabs, Ankh.'

There was a pause as Voidbringer allowed the threat to sink in, before Ankh was released.

'Now,' said the lord, holding out a skeletal hand.

'Honour me with what you came here to give.'

Bowing again, Ankh produced a shiny black orb from within the folds of his robes.

As he took it, Voidbringer's emerald eyes flashed with hunger and desire.

'A resurrection orb?'

'The very same,' Ankh replied, taking a humble step backwards.

Waving the cryptek away, his gaze still locked upon the orb, Voidbringer said, 'You may leave. Your favour will not be forgotten.'

A portal opened in reality, a long chamber stretching away from a green doorway of light that led back to the tomb and sanctuary. Ankh was pleased to be going. As he was about to go, the falsehood of Tahek's promise still ringing hollow in his mind, he stopped. He had his back to the noble but spoke anyway.

'A word of warning before I take my leave.'

'You warn me?' Voidbringer's tone betrayed his anger. The mad dog was straining for the kill.

'The Enfleshed is gone, so too are his cohorts.'

'And? He was a wretch and a ghoul. I am glad to be rid of his presence.'

Ankh turned briefly. 'The genebred ones destroyed him. There is one amongst their ranks who has power.'

Voidbringer scoffed. 'I have felt his presence. He is nothing, less than an insect.'

'He comes for you.'

Now the flames of wrath truly flared along the Void-bringer's staff. He was easy to rile and Ankh amused himself at his impotent rage.

'I fear nothing,' Voidbringer told him. 'I am invincible.'

As he disappeared through the portal, Ankh's gaze lingered on the orb and he whispered, 'Of course you are…'

ACT THREE:
SACRIFICE

CHAPTER NINETEEN

Scipio returned to the camp to find Squads Ixion and Strabo already gone.

It fell to Sergeant Vandar of the Victors to relate the news of Captain Sicarius's orders and the redeployment of the assault squads. He stepped forwards from the defensive ring of cobalt the Ultramarines had made whilst stationed in the valley and approached Tigurius.

The Chief Librarian masked his anger well as he stopped to hear Vandar's report and survey the forces he did have left at his disposal.

'Did our brother-captain mention why he was recalling the assault squads?' he asked.

To his credit, Vandar kept his eyes up and his answers brief. 'The orders were relayed through Veteran-Sergeant Daceus, my lord, and no he did not.'

'I see.' Tigurias's face was carefully neutral but the air around him visibly crackled.

Just as they had found a way to sabotage and destroy

the necron heavy guns bombarding Kellenport, Sicarius had taken away from them their chief asset in that attack. From the encounters he'd survived so far, Scipio knew it would have been tough enough to assault the Thanatos Hills. Without Ixion and Strabo, the odds of mission success had narrowed considerably. If the necron forces were led by a lord too...

Withdrawal of the assault squads left three tactical squads, including Brother-Sergeant Octavian's. They carried the honorific Swords of Judgement and were amongst the best marksmen in the Second, possibly the Chapter. Ortus had matched his skill against their best many times. The record sheet was well-balanced. With the Ultramarine's death it would forever be so.

Scipio put such maudlin thoughts from his mind as he greeted his fellow Space Marines. Despite everything, it was good to be back amongst his brothers again.

Tigurius was not done addressing the battle force. 'Fortunate then, that we bring good news.' He gestured to Scipio, inviting him to elaborate. 'Brother-sergeant?'

Several of the battle-brothers, including their sergeants, had been eyeing the humans that had joined them in the camp. For their part, the guerrillas looked wary and afraid. Only Jynn seemed unperturbed by the cobalt giants in their midst. She came forwards.

'I am Captain Evvers, and these are my men... What's left of them, anyway,' she added ruefully. 'We are your salvation.'

Sergeant Vandar was looking down on the woman when he raised his gaze to lock eyes with Scipio. 'Why does this human speak for you, Brother Vorolanus?'

'She is bold,' added Octavian. It was hard to tell through his battle-helm but he sounded mildly amused at the woman's outburst. 'And what is this "salvation" she boasts of? Are we in need of rescue?'

Scipio shot Jynn a reproachful look, before bringing his attention back to Vandar. 'She does not speak for me,' he said, before addressing Octavian, 'but she does possess some useful information, a route into the mountains behind the necron's defences.'

'Through the defensive circle?' asked Vandar, suddenly interested in the human now. Vandar was known for his tactical brilliance, yet even he could not devise a strategy that would allow the battle force to bypass the necron defences around the artillery. He wanted to know more.

'We have a way to breach the impenetrable mountain ridge, yes,' said Tigurius, 'but a plan is needed if we're to make the most of this opportunity.' His gaze fell on the three sergeants as he was walking away.

'My lord?' asked Scipio.

Tigurius didn't look back. He was heading towards an isolated promontory of rock. Much like the Librarian's thoughts, it was swathed in snow and ice. 'I must consult the Sea of Souls,' he muttered, his mind already drifting elsewhere. 'The future is uncertain.'

'Brother-Librarian,' Scipio called, risking censure for using such familiar language.

Tigurius turned. His eyes were ablaze with actinic fire. 'Are you sure that is wise, given your last attempts?'

'Experience matters not, Sergeant Vorolanus,' he replied solemnly. 'Need drives us. I must *know*.' A swell of snow spiralled up from the ground and the Librarian disappeared into it.

Scipio regarded his fellow sergeants. 'Vandar, make the most of our reduced forces.'

Vandar nodded. 'I shall bring victory to our cause, brother.'

The three departed to marshal their squads and prepare for imminent departure to the Thanatos Hills.

Scipio left Brakkius to organise the Thunderbolts, while he spoke to the humans.

Jynn returned a steely expression as he regarded her.

'Accompanying Space Marines into battle is no small thing,' Scipio told her. 'It is dangerous beyond imagining. For one, you are not equipped as we–'

'Look at us,' said Jynn, interrupting.

Scipio stayed his anger as he waited for what she was about to say. He took in the guerrillas. They were a sorry, but war-hardened sight.

'What do you see?' she asked, turning to her troops. When she looked back, there was a proud glint in her eye. 'I see survivors. I see men and women who have lost their homes, their families, everything they have ever known or will know, and have only vengeance to drive them. We are aware of the dangers and we are not Space Marines, it is true, but do not say that we're not equipped for this fight; months scrapping for our survival against these bloody things in the ice wastes says otherwise. We will fight, and we will die, but don't expect us to slow you down – we won't. We know these hills, this land. Dead or alive, I'll get you through that cordon. Promise me one thing: make those soulless bastards pay for what they've done.'

Scipio met her fearless eyes and his anger ebbed in the face of Jynn's glorious pride. 'By Guilliman's blood, I swear it,' he said. He held out his massive gauntleted hand, and uttered in a quieter voice. 'For I desire revenge too.'

She nodded. Her tiny hand was engulfed by his but the gesture was all-important. A compact had been struck, a swearing of an oath that only death could break. In that moment, Scipio saw the grief in her eyes at her loss, and recognised it instantly.

Karthax, forty-five years after
the Black Reach Campaign

THE LAST REMNANTS of the cultist army were being driven back from their walls by the guns of Helios's Terminators. Enfilading storm bolter fire cut the wretches to fleshy ribbons, whilst bursts of heavy flamer cleansed any lingering heretics from the roadside bunkers.

The Fortress of Ardant had once been a bastion to the Imperial faith; now it was an abomination. Filth caked its walls, hell ruled its halls. Blood and flesh, not mortar, held its bricks together. The emblems of the aquila, soaring proudly from its minarets and looking on imperiously from its crenellations were defaced. It was rotten with cracked timbers and pitted stone, rusted metal and moth-eaten banners – yet it stood. Somehow this festering palace was more resilient than a bunker, in spite of its obvious decay.

With a thundercrack, the incendiary charges placed by Tenth ignited and the gates to the Chaos bastion were blasted open. Severed from the fortress itself they quickly crumbled to dust. From within the gaping maw behind the gates, a swarm of mutated cultists emerged in a frothing frenzy. Other beings came with them, once flesh but now something else, something terrible. They stretched the skin of their hosts, manifesting in the corporeal world as disgusting horrors dredged from man's worst imaginings.

'Warp creatures!' bellowed Helios, a statement of damnation as much as a warning. The First unleashed their weapons. The horde withered as assault cannons and cyclone missile launchers cycled up and let rip. Explosive payloads ruptured the throng, painting bloody welts across the smoke-blackened roadway. Half-putrefied cultists, little more than the walking dead, were blasted explosively apart.

Guard units from the Mordian VI, the Stygian Hounds, were ordered into the breach. Armoured formations began the slow grind towards the bastion; Leman Russ to pound, Hellhounds to burn and purify. In a single day, the Ultramarines had cracked open the enemy resistance, a feat the Imperial Guard couldn't manage after over three months of continuous siege. But it wasn't over yet. The broken gate led into a deeper heart of evil. It had to be excised.

Helios waved on the Ultramarines waiting by the Rhino transports on his right.

'Advance, brothers. In the name of Agemman and the Chapter Master!'

Orad gave the signal to embark. The black-clad Chaplain was last aboard the transport, the access hatch still closing as he stepped inside and the tank drove off at speed.

Nine Ultramarines met him inside, down on one knee with their heads bowed as he entered the troop hold.

Scipio Vorolanus was amongst them.

Outside the patter of small-arms resonated through the hull. The Chaplain hardly noticed it.

'Reject the taint in all its perfidy,' Orad began, spitting vitriol against the inner surface of his skull-mask. 'Resist and crush those who worship Chaos. Know in your hearts you are pure of purpose and that the Emperor walks with you. His light will vanquish the traitor and the daemon.' As the engines thrashed, the sound reverberated and intensified around the hold. Orad fought it, his oratory rising from a shout to a scream. An explosion nearby rocked the Rhino on its tracks, but he kept his feet. 'The Ultramarines fight with clenched fist around bolter and blade. We are the inheritors of Guilliman, the heirs of Ultramar. They know our names and they quail as we recite them with bolters as our voice.'

The engine slowed as the Rhino struck the enemy. A lethal rank of spikes gave the hard nose of the tank a killing edge. Crunching bone, the spatter of blood and the screams of the dead came dully through the hull. A body rolled under the tracks – something big – and the Rhino lurched up and over it before landing square.

'For the glory of Ultramar, we shall know no fear!'

Screeching to a halt, the tank's hatch slammed open and the Ultramarines charged out with Orad at their head.

Blood and death greeted their arrival. Cultists clad in rags, wrapped in pus-soaked bandages pressed in, a horde of the unwashed. The Chaplain cut through them, his crozius blooded, leaving a string of enemy corpses in his wake.

Scipio was behind him, he had a perfect view of Orad's back. His shoulder plates compensated for the movement allowing his arm to rise and fall like a piston as he bludgeoned. Rancid flesh gummed the brunt of his crozius. He flicked it off with a desultory gesture as a sporadic muzzle flare lit the end of his bolt pistol. Punished heretics exploded as the mass-reactive shells did their holy work. He'd engraved every one with a litany of hate and purging. Orad knew their order in the weapon's chamber and spoke each and every one as it killed a traitor. Nothing stayed his wrath.

It was… *inspiring*.

Chainsword chugging on the flesh of a dying cultist, Scipio forged himself a little space and briefly examined the battlefield.

Across the roadway, on the opposite side of the gate, a second squad of Ultramarines had deployed. Like Scipio's Thunderbolts, they were swarmed by enemies. He recognised Sergeant Solinus immediately and felt an urge to breach the gatehouse before him. Given Orad's fervour, the Chaplain wanted that honour too.

'Repel them!' he roared. 'Smite them! Become the Angels of Death!'

He was locked in battle with a ferocious warp-thing, a possessed flesh puppet of some daemon from the abyss. Tentacled appendages spewed from the creature's distended maw. Several fizzed and burned against the Chaplain's rosarius field impelled from the icon chained around his gorget, but at least one got through and bit into his power armour.

Pressed by his own opponents, Scipio thought he heard Orad grunt and saw the protective energy field flicker for but a moment when the Chaplain dispatched the bloated hell-beast with a hate-filled curse.

Sensing a shift in momentum, Scipio ordered his warriors with even more aggressive tactics. Bolters were slung in favour of gladius and pistol as the Thunderbolts closed hand-to-hand. Brakkius snapped a cultist in two across his armoured knee, whilst Ortus stabbed another in the throat and crushed the skull of a second in his gauntlet.

Cator unleashed a ragged line of fiery promethium into the decaying ranks from his flamer and they burned. Combined with the furious blade assault it tore enough of a gap for the Thunderbolts to advance, gaining precious ground into the gatehouse and the inner citadel beyond.

The horde of traitors that had sallied forth was slowly being cut down. Helios kept up a furious but disciplined barrage from the edge of the Ultramarines battle line, withering the enemy troops that had sought to flee the fighting.

Nothing must survive. Those were Calgar's orders.

Ground under the tracks of tanks, eviscerated by blades or crushed underfoot, it didn't matter – the only sure way to cleanse the fortress was to systematically eradicate everything inside.

Once the tactical squads were in, the Terminators would begin their implacable march to the gates. The Mordians would follow, bringing tanks and more flamers for the purge.

Elsewhere on the battlefield the Tenth were taking down gun towers, cutting off supply points and collapsing defences under Master Telion's expert direction. Several weapon emplacements had already been sabotaged, leaving behind twisted metal and blast-scarred sandbags.

A plasma cannon turret, protected inside a mobile bunker, slowly turned to draw a bead on the Thunderbolts. Its rotational axle was slicked with pus instead of oil, and the bulbous maw of the weapon that extruded from the firing slit was malformed with corrosion. The weapon had almost built to expulsion when an explosive typhoon engulfed it – more of the Scouts' unseen work. Shrapnel and flesh-parts pattered against Scipio's armour as the Ultramarines fought through the last of the cultists and entered the courtyard behind them.

'Glory to the Thunderbolts,' said Scipio quickly but good-naturedly to Solinus.

'It is for the Chapter, Brother-Sergeant Vorolanus,' Orad said before Solinus could reply.

Both sergeants bowed to the Chaplain's wisdom before moving into a slow run towards the inner citadel, a craggy, gore-stained structure that poked out of the centre of the bastion like a diseased talon.

It was the briefest of respites as they crossed the

courtyard, which was littered with the dead but otherwise empty of threat, and reached the portal to the inner citadel. The door was like an open wound, festering with decay. Veins pulsed in the marblesque rock, like arteries swollen with plague. But it was unbarred.

Orad held the others back with his outstretched arm as he stood at the threshold of the inner citadel, staring. 'It is dark as sin, but the way is open to us,' he said. As he led them onwards down a shallow set of steps, Scipio thought he heard Orad's sharp intake of breath. It sounded like pain.

'Brother-Chaplain?'

'It's nothing,' said Orad, though the timbre of his voice suggested he was injured. It had a faint gurgling quality, like there was blood or mucus in his throat.

One of the warp-thing's barbs had got past his rosarius field and penetrated his power armour too. Scipio noticed crusting around the wound and some of the ceramite had even started to corrode.

Scipio paused, uncertain what to do.

'It's nothing,' Orad said more vehemently and just for the sergeant this time. 'Our enemy is close. We must destroy it. I will seek out an Apothecary later.'

He turned, signalling an end to it, and beckoned the Ultramarines on, closer to the nest of evil.

There was a stink upon the air, copper-blood and the reek of putrefaction. Corpse-fattened spiders and bloated flies skittered from the light as the Ultramarines switched on their lamp-packs. Grainy lances of magnesium white stabbed into the blackness in all directions. There were alcoves where more corpses lingered, slumped against columns or strewn over debris from the fallen ceiling. The only route further into the citadel was ahead, over a stinking carpet of mould that stuck to the Ultramarines' boots and led to a temple of horrors.

'Steel yourselves,' hissed Orad as they arrived at the entrance, the oleaginous glow of rancid lanterns spilling sticky light ahead of it.

As he touched the rim of the light, Scipio could almost feel it coating his armour in a film of decay. He suppressed the urge to remove his trappings and be free of the taint, wanting nothing more than to experience the cleansing fury of his ritual ablutions.

The foetid temple was no better.

Rusted chains hung lankly from a pitted ceiling, strung with flayed corpses and gossamer-thin webs of flesh-dust. Filth-streaked columns were inscribed with ruinous sigils and contained alcoves bearing cadaverous, half-fleshed skulls. A pit was hewn in the centre of the room, which had once been some kind of great hall but was now divested of its former use and put towards corruption. Something boiled within it, wallowing in a soup of pestilence. Noxious bubbles belched to the surface as the creature moved, disturbing bleached skulls and half-digested viscera.

So it wasn't only a temple, it was also the abomination's feasting chamber. It was the very root of evil on Karthax.

Orad had seen enough.

'Destroy it!'

Squads Scipio and Solinus unleashed their weapons in a terrifying storm at the loathsome spawn in the filth-pool. For a moment, it was utterly obscured from view by the Ultramarines' blistering salvo.

After a full minute of the hell-storm, the reports of bolters and the hiss of flamers slowly echoed away around the circular room. Smoke and fire trailed from the pit afterwards. Most of its disgusting contents had been splattered around the walls or flecked the Ultramarines' power armour.

As the smoke cleared, Orad ordered Solinus forwards. The sergeant acknowledged, and approached the edge of the pit warily. He used his boot to nudge something within it, leaning back from the sight suddenly repulsed.

'There is a body,' Solinus waved the others forwards.

Scipio crouched by the ragged corpse of a man. He was wearing robes and his flesh and bones had been utterly sundered. Bolt impacts marked his body. His exploded limbs and innards, the shattered bones and scorched skin were testament to the effectiveness of the Ultramarines' weapons.

'A sanctioned psyker of some sort,' he decided, noting sigil-marks on the skin the fusillade hadn't obliterated. 'Cursed by Nurgle.'

'So where is it?' asked Solinus.

Scipio met his gaze, questioning.

'Where is the beast?' the other sergeant clarified.

'That was not the creature I burned,' offered Cator.

His battle-brothers were right. This thing was a puppet; no more than a vessel for whatever entity had claimed this place and transformed it into its own wretched domain. Where was the plaguebearer that had claimed the soul of this man?

Scipio turned around at the sound of ceramite clattering against stone behind them.

'Brother-Chaplain, replace your battle-helm. This place is unclean!'

He went to go to Orad but was held back by the Chaplain's warding hand. The wound in his power armour was seeping gore and pus. It crusted his entire forearm and was spreading.

His words were thick with phlegm. 'Stay back.'

'Lords of Ultramar,' Solinus gasped and reached for his bolt pistol. 'It has taken him, it has taken our Chaplain.'

Scipio pushed down his aim. 'Wait!'

Orad went to speak again but bent double and vomited a stream of corruption. Chin drooling with sick, he spat a last gobbet of the stuff from his mouth. His eyes were sunken in his skull, the old wounds on his face throbbing, raw and reopened. He sank down, knee deep in the filth. His crozius fell from his grasp.

'What are you doing?' snapped Solinus. 'He has the taint – we must end him now!' He shook off Scipio's grasp and brought up the weapon again.

Scipio stepped into his line of sight. 'He is our Chaplain. Of us all, his faith is the most devout. How can this be?'

'It matters not. Stand aside, now.'

Ever since Scipio had been a Scout, Orad had been his Chaplain. He had counselled his doubts on Black Reach, had instilled the power of his faith in him. And now he was damned, reduced to no more than a vessel for an insidious terror. The taint of Chaos had claimed him. It had breached his aegis through the smallest of cracks, widened it and rotted him from within.

Scipio drew his own sidearm. His voice was low and solemn. 'I will do it.'

Nodding, Solinus lowered his aim. 'Then do it quickly, before it is too late.'

Orad had wrapped his arms around his torso and was convulsing violently in the pool of filth he had created. There was no sentience in his eyes any more. He was a gibbering wreck, a once proud servant of Ultramar brought low.

But when Scipio drew a bead upon the Chaplain he hesitated.

There must be a way. Orad can repulse it.

In eerie synchronicity with the sergeant's thoughts, the Chaplain's neck snapped up and his dead eyes fixed onto Scipio's pitiless retinal lenses.

'*Mercy...*'

The trigger squeezed a little tighter in Scipio's grasp, but he couldn't do it. Orad shook with a sudden palsy. Something within the Chaplain was changing.

The sergeant felt a hand on his pauldron. The world was slowing as if mired in the very foul stuff that pervaded the temple. The reek of death and decay overtook the chamber, more noisome than ever.

'Kill it! Do it now!'

Scipio was only dimly aware of Solinus's urgent voice, of the slow *chank* of bolter shells filling their chambers, of the bounds of Orad's armour bursting apart like an overfilled lung.

Too late the first shell spat from Scipio's pistol, its burning contrails flashing in the air. The sheer lassitude of its trajectory brought on by the hell-transformation unfolding before him allowed Scipio to appreciate every spark, every mote of flame.

Too late, other shells joined it from the battle-brothers around him; nascent spits of flamer too and the glowing coruscation from a plasma gun.

Too late, Scipio realised what his hesitancy had cost them and shouted a warning to Brother Naius.

The husk of Orad's armour broke apart under the barrage but the creature that had stolen the Chaplain's flesh was no longer there. It had leapt onto the ceiling, latching to the rock with the acid-slime on its claws, spewing out barbed tendrils from a distended maw.

Three of the tendrils punched through Naius's chestplate and he fell, bolter loosing off wild rounds as he died and his death grip clenched.

Scipio reached him a fraction too late. He bundled Naius over with the barbs still hooked in him. They stretched and ripped free as he went down, breaking open ceramite and taking chunks of flesh into the darkness above as the beast retracted them. Then it was gone.

'Naius!' Scipio unleashed a burst into the gloom but hit only rockcrete. It was a pointless act, save for the fact of venting his anger. Resting a hand over the neck where Naius's only intact progenoid was still harboured, Scipio got to his feet. He had been one of Solinus's squad and now his legacy had ended – all because Scipio had hesitated. The Ultramarines were on the offensive, searching the vaults in the temple above, throwing out random bursts of fire as someone saw a shadow or detected the insidious scuttling of the daemon.

Avoiding Solinus's furious gaze, Scipio went on the hunt for the thing too, determined to avenge Naius. It was Orad no longer. Trapped for a moment in the lurid glare of a pestilential lantern, the Ultramarines saw an abomination where once had been their Chaplain. Gelid-skinned, surrounded by flies, it was more corpse than man. A horn had sprouted from the daemon's head; claws replaced hands; it had hooves instead of feet. It was emaciated, its innards showing through diaphanous skin. Pustules and boils puckered flesh that sagged like melted wax and a grotesque hump bent the monster's back.

Seeing the Ultramarines' obvious disgust, it chuckled.

'What's wrong... *brothers*?' Its hideous voice was a slurred parody of Orad's.

Bolter impacts riddled the wall where it was clinging like some human spider, but went wide of the mark. For such a diseased beast it was quick, racing up pillars and skittering through the shadows too fast for the Space Marines to bring it down.

'Keep it pinned,' shouted Solinus, directing warriors left and right in pairs. Three battle-brothers guarded the temple entrance and were primed to release a deadly salvo if the creature came within range and sight.

Scipio did the same and was about to give chase, determined the beast that had killed Orad would not escape, when something seized his arm. At first, he thought it might be Solinus and he turned with defiance on his lips. That emotion turned to horror when he realised it was Brother Naius. His armour was corroding from the inside out. A bloodshot eye, rampant with pestilence, glared madly from a wound in his eye socket. The point where the tendrils had pierced his chest bulged, cracking his plastron.

Swinging round his chainsword, Scipio cut Naius down – the second son of Ultramar he had condemned by his inaction – finishing him with a blast from his pistol.

Or so he thought.

Partially exploded, a huge cavity in his stomach yawning open with pustulant debris, the undead-Naius rose on twisted limbs. The chainsword had chewed off part of his helmet. Blackened nubs of teeth bared in a snarl as the creature came at Scipio.

'Brother!' The sergeant ducked when he recognised Cator's voice. A *whoosh* of rapidly expelled promethium followed, sending heat spikes registering on Scipio's retinal display when the flamer burst just missed him. It engulfed the undead-Naius, though, eliciting a scream that was no longer wrenched from his former brother's lips.

'Don't let the mouth barbs touch you,' Scipio warned,

backing up and searching the shadows. Behind him, Naius burned away to ash, leaving rotten armour in his wake.

Seven grotesque pillars supported the vaulted ceiling of the plague temple. The daemon weaved and scuttled between them, using the darkness to thwart the Ultramarines.

'Herd it!' Solinus bellowed, his voice echoing from somewhere deeper in the vast room. Sporadic bolter fire followed and Scipio thought he saw the silhouette of something unholy coming his way. He pressed his body against one of the pillars and waited. He couldn't see the daemon but he could sense it. Not in a psychic way, Scipio was no Librarian. But it was in his nose, despite his olfactory filters; it veneered his skin, though he wore power armour over a mesh bodyglove; it buzzed in his ears like the droning of flies.

Scipio shut his eyes and focussed on his instincts. The creature was fast but not impossibly so. He owed it to Orad, to Naius, to kill it.

Close now. The shouting of his battle-brothers was getting nearer. They were operating in a dispersed formation in order to cover the most ground. He heard Cator and Brakkius, the clipped shots of Ortus in the vicinity.

Not yet. He pressed against the pillar, denying the urge to engage, to wreak bloody havoc as an avenging Angel of Death. He needed for it to come closer.

When the moment arrived it almost took him by surprise, but Scipio's body was honed, conditioned to preternatural levels and it reacted out of instinct. He opened his eyes. Springing from cover, his chainsword was already swinging. The mouth tendrils spilled like dead worms as the blade-teeth cut through them. The blade continued its buzzing trajectory, embedding in the rib bone all the way to the base of the sternum. Face-to-face with the daemon, Scipio levelled his bolt pistol and for a split second it was Orad there and not a plaguebearer.

'*Brother–*' it began to mouth, a look of anguish on its diseased face.

'Get back to the abyss!' The bolt pistol fired and the shell struck the daemon in the eye, turning the creature back to its true form. It still wore Orad's flesh, strips of body-mesh clung tenaciously to his enhanced musculature, but it was not him.

It isn't him...

The plaguebearer's visage exploded in a bloom of viscera and bone-chips as the mass reactive shell detonated, leaving it without a head. It sagged, deflated almost, as a keening wail ripped the air like a fat blade. Ichor exuded from the orifice in the neck, pooling about the dead Chaplain's shoulders. The daemon was banished; its meat puppet was Orad again. A dead and decapitated Orad, but it was him.

Scipio nearly sank to his knees at the sight. Solinus steadied him. His voice was stern but genuine. 'That thing would have killed us all. You had no choice, brother.'

But Scipio felt differently. His inaction had caused Naius's demise; his bolter hand had slain what was left of Orad.

'I made my choice too late,' he breathed, avowing silently never to do so again. 'And it killed Orad. It killed them both.'

CHAPTER TWENTY

SICARIUS SIGNALLED THE retreat. He'd cut a path through the necrons, dispatching one with every blow of the Tempest Blade. The air was thick with the stench of phasal shift. At their captain's command, the Ultramarines bled back into the ice-fog, their forms lit by the star-flash of bolter muzzle flares. Slow to react to the lightning assault, the necrons didn't even attempt to give chase. They settled for a desultory salvo of gauss-fire and then continued their advance towards Kellenport.

'Does this seem too easy to you, brother-captain?' asked Daceus when they were clear. He reaped a heavy toll with his power fist and was sweating with the effort of killing, but they'd barely dented the enemy's forces.

Sicarius's initial silence betrayed his anger. 'It's ineffective, sergeant,' he replied at last. 'Our attacks are of no consequence.' He opened up the battle-force-wide comms-feed. Though the necrons were blocking most vox-signals, it was only long distance communication that was affected.

The leaders of the attack groups he'd deployed to harry the necron phalanxes returned with similar replies. The mechanoids were defending themselves but otherwise had ignored them. Since their first foray, this was the fifth engagement. No one had, as of yet, managed to get close enough to the core of the force to ascertain if a high-level lord were present.

Sicarius clenched his fist, his rage impotent for now. 'Regroup, all squads.'

'Sir?' asked Daceus when his captain didn't make any move.

'This isn't working. I have to draw it out, Daceus.'

'My lord,' the voice of Sergeant Manorian crackled over the feed.

Sicarius was brusque. 'Speak.'

'The necrons have stopped moving.'

Sicarius acknowledged then cut the link. 'Something has changed.'

'A new weapon in their arsenal? Perhaps they're consolidating after our raids? They might be having an effect after all,' suggested Daceus.

'No, I don't think it's that.' Sicarius eyed the fog, as if searching it for the answer he wanted. 'But I will know the answer before we're done.'

SICARIUS STARED THROUGH Praxor's magnoculars, waiting for the rest of the force to join them. The Ultramarines would regroup in an area of sparse ruins, part of one of Arcona City's commercia districts. Most of the megalopolis had been levelled by necron heavy artillery. These blackened nubs of debris were a rare feature on an otherwise bland and flattened landscape. The squads filtered in from the north and south; west was where the necron advance was coming from – though, in truth, they dominated most of the planet – and east led back to Kellenport. Ixion and Strabo, redeployed from the Thanatos Operation, arrived first on contrails of fire.

Several of their number were wounded but they'd sustained no casualties.

Venatio was patching up the injured and stopped in front of his captain.

'I'll need to see that,' he said.

Lowering the scopes, Sicarius glared at him. 'Why do you think they've stalled their advance, Brother-Apothecary?'

'That's not my concern at this time. The injury to your shoulder is, however.'

A long cleft split part of the captain's pauldron and there was blood gumming the wound. It looked deep. Praxor had been taken aback at first when he'd seen it. He'd never known Sicarius to bleed. He knew he was flesh and blood, but Sicarius was such a peerless warrior, he had never witnessed more than a scratch against his armour. Praxor hoped it wasn't an omen.

The captain was about to protest again but Venatio's resolve was unwavering; so too was his stare. Sicarius passed the scopes back to Praxor and seated himself on a chunk of ruin for the Apothecary to examine him.

'The shoulder: how is it?' Venatio was removing the cracked pauldron and was probing the mesh layer beneath to get at the wound.

'Stiff,' admitted Sicarius, rotating the blade once the armour was removed. Acutely aware he was being observed, he turned to Praxor.

'Watch them, brother-sergeant,' he said. 'I want to know the moment anything changes.'

Praxor nodded and continued where Sicarius had left off. There was a ridge of blackened stone just ahead of the Ultramarines position. It was a better vantage point to observe the necrons so he made for it.

Agrippen met him there.

'How do you defeat an endless foe?' Praxor asked after a few moments as he looked through the scopes.

'The same as any, with courage and honour,' the Dreadnought replied.

The ridge was little more than a spur of rock, a collapsed column or statue – the damage and the ice made it hard to tell – and could just about provide enough room for Praxor and the ancient.

'Our forces are battered, though. I would follow my captain into battle until I could no longer wield bolter and blade, but it is hard to see how we will prevail.'

'The Chapter has been bloodied before. Some wars are merely harder than others. It is here that we truly test ourselves and prove our strength.'

Praxor tried not to think of the remark as facile. So much of what he knew, or thought he knew, had been tested on Damnos. Not all of it had survived the journey.

He looked below and saw that the rest of the battle force had returned. Sicarius was gathering them for something big, some fresh assault as he sought his prize.

Praxor chastened himself – such thoughts were unfitting for a Space Marine. He resolved to speak to Trajan at the earliest opportunity. He returned to the scopes.

'They are like statues. What are they waiting for?

'Perhaps they seek to gauge our next course of action,' suggested Agrippen.

Praxor lowered the magnoculars again and looked at the Dreadnought. 'Tell me, brother: how would Agemman have prosecuted this war?'

Agrippen's reply was emphatic but neutral. 'He would not have.'

'Damnos would have been left to burn?' Praxor was incredulous.

The Dreadnought fixed him with a glare from the vision slit in his sarcophagus. 'It would have been *made* to burn.'

'You think that Damnos is already lost?'

'It doesn't matter what I think. I serve the Chapter. On this field of war, on this campaign, I serve Captain Sicarius. What I believe or what I know is immaterial; duty is what matters most.'

'I am unworthy of that honour,' Praxor admitted. 'I do not see my captain's mind and I doubt our purpose on this world.'

'What do you doubt about it, brother?'

Praxor paused, weighing up his next words carefully, 'These are a broken people. Imperial citizens, yes, but unworthy of that honour. It is hard to find accord with saving a people that does not want to save itself.'

'Are you so sure they are without defiance? Courage?'

'It is what I have seen, yes.'

Agrippen considered that for a moment, before saying, 'Answer me this, brother: do you believe you are above these humans in some way?'

'In all ways,' Praxor said flatly.

'Then is it not the duty of those lofty individuals to inspire and lift those beneath them so that they too might achieve some measure of greatness?'

Praxor wasn't expecting that. The Dreadnought's logic was hard to refute, so he didn't try. Instead, he bowed his head. 'Of course it is.'

'There is more?' Agrippen pressed. Praxor's shame was not only at his discarding of the Damnosians' right to protection and life.

He lifted his head. 'I had thought you here to press Agemman's interests and secure the pre-eminence of the First by undermining Sicarius. It was an unworthy belief.'

Agrippen was sanguine. 'Your faith has been tested, that is all. It must be if it is to remain strong.' There was no hint of reproach in his rumbling sepulchral voice, 'As to the matter of Agemman, too much is made of this supposed rivalry. I trust in the wisdom and leadership of our Lord Calgar. Do you know why that is so?'

Praxor's silence bade him to continue.

'Because I have witnessed his courage and heard his words. Victory or death – one or the other awaits us on Damnos. I do not fear it. I do not let it concern me. It merely *is*. This is our duty. It is what makes us Emperor's Angels. He will protect us and He will grant Sicarius the wisdom and guile to lead us.'

Praxor bowed his head again that such a noble warrior had deigned to share his wisdom with him. '*Victoris Ultra*, venerable one.'

'*Victoris Ultra*.'

Servos whirring, gears grinding, Agrippen dismounted from the rocky spur and went to find Ultracius. He left Praxor to his thoughts and his duty.

'What do you see, brother-sergeant?' Sicarius asked a few moments later. He was done with the Apothecary and had come for a status report.

Praxor was looking through magnoculars at the distant enemy formations but the ice-fog was still thick. They'd reached the edge of Arcona City and were about to pass over its borders if they ever moved again.

'They are waiting.' In spite of the weather, Praxor could see the massive phalanxes standing shoulder-to-shoulder. Their utter stillness was unnatural. Skeletal-faced, their eye sockets aglow, they reminded him of revenants. 'Do we attack?'

Sicarius shook his head, ignoring the proffered scopes. Daceus was with him, carrying his captain's battle-helm.

'We will fall back.'

'We continue to flee?' asked Praxor.

'A Space Marine does not flee, brother-sergeant,' interjected Daceus. His bionic eye seemed to burn with indignation. 'When met by an implacable enemy, he does not throw his strength at it until he is spent. He finds a way to bring the battle to his advantage.'

'We need to level the scales, Sergeant Manorian,' asserted Sicarius. 'A warrior has many weapons in his arsenal. This,' he brandished his plasma pistol, 'and this,' then tapped the hilt of his sheathed Tempest Blade before gesturing to their surroundings, 'but he must also use his mind and mould the battlefield into a weapon too.'

He paused, peering into the mists. 'How close are they now, brother?'

'Two kilometres and static. My lord, what are they waiting for?'

'What else?' Sicarius answered, and there was a hint of a smile in his voice as his eyes narrowed. 'For their potentate, the one who wields power.'

Sicarius was right. Praxor looked back through the magnoculars and found the necron lord who commanded the army. He had just emerged in the throng. It was an ancient, terrible creature with age-tarnished trappings and a body of shimmering gold.

'I think the wait is over, sire.' He handed his captain the scopes and this time Sicarius took them.

'So it seems. Tell me something, Brother Manorian, have you heard of the Battle of Thermapylon?'

'I know a myth, from the days of the Terran battle-kings.'

'Go on.'

'Seven hundred men of warrior blood held the pass of

Thermapylon against the numberless hordes of Xeruclese from across the sea. Their sacrifice allowed the
army of King Vidus to muster and throw back the
enemy, harrying them all the way back to the beaches
where they made their berths, and burn their ships at
anchor.'

'*And the seas ran red with their blood and the sand became
as crimson night,*' added Sicarius, reciting from the epic
poem that recalled the legend.

Praxor was briefly wrong-footed; he didn't know his
captain had studied the arts. But then it was military history, mythic or not, and Sicarius was an arch-student of
war. It made a certain sense.

'Do you know how they triumphed?'

'With blood and steel, I presume.'

'Oh, their blades were red as the dawn, brother, but
that wasn't how they engaged an army of five hundred
thousand with seven hundred men. No, they achieved
their goal because they knew the lay of the land. Every
death was paid for by a hundred enemy soldiers. It was
a battle of attrition that could only end in suicide but it
wrested time from the hands of fate and used it to the
king's advantage. His army was ocean-borne and won a
great naval victory against Xeruclese's allies. Much of the
details are lost to time but the message remains true and
relevant.'

'I am ready to die for my Chapter, brother-captain,'
said Praxor.

'That is not what I mean.' Sicarius returned the magnoculars. 'This war *can* be won. But we need time. We
need our tanks – Antaro would relish this theatre of war
– and the *Valin's Revenge*. I plan to get us that time and
cut down the necron overlord into the bargain. But I do
not plan on dying to achieve it.' He turned, fixing Praxor

in a gimlet glare. 'My legacy is not yet at its end, and I would add more laurels to my banner.'

Praxor nodded. Sicarius's defiance was stirring, even if he found his arrogance a little bitter with the casualties they'd already sustained.

'Outside Kellenport, at the edges of the city wall, we will funnel the necrons into our own pass and there they will fall to our fury. Tigurius will have destroyed the Thanatos guns by then and Antaro can unleash his armoured fists.'

'The necrons are formidable, my lord. They are not the hordes of Xeruclese, nor do they merely wield spears or travel in wooden boats.'

'Indeed, but we carry bolters and are Adeptus Astartes.' He turned to Daceus. 'We make for the Kellenport outer marker,' he said. 'Signal Sergeants Ixion and Strabo to range ahead of us there and tell them to make haste. The necrons are moving.'

Both Strabo and Ixion came back to Daceus swiftly. The speed of the reply sent a tremor of unease through Praxor as did the veteran-sergeant's grim face as he related the reply to Sicarius.

'Request denied, sir.'

'Explain, brother-sergeant.'

'They cannot. There are forces coming from the east, from Kellenport. The necrons have us blocked in.'

Sicarius took his battle-helm without response. When he slammed it down against his gorget, there was a *clang* not unlike a death knell across the frozen quietude of the wastes. When the captain did finally speak it was with the grating cadence of his vox-grille.

'Gather your battle-brothers, and have the other sergeants do likewise. We make our stand here.' His tone turned belligerent as he drew the Tempest Blade and pointed towards the advancing horde and the necron overlord in its ranks. 'Death or glory awaits us – I will welcome both.'

CHAPTER TWENTY-ONE

ANKH WAS CONNECTED to all the mechanoids of the tomb. They were his workers, his messengers, his eyes and ears. Truly, he was the Architect. Most creatures of the universe – he had come to think of them as simpleton children when compared to the majesty and intellect of the necrontyr – beheld the necrons and saw only machines. They were so much more than that. Their science had fundamentally changed their race. It was so advanced that to look upon it would be to perceive what primitive cultures called magic. These humans, a race of barely evolved primates, were one such culture.

To serve the machinations of his lord, he would unleash 'magic' of a terrifying magnitude. He had activated a Doomsday Phalanx of monoliths. Through the multi-faceted eyes of one of his drones, Ankh had witnessed the destruction of one of his pyramidal engines. It had surprised him. Perhaps it was why the Undying wanted so desperately to kill this one. Was the genebred warrior really any different from the rest of his species? Certainly he attired himself more ostentatiously than any of the other armour-clad savages. Immobilising the monolith was also a feat worthy of note, especially done single-handed.

Ankh had moved the others at his overlord's command. The Undying wanted to see annihilation; the talons of the Destroyer curse had made their first incisions into his fragile engrammic sanity. Pre-eminent amongst these weapons of war was the Doomsday Monolith.

'You desire destruction, my lord,' Ankh said to the quietude of the tomb. Through the eyes of his creations he could see the trio of monoliths gliding into position; the nexus of energy between them had almost reached critical mass. 'Then you shall have it.'

Ankh unleashed his 'magic'.

'GIVE ME MORE. Break your backs if you have to but bring those things down!' Letzger was hoarse from all the shouting. Above the roaring thunder of the guns, he had to bellow to be heard.

His gun crews knew the drill, though. They knew that sweating blood was necessary, and that their lives and the lives of their people depended on it.

Hel-handed boomed again, shaking dust from its foundations and sluicing debris down to the lower levels with every seismic explosion from its barrel. From the Thanatos Hills to the monoliths converging on the meagre defenders in the Courtyard of Xiphos, Letzger had changed targets. So far, his efforts to bring down one of the necron pyramids had been in vain. There was some kind of ethereal veil protecting them all. Shots that weren't lost to the black void coiling around the machineries were otherwise absorbed by the living metal from which the monoliths were constructed.

The view down the *Hel-handed's* crosshairs was not an encouraging one.

Letzger seized the vox-horn, 'Leave 'em be and send a shell into the square.' He rattled off a series of measurements, amending the cannon's aim and trajectory. 'And give those metal bastards a half-shell. Don't want to crucify our Angels in the blast.'

Slamming the speaker cup down, Letzger was about to get settled on the scopes and watch the show when something bright blazed on the horizon.

Emerald light burned from some unseen source, forcing him to look away. He felt the heat against his skin and smelled his hair smouldering before the beam hit.

'*Merciful Emperor*,' he breathed as a green fire hit the *Hel-handed* and a god-weapon died.

ADANAR FELT THE explosion before he saw it. He felt it even before the beam hit the Kellenport wall and tore the *Hel-handed* open. Letzger had been on that platform, the ornery old dog. After the emerald flash faded he simply wasn't there anymore; neither were his gun crews. The weapon was a twisted mess. There was little of it left. Most of the wall and the troops nearby, even those who had hunkered down on the lower level, had also been obliterated.

He turned to Humis, who had ducked behind the barricade. Part of the corporal's uniform was on fire, ignited by the heat wave. Adanar was patting it down when he realised his own face was burned raw. It stung to the touch.

'Throne of Earth,' mewled the corporal. 'We are all dead men.'

Adanar was getting to his feet. He'd only realised belatedly that he'd been knocked down – must have been from the void shields breaking. 'We were dead men before now,' he said, snarling at the pain in his face. 'Yet here we are.' He pulled his pistol. Something was materialising on the wrecked battlements amidst the fire-blackened debris of the *Hel-handed*.

Necrons.

The first of the men inside Kellenport died without realising what killed them. Their faces were still etched in terror as they turned to ash.

Adanar loosed off a shot that struck a steel skull in the jaw, making the mechanoid jerk its neck. It didn't stop it from flaying the Ark Guardsmen in front of it.

'Turn and fight!' the commander raged. He was further away than he remembered and his right leg hurt with all the fires of the warp.

Slowly, the troopers below the battlements started to fight back. A sergeant was even shouting for order before a gauss-blast reduced his head to a greasy memory. He toppled, his neck wound cauterised, before someone else took his place.

Humis was running alongside Adanar, dodging the stray emerald beams and vaulting chunks of rubble. The platform wasn't that far; the enemy even less so. 'They must have used a weapon on us,' he said. There was a hollow sound in his breathing, as if he had a punctured lung. Perhaps he had. Humis didn't complain, though. 'It must have been powerful to cut through the shield.'

How were they even functioning? Adanar had no clue. They'd been punched across the battlements, caught in the blast wave – he knew that now. Somehow they'd stayed on the wall instead of being pitched to their doom, but they were both hurt.

Following their commander's example, more of the Ark Guard got up from their posts and joined Adanar and Humis. There weren't that many necrons on the wall yet; there was still time to block the attack.

'And now they're phasing in their raiders to finish the job.'

Adanar didn't talk. He assumed Humis needed to or he'd realise what they were doing and flee, or lose what scrap of sanity he had left.

A half-glance below revealed the Space Marines and some of the conscripts were exchanging fire with the mechanoids assaulting the square. The necrons obviously didn't possess the capacity to phase all of their troops onto the walls or they'd already be overrun. Silently, he wished the Angels luck. It seemed an odd thing to have to do. Over the last few hours, the Emperor's avengers had seemed altogether more human than Adanar had ever given them credit for. It was to the good and the bad, he supposed.

He was running past a vox-officer when a gauss-beam jagged out and took the poor swine in the gut. His innards were dissolved to atoms and he slumped with a gurgle. Adanar crouched behind a broken crenellation, taking cover for the first time since the surge towards the gun platform. Hot, green energy flashed overhead as he stooped for the fallen vox-cup. A few seconds later, Humis was right there with him. The man had blood on his collar from where he'd been coughing. Adanar boosted the vox-signal as high as it would go and yelled into the cup.

'This is Commander Adanar Sonne. All forces to the gun platform on the east wall. Repel the enemy at all costs.'

The barrage lessened as more troops joined the effort

of dislodging the necron invaders, and Adanar was on his feet again. He patted Humis on the shoulder, indicating they needed to get going, but the corporal didn't move. When he looked back, Adanar saw the pallor of his face and the glass in his eyes. Humis was dead.

He carried on.

Las-beams were hammering the necrons now, who didn't bother to seek cover or retreat. They merely advanced, implacable as death.

Something was happening up ahead. He thought he recognised a desperate figure fleeing from the mechanoids, taking several squads with him. Adanar's fists clenched when he realised it was Rancourt. The cowardly worm was trying to save his own skin but had opened the trap the Ark Guard had forged around the raiders.

He wanted to shout, to tell them to turn back, but he was too far away and the din of gunfire was too loud. Instead, Adanar carried on. He was racing to his doom, and he knew it. He didn't care. This was the moment he had been waiting for. At last he would know peace. He couldn't just throw his life away, *she* wouldn't like that. But this was different. Adanar's sacrifice might save the lives of those Rancourt had endangered. His only regret was he wouldn't get to see the bastard suffer for it.

Just a few more metres and he'd be on them. He nearly tripped on a corpse. The poor wretch had been sliced in two by a necron beam. Though hard to tell, Adanar knew it was Kador and that Rancourt had bolted when his bodyguard was slain.

The locket-charm around his wrist dug into his skin where his arm was blistered by the terrible emerald flash. Adanar tore it free and gripped it in his hand.

I'm coming… The words echoed inside his head,

meant for those who had waited long enough already. Leaping the half-flayed wreckage of a gun crew, Adanar made it onto the platform and was ready to meet his end.

THE COURTYARD OF Xiphos had lit up like some infernal flare. Snow and ice melted instantly before evaporating into steam as the beam struck the wall and fire washed over those below.

Some of the men closer to the impact point were flattened. Their uniforms caught alight and there was screaming. Other conscript squads were fleeing; some stayed to help the injured but Iulus waved them on.

'Forward as one, bolter and blade!'

Except these men didn't carry bolters, nor did they wear power amour or possess the strength and skill of a Space Marine. For more times than he needed to count, Iulus was impressed by the fortitude of men. The conscripts took up their weapons and kept up the fight.

The beam that slew the god-weapon on the wall hadn't come from the Thanatos Hills. That barrage, as potent as it was and still persisting even now, was unable to knock out the void shields. The range was too far. No, the killing blow that ruptured the massive cannon's aegis came from the monoliths. The pyramids had fired as a collective, unleashing a beam of such potency that it had overloaded a void shield.

'We will die in this hell storm,' shouted Kolpeck beside him. It brought Iulus from his thoughts.

The two sides traded intense fire across the Courtyard of Xiphos. Most of the Imperials had found cover and this mitigated the fact that their armour paled in comparison to that of the necrons. As each force advanced, the carnage only intensified.

Iulus nodded, 'Glory or death,' he cried to the rig-hand turned soldier. 'Embrace it and the Emperor will take you to his side when it is done.'

This *was* death. Iulus had a mind for tactical acumen, just like any Space Marine. He knew odds and strategy, and he could recognise a last stand. With the Ordinatus on the wall destroyed, so too went their final chance of survival. A sense of inevitability had crept into the ebb and flow of the fight. Iulus meant to sell his life dearly.

'Brothers!' he bellowed as the roar of bolters and heavy weapons pummelled the air.

Around him, the last of the Immortals gathered.

Aristaeus gave a nod. Galvia held up a clenched fist. Wherever he looked, Iulus saw his warriors proud and defiant in the face of certain destruction. Since he had been instated the squad's sergeant, they had never lost a battle-brother and had become dubbed the 'Immortals' on that account. It was fitting then that if that honorific was to be broken now they would die as one.

'Immortals to the end!' said Brother Pention and the cry was taken up by them all, the conscripts and Ark Guard too.

A beam took Uklidese in the shoulder and chest. He fell but was dragged up by Illion and Menalus. Venkelius was the next to drop, clutching at his gorget.

Then Aristaeus. Iulus reacted quickly, supporting him under the arm.

'Stand, brother,' he growled. 'We'll meet them on our feet.'

Agnathio was punctured by a dozen beams, the Dreadnought lanced through and spewing fire, smoke and fluids. The venerable warrior ground to a halt and his weapons cycled down to dormancy.

'Ultramar!' Iulus wanted it to be the last word on his

lips. He spat it at the necrons, as if his will and vitriol could destroy them in an all-consuming wave. 'Ultramar!'

The Ultramarines took up the call, even those who were injured, even Venkelius who could barely speak at all.

'Ultramar!'

It was an end worthy of note. Iulus found the admission of that strange. He had never considered death before or what it meant. He had always only thought in terms of function and need.

I am a warrior and my function is to kill in the Emperor's name.

He had not believed his legacy was important, save to pass on to the next Ultramarine who succeeded him; that his deeds and actions really mattered. Faced with the imminence of mortality, he found his opinion changed. Dying well mattered and this was a manner of death that Iulus could be proud of.

'Stand with me, Kolpeck,' he said, using his body to protect the rig-hand, 'and let us die well together.'

'While I have breath, I will,' Kolpeck replied. 'For her, for Jynn.'

Iulus didn't know who this person was but he understood the sentiment. Men were more than just materiel that could wield a gun, throw a grenade or drive a tank. They were flesh and blood, with hearts and minds. And it hadn't been an honoured warrior, a stern-faced veteran consigned to the lectorum or even a Chaplain that had taught the sergeant this. It had merely been a man, a miner at that. The Ultramarine felt humbled and wished it could end differently for Falka Kolpeck.

Abruptly, at no outward or fathomable sign, the necrons stopped. A radiant emerald flash filled the

Courtyard of Xiphos again but not from some dooms-day weapon, it was translocation. Iulus detected the scent of phasal shift and as he opened his eyes saw that the raiders were gone. All of the necron cohorts had simply vanished.

A reprieve. He felt slightly robbed. The practical side of his character exerted its will over his emotions quickly, though – they were alive. Most of the humans, too, had survived. For Agnathio, they mourned. The Dreadnought was a steaming husk of blast-scarred armour. His life had left him.

'Where did they go?' Aristaeus asked the question as dumbstruck Guardsmen gazed around the walls or the square. They lived, but they didn't know how or why. Even the tunnellers had fled, leaving nothing but rubble in their wake.

Iulus looked around too, trying to reason what had just happened.

Snow was forming, laying a fresh patina across the courtyard. Ice already crusted the wall as the bitter cold reasserted itself after the fire storm. Soon the scene would be virginal again, a chilling graveyard where the dead do not sleep.

Why does a force retreat? Either they are on the brink of defeat or they've found a better fight elsewhere.

Clearly it was the latter.

He uttered one word. 'Sicarius.'

ADANAR WASN'T DEAD and the revelation weighed upon him like an anvil around his neck. He should be dead. This was supposed to be his moment; this was when he was to be reunited with them. But the Emperor – damn his capricious will – wasn't done with Adanar Sonne, it seemed.

Relief, not despair, washed off the other men on the wall. He could feel it almost palpably, see it in their surprised faces. They hugged each other; some even cheered, though the gesture was only half indulged. Fatigue seized them now that the adrenaline of trying to stay breathing faded. Life for another few minutes at least. Adanar half-expected the necron artillery to release such a blistering barrage from some other *uber-*weapon that it obliterated the entire city and everything in it, but they didn't. The necrons had retreated.

He was about to ask Humis to contact the army's officers for a report when he remembered the corporal was dead. A screeching sound arrested his attention. His despair and confusion turned to anger as he was confronted by Rancourt.

'Blessed Emperor, we are saved!' He was ebullient, but on the point of hysteria. 'Our saviours are victorious.' Rancourt looked at Adanar nonplussed. 'Why aren't you cheering, commander? We have won. Damnos is saved.'

Adanar slapped him hard across the face with the back of his gloved hand. The blow drew blood from the acting governor's lip.

'Shut up, you idiot. They are not defeated. There is no victory to be had here.'

A group of officers and troopers had gathered around the altercation, drawn by the raised voices.

Now it was Rancourt's turn to be incensed. He touched his chin, but it wasn't just his skin that had been stung by the commander's reprimand. 'How dare you strike a member of the Administratum?' He looked around for an ally in the throng, and pointed at a trooper. 'You,' he said. 'Shoot him, shoot Commander Sonne at once.'

At first the Ark Guard trooper looked shocked and

distinctly uncomfortable that he'd been singled out. He held up his hands, wanting no part of it.

Frustrated, Rancourt's attention went to someone else. 'You then,' he bawled. 'Shoot them both. I command you to execute them in the name of the Emperor and the Imperium.'

'No.'

Rancourt was looking around rapidly, his gaze flitting from one soldier to the next. 'You're all in on it.' He spat at Adanar's feet. 'Your personal guard, no doubt.' Pointing a finger that he swept around the onlookers, he added, 'You'll all be shot for this. Disobedience, dissension–'

Adanar hit him again and this time put the administrator on the floor. Seizing him by the scruff of the neck, he lifted Rancourt up so he could glare into his eyes. He saw fear in them.

'You are a loathsome worm, Zeph Rancourt,' he declared, 'and your cowardice nearly killed us all. I suspect it may have killed Sergeant Kador, a good man and a good soldier.'

'Kador was a traitor,' spat Rancourt. 'He tried to leave my side.'

Adanar's eyes widened when he saw the butt of a pistol sticking out of the administrator's robes. 'What did you do?' he rasped.

'I didn't kill him if that's what you mean. It was a warning shot. I only winged him.' Rancourt saw the change come over Adanar's face and quailed. 'What are you going to do?'

'Did you hit him in the leg, slow him down and lower his guard? Eh? Is that when the beam hit him?' Adanar tightened his grip around the other man's collar.

Rancourt's feet were almost dangling off the ground. 'Let me go, let me go,' he pleaded.

Adanar brought him closer, eye-to-eye. 'Oh, I'll let you go,' he whispered. With a grunt of effort, he lifted the administrator above his head.

'Unhand me!' Rancourt shrieked.

Adanar had him poised at the edge of the battlements. 'As you wish,' he said, and threw him off.

There was a wet crunch as the ex-governor hit the ground. Blood pooled in the snow, turning it crimson. Not one of the men on the wall emitted so much as a gasp, let alone tried to arrest their commander for murdering an Imperial official. But they all turned as the massive shadow drew over them.

One of the cobalt giants was walking up the steps and had reached the battlements.

Adanar nodded. 'Sergeant Fennion.'

Iulus nodded back as the man went down on one knee.

'Execute me if you must. I would have gladly done it again.'

The Ultramarine growled. 'Get up. I've not come for your life nor do I care about what you've done. We are at war. There is no time for bureaucracy.'

Adanar got to his feet, frowning. 'Then what is it you need?'

'Your men,' replied the cobalt giant. 'Enough to make a difference.'

CHAPTER TWENTY-TWO

THREE GROUPS TRACKED through the mountains. Scipio was up front just behind Captain Evvers. He could see now why the Ultramarines had struggled to find a route through. She took them on a winding route, through almost invisible canyons, secret passes and sunken valleys. It was treacherous but no one fell to their deaths, the humans more sure-footed than their armoured protectors.

Scipio activated the comm-feed. 'Brothers. Vox-silence from this point.'

They'd reached an outer marker of five hundred metres. Both Vandar and Octavian, who were in the other two assault groups, replied with affirmation runes that lit up Scipio's retinal display.

'What's wrong?' he called ahead.

Evvers, with three of her kinsmen arrayed around her, held up a hand. They were making certain of the route. Snow-shawled crags surrounded them, barely visible against the high mountain drifts. A wicked wind was howling in from the north and the humans had to keep low to avoid being blown off the peaks. Scipio approved of their caution; one false step could be terminal in this white-out.

Tigurius joined him, the inner glow of his eyes only just fading.

'The truth is still veiled to me,' said the Librarian.

'What of our endeavours here? Can your prescience divine a path, my lord?'

He shook his head. 'I cannot breach the veil. Something is blocking my sight.' Tigurius looked down into the impenetrable fog and gloom. 'Below,' he added.

Although he could not see them, Scipio knew that a small army of the necrons awaited them there. The route through the mountains would allow them the element of surprise and they would need to make the most of it. Outnumbered and likely outgunned, the Ultramarines' plan was predicated on causing as much damage to the artillery as possible before the defenders roused into action. There was a lord amongst the mechanoids, too, the one Tigurius called the 'Voidbringer'. From their encounter with the ghoulish necron commander at camp, Scipio was well aware of their power. He wondered briefly what abilities this one would possess.

Evvers was waving them on.

Scipio would find out soon enough.

VOIDBRINGER WAS FRUSTRATED. By attaching him to the artillery in the Thanatos Hills, the Monarch had effectively leashed him. He wanted to cow these worms, eradicate them from the face of the earth and reclaim it for the necrontyr.

'I am a conqueror,' he decided, visions of conquest

flashing across his memory engrams in a blur, 'not a custodian.'

It only convinced him further that the Undying had submitted to the Destroyer curse and his sanity was all but eroded. The long sleep had taken a heavy toll and as such he would not be able to lead the tomb. Cast out by the other lords he would be reduced to a king of madmen, those who would butcher their metal bodies to the cause of annihilation.

Voidbringer wanted to annihilate but he also wanted to rule. He felt the pull of the infinite, time-eternal stretching before him like an endless conduit, but he did not fear it. He embraced it. His glory would be everlasting.

The orb given unto him by Ankh hummed with power. He regarded it idly as the gauss-obliterators thundered all around him. He did not pretend to understand the arcane science of the crypteks; his own technologies were esoteric and well-guarded by just a few of the royal cohort. Energy whorls shimmered inside it, like trapped event horizons collapsing and coalescing in microcosm. If he stared long enough, Voidbringer fancied he could unravel the inner secrets of the universe, unlock the vagaries of chronomancy and the manipulation of living metal. Such things didn't interest him. Let the crypteks be distracted by such petty diversions. Rulership required action not contemplation.

Even still, the resurrection orb was fascinating. With it his ascendancy would be assured. A subliminal command, like a muscle reflex, opened a chamber in his metal breastbone. The chest cavity opened wide enough to accommodate the orb and Voidbringer placed it carefully within. It glowed briefly, connecting with the

necron's systems and enhanced physiology. The surge of
power it radiated through him made Voidbringer shud-
der. His staff of light crackled in sympathetic symbiosis.
The cryptek could be useful, he supposed, but he also
didn't trust him. Voidbringer also hated the fact he
referred to him by his old name. *That* appellation was
no longer fitting. None whose memory engrams still
functioned remembered the royarch's name, he was just
the Undying. It gave him power, a resonance that elevated him above the other nobles.

Voidbringer wanted that. He also wanted an advisor
who was more pliable and less likely to betray him. The
pact with Ankh was ended; Voidbringer resolved to
destroy him once they had achieved victory on this
world.

If he could have smiled, he would have.

'Soon,' he whispered to himself, the thought caressing
his ego, 'I will rise above all.'

Cocooned by images of his ambition, the Voidbringer
failed to notice the figures creeping closer. Perhaps his
awareness had been dulled by some outside agent, perhaps the dulcetly throbbing orb embedded in his chest
played a part...

ANKH SAW ALL. His tiny burrowing machines kept close to
the genebred humans, followed them through the pass
and into the mountainous peaks. They kept out of sight;
the Architect ensured they remained undetected. Tahek
had activated the orb, or at least begun its cycle – Ankh
felt this too.

Multiple futures played out across his synapses, each
one a subtle variation of the last. The attack of the
artillery would cripple the necrontyr and cause a chain
reaction throughout the royal court. Nobles would be

destroyed, their memory engrams forever degraded. But then Ankh was not a noble, he was merely an elevated servant with certain skills. The rule of law in the tomb was about to change and he, in part, would bring about its apotheosis. His actions, or inactions, had helped to bring this about. The war on Damnos was about to take a debilitating turn.

Ankh was a necron, his loyalties were unquestionable in that regard, but he was also a survivor.

THE RAIDER SENTRIES patrolled the perimeter with predictable regularity. Like automatons, they marched back and forth, gauss-flayers at rest, their fell eyes aglow. A blizzard was rolling down off the mountain, bringing with it a shrieking wind and veiling snow. It built up on their joints, settled on their vast shoulder plates. They betrayed no signs of discomfort. Essentially they were dead things, barely sentient and moving only through the borrowed will and animus of other more powerful beings.

Three pairs performed sentry rotations on the small section of the perimeter that abutted the sheer-sided cliffs of the Thanatos mountain range. One of the necrons paused in its cycle, alerted to something in the icy mists. Its sockets flared with baleful energy as its twin also stopped, a few metres away. The inquisitive raider took two steps forwards – at this sector of the perimeter they were largely isolated until the other sentry pairs crossed them again – before its head jerked violently to the side. It raised a hand, releasing its grip on the barrel of the gauss-flayer, to touch the brass shell lodged in its cranium. Emitting a low-pitched whine the shell exploded, taking the necron's head and most of its torso with it.

Realising it was under attack the other raider switched to defensive protocols and was about to unleash its gauss-flayer in a spread firing pattern before a second shell punched through its eye socket to similar effect. Both mechanoids phased out instantly.

Seconds later, Sergeant Octavian and his Swords of Judgement were tracking low across the rugged hill line. The heat from the capacitors on the artillery was turning the snow into a thick, obscuring mist. It was above waist height and utterly occluded the Ultramarines from view. Reaching the site of the sentries' demise, Octavian opened the closed comm-feed by tapping the side of his helmet, red against the starkness of the ice-fog – with the first kills, vox-silence was no longer necessary.

'Attack group "Iron Sights": Hellfires away and mission achieved.'

THE AFFIRMATIONS FROM the other sergeants came swiftly through Scipio's comm-feed. The sentries were down and all Ultramarines were in position. With the perimeter breached, the way to the necron artillery was open. It was a minute aperture for a small commando force to enter and Scipio meant to exploit it to the full.

The necrons had used machineries, perhaps tunnellers and other large mechanoids to reshape and flatten a section of the Thanatos Hills. He'd taken vantage from the cliff top, just before they'd descended to the base. Thermal-imaging through the scopes revealed a roughly diamond-shaped area, with the artillery pieces arranged around it, one at each point and another weapon in the centre. Five targets for three assault groups – they'd miss Strabo and Ixion, but it couldn't be helped. Evvers and her guerrillas would have to do their part.

He regarded her through the uncompromising slits of

his retinal lenses. She was watching the route ahead through a pair of infra-goggles, and seemed tense – her heart rate and breathing were elevated. Only Adeptus Astartes could undertake a mission of this magnitude and hope to survive. Some might consider it reckless for Scipio to throw the humans into it without consideration for their safety. He cast any lingering doubts aside as he felt an iron fist clench around his heart. Orad had paid the price for his lack of resolve. It would not happen again. They would do their part or they would die in the attempt.

Tigurius emerged out of the fog next to him. He kept low, just like the rest. The Ultramarines were crouching, whereas the humans only had to stoop to become invisible. If the Librarian knew what Scipio was thinking, it didn't show. He seemed preoccupied.

'I must seek out the veil across my sight and cut it loose,' he said, as if penetrating Scipio's mind after all. 'Lead them in, Sergeant Vorolanus, but wait for my signal. Courage and honour.'

The Librarian moved off into the fog on his own private mission.

Scipio watched him go until he was lost to the mist. He opened up the comm-feed again, 'All Ultramarines: close on targets.'

A TREMOR OF unease rippled through the aeons-old consciousness of Voidbringer. It niggled insistently at the edge of his awareness but he allowed the reassuring drone of the orb to comfort him and eclipse it.

TIGURIUS HUNTED THROUGH the mist. He stayed clear of the places where the necron forces were most concentrated, guided psychically. They were little more than

unmoving shadows, statues in the ice-fog. Emerald fire
in their eyes was the only evidence of unnatural anima-
tion in the necrons and even that was dampened by the
mist. Not that he truly needed to see. The Librarian's
witch-sight might be temporarily blinded, the strands of
fate shut to him, but he could still feel...

It was close, the void blanketing his thoughts, that
which had almost destroyed him with its malice when
he had ridden the Sea of Souls as a psychic avatar. The
hulking silhouettes of the pylons and massive gauss-
cannons loomed here and there in the ice-fog, rising
above the artificial white tide. In part of his mind, that
which was largely committed to his subconscious for
now, he was aware of his battle-brothers closing swiftly
on the structures. Before they committed fully to the
attack, he needed to find the one called 'Voidbringer'.

Emotions were easy things for a psyker to detect, even
a nascent one. Hatred bled off this monster, as hot and
acerbic as acid. Tigurius followed it, a jagged trail of red
in his mind. At the end of it he knew he'd find his
nemesis.

WITHOUT ANY SCOUTS, the attack force's best chance of
making stealth an effective option was through the
Thunderbolts. Scipio had drilled his warriors in the arts
of subterfuge and operating behind enemy lines, much
of his skill imparted by Torias Telion. They were not
even close to matching the Master Scout's abilities but
the blizzard and the fog were useful tools he could
exploit, as was the fact the necrons seemed uncharacter-
istically sluggish.

Hugging close to the ground and sticking to the channels where the ice-fog was thickest, Scipio and his
battle-brothers had crossed almost half the distance to

their target without raising an alarm. The stillness of the necron defenders, eerie as it was, made the task of avoiding them easier. If they possessed some kind of sensors or form of auspex that didn't require visual confirmation they were either fouled by the weather or simply not attuned to the presence of the Space Marines.

A strange, preternatural darkness lapped at the edges of the artillery zone. Tigurius had described it as the 'Night Shroud', some piece of necron technology and part of the reason for his psychic blindness. Scipio tried not to look at the darkness too long. They'd penetrated it easily enough at the perimeter and once through the veil, it was just the ice-fog in front of them.

The Thunderbolts' target was a pylon, situated at the farthest apex of the diamond. He checked the melta bombs mag-locked to his armour. Upon returning to the encampment after the encounter with the flayed ones, they'd re-equipped and resupplied. The original plan was a lightning attack, spearheaded by the assault squads and supported by tactical squads, but without Ixion and Strabo that strategy was no longer viable. They'd stealth their way to the objectives instead, attach incendiaries and ignite them at once in a single hammer-strike. Whatever the explosives only managed to cripple, the heavy weapons would finish.

For their part, the guerrilla fighters were well tooled. Carrying improvised bombs and grenades, as well as some of the magnetic foiling devices they'd used to prevent necron phase-out, they were capable of delivering a significant punch of their own. It was insanely dangerous, but Scipio had no compunction about throwing them into the battle just like his brothers.

He stopped a second to interrogate his retinal display. A series of runic indicators were making their way across his plane of vision. Distance notifiers expressed formation and proximity to the targets. All were making solid progress but a further engagement was nearing.

Each of the artillery pieces, pylon or heavy gauss-cannon, were manned by a small group of raider constructs. Scipio doubted the machineries needed crew to function. He didn't understand necron technology but he had discerned enough to realise that much of it was autonomous or controlled by the lords. Whatever their role, the raiders would need to be dispatched first before incendiaries could be deployed. The attack also had to be simultaneous. Wits dulled as they appeared to be, the necrons would still activate with defensive protocols as soon as they realised their perimeter was breached and were under fire.

A rune flashed silently on Scipio's retinal display. Vandar was already in position. He judged Octavian wasn't far either. Casting caution aside he increased the pace, not realising he'd attracted the attention of something dwelling in the Night Shroud.

As THE FORCE rod grew hot in his gauntleted fist, Tigurius knew he was getting close to his prey. The crimson energies he'd been following sparked and forked with almost palpable expression. Briefly, he portioned out a small part of his mind to check on the situation of his battle-brothers – they were nearing final positions.

Perfect synchronicity was needed, but the slow-returning threads of his prescience told him that would be so. Satisfied, Tigurius shut them out and focussed all of his thought on finding the Voidbringer. Though he didn't know why, the veil was thinning. Visions swirled in his psychic eye, the fragments of those he'd tried to grasp before slowly coming together.

Marshal your thoughts.

Now was not the time to seek out the elusive truth and uncover the forbidding threat that had dogged him since the mission began; now was destruction and the unleashing of his psychic might. At last, he caught his prey, surrounded by a hot corona of red light. It was standing alone on a desolate ridge, surveying its majesty.

Inside his mind, Tigurius coaxed a ball of lightning into being.

SCIPIO BECAME AWARE they were under attack when Densk was lifted off his feet as if a set of invisible hooks had caught him and begun reeling the guerrilla fighter in.

Jynn screamed, swinging her gun around to try and draw a bead on his attacker, but it was as if the fog had come alive to take him. Blood was spewing down Densk's beard, his cries of pain muffled by the fact he had no tongue. It was an odd, discordant sound. When a slash of crimson washed the ground like the insouciant sweep of a painter's brush, Densk fell apart. His body disintegrated into shreds as his assailant revealed itself through the red haze.

Serpentine, with a necron's torso and a set of wicked talon-blades on each hand, it was a wraith. Only partially corporeal, the thing was half-blended into the ice-fog. Its eyes blazed with a yearning for further carnage.

Jynn's snap-shot went wild. She half-fell, backing up because the monster was so close. Scipio pushed her down as the necron's tail whipped out and the barbed tip missed her head by the smallest margin. He roared, weighing in with his chainsword. Like an adder, the wraith jinked aside and the blade-teeth bit ice-frozen earth. It flicked out a talon, which Scipio fended off with his forearm. Gouges raked down his vambrace but they weren't deep enough to penetrate.

Cator appeared behind it and thrust his gladius between its neck and collarbone. The wraith emitted a sort of part-scream, part machine-whine and twisted to slash at the Ultramarine. Scipio took his chance and cut off the monster's head with his chainsword. Critically damaged, it phased out, leaving only blood in its wake.

Jynn knelt by Densk's remains, sobbing. Scipio seized her by the shoulder and pulled her up. Their subterfuge was exposed. They had to act.

Furious at his impatience, for sealing Densk's death warrant on account of it, Scipio snarled down the comm-feed. 'All Ultramarines, attack now!'

PSYCHIC LIGHTNING ARCED from Tigurius's force rod. It struck Voidbringer's staff as he turned, breaking his strange torpor. A serpent of light and energy, the discharged psychics roiled down the haft of the weapon. He wrestled with it, trapping the force as it coursed across the staff and asserting dominance.

Tigurius's eyes widened. That bolt should have ripped the creature apart.

Energies dissipating from the psychic attack, Voidbringer turned his attention to the Librarian facing off against him on the ridge. A nimbus of power was playing across the psychic hood the Ultramarine wore and his eyes were alive with actinic force. He held the rod out in front of him, so it formed a cross with his body as the spine.

'Fell creature of the void, oblivion awaits you.'

Unmoved by the threat, Voidbringer only glared. The necron lord appeared... curious.

Again, Tigurius was surprised and horrified at the ancient intelligence in that gaze. It was like the mechanoid was appraising a laboratorium specimen. The sensation was unsettling. Tigurius knew enough of the galaxy and its species to realise mankind's pre-eminence was far from assured. Alien races clamoured to devour, usurp or study humans. It was part of the reason the Emperor had created Space Marines. But the necrontyr were something different, something so old and enduring that even an Adeptus Astartes as powerful as Tigurius was given pause.

Victory against this aeons-old culture with all their knowledge of the universe, their advanced technology, it was… *impossible*. They should give in now, submit to will of the necrons and accept annihilation. They should–

Stop! The psychic echo was as much a command to his own subconscious as it was to the metal monster. Reasserting his composure, Tigurius smiled mirthlessly at the Voidbringer. 'I thought the other one was the Herald of Dismay.'

Though his rictus jaw didn't move, a metallic voice, edged with the bitterness of millennia and abyssal deep, droned from the Voidbringer. *'You are the one who tried to penetrate the veil.'*

Tigurius nodded slowly. He felt like an insect being studied beneath a slide, but his resolve was as steel now.

'I am your doom, creature.'

A tinny, grating sound rattled from the necron's mouth. It was laughter, or what passed for it at least.

Describing arcane sigils of warding that lingered in the air in fire, Tigurius beckoned the monster on.

Voidbringer's eyes narrowed. *'Are you a pyromancer, worm?'*

A flash of light burst from the staff before the Librarian could stop it and hit him square in the chest. Tigurius was spun off his feet and sent sprawling from the ridge.

'Not a very good one,' he heard the necron lord remark.

Picking himself up, the Librarian scowled. 'I think I loathed your race less when I assumed you were humourless machines.' Fire sprang from his fingertips, reaching up towards the ridge line above and forcing the Voidbringer to retreat. Earth blackened and cracked as the flames lapped at the edge of the spur, spilling over the lip of rock rising higher and growing hotter. Snow condensed into steam in an eyeblink, scalding the air.

The necron's withdrawal didn't last. A hazy silhouette resolved through the conflagration and the Voidbringer leapt through it, fire trailing on his ancient vestments.

Ice cracked under the impact as the necron lord landed next to Tigurius. He threw out an arm, bodily catching the Librarian who was smashed aside and scraped across the ground. Blood was drooling down his lip as he rose; he could taste the tang of it in his mouth too.

Voidbringer was strong, much more unyielding than the lesser constructs. And he possessed cunning beyond mere programmed response to attack and external stimulus. The necrons, especially these noble castes, were far from machines. Even artificial intelligence didn't describe them accurately. They were something else, something vengeful and terrible. Spite, hatred, malice – the emotions were raw and tangible. Tigurius could feel them like tiny blades rubbing against his skin, like acid-edged pins in his mind.

Though the creature was not a psyker – it bore no

warp-aura that the Librarian could detect – the artefacts he wielded were formidable.

As the Voidbringer rose, energy crackled the length of its arcane staff. It coruscated around the tip, a strange pronged sigil Tigurius had seen emblazoned on the carapace of some of the larger constructs. Darkness exuded from his body. Tendrils of night coiled around his limbs and weaved through the necron's skeletal frame.

The monster was well named. Casting about, the Voidbringer assessed the level of infiltration by the Ultramarines and acted accordingly. Shadows stirred in the mist around Tigurius as the necron constructs guarding the artillery began to animate.

'You are no warp sorcerer,' said the Librarian, his voice echoing with gathering power.

The Voidbringer's eye sockets flared emerald-bright and Tigurius was transported back to his narrow escape in the world-between-worlds. *'I am more than you could ever comprehend, human. I am eternal!'* A cascade of magnesium fire coursed from the necron's staff.

Tigurius was ready for the attack and quickly fashioned a defensive sigil in the air. The arc of flame spilled against it, dispersing around the edges of a cerulean shield. It struck again, the necron throwing more force behind the blow. Staggered, Tigurius struggled to maintain his footing but repelled the energies. Sweat froze upon his brow as quickly as it formed, only to melt into hot steam a moment later. He needed to assert dominance in the duel and threw a bolt of chained lightning.

Voidbringer's body became as incorporeal as mist as the darkling mantle he wore engulfed him, rendering the psychic attack ineffective. The Night Shroud expanded, drawing strength from the blackness surrounding the artillery. Shreds of shadow became as hard as onyx as they wrapped themselves around Tigurius and all light was eclipsed. As the baleful gaze of the Voidbringer filled his vision, the Librarian felt his armour contract.

Seals cracked, ancient parchments and votive charms tore and broke apart as the necron lord exerted his cruel will.

'All is night. All is black at the end of days...'

Tigurius was fading. His mind was awash with endless darkness. It filled his senses, overwhelmed his thoughts and in that moment of near-destruction he achieved a mote of clarity. The visions, those that had dogged the Librarian since he'd made landfall on Damnos, became as clear as crystal. Death, it was death that he saw. Not the death of a world but the death of a hero. At first he believed it was him and this was, now, the instant of his demise. But the visions sharpened, just as the real world dimmed, and became more lucid. The truth was opened to him, a final torment before the end.

Tigurius saw...

SCIPIO HACKED THE last of the sentries apart. Its spinal column shattered and the necron phased out, but more were coming.

'Attach explosives.' He slammed the melta bomb against the base of the pylon, mag-locking to the strange metal. Cator and Herdantes provided covering fire. Bolt shells and incandescent plasma chopped into the ice-fog and the advancing silhouettes were blasted apart. Gauss-fire answered from the reinforcements coming in their wake as the damaged necrons reassembled and rejoined the attack.

'Will this even work?'

Scipio turned at Jynn's voice. She was hunkered down with Sia, returning fire when they could. She looked afraid. Densk's death had clearly rocked her, but she remained determined to fight.

'I don't know,' said Scipio. 'That's why we need to use everything.' He glanced briefly at the tactical display in his retinal lens. All attack groups were in position. Then he saw Tigurius's rune.

It was amber. The Librarian's vitals were weakening. Scipio looked across the ice-shrouded plateau and found Tigurius locked in battle with a necron lord. He was slowly being crushed, enveloped by a veil of darkness.

'Cator, bring your plasma gun and follow me.'

Scipio ran off towards the Librarian, his brother in tow.

'Wait!' shouted Jynn. 'Don't leave us!'

Brakkius, Herdantes and the others were engaging the necrons closing on the pylon. They were stretched and more wraiths were moving sinuously on the undefended humans.

Scipio paused, torn. He had brought them into this fight. After they'd penetrated the mountains, he could have left Jynn and her guerrilla fighters behind. They could have watched from a safe distance. But he wanted to destroy the necrons utterly, smash their artillery and grab glory for gaining the Thanatos Hills. It was too late to turn back. The humans had chosen their fate. He ran to Tigurius.

'Scipio!' Jynn's impassioned cries followed him all the way like a curse.

CHAPTER TWENTY-THREE

EVER SINCE BECOMING a battle-brother, Sergeant Atavian had been in the Second Company Devastators. It was a full-fledged Ultramarine's first calling in the Chapter proper – Maxima Atavian had simply never left. His squad were known as the Titan Slayers, a name which they'd earned for obvious reasons. As a heavy weapon trooper, Atavian had principally been responsible for the lascannon. It was his favoured weapon. Tank-killer it was also called. Atavian's motto had always been, 'Why stop at tanks?'

The honour of carrying the Slayers' lascannon went to Brothers Hektar and Ulius. Sergeant Atavian had to satisfy himself with guiding their destructive fury. During his century of service, he had seen many monsters and machineries felled by the hot beams of a lascannon. Tyranid bio-forms, daemonic engines of the Great Enemy, ramshackle ork battle-fortresses – Atavian had seen them all undone by this stalwart weapon. For a

Space Marine on foot and at range, there was nothing so powerful. But here on Damnos, he had seen such technologies that he wondered if even a lascannon would prevail against them. Floating obelisks of living metal, skeletal warriors utterly destroyed only to rise as if unscathed, small beetle-like creatures capable of twisting a weapon's machine-spirit and turning it on its wielder – this was what the Second were up against, the necrontyr.

On bended knee and with their heads bowed, Atavian recited the litanies of accuracy and function with his brothers. They had formed a half-circle, heavies in the middle either side of their sergeant and bolters at the ends. A flattened column offered them little cover but a good vantage point to overlook the wasteland tundra between the edge of Arcona City and Kellenport.

Across from the Titan Slayers were their brother Devastators, led by Sergeant Tirian. Atavian gave him a curt salute when he'd finished the litanies and was on his feet again, to which Tirian replied by holding his power fist aloft and giving a slow nod. His squad, Guilliman's Hammer, occupied a staggered platform of rock. It might once have been the tiered steps of a temple but was all but obliterated now. Heavy bolters took the first level, the missile-launchers behind them crouched down and pointing eastwards towards the advancing necrons.

The shadows of the monoliths were easy to pick out as the sun faded quickly on the horizon. These would be Atavian's principal targets, the living metal pyramids that fired death from the crystals at their zeniths. There was a larger monstrosity moving amongst the still-gargantuan smaller ones. It was taller, a tower of long tubular crystal attached to a conventional monolith base. Energies crackled between this one and the other two surrounding it. A node of some sort, Atavian decided. He put the targeting scope back on the stock of his bolter and addressed his warriors.

'Steel and death! Meltas and plasma to the fore, tank-killers with me at the rear. Remember how we took the *Soulmauler* apart, a Renegade Titan, no less! Remind me why we earned the Principex Maxima that day and why our name shall pass in legend when we are dead.'

Shouts of approval and affirmation met the sergeant's words. These were campaign veterans, despite their role as Devastators. He trusted each and every one.

'Glory to the Titan Slayers and may the God-Emperor revel in our furious thunder!'

A collective roar belted from the Ultramarines' mouths.

Sergeant Atavian had never been prouder. The cries of his Titan Slayers echoed into silence, as did the shouts of Tirian's warriors across from them. One last look down the targeter revealed the necron hordes were coming within range. Emerald energy was building between the phalanx of monoliths. Everything depended on their incapacitation. Atavian prepared to give the order to fire.

'PINION', THE TUTORS of the Chapter, Praxor's old masters, had called it. 'When one force manages to outflank and surround another.'

To the west, the necrons from the tomb itself, amongst them their overlord and the one Sicarius wanted to bring to single combat. To the east, the forces that had got around them to assault Kellenport, recently recalled to close the Ultramarines in a trap they might not escape from.

Knowing he faced a foe on two fronts, Sicarius had arranged his forces in two semi-circles each facing an aspect of where a threat was coming from. To the rear he positioned the Devastators. The necrons had brought machineries; the hulking monoliths Praxor had seen the captain take on single-handedly. Through sheer bravura, he had destroyed one of them, or at least immobilised it. If only they had three more Sicariuses with the same fortune, the same skill to achieve that feat three more times. Tactical Squad Solinus completed the rearguard, ready to wade in once the heavy guns had done all they could.

Praxor was amongst the force facing the brunt of the necron infantry as well its command echelon. The Dreadnoughts Ultracius and Agrippen joined them, stoic alongside the Lions of Macragge. At either flank, Sicarius had used the assault squads as anchor. They would strike at the heart of the phalanxes, cutting a way through so that the captain of Second might get his opportunity to kill the necron overlord.

Chaplain Trajan knelt in the centre, between the two semi-circles of Ultramarines. Their last stand was apparently on top of the remains of some ancient basilica. Long toppled by necron aggression, the Chaplain had nonetheless discovered a large stone aquila buried under all the fallen snow. He performed a final blessing on top of the ruins, beseeching the Emperor to protect and grant them courage.

In his heart, Praxor knew this would be the single biggest and hardest battle he would ever fight as an Ultramarine. Making the sign of the Imperial eagle over his breast, he hoped it would not be his last. His gaze fell on Sicarius.

The captain was looking to the north, towards the Thanatos Hills.

'It's quiet,' he said underneath his breath. His Lions, including Daceus, stood by silently.

Praxor spoke up. 'A cessation to the barrage could mean that Scipio...' he paused to correct himself. 'Sergeant Vorolanus and Lord Tigurius have been successful in their mission.'

Sicarius turned. His eyes were hard like granite as they appraised Praxor. He hadn't realised he'd intruded on the captain's private thoughts.

'*Scipio?*'

'He is – was – my friend, brother-captain.'

Sicarius looked to the west. Battle was approaching rapidly.

'We are, all of us, linked by a shared brotherhood. Our blood is the distilled life essence of our primarch, may he one day stir from slumber in the Temple of Correction. But some bonds are stronger than others. Do you understand?'

Praxor nodded humbly.

Satisfied he was understood, Sicarius drew his Tempest Blade and levelled it at the oncoming necrons. It was a gesture he was overfond of making.

'Do you know what I see out there, brother-sergeant?' he said. 'I see destiny. I see our names alongside the legends of our Chapter's greatest heroes, inscribed for all time on the walls of the Temple of Hera. Are you ready to embrace it?'

He didn't wait for an answer. Instead, Sicarius summoned his Lions and advanced to the front of the line. Agrippen was close by.

'You wish to share in the glory of this moment, venerable one?' asked the captain.

'It is only fitting that I am by my liege-lord's right hand. It is the Chapter's will.'

Sicarius laughed, loud and belligerent, before putting on his helmet. So close now, the necrons seemed endless. The Lions appeared unfazed, their demeanour stoic. It had been Praxor's desire to join them, to be like Gaius Prabian or Daceus. In these last moments before the final clash, he found himself questioning whether he could stare into the void and not blink.

He caught Vandius looking at him. Perhaps the Company Banner Bearer could guess what was on his mind. What he thought of Praxor's ambitions was unknown; he merely nodded to the sergeant and fixed his standard high. The gilded twin-headed eagle perched upon the Ultima symbol around a deathless skull stared down upon the Space Marines as if measuring them. 'Guardians of the Temple', warriors of the Second – if they survived, even achieved victory here, it would be spoken about for hundreds of years to come.

Sicarius seemed attuned to the magnitude of the moment.

'Destiny!' His voice echoed around the shattered basilica like a clarion call. 'Sons of Ultramar, if you seek renown eternal then it is before you. Ours is a proud line, it is cobalt and steel, it is unbreakable, it is spirit as adamantium. We are kings, you and I, like the old lords of Macragge in bygone days. On this soil, this frozen earth, we will make our stand and live forever in the annals of our brothers. Fight for the fallen, fight for the Second and the legacy left by those who came before us. Honour them with your deeds, your sacrifice.' He extended his open hand and clenched it tight, 'Reach out for immortality with your gauntleted fist and seize it!' The Tempest Blade was held aloft. Its edge shimmered in the fading sunlight, casting it in visceral red. 'In the name of Roboute Guilliman, *Victoris Ultra!*'

The call to arms resonated throughout the ruins, repeated by every Ultramarine who was about to give his blood to war. As the roar of it slowly faded, the sound was replaced by the merciless, clanking march of the necrons.

Sicarius turned away from the hordes for a moment to look at Praxor. 'Sergeant Manorian, you and your Shieldbearers will be at my side.'

'It is our honour, my lord,' Praxor replied. Yet after everything he'd seen on Damnos, it didn't feel as glorious as he'd expected.

ONLY THE LIONS were listening. Only they, his honour guard and inner circle knights, could hear what Sicarius had to say next.

'No battle cries for them, no rousing speeches,' he murmured. The Lions maintained their silence. 'They are devoid of humanity, these necrons. They have no capacity for compassion or pity, or any notions of glory or comradeship.' He spat the words, repulsed at such hollow creatures. Sicarius shook his head slowly. 'I will need to get into the heart of their ranks. Your blades and bolters will open the way.'

'We are your unsheathed swords, sire,' snarled Gaius Prabian with a vertical blade salute. He was eager for battle.

'When it comes, Gaius, you must lower your sword and allow me to fight it alone.'

The Champion assented but did so reluctantly.

'Daceus, you will lead them once I am engaged. Vandius, the banner must not fall.'

Both nodding, the veteran-sergeant clanged his power fist against his right pauldron, whilst the Second Company's standard bearer replied, 'To my dying breath, lord.'

'And you, Apothecary,' Sicarius turned his head to look at Venatio. 'You know what your duty is.'

'I hope not to have to perform it, but the legacy of Ultramar will be preserved, rest assured of that, my captain.'

Lastly, Sicarius spoke to them all again as one. 'You are my brothers, my equals and peers. I expect of you what I expect from myself – duty unflinching, courage unwavering, blade unswerving. These soulless automatons will drown the galaxy in darkness if they are left unchecked. I care not for Damnos, I care that this foe is taught to fear the Adeptus Astartes. Mankind will not be destroyed without a fight. Let it begin here, on these frozen wastes. Whatever else, the Ultramarines must not fail. The necrons have to be stopped, one way or another.'

VAST PHALANXES OF raiders had been roused from the tomb. The Architect had done well, but the Undying was finding it increasingly difficult to keep hold of that thought. His mind was awash with visions of destruction and annihilation. The cold emptiness of eternity clawed at his resolve. Far from being an unfeeling golem of metal and machinery, he was deeply afraid of the long dark. He had already slept, it had seemed endlessly, and now awake he was confronted by oblivion of an altogether different stripe.

Destroyers glided on their repulsor platforms, moving slowly into formation at either end of the necron battle line. Abhorred by those who could still comprehend such an emotion, simply avoided by those with simpler engrams left to them after the long sleep, the destroyers were both loathsome and terrifying at the same time. Unlike most of the necrontyr, even those of the basest

level, the destroyers had abandoned all hope of returning to *fleshtime*. Their bodies were... amended, given
over to the pursuit of decimation. Though it scared him
to admit it, the Undying liked the idea. He could imagine repulsors where his legs now were, a gauss-cannon
to replace his arm; perhaps his war-scythe could be
merged with the other limb too.

Such carnage I will reap... All the souls of this world.

Out in front, ahead of his bodyguard who crowded
around him with glaives crackling with eldritch light,
were the immortals. Stoic and implacable, these superior constructs would spearhead the advance. Anything
that survived them was obviously worthy indeed and
something the Undying should test his prowess against.
Hubris then, and arrogance, still stirred in his cruel
machine heart.

He surveyed the metal multitudes of skeletal warriors,
each the same as the last, without need for banners or
laurels of any kind, and knew the days of humankind
were finite. These warriors were but a fraction of the
cohorts still slumbering within the tomb. With a wordless command, the Undying impelled his army forwards
and imagined the slaughter to come.

CHAPTER TWENTY-FOUR

JYNN EVVERS WAS strong-willed, some might even say fearless. She'd had to be. After losing her husband to the quakes – it seemed longer than a couple of years, more like lifetimes – she'd needed courage, and had dug down into herself to find it. For a while, during the darkest days, Jynn had wondered if she'd come back from that insular place at all. Buried so deeply, she'd returned a different person when she'd finally emerged. The prospect of living her life alone, without Korve, terrified her. She would have gladly spent all of eternity with that man. Even the ice and the long, relentless days didn't seem so bad when he was still there. When Korve died, a part of Jynn died too. She became as hard and unyielding as the rock face she laboured over for the greater glories of the Imperium.

She saw the same sense of disconnection in Scipio. He was a Space Marine, as far from humankind as was possible without actually being a different species. Jynn was in awe of these warriors from beyond the stars, they all were, but she also pitied them. Never at peace, incapable of love. Bonds of duty bound them to their purpose, it was a noble one, and they valued honour, like any soldier, but had little else. Bred without fear, without compassion and only the will to act, they were the warriors that mankind needed. But why then did they feel grief? Perhaps it was to separate them, however thinly, from the unliving automatons that were trying to eradicate the people of Damnos? Perhaps it was some anachronism of humanity that had endured whatever process it took to become a Space Marine?

There was a hardness to Scipio. Jynn had once believed she was devoid of emotion too and then the attack on the Thanatos Hills came and all of that changed. Guerrilla warfare was one thing, striking from the dark, ambushing small groups – it was dangerous but doable. This was insane. Out here in the open, Jynn felt exposed. She felt threatened. Most of all, she felt fear. She'd believed she'd given up on life, that it didn't matter if she died. She was wrong and it took mortality staring her in the face for her to realise that.

'Sia, get down!'

Though the Space Marines bore the brunt of the fighting, there were too many necrons for them to repel at once. Without Scipio and the others, the humans were in tremendous danger. If they died here, their names would not be put on a plaque and venerated in some dusty temple. Their legacy would not live on for future generations. They would be dead and that would be an end to it.

Jynn grabbed Sia by the collar of her jacket and dragged her down behind the massive platform supporting the necron weapon. She'd heard Scipio call it a 'pylon'. It was huge and terrifying, an arc of black metal spitting emerald-tinged death into the sky. The noise of it hurt her ears. Jynn had gritted her teeth so long that when she'd shouted to Sia she'd found it hard to dislodge them.

Sia went down with a grunt. She was clutching a pack filled with explosive. 'We need to get this attached to the gun, bring it down. It's what Densk, Holdst – what all the others – would have wanted.'

Gauss-fire flashed overhead, burning the air with its acrid stench. Below the fog line everything else was hazy white. Necron silhouettes were moving in the mist, though. Their eyes were the first things that became visible. Jynn saw them everywhere. Lucky for her and Sia, they had yet to turn in their direction.

'You can't avenge them if you're dead. We have to stay down for a while.'

Sia shook her head. There was a wildness in her eyes, a sense of abandon that said she'd cracked under the pressure of it all.

'It's now or never, captain.'

Jynn reaffirmed her grip, 'Sia, no.'

'I can't stay like this. Ever since the camp, ever since…' She was crying. Sia threw off Jynn's hand and was on her feet. She got a couple of metres with the pack and was unclasping it when the beam caught her in the chest.

Jynn cried out but Sia was gone, her torso vaporised by the flayer blast. She slumped, gurgling blood, and died.

Holding her breath, Jynn was waiting to see if the necron would follow up on its kill. The hard bang of bolter fire caught its attention and it moved away. Sia was right, even if her attempt at completing the mission was suicidal – they needed to attach the bombs. Jynn got down on her belly – even through the thermal layers, the icy ground felt cold – and started to elbow her way towards the fallen pack. She had explosives of her own, tied up in webbing around her back, but they'd need Sia's too.

Screaming came through the fog, perversely crystal clear despite the hammering artillery. Jynn recognised the voices and knew they were getting slaughtered. It could have only been minutes, but it felt like hours. For the fifth time, she inwardly cursed Scipio. A means to an end, that's all she and her men were to him.

Fear closed in again when she reached the pack. Her fingers were shaking almost uncontrollably, and not from the cold, as she tried to remove the improvised bomb. Jynn breathed deeply, trying to master her terror, and achieved a small amount of calm. It was just enough to remove the explosive payload from the pack, arm it and attach the whole thing to the pylon. She wanted to detonate it immediately, but the resulting firestorm would kill her if she didn't get clear. Instead, she pulled out her pistol and made for the next artillery piece.

One down, one more to go.

SCIPIO WAS RUNNING. The sound of Jynn's voice still echoed on the air, but he banished it from his mind. Necrons were flooding the artillery now, summoned by their lord. The Ultramarines had nearly run out of time.

A glance at his retinal display showed that Vandar and Octavian had attached explosives and were ready to proceed. Scipio opened up the comm-feed to them both. 'Execute now!'

Plumes of fire erupted from locations around the plateau a few seconds later. In the distance, one of the pylons collapsed. Its weapon-arc crumpled as it struck the base, severed by the explosion. Emerald energy rippled across the remains frenziedly.

Scipio drove on, Cator just behind him.

The sergeant dispatched a necron warrior that loomed in their path with his chainsword. It came out of the mist late and Scipio had to react quickly. Instinct and urgency were guiding him. Consequence became secondary. All that mattered was Tigurius.

Cator blasted another off its feet with a quick burst from his plasma gun. The blue beam cut through its spinal column, ate up some of the torso and the mechanisms within. It was enough damage to make it phase out. But the necrons didn't stop. The Ultramarines were being overrun. Scipio shut off the urgent pleas for reinforcement from Brakkius. A blow-by-blow report was unfolding from the other Thunderbolts. He was pulling back, along with Herdantes. Largo too, together with Garrik and Auris, were trying to retreat. Scipio wasn't listening any more. He had to get to Tigurius. With a single act of bravura, he could save them all and atone for Orad's death.

Cutting down another of the advancing necrons, he yelled, 'Brother, are you still with me?'

Cator was resolute. 'Heading straight into the jaws of death, sergeant.'

An explosion tore up the ground nearby as another of the necron guns was ripped apart. It rocked Scipio and Cator on their feet and pushed away the ice-fog with a belt of emerald-tinged smoke. The Ultramarines let it roll over them.

The pall of smoke and debris was thick. They had to fight just to be free of it.

Largo was shouting down the comm-feed, 'Necron artillery sixty per cent effective, damaged but still operational. Our incendiaries haven't worked.'

Grey cloud was everywhere, a directionless void without end.

Largo was insistent. 'Your orders, brother-sergeant.'

Checking the retinal display, knowing they were close to Tigurius but not yet within striking distance, Scipio found similar reports coming from Octavian and Vandar. Two of the artillery pieces were down, but the others were still functional.

'Get heavies and whatever grenades you have left on those guns, brother.'

'Negative, sir. We are no longer in control of the strike area. Necron aggression is too heavy. Falling back to the centre.'

Scipio cursed. Without the assault squads there was no backup plan, no route of egress should the mission fail. His voice was bitter. 'I've led us to our deaths.'

He felt something seize his wrist and was about to lash out when he saw it was Cator. 'We're not done yet, Scipio. Courage and honour.'

Scipio clapped him on the shoulder and nodded once.

The smoke cleared. As the two Ultramarines emerged from the cloud, their objective came into sight – they'd reached Tigurius. At least they could achieve something.

Another necron was coming at them out of the ice-fog and Scipio was forced to meet it. He only had time to point at the darkness crushing Tigurius.

'Shoot it!'

Cator hesitated. 'I might hit Lord Tigurius.'

'Do it now, brother!' The shriek of chainblade teeth striking metal sounded close by.

Muttering an oath to the primarch, Cator took aim into the dark veil and fired.

* * *

PAIN WAS AN outmoded concept in the experiential range of the Voidbringer. He had long ago outgrown the capacity to feel the sensation. Even so, he knew he was injured and the desire for self-preservation still influenced his actions. In order to find his attacker, he had to release the pyromancer. He was nearly dead, anyway. Voidbringer resolved to eradicate this new threat and then finish what he had started. Darkness billowing about him, withdrawn from crushing the pyromancer, the necron lord searched the battlefield. He unleashed the power of his staff and the hot beam found Voidbringer's enemy and pitched him off his feet.

'Insect!'

The brief moment of pique cost him. When he turned his attention back to the pyromancer he saw his enemy was far from defeated, he was glowing.

AN AURA OF power surrounded Tigurius, chasing away the darkness from the necron lord's unnatural veil. It was a magnesium-bright sun, banishing the shadow with the Librarian as its focus. Jagged forks of lightning peeled off from the aura around his body. His eyes were alive with a captured storm, mirroring the tumultuous thunderhead surging into being around him.

The air cracked with the sound of his voice. 'Now you die, machine.'

Bolt after bolt of psychic lightning hammered into the Voidbringer, who reeled beneath the blows. A crack split the monster's chest, tore off an arm. His arcane staff spilled away on the eldritch wind summoned by the Librarian. Harsh and metallic, the necron lord roared as if in agony. Tigurius doubted it could feel, it was merely railing against its imminent demise. Even when the Voidbringer was nearly sundered, he didn't stop –

Tigurius poured it on, opening his mind to the warp and releasing its terrible power.

PSYCHIC LIGHTNING WAS ripping into his body, tearing away strips, burning mechanisms so old and complex that no human mind could ever hope to understand them. It was happening too fast – even the Voidbringer's enhanced regenerative abilities couldn't self-repair quickly enough. A mote of something cold and unpleasant flickered in his engrammic circuitry. Something akin to anxiety seized his aeons-old mind for just a moment as the necron lord contemplated the long dark.

I am the master of darkness, not its slave…

The self-declaration seemed pointless in the circumstances. Escape was still possible. He would not submit yet. Voidbringer *would* be royarch. He would self-repair, kill this worm that had stung him and assume the throne. Ankh, the self-aggrandising plebeian, had given him the means to do it. Before he was lost, Voidbringer activated the resurrection orb.

THE MONSTER WAS almost destroyed. Scipio watched from a safe distance, the broken body of Cator in his arms. A long burn marred the Imperial eagle on his plastron, but at least Cator was still alive. He glared, willing retribution on the necron lord. Leaking fluids, machine parts crackling and fizzing in his skeletal armature, the Voidbringer was done. Tigurius was relentless and so too was the storm blazing from his fingertips. It lit up the plateau, searing away the ice-fog.

Scipio's eyes narrowed. Something was happening amidst the storm. Impossibly, the necron lord was self-repairing. Despite the fact his form was being stripped apart by psychic fire, the Voidbringer was regenerating!

Living metal pooled together, running in rivulets over his shattered body, and started to form fresh carapace. Seemingly terminal wounds in the necron were reknitting, sealing. Scipio noticed the orb in the monster's chest. It was black like onyx and shimmered as the regeneration process perpetuated itself.

Thumbing the activation stud on his chainsword, Scipio knew what he had to do. To step into that lightning meant certain death. It was a small price. He only hoped his sacrifice would be enough.

VOIDBRINGER WAS LAUGHING. He glared down at the pyromancer who forced more of his crude sorcery into being.

It is to no avail, worm. I am eternal. I am–

He stopped laughing. Voidbringer's savage joy turned to anguish and horror. His wounds were reopening, his body was disintegrating. The pull of the long dark returned, teasing at his consciousness.

No, no…

An inner chill swept over him. The scent of the tomb and the dust of the long sleep filled his olfactory sensors. It was simulation, he was sure of it. His memory engrams were reacting to his approaching destruction. Voidbringer tried to engage with the resurrection orb, to shut off the process, but it was too late. Instead of healing him, it was disassembling his body, unravelling systems and the technology of his entire being. As the genebred ones closed with their weapons, sensing his demise, Voidbringer cursed Ankh. The Architect had tricked him.

TIGURIUS HELD UP a warding hand.

'Wait!'

The lightning was ebbing as he recalled the power of the warp back into check, marshalling the destructive forces he'd called upon by using his psychic hood as a cerebral dampener. It was a complex procedure and he created sigils of temperance and control in the air to focus his thoughts. Instead of a conduit, the Librarian's force rod became a vacuum channelling the psychic energies away to dissipate harmlessly.

'Wait,' he breathed, feeling the pull on his physical strength as he asserted mastery of his mental power. Light gave way to dark, the ice-fog came back and the plateau was stilled. An intense fatigue washed over the Librarian, as if his entire body was a tensed muscle allowed to relax. He staggered and fell, but waved Scipio away as he came to help him.

He scarcely had the breath to command: 'Finish it. Do it now.'

CHAPTER TWENTY-FIVE

ATAVIAN SAW THE energy lances cut into the hard metal of the monoliths only for the damage to be absorbed and nullified a second later.

'Mercy of Hera, are they impervious to all harm?'

Tirian's voice came over the feed – Sergeant Atavian hadn't realised he'd broadcast his words to the other Devastators. They were on an open channel, in order to better coordinate their fire. In the fury of the barrage, that fact had slipped Atavian's mind. 'I heard that Captain Sicarius destroyed one single-handedly,' said Tirian.

'I don't doubt it, brother. Perhaps he'd be willing to come over from the front line, run the three hundred or so metres between us and it, and show us how he did the first time.'

Tirian's booming laughter was at odds with the seriousness of the situation, but it made Atavian smile.

A few hundred metres was no distance at all. It was

optimum range for lascannons but then most decent distances were – Atavian had never known a more accurate, more relentlessly deadly weapon. Hektar and Ulius hammered the advancing monoliths that were using their energies to transport necron phalanxes from outside Kellenport to the force attacking the Ultramarine rearguard in the ruins of Arcona City.

Tirian's squad drilled the infantry. The muzzle flashes of the heavy bolters were almost constant, burning through their belt-feeds in seconds rather than minutes. It was testament to the sergeant's skill and preparation as well as that of his gunners that not one of the heavies had jammed. He was no Techmarine, but Atavian muttered a blessing to the Omnissiah for that. Explosions blossomed in the packed necron ranks as high-velocity bolt shells smashed into the front ranks. It was like throwing rocks into the ocean. There was a ripple as some of the mechanoids were destroyed but then the sea of metal subsided again, the casualties swallowed into the horde or simply redeployed through the monolith portals.

The floating pyramids had to go, Atavian decided. By crippling the enemy's ability to recycle its fallen troops directly into the battle the Ultramarines at least stood a chance of slowing them down. As things stood, they couldn't even do that.

'Aim for the crystal nodes,' Atavian told his heavies. 'All weapons.'

As the Titan Slayers lifted their aim, a shadow fell across them. The whine of repulsor engines promoted Atavian to shout, 'Down!'

A pair of necron gun-platforms hovered overhead at speed.

'I can vanquish them!' It was Brother Ikus – he'd

stayed on his feet. 'In the Emperor's name!' The burst from his plasma cannon engulfed the lead gun-platform, turning it into a mass of plummeting fire-wreathed wreckage. The second jinked out of the plasma bolt's path, avoiding the worst of its fury, and returned fire.

Ikus swung the heavy weapon around, grunting with the effort. The plasma coils on his back-mounted generator were still cycling. The necron's heavy gauss-cannon sent out a pulse of emerald light that bored through the Ultramarine's armour, transfixing him. Ikus shook as most of his internal organs were flayed to atoms and then crashed head-first down the steps.

'Neutralise it!' Atavian was pointing towards the gun-platform, which was wheeling around for another pass until one of Tirian's missile launchers tore it open in mid-air. The necron plummeted to the earth just in front of the other Devastators, twisted and on fire.

Brother Korvus of the Titan Slayers slung his bolter as he went to take up Ikus's fallen plasma cannon. Meanwhile, one of Tirian's warriors had made it to the gun-platform's crash site to execute the stricken necron in the debris.

'Still alive,' said Korvus, checking Ikus's vitals.

'Put that cannon on the monoliths,' ordered Atavian, sending another of the bolter-armed battle-brothers to drag Ikus to relative safety. He turned his attention back to the monoliths. In the distance, they were turning their energy to something new. A web of light was growing between the three hovering structures, the larger one at its nexus.

'That can't be good,' Atavian muttered, before ordering the lascannons to intensify fire on the middle monolith. The tactics had changed. Rather than overwhelm the

Ultramarines with infantry, the necrons would scour their bodies from the very earth with hellish firepower.

Watching their implacable advance, knowing there was little else he could do to resist the monoliths, Atavian wished he had more lascannons.

ULLYIOUS IXION CURSED as the necron gun-platforms escaped his wrath. He was still shaking loose the wreckage of the last machine he had crushed when he landed. The end of his jump took him into a phalanx of raiders and he immediately set about them with a deadly arsenal of plasma pistol and power fist. Alongside their sergeant, Macragge's Avengers were imperious and brutal. A spew of flame ripped through the packed necron ranks from Ptolon's flamer. His brothers leapt on the burning mechanoids and cut them apart with chainswords. It was tough work; the necrons were hard, but the raiders fell back before the assault squad's onslaught.

More gun-platforms, a different group, were coming around again as Ixion looked to the skies. Engage, destroy, manoeuvre and repeat: these were the tactical rotas of an Assault Marine. At their sergeant's sub-vocal command, Macragge's Avengers boosted into the air leaving scorched earth behind them.

Near the apex of the jump, Ixion asked, 'How does Strabo fare?'

The other assault squad, the self-dubbed Heroes of Selonopolis, were on the opposite flank to the Macragge's Avengers and focussed on similar targets. Ixion had instructed Brother Ptolon to keep a tally.

'They outstrip us by a single gun-platform, sergeant.'

Targets, urgent and red, were coming into view through Ixion's retinal lenses. He took aim down the small barrel of his plasma pistol. 'Then let us even the score.'

Even in desperate battle, squad rivalry was evident. Sicarius liked it that way – it kept his warrior-brothers sharp. So did Ixion.

The necrons were everywhere. It was a battle without end. Ixion revelled in it.

'Death from the heavens, fire and wrath! For Ultramar!'

BELOW THE AERIAL duelling between the assault squads and the necron gun-platforms, Praxor was cutting apart the last of a raider group sent to blunt his attack. The Shieldbearers were rampant through the mechanoids' ranks; Praxor had never fought beside his warriors this fired-up. He, too, was at the peak of his prowess. Deep within the thick of the necrons, they needed to be.

He saw Sicarius just ahead of him through the melee. It was close-up work, bolters and blades, just what Space Marines were made for. Though tough, the raiders were not as adept at close combat as the Space Marines – it put them at a disadvantage despite their regenerative capability. In hand-to-hand, or at close range, it was easier to ensure a necron was badly damaged enough that they phased out; at distance, where the Ultramarines had first engaged, too many were self-repairing and getting back up.

Though not equipped specifically for assault, Praxor had ordered his squad to switch to gladius and bolt pistols as soon as the necrons were within range. Advancing in a 'V' formation with the sergeant at the tip, the Shieldbearers were brutal and shredded the mechanoids' ranks.

Agrippen was merciless.

Both he and Ultracius had waded into the enemy throng a few seconds behind Sicarius. They ranged at either flank of the captain and his Lions, crushing bodies with their power fists and unleashing close-proximity barrages with their main weapons.

Against the Dreadnoughts, the necrons had no answer. Their flying gun-platforms couldn't get close; Ixion and Strabo were marshalling the skies. Nothing else could touch them. Unable to draw significant firepower against the venerable warriors, the necrons were getting slaughtered. But where one raider fell, another three replaced it. And these were just the rank and file; the elites would be a much tougher prospect. Sicarius's plan was a risky one. If he didn't draw the necron overlord into battle soon, all of the Dreadnoughts' efforts, the efforts of all the Ultramarines, would be for nothing.

A moment of calm descended over Praxor, his closest foes all dispatched for now. It enabled him to take stock of the battle. The Ultramarines had ventured quite far from the ruined basilica and driven a small wedge of cobalt into the necron sea of metal. As it got further, the wedge narrowed like a slow-moving lance seeking out the heart of its foes – in this case, the necron overlord. Another phalanx was moving around to try and stymie the daring Ultramarines' attack.

Its machine-spirit humming for further death, Praxor pressed his power sword up to his battle-helm to beseech the blessing of the Emperor and the primarch before thrusting back into the fray.

THE GILDED NECRON overlord was not easy to miss. Sicarius had the creature target-locked in his left retinal lens. Schemata scrolled across the right, overlaying his vision.

Weaknesses were hard to identify in the monster's metal armature. He was plated like the other necrons, but bigger, the same size as the elites pressing ahead of him in a tight warrior-cohort.

They were of a different caste, these mechanoids; just as implacable but better drilled. The elites stayed close to their lord, just in front of a tight ring of bodyguards. The latter wielded shimmering war-glaives that looked like they'd shear straight through power armour. Much like the elites, these too would need to be broken open in order to reach the overlord.

He had gambled with the Ultramarines under his command, allowed them to fall into the necron lord's web all so he could draw the monster out.

'You have me, creature,' he whispered to the confines of his battle-helm. 'Now come and claim me.'

Sicarius's mind was set: one way or another this war would end between him and the gilded necron. Even if he had to kill every one of the elites and then destroy the honour guard, he would do it. To the death.

The comm-feed in the captain's ear crackled, indicating long-range interference. He severed a raider's torso with his Tempest Blade, immolating another with a close burst from his plasma pistol.

'This is Sicarius. Proceed,' he growled.

The voice that answered was not who he expected but the news it brought allowed another plan to form in the captain's mind.

Cato Sicarius smiled.

'Daceus,' he said, turning to his second-in-command. 'Prepare the force to withdraw.'

The veteran-sergeant was pummelling a raider with his power fist as he looked up. 'Sir?'

'We fall back to Kellenport as originally planned.'

'Our forces are boxed in, brother-captain. We have no route of retreat.'

'Not yet. Defensive postures for all troops. Do it now, brother-sergeant.'

The order was relayed. The Ultramarines who'd fought the necrons back this far were told to give up the ground they'd won and consolidate at the ruins.

'I HAVE AN attack vector to the elites. We can engage. I repeat, we can engage.'

Ixion was soaring on the flaming pillars of his jump pack, locking onto his next target, when Daceus's voice brought his imagined glory crashing down to earth.

'Negative. Pull back to the ruins, all squads.'

The feed was cut. Ixion pulled up short, landing in a patch of no-man's-land with his squad.

Brother Ptolon thundered down alongside him. 'Sergeant?'

'We're falling back to the basilica ruins, all of us.'

Ixion looked heavenwards and saw Strabo was already on his way. He did not question, he did not doubt – he merely obeyed. But Ullyious Ixion did feel his wrath magnified at the denial of his warrior-urge.

He craned his neck, looking up into the stars appearing in the sky, and ignited his jump-jets in a stream of fire. 'Fly, Avengers!'

'BRING IT DOWN!'

Hektar and Ulius struck the lead monolith time and again but every blazing bolt was simply absorbed by the machine. Inexorably, it came forwards with the other two monoliths moving behind it in perfect unison. Slow and ponderous, whatever the triumvirate was about to unleash would be terrible. As he shouted the order, Atavian knew they had to stop it. But as the energy nexus strung between the crystal nodes of each of the pyramids grew into a blazing coruscation, the sergeant was struck by a solemn truth.

We are going to fail.

Emerald lightning crackled around the lead monolith's apex as the energy tendrils were drawn up its tubular conduits and into its crystal matrix. A corona of light built around the crystal, increasing in intensity with the passing of each second.

Atavian gave the only order he could think of that would make any difference. 'Get into cover!'

A thick beam of power pulsed from the lead monolith's crystal. It struck the steps just below the Titan Slayers' position, turning the air to steam and the world to fire around them. The shockwave lifted the Ultramarines off their feet. Motes of dust and debris were suspended briefly in the blast radius. It resonated outwards like an earthquake, splitting the ground with a web of cracks centred at the origin point.

Despite the dampeners built into his helmet's systems, Atavian's auditory canal was overloaded with sound. Blood vessels burst in his nose and ears, nulling two of his senses instantly. Retinal lenses couldn't process the sudden influx of intense light; excessive heat warnings raced across the internal display before they too capitulated against the sheer strength of the blast. He remembered crouching down before the blast hit and the section of wall disintegrating in front of him. It was what he imagined an atomic explosion to be like. A sense of weightlessness overtook his body as Atavian realised he'd been lifted off his feet. Propelled backwards he slammed into a still-standing column and slumped, knocked onto his backside.

Ultramarines lay scattered around him, some Tirian's, some his own. They were thrown like debris before a storm – the deadly emerald beam showed no respect for the heirs of Guilliman. It was death. Pure and undistilled. Despite himself, Atavian couldn't help but feel awed by its incredible power. It didn't stop him from wanting to destroy it.

Cobalt-armoured bodies were stirring. Smoke and fire wafted and flickered between them. The stone steps were levelled, most of what was left of the ruins too. The sound of scraping battle-plate came from all around him as Atavian's battle-brothers got up and tried to regroup. Defeat was not a word in an Ultramarine's vocabulary, or so the sergeant believed. Pain-suppressing drugs were already flooding his nervous system and Larraman cells began the process of rapid blood-clotting as Atavian rose to his feet. A farinaceous pall swathed the atmosphere from the displaced dust and debris. Patches of steam lingered in tiny squalls before crystallising as the cold reasserted dominance.

Atavian's tactical display revealed a lot of amber runes – almost all of the Ultramarines in the rearguard were injured. There were some red icons too, the disabled or dead. Ineffective battle-brothers were not his concern right now; he needed firepower, and quickly. He'd reached the end of the blast zone – perversely, the resulting crater provided some rudimentary cover. Several of his squad and what was left of Tirian's, including the sergeant himself, were already hunkering down.

Tirian handed Atavian his magnoculars.

'Barely even a scratch.'

Atavian had to agree. It was a slow march that brought the necrons and their monoliths to the rear of the Ultramarines lines but for all the damage done to them they could have been advancing one step a minute and they'd still reach the Devastators intact.

He handed the scopes back. 'Its weak point is the crystal power matrix at the machine's apex.'

Tirian nodded. 'An easy enough target.'

Ulius was crouched down next to Atavian and said, 'If something weren't fouling our auto-aiming systems.'

Removing the targeter from Ulius's lascannon, Atavian took a look. 'Trajectory is off.' He made some adjustments, looked again. 'Still off.' He gave the device back to Ulius and glanced around the crater. 'Where is Hektar?'

'Dead, sir.'

'Where is his lascannon?'

'With his body, brother-sergeant.'

Atavian's gaze was on the advancing monoliths.

'Bring it here.'

Ulius did as commanded. He kept his head down as the fire from the Devastators started up again. His caution was unnecessary. The monoliths were recycling, spewing repaired and revivified necrons from their portals and undoing all the damage inflicted by Guilliman's Hammer. Tirian was unimpressed.

'We're wasting ammunition,' he growled, calling for a cease-fire. Missile-launchers stayed primed but still; heavy bolters stalled with belts ready-fed. 'The war machines must be neutralised.'

Since the blast, Atavian's Titan Slayers hadn't fired a single shot.

'While they're regenerating infantry, they're not using those crystal matrices to eradicate us. It's a cycle. Once it's complete, the monoliths will charge those conduits and unleash the beam weapon.'

Ulius returned, hefting Hektar's lascannon and setting it down next to his sergeant.

'What are you seeing, Maxima?' Tirian's use of his first name made Atavian turn to face him.

Tirian's scarred battle-helm was reflected back in his crimson lenses. 'It's what I've *seen*, brother.'

Overhead, stabbing beams of emerald were thickening the air. The necrons were within gauss-flayer range and releasing sporadic bursts as they advanced. Bolter fire answered but it was no more than a perfunctory response.

Atavian continued, 'We cannot trust our auto-targeters. The necrons are machines of a type. Affinity with mechanisms is a component of their xenos construction. We are feeling their influence.'

'The machine-spirits of our weapons are corrupted?' Tirian sounded incensed.

'No, but they've been compromised. The adjustments I made to Ulius's targeter should have corrected the aim – they didn't. Destroying those crystals will take accuracy but it must be done by instinct.' Detaching the seals on his gorget, Atavian removed his battle-helm. Without the voice-augmentation of his armour, he had to shout to be heard. 'By naked eye alone.'

He hefted the lascannon onto his shoulder. The weight of it felt good, almost nostalgic. Atavian side glanced at Ulius. 'Follow my lead, brother.'

Jettisoning his helmet and mag-locking it to his thigh, Ulius tried to gauge his sergeant's aim.

'We are targeting the thirdmost machine?'

'Yes. Wait until they're powering up the main weapon. I will give the order when to shoot.'

It was sniper shooting with a lascannon. Tanks, Dreadnoughts, installations – a lascannon's usual prey was large and relatively static. The monoliths *were* slow but whatever fouling technology the necrons were employing had narrowed the target-window considerably. It required peerless accuracy.

A sniper often prepared for days, scoping out the area, finding optimum position. They would gauge all variables: light, wind speed, weather anomalies, a target's weak points. Though much more powerful, a lascannon lacked the subtlety of a rifle. Instead of days, Atavian had only had minutes to prepare his shot. He considered recoil, trajectory, projected impact point. In the end he trusted to two things: instinct and faith.

The last of the repaired raiders emerged from the portals, prompting the crystal nodes on the monoliths to energise again. Frantic lightning arcs sprang from the central machine, creating a link between the other two. Power was fed to the main crystal and the energy coruscation swelled brightly.

'On my signal...' said Atavian, adjusting his position by a fraction. Gauss-fire was chewing up the earth around the Ultramarines, taking chunks off the crater's edge and spitting the debris against their armour. Sergeant Tirian had opened up with his heavies again, trying to give the lascannons some protection.

The glow around the lead monolith's crystal was still growing. Beam release was imminent.

'Make your blow quickly, brother,' warned Tirian.

'It will fall heavily. At my signal...' Atavian muttered, bringing his cheek to the side of the lascannon and lowering the barrel tip by the smallest fraction.

When trying to disable a fast-moving target, let it come to you.

One of the rubrics of his old masters came to the forefront of his mind.

The monoliths advanced into prime firing position. It also brought them into Atavian's crosshairs. He lifted two fingers from the cannon trigger. That was the signal.

Twin lascannon beams hit the thirdmost monolith as it was feeding the last of its power to the hub-crystal, shattering the node and sending a backwash of energy into the other two.

The struck monolith shuddered as a chain reaction of catastrophic damage rolled through its structure. Cracks formed in its pyramid hull, exuding sickly emerald light. Actinic fire bloomed out of its portal as the vast machine crashed to the ground and stopped. Rampant energy spikes crippled the other two, forcibly aborting the beam projection. Stung and in sudden need of repair, the remaining monoliths began a slow retreat leaving the shattered war engine behind.

Despite himself, Atavian gave a shout of triumph.

It was echoed by some of the others in the rearguard. The defeat of the monoliths sent a ripple effect through the advancing infantry who were being chewed up by the combined fire of both Devastator squads. Without the portals they could not immediately repair and rede-ploy. At last, their numbers were thinning.

A second problem compounded the first for the necrons. Tirian saw it through the magnoculars.

'Brothers, we are reinforced.' The savage joy in his voice was obvious.

Atavian felt it too as he was given the scopes.

'I see conscripts, Guard formations too.' Increasing magnification, he added, 'Iulus Fennion and his Immortals lead them.'

Tirian laughed, surprise and relief colouring his tone. 'I confess I thought the Kellenport defenders van-quished and us an island in a sea of foes.'

Atavian handed off the lascannon to Hektar's replacement. Now the monoliths were neutralised, at least for a time, he resumed his duties as sergeant.

'We are still an island, brother,' he asserted, 'but now we have a channel taking us back to land.'

Orders from Daceus were already coming from the frontline.

A full retreat was in effect. All forces were to return to Kellenport. With the concentration of Ultramarines in the area, several necron phalanxes had rerouted to tackle them. Somewhere in their midst, a necron overlord directed their efforts. Sicarius must have irritated them and now baited the trap. Kellenport's walls were as good a staging ground for a pitched battle as any other.

'It's as if he planned it,' said Tirian. The necron infantry was being pressed on both sides.

Before he donned his battle-helm, Atavian met Tirian's gaze. 'What makes you think he didn't?'

BARRING A SKELETON force of defenders, Commander Sonne had virtually emptied Kellenport. Entrenched gun positions were dug out and formed into heavy weapon teams; the troopers from disparate squads were reappropriated into platoons; conscripts were armed and armoured from the dead and forged into their own battalions; and what was left of the Damnosian armour rode out into the wastes led by a small group of cobalt Angels.

Adanar was in the cupola of the lead tank, a Leman Russ with a damaged battle cannon but whose side-sponson heavy bolters worked well enough. Two others followed it in staggered formation, one either side. Both were damaged but still had some firepower left. Sentinel walkers, some without functioning weapons, and Hellhound tanks ranged the flanks. A stoic block of Chimera transports brought up the rear, with one exception. This

vehicle was at the head of the slow-moving armoured
column. Its roof hatch had been ripped off by a gauss-
blast, so too most of the roof. The rest of the Chimera's
hull was intact, as were its tracks and engine. It made the
perfect transport for Sergeant Fennion and four of his
men. The others were amongst the infantry platoons,
their presence more galvanising than any tank.

For the first time since the siege had begun, Adanar
felt something other than despair. It wasn't hope, only
reunion with his dead family could restore that; it was
something else, something that at least dulled the fatalism seizing him – it was vengeance.

THE ONE HUNDRED seemed to Falka like a misnomer
now. He wasn't sure there'd ever been a hundred poor
souls in his improvised regiment in the first place, not
exactly. It didn't matter, the name had resonance and
the ex-rig-hand turned soldier liked that. What was
left of the men marched with him in lockstep alongside the Ultramarines. The Chimera transport of the
Space Marines moved slowly so the conscripts could
keep up. Sergeant Fennion had initially dismissed the
idea of riding aboard the tank, wanting to march the
wastes as the humans did, but Falka had convinced
him that he needed to be seen. He was a beacon,
something for the others to look too, and more inspiring than any banner. Reluctantly, the Ultramarine had
agreed.

'What are you thinking, brother-Angel?' Falka asked,
looking up in the direction of the Chimera's ragged
hull. He caught the last dregs of the sallow sun fading
into the horizon. It painted the distant tundra red and
rimed the edge of the mountains.

Iulus glared straight ahead as if he beheld destiny.

'That you ask many questions and are impudent in the extreme, Trooper Kolpeck.'

Falka laughed.

'That is why you like me so much.'

Iulus glanced at him askance. There was the shadow of a smile on his lips then it was gone again.

'Are you ready for more war, Brother Kolpeck?'

Falka nodded. 'Aye, my time is almost up I think. I'll be happy to leave my blood here, just as long as I take a few of those metal bastards with me.'

'Fearless and well-spoken, brother. You would have made a fine Ultramarine.'

The necron lines were close now. Some of the mechanoids were turning in response to the new threat and sporadic bursts of emerald gauss-fire came rippling their way. It was different to the battle in the courtyard, even the fight to hold the walls. That was desperate, there was no choice but to take up arms or die. This was not like that. A silver sea stretched before the Imperial defenders comprised of alien killing machines Falka didn't understand or truly want to face.

Though they moved like skeletal automatons, he saw the awareness in their eyes and felt their emotions, such as they were. It was hate that burned in their balefire orbs, pure, hollow hate. The necrons would not rest until all of Damnos was gone, its population eradicated like some cancerous plague. It was this chilling fact that made Falka and his men, all of the Damnosians, march to their likely deaths. Better to fight and die, than just to die.

Mortality had never really concerned him. He didn't know if at the end there was anything more than a dark void without feeling. He hoped there would be light, maybe not a Golden Throne in the Eternal Palace of the

God-Emperor, but light enough so he could find Jynn and be reunited. That would suit him just fine.

Falka donned his helmet – it carried the markings of a sergeant inscribed with a combat blade by Iulus himself – and hollered to his troops.

'Gather your courage, men. We are the saviours of Damnos, fighting for our native soil. The Emperor is with us. He has sent His Angels to fight by our side. In the name of the Imperium, honour them!'

Las-fire whickered from the Imperial ranks meeting the gauss-beams in a lattice of energy, crisscrossing lethally over the wastes. The shuddering report of heavy bolters joined it as the battle tanks opened up. Pintle-mounts blazing on their cupolas, engines screaming – the last armoured company of Damnos went to war.

An explosion, emerald-tinged and violent, lit up the distance in a viridian flash.

The afterglow still lingered in Falka's vision when he saw two beams of light strike one of the floating necron pyramids and destroy it. Beyond the enemy masses, through the cascade of gauss-flayer death, he saw the beleaguered Ultramarines too, Sergeant Fennion's true brothers.

Even amidst the firefight – seen in cracks between the melee – they were glorious. A figure strode amongst them, his armour gilded and with a white-red crest atop his battle-helm. A cape fastened to his ornate pauldrons via taloned clasps whipped about him as he killed necrons with a glowing blade. This was the personification of a hero. It was valour made flesh. An arch-angel. It was Sicarius.

With the Emperor's name not long passed his lips, Falka wept.

* * *

'IMMORTALS, DISMOUNT!' IULUS leapt from the open-topped Chimera, landing squarely with chainsword drawn. In the next breath, he was running, a steady thud of shells spitting from his bolt pistol into the necrons. Four of his battle-brothers were alongside him, charging at full tilt, for the glory of Ultramar and all of Guilliman's heirs.

The clash was fearsome, Iulus and his four battle-brothers weathering a hail of gauss-flayer bursts before they reached the enemy. Necrons responded to force, they had to be overwhelmed, struck such a catastrophic blow that whatever arcane engines animated them would realise destruction was imminent and quit the field for the sanctity of their tomb.

Considering their frailties, the humans showed incredible bravery to be only a few metres behind the Ultramarines. As he severed the spinal column of one of the mechanoids, Iulus felt a swell of pride for these poor doomed souls. In such an intense firestorm, casualties amongst the Guard and conscripts were horrific. Without power armour or an intensely hard armature, they fell quickly and in numbers.

Iulus lost sight of Kolpeck almost immediately. Inwardly, he chastened himself for it but this was war, the great leveller, and it had no use for sentiment. His chainblade growled, eager for the kill, and he fed it. Adopting a semi-circular formation, the five Immortals advanced laying down an incessant barrage of fire. The necrons had thrown their infantry against them, a horde of raider constructs that the Second had become experts at fighting. Space Marines adapted quickly, learned the weaknesses of an enemy and how best to slay them. The Ultramarines, from Legion to Chapter, had been doing it for over ten thousand years. It was down to a fine art.

'Killing is why we were born.' Iulus recalled the words of his old trainer.

There wasn't much guile to it. The fact the bulk of the force was conscripted ruled out any intricate tactics. It didn't matter. They would employ the hammer and hope it was enough.

As he cut down a raider trying to rise, Iulus caught sight of the tanks. The one with Commander Sonne was racing in the front.

TWO BATTLE TANKS behind him were burning wrecks. He'd seen them stitched by gauss-beams and then explode. No rifle weapon had any right to be so potent against armour like that. It left a limping Hellhound and a Chimera with its multi-laser still functional to take on the monolith.

Whether reacting to their proximity or merely self-repaired and thrown back into the fray, Adanar didn't know or care, but one of the necron pyramids had turned and was heading for them. Lances of emerald death spat from the cannons arrayed around the machine's flanks. A concentrated burst chewed up the Chimera, riddling it with holes before the fuel reserve cooked off and turned the vehicle in a ball of oily flame. Adanar watched it buck and spin, before crashing down on its roof in a smoking, fiery ruin. He let the backwash of heat flow over his face, toss the cape at his back – it was ragged and dirty by now.

The Hellhound slewed to a halt soon after, its axle giving out. The engine screamed hot but it was just grinding metal. Adanar turned. The tank's crew were still fighting to get out of the escape hatches when the monolith found its new target and immolated them. It was the broken axle that killed them. Fate was cruel sometimes.

Heavy bolters on the side sponsons were throwing out shells, tearing through their belt feeds with fury. Suddenly one of the guns clunked tight and the fusillade from the right side stopped. Then it was the left. Out of ammunition – they'd run their stockpile dry.

'I want that thing down!' he cried into the darkness of the cupola below.

A stuttering salvo of emerald beams stabbed into the tank's hull before the crew could reply. The tracks slowed almost instantly, engine noise falling from a shriek to a whine to a low hum. Deceleration. It could mean only one thing: the driver was dead.

Leaping down into the tank's hold, Adanar found a scene of bloody carnage. Crimson, though it looked more like black, painted the walls where the crew had been part-flayed by gauss-beams or shredded by internal shrapnel. In such close confines it was worse than a grenade going off. Adanar's position in the cupola had been the only thing that had saved him. Everyone else was dead.

'Can't let it live,' he muttered. Somehow, the locket-charm had found its way into his grasp. He rubbed it idly, though he didn't remember retrieving it. Dragging the driver – or what was left of his half-cooked, cauterised body – out of his seat, Adanar scrambled into the self-same position and hit the accelerator pedal hard. It didn't take a crew of five men to drive a tank. It took one with the will to do what was necessary.

Through the cracked view-slit Adanar made out the bulky form of the monolith. The view was mired by dirt and blood so he wiped it with his sleeve. Collision course set, he gave it everything. Stabs of light perforated the hull as the necron machine opened up again but miraculously he was left unharmed.

Just a few more metres.

The names of his wife and daughter were on Adanar's cracked lips. The sheer side of the monolith loomed, filling the view-slit with black.

'I am coming...' he whispered, and closed his eyes.

AN EXPLOSION LIT up the battlefield. Falka saw wreckage and fire, but he was too busy fighting for his life to make out details. It was the sound more than anything that arrested his attention.

To his right, a conscript pulled a frag grenade and was halfway through a throw when a blast caught him in the neck. He fell and the grenade went off, filling the area around him with noise and hot metal. Falka's vision faded to black. He was dimly aware of being on his back and a damp sensation over his torso and legs. The dirt was soft and all sound slowly bled away to a soft susurrus. Through the encroaching darkness he thought he could see angels coming through the white mist...

VICTORY WAS AT hand. Iulus had been in enough battles over his decades of service to realise this. Attacked on both sides, at one a reserve battalion primarily made up of human soldiery, and the other a breakout force of Ultramarines, the necrons were well beaten. Smashed between such desperate and inviolable warriors, the mechanoids phased from the battlefield and left only the bodies of Imperial fallen in their wake.

He held his chainsword aloft, gazing around at the carnage they had reaped. '*Victoris Ultra!*'

Every Space Marine, every conscript and Ark Guard trooper raised their fists.

'*Victoris Ultra!*'

'And the glory of Damnos!' he added, seeking out

Kolpeck amongst the exultant masses. The trooper was nowhere to be seen. Iulus had no time to think further on his ebbing sense of triumph – the captain and his honour guard approached.

Sicarius clasped him in a firm embrace. 'Well met, brother.' He withdrew and held onto Iulus's shoulder guards to help convey his delight at their arrival. 'Well met!'

Humble, Iulus bowed. He saw Praxor just behind the captain and caught his gaze.

'All is in readiness back at Kellenport?' Sicarius pressed, letting the sergeant go.

Iulus confirmed this.

'Then we had best make haste.' Sicarius turned to indicate the larger necron army behind them. The Ultramarines had put ground between them and small longer range skirmishes were still going on between the assault squads and the necron gun-platforms, but the majority of the phalanxes had slowed to a crawl. 'The overlord rebuilds his forces but will continue the advance. We must reach the staging ground before he meets us.' Something flashed behind the captain's helmet lenses; either retribution or anger, but Iulus couldn't tell which. 'I vow this will be our last retreat.'

With that, Sicarius left him. It allowed only the briefest of reunions with Praxor.

'I am pleased to see you still alive, brother,' Iulus said genuinely. The two sergeants clasped forearms.

Where Iulus gave off a reserved ebullience, Praxor's mood was dark. 'Many are not.' From the reduced ranks of the Shieldbearers, it was obvious that his squad had suffered.

'Death or glory, brother,' said Iulus. 'It is our way, our lot.'

'We have chosen death.' Praxor saluted, though the gesture was perfunctory and intended to end the brief discourse, and tramped away with his battered squad.

The Dreadnought, Agrippen, followed in his wake.

'Immortals indeed,' said the venerable warrior, appraising Iulus's men.

'We are too stubborn to die, old one.'

'When we reach the walls of Kellenport to make our stand, that trait will be tested, I feel,' Agrippen replied before walking on.

Iulus looked out into the advancing necron sea, a silver waste bringing ruin to everything in its path. Ixion and Strabo were withdrawing too, having neutralised the vanguard of gun-platforms. The necrons were consolidating their forces. They had time and growing numbers on their side.

'Yes,' his answer came, too late for the Dreadnought to hear. 'Yes it will.'

Turning, Iulus saw the conscripts and Ark Guard gathering too. He stopped a corporal on his way. 'You!' The man looked up fearfully at the imposing cobalt warrior-knight. 'Where is Trooper Kolpeck?'

CHAPTER TWENTY-SIX

THEY STOOD SHOULDER-TO-SHOULDER, bolters locked and ready, blades drawn and gleaming with the rising of the moon.

Before them, the third wall, its gates laid open for the sally of the Damnosian defenders. The humans were behind them now, tucked into their firing holes, pressed against their battlements and looking down on their champions arrayed in the Courtyard of Xiphos.

Praxor did not turn to look, he didn't need to. The humans had made their last act of defiance; it was up to the Ultramarines to become the true saviours of Damnos now.

'Do you remember our words about King Vidus?' asked Sicarius. The Shieldbearers were next to the Lions of Macragge in the line.

'A legend of triumph over adversity, my lord,' Praxor replied.

'Indeed, brother-sergeant.' Sicarius pointed to the

third wall and its open gates, an expansive gesture of his sword-arm encompassing the courtyard. 'This is our Thermapylon, and we the seven hundred whose blades and courage blunted the cruel ambition of a tyrant. History repeats itself, Sergeant Manorian, it always does. We stand at the cusp of it now.'

The Lions stood straighter at their liege's words. Vandius thrust the banner of the Second higher and it caught the wind. Daceus sent a crackle of energy through the fingers of his power fist. Gaius Prabian drew the blade of his sword against his shield, making the metal scrape in a wordless challenge.

This was what it meant to be a Lion. It was utter devotion; it was obedience and blind trust without equal. Sicarius only brought those who followed his will without question into his inner circle. Ironically, this was the closest Praxor had ever been to joining them and it was also the moment he knew he never would.

Agrippen was close, on the other side of Sicarius's honour guard. His eternal gaze was on the battlefield ahead. The Dreadnought was not here on Damnos to report on the captain of Second Company's actions, nor was he following any agenda Agemman had set. He was merely here to fight, to honour the Chapter's name and lineage.

'I am my Chapter's unsheathed sword,' said Praxor at last.

'Then make your blade ready, brother,' Sicarius answered, the Tempest Blade held before him, 'for the enemy comes! Courage and honour!'

The Ultramarines took up the bellowed cry, their voices in unison, their purpose as one.

'Courage and honour!'

Necron raiders were the first to breach the wall. As

they did so the charges Iulus had set all those hours ago ignited, filling the Courtyard of Xiphos with rock and fire.

TONNES OF ROCK and plascrete descended on the necrons. Many metres thick, several kilometres long, the third defensive wall of Kellenport was obliterated in the blast burying everything around it. Dust and dirt rose in a massive pall to blanket the advancing necron forces. It churned across the courtyard, brushing against the assembled Ultramarines and colouring the edges of their armour. The Space Marines let the debris cloud roll over them, unmoving. It only took a few minutes for it to be swept away on the breeze and an echoing silence to eclipse them. Seconds later, green balefire orbs resolved in the gloom as the next line of mechanoids thrust into the rubble.

With much of the vanguard crushed, the necron overlord had little choice but to press his elites into the breach. By now, the phalanxes rerouted to destroy the Ultramarines had been gathered. Necron immortals stumbled over the wreckage of the wall to be met by a stern barrage of bolter fire. They were beyond mere raiders though, and weathered the storm with impunity. Gauss-blasters answered in rapid-fire bursts that shimmered like green pyrotechnic across the snowy courtyard flagstones.

Falka watched it all through his firing slit on the wall. A thick bandage was wrapped around his torso from where the shrapnel had hit him. Despite the cocktail of drugs in his system keeping him upright and battleworthy, the wound hurt like all the hells. Others weren't so lucky. Pelk lost most of his throat to the blast; Hiiken, an eye and the back of his skull. Men had died, but

Falka lived. Perhaps the Emperor had blessed him; perhaps He had blessed them all. He hoped His gaze would fall on His Angels too as the necrons poured into the courtyard.

I AM DOOM. The words echoed inside the Undying's cavernous mind. He had contemplated oblivion, his endless sentence of existence, and decided that all life must be eradicated from the universe. Cities burned, their populations reduced to ash by his wrath; worlds imploded, sucked into a vortex of obliteration; entire systems ignited into endless flame witnessed by his mind's eye.

This is death, this is all… I shall show it to the universe.

The curse was alive in his memory engrams, as pervasive as any flesh-borne contagion. It had condensed his self-awareness down into a singularity – the obsession with total destruction.

Hurl rock and earth, until the world is bare. It is as inconsequential as a speck of dust. Across the debris and the sundered remains of the defensive wall, the Undying found his prey.

This was the one who had defied him.

He glared, imaging the ending of all things, and outstretched a skeletal finger.

'Eradicate them.'

Reacting to the voice of their overlord, the immortals marched into the billowing dust cloud in phalanx. The Undying went with them. His honour guard attempted to close around him, glaives drawn up protectively in the simulated behaviour of aeons past. With a curt gesture, like he was parting the waves of some ancient sea, the Undying broke apart their circle and advanced after the immortals. Obeisant, they followed.

I am no longer flesh. I am abomination. I am destroyer.

The hollow thoughts echoed in his slowly fragmenting mind. Weapons-fire was coming from beyond the debris. War was joined again. Igniting the blade of his war-scythe, the Undying stared into the storm and felt... nothing.

TWO-HANDED, SCIPIO HAMMERED the necron lord over and again with his chainsword. Whatever the strange orb in the monster's chest had done to it, the Voidbringer was reduced to scrap. With a final cry of anguish, it phased out, seemingly drawn into the artefact only for it then to collapse in on itself in a miniature event horizon.

Scipio sagged a little, his breathing rapid. 'It is done,' he announced, but Tigurius wasn't listening. The aura was still emanating from his body and he focussed to control it.

Extending a shaking hand, he uttered in a broken rasp, 'Get me to the ridge, as high as you can.'

Surveying the immediate area, Scipio looked for further threats but the necrons had ceased their advance. In fact, in many instances, they had simply stopped. The effect of the Voidbringer's destruction was potent and debilitating it seemed. His constructs appeared slower, sluggish even, as if having to recalculate or waiting for the hole in their chain of command to be repaired. Those necrons that had to defend themselves did; those beyond the immediate reach of the battle remained still.

Scipio raised the comm-feed immediately. 'Do not engage. I repeat, do not engage enemy unless necessary. The lesser necron constructs have suffered some kind of catastrophic failure and are reverting to defensive protocols.'

Octavian and Vandar confirmed. There was a clear

zone around the artillery. None of the necrons were moving.

'What happened to them?' asked Vandar.

'I don't know, but hold your positions and prime whatever explosives we have left,' Scipio replied. 'We can level this artillery platform, bury it under the mountain. Make ready.'

The other sergeants issued clipped affirmatives before Scipio was back.

He turned to Cator. 'Are you strong enough to stand?'

The plasma gunner grunted. 'Try and stop me. I'll crawl out of this hell-hole if I have to, brother-sergeant.'

Satisfied, Scipio went to Tigurius. Weakened by his psychic exertions and not entirely lucid, Scipio had to help him up. Temperature spikes throughout his armour's systems filled his retinal display with warning icons from the heat still emanating off the Librarian's psychic aura. Lightning crackled across his arcane battle-plate again, ripples and motes at first, but growing in intensity. By the time he and Scipio had staggered to the edge of the ridge, they were developing into jags and forks. Drawn into the foci of his force rod, Tigurius began crafting them into a massive nimbus of psychic energy.

'When we reach the summit,' he said, clambering across the rocks, 'get down. Tell your brothers to do the same and seek cover.'

As soon as they'd mounted the small ridge overlooking the artillery, Scipio jumped back down again and gave the order. Crouched with Cator at his side, he watched.

Tigurius was glowing. A tumult of lightning coursed across the sigils inscribed onto his armour, illuminating their designs, and fed into the force rod. The eye sockets within the skull at its tip were bleeding power ferociously. Arcane instruments – keys, chains, scrolls, all of the Master Librarian's esoteric panoply – rose up with the quickening energies infusing him. It was as if they were partly magnetised and lifted in response to the sudden polarisation.

He lifted. Tigurius levitated off the ground, tiny thunderbolts striking the earth below his feet and leaving burn scars in their wake. A series of runic sigils lit up across the hard features of his face, unseen by the naked eye but visible with the tapping of his power.

'I am a servant of the Chapter Librarius. My body is a conduit. My will is dire and filled with the fire of retribution!'

A split-second of silence persisted where all was still and time itself simply ceased. It broke loose the instant the storm was released like a pent-up current rushing through an opened flood gate. Lightning pulsed outwards in a wave, ripping into the artillery, turning their living metal into slag and destroying them utterly. It cooked off the rest of the explosives placed by the Ultramarines and jets of fire leapt from the ground edged with a viridian lustre.

It burned the necrons too, immolating those close enough to the nexus of the storm, banishing wraiths who vanished like frost before the winter sun.

The light died as quickly as it had manifested. Tigurius slumped to his knees, his strength all but spent.

Scipio scrambled up the ridge. The Librarian waved him off.

'I am alive.' But he was also clearly weak. Tigurius's eyes grew penetrating. 'The veil is lifted. I can *see*.'

Ultramarines were emerging through the ice-fog. Brakkius and Garrik, the latter carrying his missile launcher at ease. Largo was just behind him. He carried something too, across both arms, but he was obscured by the others and Scipio didn't see what it was. He was more concerned with Tigurius.

'My lord?'

'The veil is lifted,' the Librarian repeated. His eyes were glassy, trance-like, 'and the future unfolds, like a diamond with all possible roads laid out in its facets.'

Scipio came close, put a hand gently on Tigurius's shoulder. 'My lord,' he whispered, beseeching knowledge.

'A hero will fall, struck down by a fatal blade,' he breathed. 'Futures kaleidoscope, one tumbling into another, fragmenting and resolving again. The images shatter but this is immutable. In all the facets, it is the same.'

'Who will fall, my lord? Whose protection must we look to?' The others had gathered around him, all barring Largo, drawn by Scipio's urgency.

Tigurius's eyes became clear. He seized Scipio's wrist in a fearsome grip. 'It is Sicarius!'

Something cold filled Scipio's chest and made his movements leaden. Prescience was the Master Librarian's greatest psychic talent. He was seldom, if ever, wrong.

Sicarius will fall. The words inside Scipio's mind didn't seem real. He shook off Tigurius's hand, allowing the Librarian to slump, and turned sharply. 'Are we close enough to contact Kellenport?' he asked Brakkius.

'Not while we're in the mountains.'

Scipio looked down at Tigurius. There'd be no psychic communion either.

The comm-feed crackled in Scipio's ear. It was Octavian. 'Last of the charges primed. What is happening, brother?'

'Full evacuation from Thanatos Hills, effective immediately,' he replied.

'Are we under attack?' asked Vandar across the feed.

'Negative, but dire news has reached us. Captain Sicarius is in peril.'

Scipio was on his feet. 'Help him,' he said, and rushed past Brakkius and Garrik as they moved to assist Tigurius.

Cator was up and held out his hand. He looked saddened. 'Wait–'

'There is no time, brother.' Scipio was about to dismiss him when he caught sight of Largo again. This time he saw the Ultramarine carried a body, a still and inert body.

A second spike of cold jabbed into Scipio. This time it was soured by guilt.

'What?'

Largo bowed his head, looking down on the recumbent form he cradled. 'Most of the guerrillas are dead. The humans simply weren't made for this fight.'

It was a woman in his arms, a cold and lifeless woman.

THE NECRON ELITES were tough, but Praxor's blade would not be denied. His power sword hummed as it cut through the thickened carapace of one, finding the crucial systems that animated it. He plunged the crackling blade deep, until hilt met the simulacrum of metallic bone, and the creature phased out. His Shieldbearers were fighting hard too. Close-range bolter bursts flashed in the encroaching night. A stream of liquid promethium lit a blazing conflagration in the enemy ranks. They moved together, with Sicarius and his Lions as their inspiration.

Despite the dark cloak drawn over his thoughts, Praxor felt uplifted and galvanised by his lord's presence. Before such glory, death would be a lauded thing destined for the annals of eternity. From his advanced position and proximity, Praxor had a good view of his captain.

Sicarius was imperious as he killed. The Tempest Blade flashed like a lightning bolt captured in his fist, unleashed time and again in a storm of righteous anger. It was easy to see why so many followed him, why he was spoken of in the same breath as Agemman and even Lord Calgar. He was ambition and arrogance, he was skill and courage personified, he was guile and reckless bravura. He *was* Ultramar.

Daceus and Gaius Prabian went before him, hewing a route through the necrons in order that Sicarius find his enemy, the one who led the mechanoids. Agrippen applied a similar fervour to his efforts; smashed necron bodies erupted with every swing of the Dreadnought's power fist, phasing out in mid-air before they could land. At such close quarters, he eschewed his plasma cannon and instead utilised the heavy flamer mounted to his armature. It scorched a ruddy line across the silvered necron hordes, burning their armour black. One fell beneath his foot and he crushed it.

'For Macragge and the Lords of Ultramar!'

Overhead, Praxor caught the flaming contrails of Ixion and Strabo as they duelled with the flying necron gunplatforms. One of the Assault Marines fell like a downed comet, wreathed with emerald fire, his armour flaking away before he crashed out of sight into the melee below.

Elsewhere, the Devastators at the back of the line were cutting furrows into the enemy.

Sergeant Atavian punched the air in triumph as his lascannons tore an arachnid construct in half. Bursts from the other heavies scattered the smaller beetle-like creatures, melting their bodies with intense microwaves or engulfing them in bright plasma.

Everywhere the Ultramarines pushed and fought like the Legion warriors of old, those who had trod the same earth as Guilliman. But despite their heroics, more and more necrons were spilling through the sundered defensive wall and into Xiphos. Only one thing would break the deadlock and Praxor saw it.

It stood taller than the others, wreathed in archaic vestments that hinted at a royal heritage. The necron overlord's gilded metal body shimmered, half-silvered by the moon, its ochroid nature only revealed in the flash of nearby weapons fire. Encircling its skull-like visage was a crown, a red gemstone in the centre. A blue pectoral hung around its neck and torcs banded its arms. Clenched in its skeletal fist was a rippling polearm, glaive-edged and wrought with alien iconography. As its gaze alighted on Sicarius, the overlord's eyes flared.

'I am the Undying, I am doom incarnate…'

SICARIUS HOLSTERED HIS plasma pistol as he faced down the overlord. He wanted to be on even terms with the monster. It was a moment long coming, but now arrived he was ready.

'We are the slayers of kings,' he spat, the words grating through his vox-grille. A crackle of energy coursed up the length of the Tempest Blade.

He would wreak such carnage against this thing.

Sicarius advanced, signalling his Lions to stay back. For a moment he thought he might have to kill the overlord's honour guard too but the Undying ordered them aside.

It was strangely martial, even ritualised.

Sicarius struck the first blow. Chopping with the bluntness of a broadsword, he cut into the overlord's arm. The Undying was fractionally slow to defend itself and a narrow gouge was scraped across its pristine metal. Split torcs cascaded like a fountain of unlocked treasure. A modulated cry was torn from the necron's rictus mouth but its face betrayed no emotion.

The glaive swept out in a wide arc, preventing the Ultramarine's follow-up. He parried, hot sparks dancing off the clashing blades before the combatants parted.

Sicarius came again, aiming a thrust for the necron's midriff which was turned aside by glaive's long haft. A punch dented the captain's battle-helm and he staggered, before firming up his stance and rolling away a blow heading for his gorget.

He slashed downwards, cutting a jagged furrow in the necron's torso. The glaive's haft smashed against his pauldron before he could properly defend, numbing his shoulder. Sicarius backed up again but the monster would not relent.

The Undying was slow, ponderous even, but tough. Every blow was like being hit by a tank. Sicarius went in again, unleashing a hail of blows against the necron's defences. The monster parried some, took others against its near-impervious body, before replying with a lightning-fast riposte that cut into Sicarius's plastron.

As THE CAPTAIN cried out, Praxor was filled with a terrible sense of foreboding. He moved towards the duel, as did the Lions, but a warning glance from Sicarius held the veterans at bay.

The necron overlord was gathering momentum. The Undying whirled its glaive in a circular arc, spinning it end-over-end. With a viper's speed, it snapped out, clipping Sicarius's shoulder guard. He leapt forwards, forging the extra impetus into a double-handed blow that bit into the necron's forearm. Still, the monster came on undaunted. Its cries of pain had turned to laughter.

ENRAGED, SICARIUS THREW himself at the Undying, hacking and cleaving with the Tempest Blade like it was an extension of his inner anger. He fought the Undying back a step and felt the tide turning…

…until a flash of energy from the necron's open palm overloaded his retinal lenses and sent Sicarius reeling. Light, hot and emerald-tinged, filled the captain's world. He backed off, blinded, tearing at the seals connecting his battle-helm to the rest of his armour, and ripped the headgear loose. Blinking away the after-flare, Sicarius had time to parry a blurred attack. The overhead blow *pranged* hard against his sword, forcing him to one knee.

Vision still adjusting, he tore the plasma pistol from its holster and snapped off a quick blast. It struck the Undying beneath the chin, forcing the necron's head upwards and burning off part of its jaw. Staggering back from the kinetic impact, the overlord leavened the press of its glaive and Sicarius stood.

This was it.

He was about to ram the Tempest Blade into the Undying's fleshless skull when something slammed into his side, stopping him.

Agony flared like a thousand burning needles in the captain's flank. As Sicarius looked down, disbelieving, at the glaive embedded there he felt the world grow cold. A sense of weightlessness overcame him and he realised he was being lifted off his feet. The nerves in his fingers failed him and the Tempest Blade slipped free, clattering on the ground below beside his discarded battle-helm. Blood tanged his mouth, slipped over his swollen tongue like copper filings. He spat a gobbet and it stained the Undying's gilded carapace.

AS THE WAR-SCYTHE was driven deeper, the genebred champion gave up a cry of pain. Emotionless, the Undying looked on.

'I am doom,' he rasped as the shouts of others clawed for his attention. More cobalt-armoured warriors were coming for him.

SHUCKED DESULTORILY OFF the glaive like a piece of offal, Sicarius crashed earthwards and lay still. Immediately, the Lions surrounded him just as the necron overlord's honour guard closed too.

'No!' The word fell clipped and defiant from Praxor's lips. He drove the Shieldbearers hard into the necron elites, splitting them apart so he could reach the side of his lord. It was to no avail. He lost Sicarius amidst the crowd of bodies, the image of a fallen sword next to a captain's helm imprinted onto his mind.

He saw the banner, upheld defiantly by Vandius. Brother Malican was by his side. Daceus and Gaius Prabian led the line. They struck down two of the honour guard, exchanging a few blows before dispatching them. Stalwart as statues, they stood over Sicarius's body and felled anything that came close. Venatio knelt behind them, working his ministrations. In Praxor's heart, he knew it was too late. Sicarius was dead.

CHAPTER TWENTY-SEVEN

BY THE TIME the Ultramarines reached the edge of the Thanatos Hills and left the mountains for good, Tigurius was coming back around. Strengthened by the force of his will, he stood straighter and was able to walk unaided, albeit by leaning on his staff.

Evacuation from the mountains had been conducted in silence. Led by Scipio and his Thunderbolts, the Ultramarines were driven by a frustrating sense of urgency. Their captain was likely in very real danger but until communication was restored they were powerless to do anything.

'Check again,' said Scipio as the icy fells gave way to a stretch of flat tundra. Perpetual blizzards roamed this part of Damnos, kicked up in squalls that moved from region to region on the arctic winds. Weather was still fouling the connection to their distant brothers.

Brakkius shook his head.

They marched on. Scipio spared a glance for Jynn. She was being carried on a makeshift stretcher by two of the

surviving guerrilla fighters. The rest were dead, left on
the plateau where the earth and rock would bury them.
Scipio checked the distance from the plateau on his retinal display. A few more kilometres and they could
detonate the charges that would obliterate the artillery
station.

His thoughts went back to Jynn. He'd left her, abandoned her to this fate. It was the right thing to do,
Tigurius was in danger. But he couldn't shake the guilt
that she and her troops should never have been there.
Scipio was reckless and arrogant, believing they could
take the necrons by surprise, sweep in and destroy the
guns without casualty. He gave no regard to the potential loss of human life. It made him think of the earlier
attack on the outpost and the death of Ortus. Brother
Renatus, too, had lost his life on account of injuries suffered during that ill-fated assault. Again, Scipio's lack of
temperance had done this.

Iulus's words, spoken long ago on the assembly deck
of the *Valin's Revenge*, came back to him.

'You are becoming like him.'

He was right. Orad's death had changed Scipio,
although he was only now realising it.

He hoped that Jynn would live.

The comm-feed in his battle-helm crackled. Brakkius
had made contact with the others.

AGRIPPEN BARGED THROUGH the silver horde. Scattering the
last of the necron immortals in his way, he descended
on the honour guard. One he crushed in his fist; the
other he burned, pressing the flamer so close it scorched
his armature and stripped away the paint.

The necron overlord glared up at the Dreadnought, a
hellish fire ignited in its eyes. Sicarius had wounded

it – the Undying's face was caught in the flux of self-repair. Agrippen cared not. He smashed his power fist down upon it brutally, crushing the gilded overlord into ruin.

The destruction of their lord sent a massive shockwave rippling throughout the necron ranks. As one they began to fall back. The Dreadnought was not to be denied, though, and tore apart the mechanoids as they fled.

Assuming command, he drove the Ultramarines forwards. Only the Lions remained, surrounding their fallen captain protectively.

They harried the necrons across the rubble and out into the wastes. In disarray, the automatons were easy prey. During the retreat, the warriors of Sicarius exacted their vengeance in a tally of enemies that scoured the earth and cleansed the area around Kellenport completely.

IULUS HEARD A cheer resound behind him as all the men of Damnos witnessed the necrons' defeat. Like his battle-brothers, he was swept up in the moment. When he saw the Lions of Macragge arrayed around the slumped figure of his captain in a protective cordon his exultant mood ebbed. It was replaced by vengeance and the desire to vanquish the enemy utterly.

Stationed in the rear line of the army, alongside the Devastators, Iulus pushed his Immortals forwards. He caught Sergeant Atavian's eye.

'Sicarius has fallen.'

Like Iulus, Atavian gave nothing away. 'Is he dead?'

'They watch over him like pallbearers.'

The grating rasp of Chaplain Trajan interjected. 'Rites will be spoken if he is slain. Now we must let our bolters and blades describe our litanies of hatred.'

He led them into the fleeing masses, crozius swinging. Iulus followed a little way behind. Atavian's advance was slower still with the heavy guns.

A gauntlet reached out and snatched Iulus's arm. He turned about to strike, believing a destroyed mechanoid had self-repaired, but it was Praxor. He wasn't wearing his battle-helm and his eyes were wide.

Iulus said, 'Brother?'

'He is dead. I saw him fall with my own eyes. Captain Sicarius is slain.'

Iulus's expression went from grief to resolution. 'Then we avenge him.'

For over an hour the Ultramarines pursued the retreating necrons, all the way to the far border of Arcona City. Thousands were destroyed in the rout, the mechanoids unable to mount a defence or any kind of useful tactic that might have spared their losses. Without their overlord they were less than automatons, little more than directionless drones. Even the elites appeared locked onto a single course of action – full-scale retreat.

The as-of-yet unseen phasic generator teleported some of the constructs back to the sunken tomb all the way into the northern polar wastes. No Ultramarine had laid eyes on the device, and it was likely withdrawn upon their arrival.

Only when the last of the necrons had either been teleported or damaged into instant phase-out did Agrippen call a halt, his fury sated. Then the Ultramarines began the long march back to Kellenport.

THE SUN WAS high in the ice-blue Damnos sky when Scipio reached the city. The edges of its walls were veneered in hazy umber from the light.

Led by the Thunderbolts, the Ultramarines from the Thanatos Mission passed through the Kellenport gates just as a viridian explosion lit up the distant hills. So large and destructive, the blast was even visible from the city. The pylons and gauss-obliterators would not return. For one they were buried, for another the Ultramarines had used enough explosive to level the mountainside.

'Sergeant Vorolanus.'

It was Tigurius. Scipio stopped and turned to face the Librarian.

'I will see to our captain,' he said. 'Agrippen has command.'

Scipio bowed, acknowledging.

As they parted ways, Tigurius stopped. 'I saw courage on the Thanatos Hills and a desire for self-sacrifice. Now you know who you are, brother. Remember it.'

The Librarian was heading into the distant hubbub of the city. Already, preparations were being made for the arrival of the Ultramarines armour. Several squads stood watchful upon the battlements, alongside the Damnosian soldiery.

There was no sign of Agrippen or the Lions. Scipio assumed they were in council, planning the strategic defence of the city. At least two other sergeants were not present at that meeting. Leaving Brakkius in charge, Scipio dismissed the Thunderbolts. His gaze lingered on Jynn as she was carried to the nearest medical station. He banished the bleak thoughts from his mind as he went to meet his brothers.

Hugging Scipio firmly, Iulus said, 'I am glad you're alive, brother.'

Scipio laughed mirthlessly. 'You sound like you had your doubts.' He turned to Praxor. 'Brother?'

He looked downcast, his shame obvious in his bearing. Praxor had believed Sicarius dead and become like the people of Damnos he had thought weren't worth saving on account of that fatalism.

The captain was injured, badly, but lived. The truth of it was revealed later when the courtyard had cleared and Venatio announced to the Lions that their lord still drew breath. He was still in the Apothecary's care, surrounded by his inner-circle warriors. But Cato Sicarius would play no further part in the war on Damnos. As soon as possible, he would be ferried to the Apothecarion aboard the *Valin's Revenge* and allowed to recover.

Scipio put a hand on Praxor's shoulder. 'Neither of us was there, brother. We didn't witness what you did.'

'I should have known, but instead I gave in to doubt.'

'All three of us have experienced much in this campaign. I confess I never thought this ball of ice would be a place for revelation.'

At this point, Iulus stepped in. 'It's not done yet, either.' He held up a data-slate displaying the planet's northern geography. 'Necron forces are stirring in the north. Scans reveal massive tectonic activity.'

Exhaling, Scipio marshalled his anger. 'So all we have done so far has merely set them back?'

Iulus nodded. 'It would appear so.'

'We have sacrificed much for little.'

'And more is needed.'

Scipio was pensive for a moment before he straightened and clapped his brothers each on the pauldron. 'Then by the glory of Ultramar, it will be given.'

Praxor nodded determinedly. Iulus even cracked a feral smile.

All three looked skywards as a large vessel silhouetted the upper atmosphere. The sound of the battle-barge's engines was loud, even as far up as it was, and smaller ships were disgorging from it.

Valin's Revenge.

The Ultramarines on the wall, those in the courtyard, all of the Damnosian infantry looked up.

The voice of Antaro Chronus, veteran Ultramarines tank commander, came over the feed. 'The heavens are clear,' he announced, shouting above the sound of heavy machinery in the background. 'We are coming, brothers.'

EPILOGUE

ANKH HAD FORESEEN this outcome. Not through any form of prescience or sixth sense, but rather the cold logic of cause and effect. The Undying's demise was inevitable; the necron retreat likewise. Tahek's death he had engineered purposely – it meant the skies were open for the genebred warriors to bring their vessels and machineries to the surface. It would give them hope, make them believe that victory was even possible.

That thought amused the Architect. In the depths of the tomb his spyders and scarabs were revivifying in thousands, *tens of thousands*. The phalanxes in full retreat on the surface were but a fraction of what lay beneath, and there were things much more terrible in those depths. As the battles raged above, Ankh had been busy waking them.

He felt the touch of an ancient sentience in the emerald gloom of the under-caverns. It was a royal chamber where he stood. As Ankh contemplated the vast catacombs and their slumbering hordes, a pair of eyes ignited in the darkness in front of him.

Ankh took a step back and bowed almost to the floor.

'My lord,' he purred as the royarch's gaze fell upon him.

ABOUT THE AUTHOR

Nick Kyme is a writer and editor. He lives in Nottingham where he began a career at Games Workshop on White Dwarf magazine. Now Black Library's Senior Range Editor, Nick's writing credits include the Warhammer 40,000 Tome of Fire trilogy featuring the Salamanders, his Warhammer Fantasy-based dwarf novels and several short stories. Read his blog at *www.nickkyme.com*

WARHAMMER
40,000

A SPACE MARINE BATTLES NOVEL

RYNN'S WORLD

STEVE PARKER

UK ISBN 978-1-84416-802-6   US ISBN 978-1-84416-803-4

HELSREACH

AARON DEMBSKI-BOWDEN

UK ISBN 978-1-84416-862-0   US ISBN 978-1-84416-863-0

HUNT FOR VOLDORIUS

ANDY HOARE

UK ISBN 978-1-84416-513-1   US ISBN 978-1-84416-514-8

Buy this
series and read
free extracts at
www.blacklibrary.com

THE PURGING OF KADILLUS

GAV THORPE

UK ISBN 978-1-84416-896-5   US ISBN 978-1-84416-897-2